C000093020

Copyright © 2023 Clare Kirk-George

ISBN-13: 9798399084749
ISBN-10: 1477123456

Cover design by: www.alexcrumpillustration.com
Library of Congress Control Number: 2018675309
Printed in the United States of America

To the Angels that walk amongst us...
I can see you

Contents

A Note From The Author

Angels have always fascinated me, and what better way to feed that fascination than to write a book about them. The Angels that I've written about are not ones in the traditional sense, these are how I imagine them to be, Angels of my fiction and fantasy. Hopefully I can begin to bring you as the reader into a world within a world as my story progresses.

The story is written from the perspective of each character. Personally I like to look inside the mind of each individual character. To save any confusion their name is written at the start of each chapter or subheading, which makes it easy to see who's mind you have entered.

Throughout the book I make reference to music and songs that have helped inspire me during the writing process, some songs are happy, some sad, and some funny ones thrown in too. You can find these songs on my Spotify playlist, if you search for PurpleVampireGirl The hidden Angel's daughter. I urge you to listen to the lyrics, they will add enhancement to the story.

Some of the subjects broached in this book might upset some readers, remember that my inspiration is taken from real life, and a fictional world of my making. Any reference made to events that occur in this book are my interpretation of them and completely fictional. Primarily being set in England, please expect some slang words and English phrases throughout the book.

Thank you for reading, and supporting my first book,
Kindest Regards
Clare Kirk-George

Update May 2024

While writing book three, yes you read that correctly, I decided that I wasn't happy with the original artwork. Then I found a wonderful artist that has a unique and quirky style much like me!

Alex Crump brought to life the characters of Maddie and Danny with the backdrop of the fictional town of Eastleigh-On-Sea.

So a huge shout out to Alex, especially helping me with my computer woes. He can be found at www.alexcrumpillustration.com and I urge you to check out his other work.

Epigraph

When you cried, I'd wipe away all of your tears
When you'd scream, I'd fight away all of your fears
And I held your hand through all of these years
But you still have all of me

-   My Immortal, Evanescence

Prologue

Maddie, Aged Nine

Madeline Reynolds, or Maddie for short, is the name one of the nurses gave me at the hospital, the week I was abandoned. I suppose I'm fortunate really because no one bothered to give me a name before then.

I'm nine years old and according to my social worker, I'm far too grown up for my own good, whatever that supposed to mean, but when you've lived my short life it's hardly surprising.

My home is this small, sleepy, as in nothing ever happens here, seaside town. Eastleigh-On-Sea is actually a pretty decent place to live, considering I could have ended up living anywhere.

Living with my foster parent is okay it could be worse, she likes all us kids to refer to her as Nanna Jenny, I'm pretty sure she isn't anybody's real Nanna. But if she insists on being called that ridiculous name, and it keeps her happy, I don't have any problem with it.

She's never been married as far as I can tell, and I'm not about to ask. No point rocking the boat, I've got a pretty good thing going here, better than some of the places I've lived. I don't think she has any children of her own, I'd like to think that's why she took us all in. But nothings ever done out of the kindness of the heart, not in my world. I'm pretty sure it's more to do with the allowance she gets paid by social services every month for looking after us.

You see, the more of us kids she takes in, I guess the more allowance she gets? I'm not sure exactly how the system works, but that's the gist of it.

Being an orphan means I don't have any parents, and I don't know where I came from.

Nanna Jenny sat me down and told me I was abandoned when I first came to live here, but she's always been vague about the finer details, and believe me, I've asked her. I'm determined to wear her down eventually, and she will have to cave and tell me the truth.

In the future, when I'm older, I'm going to look for my parents, and find out where I came from, and who I really am. That's my dream, because it's okay to dream, and no one can take those away from you.

But until then, I'm going to keep those dreams to myself, because I'm the only person that I can ever rely on. All the adults that have ever come into my life, have let me down, and broken their promises. One social worker told me when I was five years old, that I'd get adopted soon by a nice family, but that's never going to happen now, I'm too old.

The small bedroom I have at Nanna Jenny's house is shared with another girl called Donna. We have a bunk bed, and she makes me sleep on the bottom bunk, so I get to hear her moving around and squirming about all night long. She's thirteen years old, and not all that nice to me, I've tried to be her friend, but she doesn't seem to like me very much. Sometimes I think she's jealous of me by the way she acts, the thing is I have no idea why, or what I've ever done to her. Nanna Jenny calls it "acting out" but I call it for what it is, just plain mean.

Donna hides the few possessions I have, like my toothbrush or my school bag. She's also got this nasty habit of making up crap about me. Then I seem to end up being the one in trouble with Nanna Jenny. Donna will try and start fights with me deliberately, she used to really hurt me physically, but not so much anymore, I've learnt to just run off now or try and avoid her altogether. It's the mental damage that will stay with me, that never goes away.

Nanna Jenny says I need to stop being so soft, suck it up, and grow a pair whatever that means. Learn to stick up for myself and not rely on other people to do it for me, at least Nanna Jenny got that part right.

But one thing I do know for sure, apart from the bare basics, Nanna Jenny doesn't give much of a crap about me or the other kids. The only reason she really pretends is because she likes to appear to social services to be all loving and caring, guaranteeing that monthly allowance.

Jack and Tommy also live with us. They are hands down, the cutest twins you have ever seen in your life. They're only two years old, and like my unofficial baby brothers, and I'm their self-appointed big sister. Nanna Jenny is forever moaning about how much of her time they take up, so I try to help her out as much as I can.

When they do a poop in their nappies they really stink. I'm pretty sure they save up that explosive, smelly radioactive stuff for when it's my turn to change them.

Secretly, even though I complain like hell sometimes, I don't really mind caring for them. Because I love those boys like they are my blood family.

Nanna Jenny seems to get really tired out with them, and is

usually passed out on the sofa by the time I get home from school. I usually tidy up, picking up the empty bottles, and the boys will run riot around her. It's almost like she lives in her own little world most of the time.

She seems sad, and sometimes I see her crying. Other times she just stares at trash TV, soap operas or reality crap. I feel quite bad for her.

I suppose I better come out of this little daydream now, I can hear Nanna Jenny summoning me as per usual. One of the twins has probably dropped another toxic load into their nappy.

Or it could be time for their bath, who knows?

The fun round here just never ends.

Danny, Saint Peters Church, Nine Years Ago

"Danny, can you please get your skates on son. We are going to be late for church again." My dad sighs in annoyance.

"But dad, can't I just finish up this level? I'm really close to levelling up, and if I stop now I'll have to start from the beginning again." I answer him reluctantly, with a sulk on my face knowing that I've already lost this argument. It's almost exactly the same as the one we had last Sunday, and the Sunday before that.

"If you're not down here Danny, in the next five seconds I swear to God himself I will throw that games console out of the window." Shit, dad sounds angry now, but it's just an empty threat. At least I hope it is.

I quickly reply "Yes sir, coming sir." Knowing he won't stay mad at me for very long, it's not in dads nature to get really angry.

"And you can cut the sarcasm you cheeky monster, and hurry up." He briskly retorts back.

"Sorry dad." And I try to sound sincere.

I really hate going to church every single Sunday, especially when I can think of at least a hundred other things I'd prefer to do. But dad insists it's good for the soul, and what mum would have wanted.

He's been an overly devoted catholic since my mum passed away. You'd think he'd hate God for taking her away from us, but it's the exact opposite.

So, I just go to church because it keeps him happy. But I'd much rather be playing video games or kicking my football around in the park.

"Now I can't find my damn car keys Danny, for Christs sake help me look." Dad grunts at me, throwing drawers open and searching in his pockets.

So, me being ever the antagonist replies with, "Dad stop taking the Lord's name in vain. Or you know that Father Christopher is going to force you to volunteer at senior citizens bingo again. And that never ends well." I add a cheeky smirk at him, thinking I'm pushing him now.

"Who exactly is the adult in this relationship son?" He puts on a quizzical look, directed towards me.

"You are dad. Look, I found your car keys. Can't we skip this week we're late already anyway and you know how bad parking is." I say hopefully to him, dangling the car keys in front of his face.

"Again Danny, who's the adult in the relationship here?" Dad replies, but I know he's only joking, and he playfully snatches the keys out of my hand.

"OK but don't say I didn't warn you." I sass back to him.

Now my dad's driving around looking for a parking spot, he never listens to me, every single week we go through exactly the same scenario. The church service started ten minutes ago, and now everyone is going to glare at us and gossip when we eventually walk in. Great, just great.

"Hop out the car here son, at least one of us can get inside on time, I'll circle round and look for a space." Dad states hopefully, but I'm sure he knows he's going to be driving around the whole block looking for an available space.

Oh, that's just bloody great, now I get to walk into church late and alone, I hate getting stared at by the congregation. The old ladies creep me right out, with those big fancy hats and bright red lipstick. I slam the car door as hard as I can, just so dad knows how pissed off I am, and I walk up the path to Saint Peters church. I can already hear the choir singing a badly out of tune hymn.

It's starting to drizzle rain and it's bitterly cold for the end of December, and I'm now regretting leaving my gloves in the car. I'm debating on standing outside waiting for dad when I hear a tiny cry. Sounded like something in pain. Looking around I can't see anything, but I hear something again, so I know I'm not imagining things. Just as I'm turning back around my foot kicks a small cardboard box and I almost trip over.

The tiny cry is now a really loud scream. I slowly fall to my knees and peer into the box. There inside is what looks like a faded old blanket, swaddled around a baby. An actual baby. Which is now frantic. Without thinking I lean into the box and scoop up the baby to sooth, and immediately it stops crying. It feels icy cold, that can't be good. Where's my dad when I need him?

"Danny why are you still standing out here, it's below zero?" My dad arrives just in time.

"Dad thank God you are here, look it's a baby. I found it crying in the box". And I indicate with my foot, because I'm still holding the baby.

"In a box out here?" Replies my dad. He looks really shocked at such a revelation.

"How many other boxes can you see dad? The baby, it feels cold, and I don't think that's good." I answer back at him annoyed, still clutching the baby.

"Sorry Danny, you just caught me off guard. Pass me the baby carefully. Now go and run inside the church. Get Father Christopher as fast as you can. I'll go and wait in his office around the back of the church where it's warmer. It's bloody freezing inside that church. Hurry up, I want to get this baby checked out." My dad practically barks his instructions to me. For once I don't give a smart-ass answer back. No, I just run.

I burst inside the church and spot father Christopher in the pulpit. And I run straight up to him, panting and out of breath after sprinting. I start tugging on his arm to indicate I want him to follow me. The service grinds to a halt and people start whispering loudly.

Guess I didn't avoid it after all, the old ladies will have something to really gossip about now.

At Exactly The Same Time, Outside Saint Peters Church...

Hidden behind the ivory covered stone wall next to Saint Peters church, the two individuals watch as the young boy carefully picks up the small baby girl.

They have made it look as convincing as possible, by placing her in a cardboard box wrapped in a faded blanket. A small envelope tucked into the box underneath her with future instructions, ready to be found later.

On the surface, it looks like she was unwanted, but nothing could be further from the truth. And the decision to place her in the human realm was not a difficult one, especially as she is half human after all. No, the decision to leave her here was never taken lightly. Keep her hidden in plain sight, which is now the plan to keep her safe.

The baby's father will have no idea where to start looking for her. Expecting that she will still be with her mother in the banished realm. With her power not manifesting until reaching maturity, eighteen years old in human years.

"Do you think she will be safe here with these humans?" The small female asks, the faint glow around her evident in the sunlight.

"No, I cannot form an opinion yet, but the church is a sacred space in their religion." The male companion replies, the same glow surrounding him also.

"My senses aren't picking up any immediate dangers, but that doesn't mean there won't be any." The female shares with her companion.

"The boy is going to look over her, not right away, but in the future." The male sighs. "It is the best we can do at this moment in time. For we must not stay here any longer, every minute spent in this realm we will be putting her in further danger. We must leave her and hope now, that her mother made the right decision sending her here. She will be completely safe until the dreams start to come, and complete manifestation is many years away. The boy is already connected to her now, and in time will become her protector. Of this I am more than certain."

The pair then slowly faded away leaving the future of a baby in the hands of a young human boy and his devoted father.

Chapter One

Maddie, Present Day Aged Seventeen

"**S**o are you going to apply for university Maddie, because if you keep getting these grades you can go anywhere you want too." My teacher asks.

"I don't know miss, I really want to, but things are complicated at home." I look at my teacher with sad eyes.

"Can I ask?" my teacher looks concerned.

"You know my situation miss, I've only got a few months left in the care system and then I'm on my own. So, I really need to get a full time job and not dream about things I can't have."

"You could apply for scholarships and grants, and work part time? I'm not saying it will be easy but it's certainly worth thinking about don't you think?" She smiles back at me, not really grasping what I'm trying to say to her. You have to love my teachers optimism. It's not exactly realistic, unfortunately I have to live in the real world.

"Scholarships, do you actually think they'd consider somebody like me miss?" I sigh, knowing it's never going to happen, a girl that's been in the foster care system her whole life.

"Oh Maddie, you are worth so much more than you think." The bell rings in the background. "You'd better get off to your next class, but we will continue this conversation at a later date." And my teacher waves me away to my next class. I know she means well, she just hasn't got a clue. What am I going to do?

I can't tell her there is absolutely no way in hell I can go to university. It's not about just the money. I need to apply to take over guardianship of the twins as a foster parent. I can't afford to do that and go to university. Plus, I promised I'd get them out of the care system as soon as I'm legally old enough and I turn eighteen somewhere near the end of December. Although it's only an approximation, nobody knows my real date of birth.

After hours of trailing through the internet, I managed to find this solicitor online that works for this charity, and convinced him to help me pro-bono. I'm pretty sure that he's just trying to make his resume look better, doing some charity work for the poor little orphan girl, but I'll admit we both get something out of it, so I'd call that a win, win, situation.

After Nanna Jenny died last year we all got split up into different foster homes. And it's been a nightmare for those boys at home ever since. Jack and Tommy and now stuck with a complete bitch of a foster parent and I fear for their safety on a daily basis. The woman that they live with Mrs Thompson is a complete psycho in my opinion. I managed to buy them both second hand mobile phones from eBay using my babysitting money, so at least we can stay in touch.

I never expected to have to apply to be a legal guardian as soon as I turn eighteen years old, but those boys deserve so much better, and I can't put my finger on it but I know something is drastically wrong in that house. I have no real evidence, and I can't prove a thing. But I'm going to make sure that I can take them out of that situation as soon as possible. Mark my words.

Honestly, I don't understand how some people are allowed to look after children, and how the system continues to fail them. It doesn't matter how much you complain to social services, my complaining has gotten me nowhere. But I won't give up on them, even if it means sacrificing my own future.

Nanna Jenny didn't exactly give much of a shit about us, all the time we lived with her. But she didn't physically hurt us, and on the plus side she did remember to feed us. There just wasn't any kind of love, or any emotional care involved.

If any harm comes to those boys I will blame social services and never forgive myself, because a promise is a promise.

I need to cut my last class because they have a football match today, and their school is at least a twenty -five minute walk from my college. My bike got a flat tyre this morning. I hate cutting class, but I promised them both I'd be there, and I'm not letting them down.

I unlock my bike from the bike shed and start wheeling it towards the twins school. My hands are freezing, I never seem to get warm even in the summer. Maybe it was because I was a winter baby, or maybe it was because I was found in a box. There I go again. Box baby. Box baby. Nope. I'm not going to think about that right now. I need to put those ten year old boys first.

The school field has several games happening in unison. I lock my bike to some railings and quickly spot one of the twins waving frantically at me. It's difficult to tell which twin it is from way over there. Somebody blows the whistle and claps their hands to get the teams attention.

Must be their new football Coach. As he turns around our eyes briefly meet. Recognition? DeJa'Vu? Call it what you want. Something hits me inside, some kind of familiarity, a connection. I mentally shake myself out of it.

"Maddie, you made it!" Tommy comes bounding towards me.

"Of course, I made it Tommy, how could I miss yours and Jacks first game on the team?" I say proudly to them.

"We might not actually get to play today, Maddie, we're only Subs." Frowns Jack, and looking over his shoulder towards Coach.

"Hey, Jack speak for yourself, I'm positive Coach is going to play me." Tommy pipes up, nudging his brothers shoulder.

"Come on boys don't start arguing or Coach won't play either of you." And I find myself putting on my best mum voice.

"That's right boys, he won't, now get on the field and start warming up." The Coach answers, pointing to the football pitch and blowing his whistle again.

"Yes Sir!" Jack and Tommy both reply simultaneously.

The guy I just made eye contact with is holding out his hand to me.

"You know it's customary to shake it." He grins at me with a kind smile on his face, meeting my eyes again.

"Oh my God, I'm so sorry how rude of me. I'm Maddie." And I hold out my hand so he can shake it. That's when I feel a sudden spark igniting in my hand. He looks down to where our hands are now awkwardly joined, so I quickly pull mine away.

"Hi, I'm Coach McKenzie and you must be their??" He says, waiting for a reply expectantly.

"Oh, we were in foster care together, they're like my annoying little brothers. I hope it's okay I'm here today only I promised them both." I nervously smile, and he grins back at me again.

"Of course, it's fine. I had no idea the boys were in foster care." He answers clearly surprised.

"I probably shouldn't have mentioned it Coach McKenzie, I don't want to single out or embarrass the boys. So please forget I said anything." I sigh, immediately regretting my habit of oversharing information when I get nervous.

"No of course not, it's great for them to have a big sister here. Anyway, nice to meet you, Maddie." He runs back onto the football pitch.

Very nice to meet you indeed Coach McKenzie, and I smile to myself....

Chapter Two

Coach Mckenzie

Okay, who was that girl Maddie? Why does she feel so familiar to me like I've met her somewhere before? I've been pondering this for ages, and I can't get her out of my head. Those stunning jade green eyes and red hair. With her pale complexion and that hourglass figure, she's stunningly beautiful and she's completely oblivious to it.

She looks college age possibly university, too young all the same. But this niggling feeling is trying to claw it's way out of the back of my head. The need to know more about her, and I know I'm going to be doing some slightly illegal searches on my computer once I get home tonight. I'm not exactly an angel when it comes to things like that.

I made sure to give the boys a game just so I could admire her cheering them on. Standing on the side-lines, shouting out encouragement to them both. Her magnetic energy rubbed off on everyone, and both of the boys managed to score a goal, much to the teams delight giving us a winning score. And I'm going to make sure Jack and Tommy get the game time they deserve now, feeling slightly guilty that I may have unknowingly overlooked them before now.

Wanting to speak to her after the game, I totally chickened out, using the excuse to myself that the boys were hyper excited and I didn't want to interrupt them all. Now I just wish I had just walked up to her and spoken, said actual words instead of thinking them in my head. What on earth is wrong with me?

I'm acting like a pre-pubescent teenage boy, much to my own embarrassment.

It's just a strange feeling I've got and I can't explain it. It's like I've got the sudden urge to protect them all, Maddie, Jack and Tommy. I don't know why or where it's coming from, it's the most bizarre feeling I've ever experienced.

On my drive home I spot her again in the distance, on the other side of the road from me pushing a dilapidated old bicycle along the pavement. Do they still make bikes like that one? That's how old it looks, it obviously has a flat tyre. But I don't stop, not very gentlemanly of me, dad would be disappointed. I know I should have stopped, any decent man would, but something inside stopped me.

Call it self-preservation...

Chapter Three

Maddie, Aged Ten Years

Donna slapped me around the face last night, and now I have a massive bruise just underneath my left eye and it's gone a purple colour. She caught me good this time, usually I can be faster than that. Plus, we've got school photos today, the one day a year everyone wants to look their best, just my rotten luck. Thanks Donna, thanks a lot for that little gift.

Nanna Jenny isn't very happy about it either, she wants to know what the hell I was playing at letting her bruise up my face like that. But I'm sure she's only worried that social services will think she did it to me herself, and if she loses us kids, she will lose her income. I'll give Nanna Jenny her due, she's never hit any of us. Shout, yes. Swear, occasionally. But hit us, nope.

If she lost her allowance from the social, no more couch potato for her, she'd have to find an actual job. So, she helped me cover up the bruise with her makeup, and complained the whole time. At least you can hardly see it now. It will keep the teachers and social services off my back.

Trying to stay under the radar and go unnoticed at school, that's what I try to excel at, keeping my head down and my grades up. That way no one will come knocking on our door asking unwanted or unnecessary questions.

I'm sure there are better foster homes out there, I'm just yet to find one and besides, I've been with Nanna Jenny the longest now, and I know where I stand with her. Plus, and this is the most important thing, I don't want to be split up from Jack and Tommy.

Donna is a pain, but that girl has issues and I'm sure she's hurting inside. I think her stepfather did something to her, but she doesn't talk about it, and I don't ask. So now she just acts out all the time, she definitely has anger issues. The girl needs therapy if you ask me. I really wish I could help her, but every time I try, she just pushes me away, and last night I got smacked around the face for my troubles.

One good thing came out of it though. I finally managed to ware Nanna Jenny down, and she told me about what happened when I was found as a baby. She told me that somebody left me in a box outside a church, but I don't know which church it was, and she was never told so doesn't know. So, who can I ask now? Unless I visit every single church? That could take an eternity. I guess we all have our problems, and that's a problem for another day.

Waiting in line to have my photograph taken, and I find my mind wandering off again, I swear that I'm always in a state of daydream. I can't stop thinking about this recurring dream I keep having. It's so weird.

A boy with the brightest blue eyes and shaggy brown hair, he reaches down to pick something up, but I can't see what it is. He turns around and he's holding a baby, could this baby be me? Then his body starts to morph into a man, it's still him but he's much older now. But I can't see his face it's all blurred, why can't I see his face?

I must have had this dream at least a hundred times, I'm such a weirdo.

What could it mean?

Maddie, Present Day

So, I'm standing in Halfords trying to find cheapest puncture repair kit possible, bearing in mind my knowledge of such is zero. My funds are desperately low and the babysitting jobs I've been doing after college have been scarce as of late and even when I have them they don't exactly pay a great deal. I need a real job, but it's difficult to get a proper job when your seventeen and have no real work experience. And believe me, I keep applying for them. Supermarkets, restaurants, basically anything in retail. But it's soul destroying, you either never hear back, or get told that they will put you on file.

The longer I stand in the bike section the more confused I get. I could have ordered a kit from Amazon, but I need to fix this bike before tomorrow. It's nearly closing time; I haven't found what I want and I'm starting to panic now. I haven't got a clue what to buy, I should have YouTubed it first.

"Fuck my life." I mumble to myself.

"Now that's not very polite Maddie, is it?" A deep voice says.

I nearly jump out of my skin. It's him. Mr Oh my God I'm so hot McKenzie, immediately I start to blush bright red. Kill, me, now. "Ccccoach." I start to stutter and can't get out my words into a coherent sentence. Then he grins at me. Bloody grins at me. The arrogance.

"Ccccoach that's a new one on me Mmmaddie." He laughs.

I smile and laugh back at him, even though he just took the micky out of my word jumble, he definitely has a sense of humour.

"Sorry, I'm just frustrated. I can't find what I'm looking for and it's nearly closing time." I reply, waving my hand in front of the rows and endless rows of stuff for bikes, I'm not even convinced I'm looking in the right section of the shop now.

"What exactly are you after?" He asks me, making eye contact, always making eye contact. It should make me feel nervous but it doesn't, not with him, this relative stranger.

"A dirt-cheap puncture repair kit for my bike, and I need to repair it tonight for college tomorrow." I look towards him, and there I go with the oversharing again, what is wrong with me?

"Well if it helps, I have a puncture repair kit in my car?" he indicates towards the car park, he seems like a man I can trust, they let him Coach the football team after all, so he's not a serial killer?

"Ok, strange question why have you got a puncture repair kit for a bike in your car? And you're sure you're not a serial killer?" I give him a quizzical look.

"Oh, I go off road mountain biking on the weekends Maddie, and I'm definitely not a serial killer." He laughs, not even acknowledging my off the cuff questions.

"Of course, you off road, and aren't a serial killer, my bad." I'm laughing as I say this to him, now he probably thinks I'm a complete moron.

"Let me pay for this motor oil and I'll get the kit out of my car for you." He replies walking towards the checkout counter at the front of the shop, it's the last till open and it looks like they are closing down for the night.

I look at his hand as he walks off and notice the motor oil, so he was actually shopping. He pays at the till with the girl behind the counter clearly flirting with him. For some reason that annoys the hell out of me. Thank goodness he is completely oblivious to the woman's flirtations.

Reluctantly I follow him out to the car park as the whole situation has escalated in my head, embarrassing to me beyond belief. Did I really just ask him if he's a serial killer? But like I said funds are tight, so I need to swallow my pride, and if he's offering a repair kit for free, who am I to say no to it, beggars can't be choosers?

He's currently rifling through the boot of his car when I hear him say "Found it, knew I had a spare one in here."

"Well thank you Mr organised." I say jokingly at him, using humour to cover my nerves.

"No problem, Maddie, I can't have Jack and Tommy saying I abandoned you in your hour of need." He replies back and hands me the repair kit, it's small. No wonder I couldn't find it in the bloody shop.

"Thank you, it's much appreciated, and I will return the favour. Anyway, I better get going I need to fix this puncture before tomorrow or it's going to be a long walk to college." And I try to make my escape, without making it look to obvious.

"Can I offer you a ride home, it's getting dark, and this isn't the best part of town." He looks around the badly lit car park, one of the streetlights isn't working.

"No, it's fine I live on the other side of the industrial estate, on the bad side of town." And I wink at him cheekily, trying to make my escape.

"No really, please. For my peace of mind, I just want to make sure you're safe Maddie." He says insistently, his kind eyes giving me no fear of bad intentions.

"Okay, if you insist but it's really not needed." Well, this just got more awkward I think to myself.

Getting in his car, I'm impressed, it's a very nice car for someone his age to have, it's the kind of car you'd expect some flashy business person to own. Wow, I didn't think school football coaches made that much money? He turns on the engine and his stereo automatically kicks in.

The familiar sound of the cello starts to play and Apocalyptica comes through the speakers, I know this because it's one of my favourite artists. Honestly, I'm in shock. I've never met anyone before that listens to them too, they are so obscure to most people.

I only discovered them by accident, an older CD of theirs was in a charity shop I was volunteering at last summer. It was a great gig really because you always got first dibs on all the donations before they went on the shelves. So long as you made a small donation to the charity of course.

Anyway, I saw their CD on one of the shelves and decided to play it on the ancient stereo located in the stock room, so I could listen to it while I was working. And what a revelation. I've been hooked since, watching all their YouTube videos online.

"You can turn it off if you want to, I know it's not to everyone's taste." He says and smiles at me, reaching to turn off the stereo.

"Oh no, I love this track especially the chorus, Lzzy Hales Vocals are amazing."

I then proceed to start singing along happily at the top of my voice, suddenly remembering where I am, I quickly shut my mouth. I go bright red and turn towards the car window and try to hide my embarrassment.

"Maddie, you have got some pipes on you girl, and you know it's one of my favourite bands too. You just keep on surprising me."

I have absolutely no idea how to reply to that, so I just spurt out my home address quickly, and pray we arrive there fast.

Coach Mackenzie

Maddie is enchanting me, I can feel it to my bones. There's something quite amazing about her, the way her whole persona physically glows, and she has the voice of an Angel. Yet she has got absolutely no idea about this herself, has no one ever pointed this out to her?

I want to get to know her better, because her positive energy is drawing me in, I really can't explain it. And it felt like fate intervened tonight, putting her in the same place, at the same time as me, I don't believe it was a coincidence.

But, and it's a rather large but, she's only seventeen years old. I may have done an illegal search on her as soon as I got back from football practice earlier. It was a pretty low thing to do, digging into her background like that, I'll be the first to admit that, but I had to know. Maddie is a teenager that's been in the foster care system her whole life, and basically a sister to two of my young students.

Thinking about any kind of relationship with her is probably a great big no, and starting anything would be highly inappropriate. I can't entertain these kinds of feelings, and just thinking about it while I'm in a car with her is just plain wrong. No, I just need to get her dropped off at home. Job done. Conscience clear.

We make the short drive to her house in silence apart from the stereo playing, and I notice she still looks withdrawn after singing in front of me, she's tapping her fingers along to the sound of the track playing. It's like she's trying to keep her mind busy, on anything else but me. I don't understand why she shut down like that after singing? She has nothing to be embarrassed about, perhaps I should tell her that?

Her house really is at the back of the industrial estate she wasn't kidding when she said it was close, and I find myself being disappointed the journey wasn't longer, just to be near her more. Pulling up outside a small, terraced house, I can't help but notice just how rough the area she lives in looks. It's judgemental, it's totally wrong to think, but did Maddie ever stand a chance in life?

The front garden of the house she lives at is full of car parts from an old Ford Fiesta up on bricks, who on earth does she live with? I didn't dig into that part of her life, it felt like too much of an invasion on her privacy. A neighbour's dog is barking ferociously through a window next door, itching to get outside scratching at the window. Children that look far too young to be out this late alone are kicking a football around in the street, and two rather shady looking men, smoking what I hope are just cigarettes and not drugs, are closely watching my car from across the road. The whole scene puts me on edge, and I feel uncomfortable leaving Maddie here alone.

Before I get the chance to make any comment to her, Maddie is jumping out of the car. It's like she can't get away from me fast enough. Is she afraid of me? Have I offended her in some way?

"Well thanks again for saving me from my misery in Halford's and giving me a repair kit for my puncture. You really didn't need to drop me off home." She blurts out in an over eager fashion, and blushing slightly. She still must feel embarrassed. Damn it. I hate making her feel uncomfortable.

"Always Happy to help a damsel in distress." I laugh awkwardly, then decide to add "Do you need any help fixing the puncture?" Why did I even say that to her? What is the matter with me? It's like I have absolutely no control over what I'm spirting out of my mouth.

She gives me a look of confusion, and it looks like she's about to say yes. But then a look of doubt crosses her face, she's over thinking it, and then she shakes her head. Damn. I did make her feel uncomfortable.

"Are you sure, because you don't look very sure?" I reply, trying to not come across as pushy.

"I've taken up enough of your time already Coach McKenzie. I know how to fix it, and I've got a bike pump and a few tools, it was just the repair kit I didn't have. But thanks for the offer anyway. Well, I'd best get going." She replies quickly. Before I have a chance to respond she runs into the house.

Probably for the best, but I still feel uncomfortable driving away from her knowing I could have helped. And I spend the rest of the evening thinking and worrying about her and that blasted bike.

Chapter Four

Maddie

By the time I make it indoors my heart is pounding. I've no idea why I keep getting this reaction to Coach. He just feels so familiar to me, like we've met somewhere before. But how could that be possible? The notion itself is ridiculous, I would never have crossed circles with someone like him under normal circumstances.

"Is that you Maddie?" Sam puts down the dishcloth and turns around. Sam is my foster parent, she's a nice enough lady but I don't know her well, and things still feel awkward between us at times. But her heart seems to be in the right place, and she comes across as a very genuine person. Not many of those about, but I still keep my guard up.

"Yes, sorry I'm late Sam, had to go to Halford's and get a puncture repair kit for my bike, typical it's the only thing I didn't have." I reply, feeling guilty for being late and not letting her know where I'd gone. Nanna Jenny wouldn't had bothered, I doubt she would have noticed if I was gone all night.

"That bike is a death trap Maddie. I wish I could afford to get you a new one, but things aren't great money wise at the moment, the landlord is being an arse again. All I did was ask him to kindly remove his old car from the front garden, and now he's talking about increasing the rent. Sorry kiddo. Dinner is in the microwave. I should be back before you go to college in the morning. But I'm on the end of the phone if you need me." She quickly adds, Sam works so hard trying to keep this house nice, she's already transformed the back garden with flowers and plants. I know she's keen to make the front nice too. Even though she's about the only person in the neighbourhood that bothers.

"Will do, see you later Sam, have a good shift." I reply back, she hates leaving me overnight and if the social found out she'd probably get into trouble, but with the rents as high as they are she needs to work nights to earn more. She's doing her best, and it's not like I'm a little kid. I'm eighteen at the end of December.

She grabs a small backpack, and a Tupperware container that no doubt holds sandwiches for her break, then races out of the door. Sam is a great foster parent really, and she works so hard doing night shifts at the local hospital as a staff nurse. It's no wonder that she has bags under her eyes most of the time working those crazy hours, and picking up extra shifts to make ends meet.

But one downfall living with Sam is social services wouldn't let her take the boys too when Nanna Jenny died. It was an emergency placement and we all got split up. They said something stupid about her not having enough bedrooms. I would have happily slept on the sofa to have them here, but that's not how the system works. Damn the bloody system.

I even miss Donna sometimes, which is totally crazy considering our rocky relationship. But when you share a room with someone for so long, you're bound to miss the companionship. Thinking about it Donna had already moved out of Nanna Jenny's house by this point, although she still insisted on hanging around the place anyway, so it never felt like she left.

I open the microwave door to see what dinner Sam made for me tonight, veggie lasagne, result. My favourite. I can even make a fresh salad to go with it. Sam's great like that, she always has stuff I can just help myself too. Nanna Jenny would never have allowed me to just help myself like that out of the fridge. Then I find myself worrying that Jack and Tommy got a decent meal tonight, I must text them later on and check.

Firstly, I need to repair the puncture on my bike, and then I can eat. I start to regret not taking up Coaches offer of help, but he already did enough tonight, and I didn't want to take advantage of his generosity.

Grabbing my phone I pull up YouTube, and search how to fix a bicycle puncture. Finding several video's, I click on the first one and start watching it. It doesn't appear to be too complicated, and I seem to have everything I need thank goodness. I've only had the bike a few weeks and it makes my life so much easier, just the thought of having to go back to walking everywhere makes me more determined.

Finding the bike was a complete fluke, I pulled it out of a skip walking home from college one day, no one was around and it had been disregarded, so I liberated it. Why do people throw things like this away, I just don't get it? Yes it's old, but it still does its job getting you from A to B, I call that a win. As I'm taking the wheel off the front of my bike my mind starts wandering again, thinking about a certain football Coach.

Mr hotness himself, it should be against the law to look that good. He obviously exercises and takes care of himself, and I could get lost in those bright blue eyes, I smile. Then I cringe at my inappropriate thought and slap my head repeatedly when I remember singing in his car. Why did I do that? I never sing in front of anyone, I'm strictly a singing in the shower kind of girl or with the boys when they were younger.

Looking down at the shredded inner tube of the tyre, I sigh, slightly exasperated. This is going to be like a patchwork quilt by the time I'm finished. At least it should hold for now, or I'm going to be screwed walking everywhere again.

Maddie, Six Months Ago

"Well, the stupid old bag, she finally managed to do it, drink herself to death." Donna huffs, shaking her head cringing.

"You can't possibly know that for sure Donna, are you suddenly a qualified doctor?" I retort back at her, with a shocked look on my face, that she could be so blatantly callus.

"Maddie, Maddie, Maddie, such an innocent young mind, wake up and smell the coffee. Nanna Jenny has gone bright yellow and obviously in liver failure, you don't have to be a doctor to see that." Answers Donna with an air of authority, folding her arms and looking at me smugly. She always acts like this, it's because she's older than me, and thinks she knows better than me.

"Just because you binge watched greys anatomy, doesn't make you a medical expert. Keep your voice down anyway, I don't want the twins to hear what's going on down here. They've been through enough already." I glare at her, she's so irresponsible, it drives me mad.

"Oh, come on Saint Maddie you're not their mother, let the social deal with the boys, they'll be here soon anyway, I just heard that copper on his phone." Donna sighs, trying to poke her head around the door to see what the police and the ambulance crew are doing.

"Why are you even here Donna? You don't give a shit about anyone apart from yourself! You don't even live with us anymore." I say getting increasingly angrier, my nerves are already ripped to shreds after finding Nanna Jenny lying motionless on the living room carpet.

"For your information I was only here doing my laundry, and Nanna Jenny didn't care if I used her washing machine. Saint Maddie. I think the old bag missed having me around." Donna answers glaring back at me with eyes like death rays.

"Stop calling me that Donna, you know I hate it, we're not kids anymore. And you've literally just watched the paramedics trying to resuscitate Nanna Jenny on the living room carpet. Stop talking about bloody laundry!" I angrily snap back at her, letting my mixed emotions get away from me.

Her face suddenly turns sullen, and tears start to form in her eyes. Shit, I didn't want to make her cry, that wasn't my intention at all.

"I'm sorry, my therapist says I need to try and think before I speak. God I've been such a bitch to you all these years Maddie." A single tear starts to escape from Donna's eye, this is a rarity for her. Donna doesn't show emotions like this usually.

"Hey, it's okay. We've talked about this. You were messed up, and besides, it was a long time ago now, I just happened to be an easy target at the time. And let's face it Nanna Jenny was hardly mother of the year material. God rest her soul." Donna looks like she's about to lose it now. She breaks down and starts to sob on my shoulder. Her body shaking and I can hear her using my shoulder as a handkerchief.

But while I try to comfort Donna to the best of my ability, all my mind can think is, Nanna Jenny's dead and what's going to happen to the boys and me now?

It turns out my fears are justified. I was right to worry, because social services can't find any suitable foster carers for all three of us to be placed together. Jack and Tommy end up with an even worse foster parent than Nanna Jenny. And I'm powerless to do anything about it, because I'm only seventeen. What the three of us want doesn't appear to be important to the authorities. I will never forget Jack and Tommy's little faces the night Nanna Jenny died, and social services separating us all.

The way the social worker and the police officer had to physically tear us apart. The shouting and screaming from those boys not to take them away from me, and the tears running down their angry faces. Why did Nanna Jenny do that to herself? I guess it's something we'll never learn the answer too, and I hope that she's finally at peace now. Even though it leaves Jack, Tommy and me in complete limbo...

Chapter Five

Coach Mckenzie

I loudly blow my whistle three times to indicate the team's football practice is over, it's been wet and windy today making it miserable weather to train. But that's all part of the fun, you'll never change the unpredictable weather patterns in England or the rest of the United Kingdom.

"Okay good practise boys. Jack and Tommy, a quick word please. Everyone else hit the showers." I shout to everyone on the football pitch.

"What's wrong Coach McKenzie?" The twins, Jack and Tommy reply in unison, fidgeting nervously in front of me.

"Nothing to worry about boys I was just wondering how things were going at home?" A look of sudden panic and confusion occurs from both the boys at the same time when I ask them this question.

"What's it to you Coach?" Jack replies, then elbows Tommy and shakes his head.

"Seriously boys you're not in any trouble I was just concerned. Your concentration wasn't great today from either one of you, I just wanted to check things were going okay. You can talk to me you know? About absolutely anything, if it's effecting your performance on the field I want to know. That way I can help you." I answer, hoping that they will open up to me because something is clearly wrong. Both of the boys look troubled. I notice them looking at each other slightly panicked.

"It's our football boots coach." Tommy suddenly shouts out, earning another elbow from Jack.

"I'm confused boys what's wrong with your football boots?" I ask them both, totally confused, and not expecting Tommy to shout that out at me.

Jack let's out a heavy sigh, almost in defeat. "Our football boots are too tight, and they're are pinching our feet, we keep getting blisters. It's only the beginning of the term and the lost property box is empty."

Trying to piece the puzzle before me together in my head, I realise exactly what Jack is eluding too. The boys must get their football boots out of the lost property box. Is that what Jack's trying to tell me, without actually telling me?

"Our new foster parent is too tight to by us new ones. And Maddie is still saving up from her babysitting jobs. So, we have to wait." Tommy shrugs his shoulders in defeat, looking worriedly at Jack and shaking his head.

But I'm certain there is more to this story than they are letting on, I don't doubt about the football boots story for one minute, and I plan to get to the bottom of what's bothering them both so much.

"You two hit the showers and leave it with me, I'll see what I can do. How does that sound?" I let out an exasperated sigh, I haven't made any direct promise to them. I need to gain their trust first, and I pray whatever is bothering them both, isn't something really serious.

"Okay Coach." Jack and Tommy answer at the same time, still fidgeting about. Neither of the boys look convinced.

And why is Maddie saving for two sets of football boots??? No wonder she could barely afford to buy her puncture repair kit for that clapped out old bike of hers, she's saving her money for Jack and Tommy.

I decide in my head that I need to speak to Maddie about Jack and Tommy urgently, and before I cause waves for the boys at their foster home. I'll make it my number one mission to get to the bottom of this, because something is ringing alarm bells in my head, and not in a good way.

Danny, Aged Twelve

"Dad do you ever think about the baby girl I found. Because I do, even now." I look towards my dad, thinking back to that cold December Sunday two years ago.

"Sometimes son, sometimes." He slowly removes his glasses and pinches the bridge of his nose. Dad hates it whenever I bring up the subject of the baby for some reason.

"I wonder if her mother ever came back for her." I ponder out loud, trying to imagine my own mothers face at the same time. At least I got to have a mother, even if it wasn't for long enough. That baby girl was all alone, abandoned in that cardboard box.

"Father Christopher assured me at the time social services would have found her a good home son, you have nothing to worry about. You played your part in finding her and we got her to the hospital before she became hypothermic, she was left in safe hands." My dad answers, but I can tell even he doesn't believe what he's saying to me right now.

"I just can't understand why we couldn't look after her, give her a good home..." I look disappointedly towards my dad, we have enough room in our house. We could have easily taken her in and given her a home. But I don't say that part to him.

"Danny, son you know why. We hadn't long lost your mother and I was hanging on by a thread at the time. There's just no way I could have taken a baby on too. It wouldn't have been fair on her, and it wouldn't have been fair on you." He sadly replies to me, picking up a photograph of my mother and staring into it.

"It's just not fair dad. Father Christopher never even told me where she went. Data protection crap." I say back to him exasperated, Father Christophers lips have always remained tightly sealed on the subject, almost like he's brushing it off and pretending that it never happened.

"Language Danny." Dad replies, not happy with my attitude, and I go into an immediate defiant sulk.

"Sorry dad." I reply to my dad, guiltily, regretting that I'm taking it out on him. It isn't really dad's fault and I certainly don't blame him.

"She will be with a good family I'm sure of it. Stop worrying about her. It's in the past now." He doesn't even sound convinced himself.

"If you say so dad." I reply, and I just turn away from him.

It wasn't until many years later that I found out she didn't go to a good family after all and that I was right to worry for her...

Chapter Six

Maddie

I'm trying to get through my seemingly unending mountain of sociology course work when I hear a knock at the front door. Using any excuse to take a break from the work I jump up out of the chair and shout "I'll get it Sam."

"Okay kiddo I'm just taking a quick shower before I go into work for my night shift. If it's the window cleaner at the door, his money is in an envelope on the side." Sam shouts back, from upstairs.

"No problem Sam, will do." I reply to her, and open the front door. Coach McKenzie is standing there. Right there, at my front door in the flesh, and I start to blush nervously.

"Coach McKenzie you were the last person I expected to see tonight, is everything okay?" I open the door a little wider to indicate that he can come inside. This is mainly to stop the neighbours from gawking, nothing gets past the curtain twitchers in this neighbourhood. But it a crime happened, you can guarantee no one will have witnessed a thing, people around here don't talk to the police.

"Take a seat on the sofa Coach, can I get you anything? Tea or coffee?" I wave my hand towards a rather battered up old Chesterfield sofa that's seen better days. Sam just loves the damn thing, and won't get rid of it because she intends to upcycle it at some point. One too many restoration shows on TV if you ask me...

"Thanks Maddie, I won't keep you long, I'm fine for a drink right now. It's about Jack and Tommy." Coach McKenzie replies, sitting down on the Chesterfield clearly admiring it.

"Oh my God are they both okay?" I immediately start to panic inside, at the mention of Jack and Tommy.

"They're both fine Maddie. I didn't mean to worry you, but I just had a couple of questions I wanted to ask, if that's okay?" And he waits for my answer patiently, wanting to go ahead with his question.

"Go ahead, shoot. Sorry bad football pun. I'm used to a ten year old boys sense of humour." I laugh, embarrassed at my feeble attempt at a joke.

"So am I, I might use that one next football practise." Coach laughs back at me, pretending to write the joke down in an imaginary notebook.

"So, what have the little terrors been up to now? Please tell me it's got nothing to do with toads." And I think back to a practical joke they sprung on fellow classmates last term, I can't go through that drama again. It took hours to catch the damn slimy creatures, and their teacher was less than amused.

"No, nothing like that Maddie. But you're going to have to tell me the story about the toads sometime, that sounds like an amusing tale. What I really needed to ask you, it's about is who's responsible for buying them new football boots?" And again, Coach patiently awaits my answer.

"Well, technically speaking the foster parent is given an allowance by social services to provide things like that, you know school uniform, PE kits. But in my experience that doesn't always happen, the money gets spent elsewhere, and it's Jack and Tommy that miss out. I've tried speaking to their foster parent, but it would be easier getting blood out of a stone. Last time I went to the boys house I got the door slammed in my face and told to stop poking my nose in where it doesn't belong. You have to understand that up until six months ago that I'd been with those boys since they were two years old. They're like siblings to me." Tears come to my eyes, but I quickly blink them away, hoping that he doesn't notice. I don't want to reveal my vulnerabilities to him about the boys.

"I had no idea Maddie things were that bad with the foster parent, the boys they mentioned something. Is that why you're the one saving up for them? Don't worry Maddie, I had to practically pry the information out of them, it's not your fault." Replied Coach, looking deeply concerned.

"Yes, it's that bad. As soon as I turn eighteen, I plan to become their legal guardian and foster parent. I've got a solicitor helping me with the details. Social services legally need to help me find accommodation when I'm eighteen. I'm already looking and applying for a full time job, I'll be finished with college by then. Social services will give me an allowance to help look after the boys too. I've got a plan." I give him a sad smile, my future already set in stone, but it's a small sacrifice for my little brothers.

"You know Maddie, you don't have to take the weight of the world on your shoulders yourself." He says kindly to me, looking into my eyes again. Those beautiful blue eyes of his shining back.

"There isn't anybody else to care. But that's fine, I'm used to it." I reply, slightly abrupt, used to having to defend my actions.

"What about your foster parent?" he looks around the room as if seeking her out.

"Sam is great, but I've only been here a few months. It's not really her problem. Anyway, she did try to help but they wouldn't let her take the boys because there aren't enough bedrooms here, and it's a strict criteria they have. And Sam can't afford to move anywhere bigger, the rents are just too high. Everyone is in the same situation. Not enough money, it is what it is." I reply to him stating the bitter truth, gulping at the harshness in my trembling voice.

"How about this as an idea? Call it a temporary solution if you want. I can lend you the money for the football boots and you can pay me back? It will be difficult for them to continue to play good football if they haven't got boots that fit properly." He says looking hopeful.

"So, what your saying is, I'm stuck between a rock and a hard place. You have to know that I really hate borrowing money from other people, but I'll do it for the boys. Thank you for caring enough about them too." I reply starting to feel emotional, and I blink back tears quickly. Someone else is sticking their neck out for Jack and Tommy, and that means a lot to me.

"Hey, don't look so sad Maddie. It will be OK." Coach tries to reassure me. He gently places his hand on top of mine and gives it a comforting squeeze. I feel that invisible spark of electricity again. What is happening between us? He gives me an equally confused look, as if to say what on earth was that? He's feeling it too. I just know it, this connection, this thing.

Standing up to leave he says, "How about I run you and the boys into town shopping tomorrow after school? That way they will have the new boots before their next game?" he asks eagerly, hoping I'll say yes and agree.

"Are you sure that will be, okay? Because I feel like I've already been enough bother to you, I can take the boys myself." I reply looking unsure, trying to read his body language.

"Yes, I wouldn't be offering if it wasn't okay. I'll meet you and the boys after school, I'll send them a message to come and see me when school finishes. Then you can wait outside for us all. How does that sound?" I can see he's trying to be helpful, without sounding pushy.

"Coach I'll do anything for those boys, because they come first as far as I'm concerned." I answer smiling at him.

Well, it looks like we're going shopping after college and school tomorrow...

Coach Mckenzie

What on earth am I doing? Why do I suddenly care so much about what happens to this young girl and those boys? I'll admit that I'm concerned about Jack and Tommy's welfare, but without any solid proof there is very little that I can do. That's why it's so important to get them to open up to someone. That's one reason, but I have a second one that I'm not proud of, my inner ulterior motive. An excuse to see Maddie again. I feel really protective of this young girl, or should I say practically a woman? And I feel like I need to also earn her trust, which takes me back to reason one, Jack and Tommy. I have to admit it broke my heart when she told me about the kind of life these boys were living. I couldn't imagine having football boots that didn't fit when I was their age, how many other things do they have to go without? And what other things are happening behind the scenes that we don't know about?

Seeing how much Maddie cares for them both, and clearly loving them more like a mother. She's so much more than just a concerned sibling. Has Maddie ever even been allowed to be a child herself?

I never anticipated anything like this happening when I agreed to volunteer as a football coach. Of course, it was my dad that talked me into it, and then Father Christopher that gave me that final nudge in the right direction. They were both worried I was losing touch with the real world. They reminded me that charity begins at home, and in this case close to home, as in my former school. I happen to think there is some saving my soul business going on too, that pair are always conspiring together. But rather than just donating money to the school as my dad so ungraciously worded it, I decided to donate my time instead.

Okay, so I admit that I may have donated the money for a new roof on the school. And maybe I provided the state-of-the-art computer suite. But no one else needs to know who the anonymous beneficiary is.

I haven't really got much family now just my dad, no brothers or sisters. Both sets of grandparents died when I was younger, and of course my dear mother died of cancer when I was even younger than that. Perhaps I never really got over her death, and I know I still miss her every single day, that pain in my heart never really goes away, even after all these years.

That's the reason I became so motivated at such a young age. You could say I became an entrepreneur, totally driven, focusing on anything to take me away from my mother's death. So completely buried away in my studies or kicking a football around with little time for anything else.

Then I really got into computer programming, and by the time I was sixteen years old I'd already sold my first app for a ridiculous amount of money. From there I started investing my money into properties mainly, and a few more overseas investments. So of course, that money started to grow and grow and grow. I don't have to even think about money now, and I certainly don't think even my own father realises how much I'm worth.

But just speaking to Maddie puts things into perspective. You can't buy happiness, although money can certainly help. So, I'm going to have to be sneaky about how I do this, what I'm going to do, and how I'm going to help.

I'm snapping myself out of my daydream, just as the last bell of the day sounds throughout the school. A few minutes later the twins are excitedly running towards me in the gym where I'm tidying away the equipment from the last lesson, cones and footballs are scattered everywhere. The class couldn't get out of here fast enough once that last bell rang, leaving me to tidy up.

"Coach McKenzie we got your message you wanted to see us?" Jack says in slight confusion, walking towards me and picking up a football and dumping it in the box in the corner of the gym.

"Whatever it is we didn't do it." Tommy laughs jokingly, following Jack in unison, automatically picking up another ball to tidy away.

"Nothing to worry about boys. I had a little chat with Maddie last night and she's taking you both football boots shopping after school today. I've got to run into town myself, so I offered to give you guys a lift as well. How does that sound to you?" I answer looking at them both, trying to read what's going through their heads. The boys look at each other in surprise but then simultaneously grin. Good. That's the reaction that I was hoping for.

"Just help me put the rest of this equipment away in the cupboard and then we can go and wait for Maddie out front." The boys both jump into action, practically throwing the equipment into the back of the sports cupboard, I have to smile to myself while they do this.

We walk outside to the front of the school just as Maddie is locking her bike up to the fence. She looks cold. Even though autumn has only just started, her face is already red from the slight breeze in the air. She's already wearing some fingerless gloves and the cutest bobble hat I've ever seen. Her backpack looks really heavy, with textbooks poking out of the top where the zip is broken. A small safety pin is barely holding it together and it looks like it could rip apart at any moment.

"Maddie!" Jack and Tommy run towards her, then throw their arms around her at the same time and nearly knock her to the ground.

"Miss me much." She laughs, hugging them both smiling, and she almost glows in the autumn sunlight, her red hair strikingly poking out from underneath her hat.

"Coach said that you are taking us football boots shopping and offered us a ride into town, how cool is that? We get to go in his car." Tommy announces with a beaming grin on his face.

"Did you save the money already Maddie? I thought you said it was going to take a while to get the cash together not that I'm complaining or anything." Tommy asks thoughtfully, and looks towards Maddie, you can almost see the cogs turning in his head. I doubt much gets past him.

I decide to jump in and save Maddie from any embarrassment about borrowing the money. Jack and Tommy don't need to know that, it's between me and Maddie.

"Maddie was telling me how she's been doing some extra babysitting jobs recently. Come on let's get into the car before the traffic gets bad." I smile at Maddie, and she gives me a look of appreciation, and getting her out of a tight spot with Tommy.

The boys pile into the back of the car and Maddie sits up front.

"Seat belts on boys." Maddie instructs with authority.

"Yes, mam." I decide to cheekily reply, and she laughs along with the boys.

"So, can we go to that new sports shop that just opened? It's got the latest football boots, and all the coolest styles. Zach got some new boots from there last week and they look amazing." Chirps Jack, practically bouncing with excitement in the back of the car.

"I'm sorry Jack but I'm not sure my budget will stretch that far, unless I just buy one pair of boots and you both share them. You could wear one each and hop." Maddie says, trying not to laugh.

I look in my rear view mirror and can see that both the boys look horrified at this idea. Maddie has her eyes closed, now. She's probably trying to work out what to say to them both without hurting their feelings.

"Let's see when we get there, maybe something will be on sale. You know boys, it's not about how expensive the boots are or what make they are. It's all about the player, and what that player makes those boots do." I look across at Maddie and she words a silent "Thank you" to me. I nod to her in acknowledgement.

The boys are chatty in the back of the car on the relatively short journey into town, Maddie's very quiet though. She's obviously thinking about how much these boots are going to cost, and she's clearly worried. I wish I could take her fears away, and the worry from her face.

I decide to get a parking space in the multi-Storey car park because it's nearer to where all the shops are. As soon as I park up inside, the boys are excitedly out of the car, and go running off towards the lifts that go directly down to the shopping centre.

"Wait at the lifts boys." Maddie shouts, shaking her head in frustration.

"They're quite the handful, aren't they?" I grin at her.

"You could say that." She laughs at me. "Thanks for saving my arse back there. That shop is super expensive and totally out of my price range."

"Hey, don't worry we can work something out, for sure." And I nod towards the boys.

Chapter Seven

Maddie

Jack and Tommy are both having their feet measured in the sports shop by a shop assistant, they've gone up nearly two whole shoe sizes, and I failed to notice. Their poor feet, it must have been so painful for them running around and kicking a football. I'm a terrible person I should have realised, how did I overlook something so important? Now I'm worried about how long their trainers are going to last, and don't even start me on their school shoes. There's no way social services will let me take over their care if I can't even get the basics right.

I start to hyperventilate thinking about my impending failure, and letting Jack and Tommy down again, not now, not here in the middle of the shop. I bend over, with my hands on my hips, I'm trying my best to take deep breaths. Feeling my airway closing up, I start to feel dizzy and I can feel myself swaying slightly, it's all getting too much. I keep letting Jack and Tommy down. How can I be ever good enough to look after them? I must be deluding myself.

"Maddie, Maddie are you okay?" Asks Coach looking concerned. He's starting to go blurry, am I about to pass out?

Trying to wave my hand at him and indicate that I'm okay, feeling faint and dizzy, I stupidly attempt to speak,"Pppp panic…" I can't even get the words out.

"You're having a panic attack??? Oh Maddie." He gently guides me to one of the chairs in the fitting area of the shop, and I don't know how I manage to drag my feet to get there, swaying from side to side.

Coach kneels down in front of me, "Maddie, I need you to try and take deep breaths for me, look at me, don't think of anything else, breathe with me, yes that's it sweetheart. Breathe with me, in and out, in and out." He continues to do this for about five minutes, it could be longer I'm not sure. But my breathing has calmed down and I'm starting to feel better, my head is clearing and the dizzy feeling is going away. My airways have opened up, and I can feel my breathing return to normal.

Jack and Tommy must of wondered where we were. They have come over to find out what's going on, I'm getting an audience. Great. Just great. Kill, me, now.

"Is Maddie okay?" Jack asks Coach, but looking at me with concern.

"She's having another panic attack you idiot." Pipes up Tommy, giving the evil eye to his brother.

"Hey boys, now is not the time to start bickering with each other. Why don't you go back over there and look at the football boots while she's calming her breathing down." Coach firmly says, and points towards the rows of football boots just besides the fitting area.

Looking up at coach, my breathing is much better, thanks to him and it's slowing down. It wasn't a bad attack, not this time, all because I had him here talking me through it. Giving me the reassurance that I so desperately needed to hear.

"I'm so sorry I, I, I..." Nope, still too soon to get my words out yet, let alone form a whole coherent sentence. He must think that I'm a complete basket case acting like this.

"Maddie, I can tell you were totally overwhelmed, and the situation got too much to deal with. All you need to do is sit there for now, and gather your composure. Let me handle the boys and don't worry, it will be okay." Coach says in a gentle voice, and I nod as a reply to him.

I'm feeling much better, but my legs still don't want to move, so I continue to sit on the chair, watching Coach with Jack and Tommy. They're obviously having fun together trying on various football boots, Jack and Tommy never normally get to go shopping like this. It makes me wonder if Coach has younger siblings because he's really good with them both.

The boys don't always take to people immediately, especially men. I think it's because they've never really had any real male role models in their short lives. Jack and Tommy obviously respond well to him, I guess he must be a good football Coach.

Standing up, and feeling much better, Jack notices and immediately runs over towards me.

"Sorry about before Maddie, it was insensitive of me." Jack frowns, looking guilty.

"That's okay Jack. I'm not sure what came over me. But I'm okay now. How are you getting on picking out boots? Found anything in the price range yet?" I reply to him, trying to change the subject, and steer it away from my panic attack.

"We're all finished. Let's get out of this stuffy shop and get Maddie some fresh air." Coach appears beside me, and starts to guide me towards the door of the shop, by placing his hand on my back.

"What?? You can't have picked out something already, I haven't even seen them. And what about the price of..." Coach cuts me off, before I have a chance to start spiralling out of control again.

"Don't worry Maddie, let Jack and Tommy have this moment and we can talk about it later." Coach smiles, trying to reassure me. What on earth is he playing at?? Have I suddenly fallen into an alternate universe? I'm not sure what's happening, and

I don't want to cause another scene, so I just nod at him in agreement.

Jack and Tommy of course, are now both hyper excited. Both wanting to show me their new boots at exactly the same time, both talking over each other's voices about a million miles an hour.

"One of you at a time please, one at a time, or I can't hear what you're saying." I indicate with my hands to calm them both down.

"We got the exact same boots but mine are red, and Jacks are blue." Tommy announces proudly, with a giant smile on his face.

"Then they're not the exact same boots if they're different colours, you idiot." Jack answers his brother smugly.

It's really hard not to laugh at this, it's such a silly thing to disagree on. But so perfectly normal for them both, these boys crack me up, they're hilarious.

"Okay, okay." I say in between laughing. "You can both show me you're new boots in the car. Coach do you mind dropping us off again?" And Coach just nods his head in agreement, I really hope he doesn't think I'm trying to take advantage of his kindness though.

"If you can drop the boys off first, and then me at the school so I can pick up my bike. Thanks, it would be really helpful." I hate to keep asking for favours like this. But I really need to get him alone to speak to him about what's just happened, and this will be my only opportunity.

"Yes, that's fine Maddie, sounds like a good plan." Coach smiles at me, and we slowly walk back to the multi storey car park. The boys both chattering away, swinging their shopping bags in their hands.

We arrive at the boys foster parents house, slightly later than expected after getting caught in heavy traffic on the way back. The lights are all clearly turned off and the house is in darkness. Their foster parent Mrs Thompson should be at the house. But she doesn't appear to be at home. I turn around to face the boys in the back of the car, so that I can see them both.

"Home alone again? We've talked about this; you need to tell me when this happens. What about dinner? Who's even cooking for you? I need to speak to your bloody social worker again." I'm beyond frustrated with the situation. I know it's not the boy's fault, and I can feel my temper starting to flare. Coach puts his hand on my shoulder to calm me down, and he shakes his head. And I feel embarrassed for almost losing my temper in front of him. Can I sink any lower today?

"How about I turn the car around and swing by the McDonald's Drive thru near the roundabout? My treat, I'm starving, and I hate eating alone, you'd be doing me a favour." Coach nods to me again, and turns the car around driving back the way we've just been. To be honest, I'm still fuming with Jack and Tommy's so-called foster parent, Mrs Thompson. I really need to speak to Coach about what's happening here. He needs to understand the bigger picture.

The car pulls up at the drive -thru and Coach lets the boys put in their order. Of course they've ordered the complete works, I should have warned him first. Large fries, double cheeseburgers and of course chocolate milkshakes, I certainly don't want to be their poor stomachs tonight. Coach orders a burger and coffee. For someone that's supposedly hungry and hates eating alone it's not much of a meal. Then he turns towards me, and asks, "What would you like Maddie? My treat remember."

"She won't eat anything from McDonald's in case it's contaminated, she's a vegetarian and a really fussy eater." Tommy sasses at me, smirking smugly.

"Manners, remember Tommy? Those things you use when you're trying to be polite?" I look across at Coach and apologetically say, "I'll just have a diet coke if that's okay, Sam's cooking for me tonight and if I eat now, I won't be hungry later." And then I glare at Tommy in the rear view mirror, annoyed with his little outburst.

"Okay Maddie one diet cola coming up." Coach answers, and adds my coke to the order.

We drive down to the next window of the drive-thru to collect the food and beverages. While we are waiting to collect the order, the boys start showing me their new boots. They look expensive, expensive, as in they must of cost a fortune. I look on one of the boxes for a price, at the same time trying not to make it look too obvious. I also look inside the carrier bag for a receipt, but that has also mysteriously disappeared. I smell a rat here, something is going on.

Coach decides to pull up in the car park so the boys can eat their food, and I'm surprised that he doesn't mind them eating in the back of his flashy car. I hope they don't spill anything, it would cost a fortune to get cleaned professionally.

I slowly sip down my cola. It's like heaven, icy cold and sickly sweet. I don't drink cola very often but whenever I do I savour the taste.

"Can't remember the last time I had one of these, I must have been a teenager." Coach takes a large bite out of his burger with the look of contentment on his face.

"You haven't had a burger since you were a teenager? That's weird coach." Tommy answers, in-between a mouthful of burger.

"Tommy, don't be so rude, Coach just brought you dinner." I snap at him annoyed. Coach immediately chuckles.

"What I meant to say was I haven't had a McDonald's burger since I was a teenager, not burgers in general. You're right that would be weird." Laughs Coach, not in the least offended. But now I feel awkward letting my mouth run off at Tommy like that.

"But it still makes no sense Coach, why you would not eat at McDonald's?" Jack asks confused, as if it's the strangest thing in the world not eating at McDonald's.

"I've just never really eaten much fast food. It was just me and my dad growing up, and we used to cook together. Now I'm older I just really enjoy cooking and trying out new recipes, and you don't get abs eating fast food all the time." Coach laughs again, tapping is abdomen, then taking a sip from his coffee.

"Why didn't your mum teach you how to cook?" Tommy cuts in, trust him to pick up on that.

"Hey, don't get so personal Tommy. I'm so sorry Coach I don't know where they left their manners today." And I glare at Tommy again, wishing he knew when to quit asking questions.

"No, it's fine really, I don't mind you asking. My mum died of cancer when I was young, so it's just been me and dad." Coach looks off into the distance obviously thinking about her, and I silently curse Tommy for bringing up such a sensitive subject. The car goes into an awkward silence, and everyone just continues eating and drinking. Pretending like the last five minutes didn't happen.

Coach Mckenzie

The ride back to Jack and Tommy's house isn't far, we all revert to small talk. The previous conversation quickly brushed away. But that's probably my fault because I didn't really elaborate much, but talking about my mother is hard sometimes. I just hope that I didn't make things too awkward in the car.

Maddie is just walking the twins up to their front door, when it suddenly swings open with a harsh velocity. There's now a rather angry looking older lady standing there, and she's pointing her finger fiercely at Maddie, and going red in the face. This must be the infamous Mrs Thompson, Jack and Tommy's foster parent.

I observe a rather heated exchange of words, clearly happening between Maddie and the older woman, and Jack and Tommy are standing either side of Maddie in a protective stance. Looking like they'd protect her in a heartbeat.

Without even thinking about it, I jump out of the car and stroll briskly up the garden path to find out what's going on, and intervene if necessary. I can play mediator if needs be. The further I walk up the path the more raised the voices start to become, and it's clear that this is not a friendly exchange of words.

"You've got no right just taking those boys off gallivanting without me knowing." The older woman screams at Maddie, still shaking her finger at her and getting right into her personal space. Social services lets this woman foster children?

"Please listen to me Mrs Thompson, no one was even at home when we got here, so we went for a burger. Had you even thought about feeding the boys dinner tonight?" Maddie does not look happy, and I'll give her, her due. She's managing to keep her cool.

"Always interfering, causing trouble for me with the social, miss high and mighty." Mrs Thompson looks about ready to blow a gasket.

Before they come to blows, I decide to interject. I hold out my hand to Mrs Thompson. "Hi, I'm the boys football Coach, Mr McKenzie I gave Maddie and the boys a lift into town to pick up their new football boots. I was starving and fancied a burger afterwards and I asked Maddie and the boys to tag along with me. I'm sorry if that's caused problems. But it's not Maddie's fault." And I smile at the old battle-axe, giving her a giant grin using all my best charisma, laying it on as thick as I can.

Mrs Thompson gingerly takes my hand and shakes it, suddenly lost for words. After a few seconds she replies "Well if that's the case I suppose it's alright. But just let me know in the future, and we won't have any more misunderstandings." But she still glares directly at Maddie, while being polite towards me. I've taken an instant disliking of the woman, and I have a really uneasy feeling about her.

Jack and Tommy are both unusually quiet, which is out of character for them. It's obvious this foster home is a toxic environment. No wonder Maddie is so keen to take over the boy's care as soon as possible. I've decided I'm going to do everything I can to help them all, they need to get away from this horrible woman. We say our goodbyes and the boys go inside. Mrs Thompson closes the door with a smug look on her face, knowing she's won this battle.

Maddie goes stomping back towards the car and gets inside slamming the door.

"Shall we talk about what just happened?" I look towards her, and she turns to me swinging her hands around in frustration.

"Talk, Talk!! Which bloody part do you want to talk about? Me being permanently skint? Me having a panic attack in the shop? Or how about we talk about you buying the really expensive boots? Ones that I'm never going to be able to afford to pay you back for in this lifetime? Okay maybe that's a slight over exaggeration, but it's still going to take me forever. Perhaps we should talk about that cow Mrs Thompson back there, the so called responsible foster parent? And I use the word parent in the loosest of terms possible." Her eyes are glazing over and she's so angry, she's practically snarling, and her breathing is tense. The last thing I want is for her to have another panic attack.

"I want to talk about all of the above, but not right now. I just want you to breathe slowly and relax." I start the car and my stereo comes on. I skip through a few tracks to get to the one I want.

Sigrid and Bring me the horizon, the track Bad life, starts to come through the speaker. And I just start to drive...

Maddie

Out of all the songs in the world he could have put on, he chooses this one. I love this song, the lyrics, the melody and let's face it the vocal chemistry between the two singers is outstanding. But what's Coach trying to convey to me with this song? Am I reading too much into the lyrics and taking them too literally? I turn my head away from him, so he can't see my eyes. I will not cry; I will not cry. I dig my fingernails into my hand instead and concentrate on the bite of pain. Better, much better. I'm not going to embarrass myself again in front of him today. But I'm still lost for words, so I don't say anything at all, and continue to look out of the car window while the song plays.

"Maddie, are you okay? I just thought this might help, I've just made it worse, haven't I?" He asks, and I know Coach is looking at me because I can feel his eyes burning through the back of my head.

I let out a sigh, and turn to face him. "No, I'm really not okay. Not at all. I'm sorry, I know all you're trying to do is help but I just feel like I'm sinking at the moment. But I do love this song. You have great taste in music." I sadly smile, and turn away from him again in a moment of self-pity that I don't want him to witness.

Coach pulls up outside Jack and Tommy's school so I can collect my bike, and ride home.

"Look Maddie, I will be honest with you, those boys needed

new boots. And I want what's best for the team. They have both proven they are great players, but they can't continue playing well in boots that don't fit them. How can they perform at their best if their feet are painful? I know you're probably worried about paying me back, but how about this for an idea? You could come and volunteer at their practises and games. I've not been doing coaching that long and I could do with the help. Plus, I really hate washing muddy smelly football kits so you'd be doing me a favour, and that will be plenty payment for those boots believe me." And he gives me the biggest puppy dog eyes ever, the cheek! Who can resist puppy dog eyes? Because I know I can't. Getting out of the car I walk towards my bike, and take the keys to my padlock out of my coat pocket. I start to unlock my bike and turn back around to face him.

Then I put on my biggest, brightest smile and say, "I mean who could resist the offer of washing smelly muddy football kits. Seems like I'm getting the best deal here." And then I laugh at him, and he grins back at me.

"So, it's a deal then? Practise is Monday and Thursday after school. Don't worry if you can't make every practise, I know you have college. If the days change, I'll let you know. Sometimes the school just drops things on me at the last minute." Coach replies looking chuffed that I've agreed.

"Both days' work for me, Mondays I have study time last period, so it won't matter if I leave five or ten minutes early. Thursdays I have a half day anyway, so it's not a problem." I smile at him and then go on to say, "I just wanted to say thanks for today, for everything. I know you don't have to do this stuff for us, but it's really appreciated, I'm just not used to somebody caring enough to help. So, if I came across as a bitch before I'm really, really sorry." I look at him apologetically.

"Hey, stop apologising. You have nothing to apologise for as far as I'm concerned. Do you want me to drop you off? I can put the bike on the back, I've got a special bracket fixed to the car for my bike already." He replies looking almost hopeful that I'll say yes, but I've already taken up too much of his time today, and I'm certain he has better things to do than ferry me around.

"No, it's fine, I could use the ride home to clear my head and get some fresh air. I'll see you Thursday at practice." I turn around, get onto my bike and ride off humming the song in my head he played for me in the car.

Coach shouts after me "Thursday then." And I smile to myself as I ride along the road…

Chapter Eight

Maddie

"Hey Maddie, wait up." Bryan Johnson is calling out to me. That's strange he doesn't normally talk to me apart from the odd question in class. I've always got on well with him doing class projects or brainstorming during group work. He has a kind of cheeky laddish persona, quick witted, and he normally hangs out with the popular crowd.

"Hey Bryan, something I can do for you? I've got notes from the last lesson if you need to borrow some." I've got no idea where that came from. I can feel myself blushing. People don't normally stop and talk to me in the corridor at college. And he isn't exactly looking comfortable, so I start looking in my bag for my sociology notes, just for something to do.

"Um, I was wondering if you could help me out with something? I've noticed you're not like the other girls here." He whispers to me, nervously looking around, like he's scanning the area for signs of trouble.

I stare back at Bryan with a puzzled look on my face, and tilt my head to the side trying to work him out. Where exactly is he going with this question?

"No, no, no, I didn't mean it in a bad way. Crap I'm messing this up, what I really meant to say is you seem really nice and don't gossip like everyone else does, it's hard to meet genuine people here." Bryan looks apologetically at me, and shrugs his shoulders. He looks like he's going to say something else so I don't immediately reply.

"Would you mind visiting somewhere with me? I could really do with the moral support, and I don't really have any friends that I can ask. Friends that will understand anyway. And I noticed the pin you've got on your backpack." Bryan points towards the rainbow pin I have fastened on my backpack, with a glint of hope in his eyes.

It's a pin they were handing out when I took the boys to Pride last year, which was held on our seafront. Jack and Tommy had been asking me questions about sexuality and diversity after watching something on TV, so I decided taking that them to Pride would be a good starting point.

"Sure, Bryan where were you thinking of going?" I smile back at him, happy at the possibility of having a friend outside of college, and that out of all the people he could choose to speak to he spoke to me.

"There's this bar in town that has drag queens, and I've always wanted to see one live, but haven't had the guts to go by myself yet. I heard they don't bother much checking out your ID's as long as you don't cause any trouble." He shrugs his shoulders, looking slightly unsure. I'm getting the impression he's uncomfortable talking about this, and doesn't want to be overheard in the corridor.

"I know the one you mean, what night were you thinking of going?" I reply, keeping what we're talking about vague in case anyone is eavesdropping.

"How about we swap digits then I can message you with the details when I get them?" Bryan answers taking the latest iPhone out of his back pocket, and tapping the screen.

I remove my embarrassing almost obsolete smartphone, the one with the cracked screen, out of my backpack. It's one I picked up in a job lot on eBay so I could message with Jack and

Tommy, I kept the phone that was in the worst condition for myself. I gave the boys the best two in the lot, at least they were cheap and they work. I've never actually owned a new phone, and I look at Bryans in admiration.

Bryan stares at my cracked screen, and I hand him my phone so he can type his number into it. But he doesn't say anything about the screen, no remarks, no judgement, and we go ahead and swap numbers.

"Thanks Maddie, you don't know how much this means to me." He replies, sporting a massive grin on his face, and a look of relief. Making me wonder just how long he's been wanting to share this with me, and I feel bad that he didn't feel he could talk to his friends.

"Not a problem sounds like a good night out to me. I wonder if they will do any lip sync battles?" I say in a whisper, I'm actually excited about this I'm a massive fan of RuPaul. This is going to be so much fun.

"Oh, tell me about it, I will lose my shit if they do Britney or Gaga." He whispers back, and he's glowing with enthusiasm now.

"You know what Bryan; I think this is going to be the start of a beautiful friendship." And I grin right back at him.

Bryan, Later That Evening...

Well, I've taken the first step and I think I've made the right decision. I've been talking to Maddie Reynolds in class on and off for weeks now, just making small talk with her, to make sure she's a genuine person first. After all you can't be too careful, I've been burnt before with people pretending to be a real friend, and I'm not about to make that kind of mistake again. And I shudder at the thought of Chelsea Swanson, and the narrow escape I had with her. Pretending to be my friend to try and get into my pants, no thank you very much.

It's time that I made a real friend, someone that isn't superficial and toxic, someone that I can trust. Maddie just gives off this natural vibe of positivity and goodness, and she's so much different than anyone I've had in my life before. I'm totally over toxic friendships, I refuse to take second best anymore, I've been surrounded by those kinds of people most of my life. People that like to pretend they're something, when they're not. My mind wanders closer to home and I think about my own parents fitting into that category, and I flinch. If my family found out that I'm attracted to men, they would totally disown me. Coming from a reasonably strict Catholic background, I'm going to burn in hell as it is, but I might as well have some fun first.

Asking Maddie to come to the bar with me to watch a real life drag queen, she didn't judge me one little bit. Didn't ask loads of awkward personal questions, she just took it completely at face value, and I never felt judged. I can't explain it, but I'm strangely drawn towards her as a person. I just feel like I can trust her now with anything, it's like a magnetic pull and I can't explain it.

I decide to drop her a WhatsApp message with the details from the bar's website. The next drag night is in just under a week, next Tuesday. It's annoying because it's a school night but we don't have to stay late, late. I just want to check it out and get the lay of the land.

I open the WhatsApp messenger service on my phone:

Hi this is Bryan. The next drag night is on Tuesday.

Not thirty seconds pass before my phone pings, and I get to reply.

Hi Bryan, next Tuesday works for me. I've got a babysitting job until 8:30 pm so I will have to meet you there. But we can sort the details out later.

I quickly respond back.

That's fine Maddie, doesn't start until 9:30 PM anyway. Just want to hover in the back, check the place out this time.

My phone pings again.

Whatever makes you feel comfortable no pressure from me.

I quickly type back.

Glad I finally got the guts to ask you to go with me.

I breathe in a sigh of relief. Ping, another incoming message.

So am I Bryan I'm really looking forward to it:)

I grin like a complete idiot to myself, I'm so happy right now. Yes, I made the right decision after all.

Maddie

"How come your lunch looks about a million times more appetising than mine?" Bryan says as he sits opposite me at the table in the canteen, looking enviously at my food like a predator about to pounce.

"Probably because I made my salad fresh this morning, and yours came out of a plastic container, made three days ago in a factory." I laugh back at him, and push my salad towards him so he can sample some, and he pinches an olive and a cube of feta cheese. Bryans never sat with me in the canteen before, he's normally with the popular crowd near the back, and I feel a sense of happiness that he's sitting over here with me.

"Yes, lesson learned. Stop buying crappy canteen food and learn to make my own lunch." Bryan smiles, dragging his fork through what looks like a very limp looking chicken salad, taking pity on him, I push my Tupperware container in front of him, so he can finish mine. And I take a protein bar and an apple out of my backpack to eat instead.

"Well, it's cheaper and healthier to bring lunch from home, I save myself a ton of money that way. And I like to know what I'm eating, although today that didn't work out so well for me." I laugh as Bryan now tucks into my lunch, and I take a bite out of my apple.

"Respect. I'm just too damn lazy. Banging salad Maddie, make this one again. Anyways, I just wanted to thank you for getting back to me so quickly last night. I was so nervous you wouldn't reply. It was kind of a big step for me." Bryan looks at me still slightly unsure, chewing a mouthful of salad.

"It actually made me really happy; I don't always find it easy making friends. I was just surprised that you approached me, you normally hang out with the popular crowd." And I indicate towards the back of the canteen, where a large crowd is gathered around tables pushed together.

"Believe me Maddie when I say they're not all they cracked up to be. Fun for a while, but the superficial becomes old quickly. I just wish I'd taken a step back sooner." He looks down, and shakes his head like he's embarrassed.

"Hey, baby steps. So, did you want to discuss next week now? Or you can swing by and meet me after football practise?" I ask Bryan just in case he doesn't want our conversation to be overheard in the open canteen, I know how sensitive he is about it.

"Football practise?? Yes, I'd prefer to meet somewhere else if that's okay. But I didn't take you to be a footie kind of girl." Bryan laughs, pushing a now empty Tupperware container back towards me, and rubbing his stomach in satisfaction.

"Oh, I'm not really, my little brothers have a football game after school, and I help with the team as a volunteer. So if you want to meet me on the field at the Junior School on the hill that would be great." I reply to him, with enthusiasm.

"Muddy field it is then. Not where I expected our planning meeting to be, but I'll take it." Bryan laughs, just don't expect me to dress up for the occasion.

"Yes, I can guarantee I will take you to all the best places." I laugh back, enjoying Bryans company and his constant bantering.

"Isn't this cosy? Introduce me to your friend Bryan. You don't normally slum it down this end of the canteen." Chelsea Swanson sits on the edge of the table looking down her nose at me. It's a shame her insides aren't as beautiful as the outsides of her. She has a tongue like a viper, or so I've overheard people say, but I try not to take notice of gossip.

"Don't be a bitch, Chelsea. Be nice. This is Maddie." Bryan quickly snaps back at her, in my defence. He's sticking up for me, people don't usually do that.

"Charmed, I'm sure." Chelsea replies sarcastically, fluffing her hair and batting her eyes at Bryan. I can't help smirking because it's not going to get her anywhere with him.

"Hi I'm Maddie." I decide to play nice, sticking my hand out to her to shake.

Chelsea then proceeds to totally ignore me and turns to Bryan saying, "So are you coming to Ashley's party Friday night? You can even bring your friend if you want." And Chelsea glares at me, as if to say, don't turn up, the invitation isn't for you. I'm not stupid, I know she only said it for Bryans benefit, and so she won't look bad in front of him.

"I'm busy." Bryan quickly replies to her, and gives Chelsea the cold shoulder, like she gave me.

"Well let me know when you change your mind." And she stomps off towards the back of the canteen, swinging her hips trying to look sexy. All it does is make her look ridiculous, and I kind of feel sorry for her.

"That was rude. I can see exactly why you want to change your friend group now. I've also got a sneaky feeling that Chelsea might have a bit of a thing for you Bryan. Did you see the way she was looking at you?" I comment to Bryan when Chelsea's out of earshot.

"Tell me about it, that girl scares the bejeezus out of me. She just won't get through her head that I'm not interested in her. No wonder I'm attracted to you know what." He grins, like a loon, letting out a laugh. Obviously, he's still very nervous about his sexuality. But I'm not going to call him out on it, I just nod in agreement.

We continue to make small talk over lunch, chatting about anything and everything. It's very comfortable and feels like we've already been friends for ages. It looks like things are starting to look up in my world...

A Few Minutes Later, In The Girls Toilets...

I'm about to come out of the cubicle in the girls toilets when I hear someone mention my name. So, I decide to hang back and listen. Call it instinct, but I instinctively know I'm going to need to hear this conversation. Eavesdropping isn't my thing, but sometimes, needs must.

"You should have seen who Bryan was sitting with at lunch today. That skank foster kid Maddie. I don't know what's gotten into him recently." A girl says and I can hear her sniggering to another girl. I think it's Chelsea from lunch talking, although I can't be positive because I don't know her voice well enough. Then I hear another girls voice speak back to the girl who I think is Chelsea.

"He's been acting weirdly. You don't think he's slumming it with her, do you? She looks like the type who would lead a prime specimen like Bryan astray, I bet she's already sleeping with him." I can hear cruel sniggers and then the bathroom door slams shut.

I'm frozen, is that what people really think about me? This is exactly why I don't make friends, what was I thinking hanging out with a boy from the popular crowd? I've effectively drawn a big red target on my back, leaving me open to ridicule and speculation, I can feel tears threatening. I will not cry. I will not cry. My never-ending mantra. Why are people so cruel towards me, what did I ever do to hurt those girls? I Take a deep breath and exit the cubicle, turn the taps on at the sink and splash cold water over my face in an effort to calm myself down, better. Breathe, Maddie breathe. Words can't hurt you, but who am I kidding, only myself sadly...

Maddie

I honestly don't know how I got through the last two lessons of the day. I'm still shaken up about what I overheard in the girls toilets and now I'm referring to it in my head as the Mean Girls incident. Which immediately makes me think of the movie with Lindsey Lohan. What a mess. I don't want to let Bryan down but at the same time I can't cope with pathetic privileged Mean Girls, I have enough on my plate now. I don't want to be selfish, but I don't know what the hell am I going to do now? Yes, I'll talk to Bryan. He'll understand I can't get involved in this kind of shit. I need to focus and concentrate on Jack and Tommy, getting them out of care and finding a job. These have got to be my main priorities. I don't have time for any other dramas in my life right now.

The last whistle sounds signalling the football game is over. It was a draw with a rival school from the other side of town, and Jack and Tommy are fast becoming the star players on the team. And they looked so smart in their new football boots. Coach McKenzie currently has the team standing in a group huddle, discussing the game. It wasn't the worst game, but mistakes were made. It's like a match analysis in the premiership, and it's all being taken very seriously. I have to smile to myself; the twins look absolutely engrossed and are hanging off Coaches every word.

I start passing out water bottles and protein bars to the team, and then I go onto the pitch to start gathering up the flags from each corner. To be honest I haven't really been needed to do that much so far. But I will have the kits to wash tonight as the team aren't allowed to take match day shirts home in case, they lose them. Funding is tight, and equipment is shared between teams at this school. There is a lot of poverty in East-Leigh- On- Sea, schools are desperately underfunded, so they have to make do as best they can. I can see that Coach is almost finished.

"Okay boys, remember practise is postponed on Thursday because it's parents evening." Coach reminds the team, and all the boys are now moaning and groaning. "I know, I know. It just means we have to work doubly hard next practise. Now hit the showers and hand your empty water bottles back to Maddie please so she can get them rinsed out. Dirty shirts go in the white laundry bag in the changing rooms because they need to get washed tonight. Don't forget, the girls team have a match tomorrow so I need the shirts." Shouts out Coach, as the team are dispersing back into the changing rooms.

"They don't want our manly scent, I'm shocked." Jack laughs, sniffing the armpit of his football shirt.

"Sucks to be you Maddie, you get to wash them tonight." Tommy responds, following Jacks actions and then regretting smelling his own armpit, it must smell pretty bad.

"Go shower, or I'll make you hand wash them with soap and cold water you little monkeys." I laugh, chasing them towards the changing rooms.

"Okay, now I'm officially scared too." I turn around and Bryan is walking onto the pitch.

"Bryan. Didn't spot you coming, I won't be much longer, I just need to wait for the football shirts to wash and I'll be finished here." I reply to Bryan, smiling that he turned up.

Coach approaches us both. "Bryan how are you? I didn't expect to see you here. Hope your dads feeling better, that was a nasty flu going around." Coach asks Bryan. They must know each other, small town life, I guess.

"We go to the same church and our fathers have been best friends since infant school." Coach says seeing my look of confusion, and answering the question in my head, it is a small world indeed.

"Haven't seen you in the congregation much recently, Father Christopher made you do the coaching didn't he?" Bryan laughs at him, chuckling away to himself.

"I'm confused, you volunteer too. I thought this was your actual job?" My head turns towards Coach, I've got no idea what to make out of this new information. But it's Bryan that answers the next question in my head.

"Only in his dreams is this his job." Bryan laughs, and Coach gives Bryan a knowing look, unspoken words pass between the two of them.

"I'm into computer programming, nothing particularly interesting." Coach briskly answers, and Bryan snorts at this loudly. What is it with these two?

"I'll let you both catch up; I need to make sure the team isn't destroying the changing rooms. Good seeing you, Bryan." And Coach disappears inside the building, leaving me standing in a muddy field with Bryan.

"So, you two guys know each other." I awkwardly say to Bryan, stating the obvious.

"Yes. I've known him all my life. Please, you can't mention anything to him about where we're going. It's not that I think he will have a problem, but if it gets back to my family..." Bryan looks genuinely worried, and the humour in his face from a moment ago has faded away.

"Hey, I would never betray something said in confidence to me, but I'm having second thoughts about going now." I reply, back to him, feeling guilty about my selfish reasons to back out.

"Maddie why? You were so up for it earlier, what suddenly changed since lunchtime?" Bryan looks at me with a worried expression on his face, and a hint of hurt.

"There was a bit of an incident, it's silly really, something I overheard in the girls toilets after lunch. It just made me second guess myself." I turn and look away from him, not able to meet him in the eye right now.

"Who said what about you? No let me guess, does this have something to do with Chelsea?" Bryan places his hands on his hips trying to look serious, but it's actually really adorable.

I start to laugh at him. "Sorry I can't take you seriously standing like that."

"How about this then." And he does a ridiculous catwalk pose, strutting up and down the football pitch. I'm cracking up now, I'm laughing so hard at his antics.

"Stop Bryan, please, have mercy." My stomach is starting to hurt now with all the laughing, it's just what I needed.

"You don't have to tell me what she said but please just take no notice of her. She pulls this shit all the time, she'll get bored and move on to the next person. Please still come out with me. Pretty please?" He's blinking his eyes at me now, and framing his face with his hands.

"OK fine. But if she says anything else I'm totally calling her out on it. I won't have anyone telling lies or spreading rumours about me." Wow, I'm feeling brave now. Where did that new found confidence come from?

By the time we have finished making our plans Coach appears with a large very laundry bag, I'm not entirely sure how I'm going to manage it on my bike. I clearly didn't think this arrangement through. Guess I'm wheeling my bike and walking home tonight with a laundry bag balanced on the seat. That's going to be a barrel of laughs.

"That must be for me." I reach towards the bag expecting Coach to hand it to me.

"I was only joking Maddie when I said about you washing the shirts. It's not a problem I've got a washer and dryer at home, and I know how to use them." Coach grins at me cheekily, hanging onto the bag of laundry.

"But it was part of our deal. I agreed to do it for you, to pay for the boots remember?" I'm totally confused now, and slightly annoyed that he would suddenly change a perfectly fair deal, now how am I going to pay him back for the boots? Thinking to myself that perhaps I could tidy the equipment cupboard instead, that's always in a mess. I'm about to suggest it to him, but he beats me to it, speaking first.

"Tell you what, how about you help me instead, and you and Bryan can join me for dinner? I made a vegetable casserole earlier and it's way too much for me to eat alone. Dads not at home tonight so it's just me." Coach asks us both, much to my surprise at such a nice offer.

"Well, I'm totally up for one of your meals, he cooks like Gordon Ramsay you know Maddie. But I do draw the line at washing football kits." And Bryan wiggles his nose in a show of disgust.

Coach and I both start laughing at the same time, Bryan is hilarious. Looks like tonight is going to be an interesting evening.

Chapter Nine

Coach Mckenzie

So, I've driven back to my dad's house, with Maddie and Bryan in tow. It wasn't exactly my intention but it's just the way things played out. I needed to get Maddie to my house with the laundry, and it was the first thing that popped into my head. No way was she managing that heavy bag on that bloody bike of hers. I can't believe she thought I'd make her wash the kits, I was only kidding when I said it to her. I didn't realise Maddie actually thought I was serious about her doing the laundry for the team, and besides, how would she even have got it home on the back of her bike? That would have been interesting to watch.

I'm just putting the casserole into the oven that I made this morning when I hear Maddie shout from my utility room housing the washing machine and dryer.

"Coach which cupboard is the laundry powder kept in? And what temperature do you usually put the kits on to wash? Oh, and do you have any of that stain removing stuff?" She barks out her questions to me. Maddie's now appeared at the kitchen door.

"Left cupboard, 60 degrees, and I haven't got any, but I'll get some next shop. Does that answer everything?" I reply laughing at her multiple questions, hoping that I remembered to answer them all.

"Just checking, can't be too careful when doing important

laundry for the team." And she disappears again, leaving me smiling to myself at the pride she takes in even doing the small things. Maddie really is the most fascinating girl I've ever met.

"Is there anything I can do to help? Apart from laundry?" Bryan says, as he walks into the kitchen, grabbing a grape from the fruit bowl and eating it.

"Yes, grab some dinner plates out of the cupboards, and the cutlery is in the top drawer. And set the table please." I reply to Bryan, I don't know why I'm telling him where things are kept. Bryan's eaten with me and dad loads of times, especially recently. Making me wonder if there are problems at home? I know his dad can be slightly overbearing at times, but I'm sure I'm just imagining things.

"Yes, mum it's like being at home. Still doing chores," Bryan says laughing at me, and then jumps into action, like a whirlwind in my dad's kitchen. I walk into the dining room carrying glasses and a jug of cloudy lemonade while Bryan sets the table for the three of us.

"Dinner won't be too long." I shout towards the utility room so Maddie can hear me.

"Okay." They both reply to me at once, and I have to laugh because Bryan is standing right next to me, still setting the table.

It might be a good idea to put some music on, so I wander through to the lounge where my dad and I both have matching CD towers. We do it old school here, no streaming music through speakers from Spotify. I like to listen to an album in its entirety, especially if it's trying to tell you a story. My other reason being that I love to hold a CD physically in my hands, so I can flick through the cover or read along with the song lyrics.

Maddie appears in the lounge , and I hear her gasp out loud. "Oh my God how many CD's have you got! This is amazing. Oh, do I get to choose?" She's really excited, her eyes lighting up like a kid in a sweet shop, seeing our combined CD collection.

Bryan looks at me, then looks at Maddie, then looks back at me. "I hope you haven't got weird taste in music as well Maddie." Bryan laughs, he's never been a particular fan of rock and alternative music, I know he favours pop music.

"Then I'm weird too, because I love this kind of music. Who doesn't like a bit of alternative or rock?" Maddie answers her persona lighting up the whole room, added on with her enthusiasm, and she has the biggest grin on her face, it's nice to see the worry gone for once.

"Do you mind if I take a few CD's off the shelf to look at? Because I don't know how I'm going to decide there are just so many..." She says excitedly, flapping her arms about pointing towards the CD towers.

"Go for it." I answer taking a seat on the sofa and watching her eyes scan the towers in interest. Every now and then, she removes one from the shelf, and carefully places it on the coffee table. A few minutes later, Maddie and Bryan are sitting on the floor with CD's scattered all over the coffee table, having a discussion about different genres of music. It sounds like she has quite eclectic tastes and is willing to listen to anything once. I find the conversation totally fascinating and I could listen to her talking for hours about music, she speaks about it so passionately.

And I'm surprised to find out the taste in music that Bryan has, it's not what I expected at all, I knew about the pop music, but it seems Bryans obsessed with female Divas. Which makes me wonder??? Or am I totally off key here, Bryan always has been on the more feminine side...

They finally both decide on a Biffy Clyro CD, and now have it blasting through my speakers, and the whole atmosphere is relaxed. The timer goes off on the oven signalling the casserole is ready so I disappear into the kitchen to take care of it.

"Anything I can do to help?" Maddie shouts out to me, making me chuckle to myself.

"No, it's fine, just get yourselves sitting down at the table." I reply, as I'm now carrying the casserole through to the dining room, and we all sit around the table together, and I start to serve the food to each of them, I wouldn't normally go to this much trouble, but I feel the need to impress Maddie.

"Wow this food looks amazing Coach, I love a man that knows how to cook, especially vegetarian food." Maddie says, as she takes a taste of the casserole, making satisfied groans of enjoyment at the taste.

"I told you I said he was a good cook, you should see the cakes he makes. He won first prize at the last bake sale. That really upset the old ladies at church." Adds Bryan as he's laughing, and I glare at him, giving him the evil eye. He doesn't need to give all my secrets away.

"You bake? Oh my God, is there no end to your talents." Maddie laughs, shaking her head smiling.

"I'm going to have to check out these cakes. You may have some competition because I make a mean chocolate brownie." She adds, waving her finger at me in gest.

"Bake Off, Bake Off, Bake Off." Bryan starts chanting excitedly, clapping his hands like a little kid. Trust him to get excited about something involving food. We all look at each other and burst out laughing at his relentless bantering, trust Bryan.

"So which church do you both go to?" Maddie enquires with genuine interest, digging into her food and waiting for me to answer.

"Saint Peters church, I mainly go because of my dad." I look down and close my eyes. Religion is always a tricky subject for me, since my mum passed away. I don't really know what I believe in anymore, and I've never really enjoyed church. Father Christopher is a good man, but his sermons go on forever sometimes.

"Sorry I didn't mean to be so personal." Maddie gently smiles, and I try shaking myself out of negative thoughts on the subject.

"No, it's absolutely fine, it's just stuff to do with my mum, old wounds that run deep." I sigh, dejectedly at myself.

"I totally get it, we always make sacrifices for the ones we love." Maddie smiles at me again, in support. She can tell I'm struggling with the subject, the girl is so intuitive.

"Same with me too, I go to church because of my family." Bryan suddenly says, and Maddie and I both look at him at the same time. I had no idea that he felt that way about going to church. Seems to me we all have something in common, putting family first.

We settle into a pleasant chatter and have an enjoyable meal. All the plates are clean, so I know my casserole was a hit. I'm glad now that I decided to make a vegetable one because Maddie is a vegetarian, but maybe I subconsciously did that on purpose, just in case she came over. Who am I trying to kid? I looked for any excuse to invite her over for dinner tonight knowing my dad would be out at a function. Bryans phone starts to vibrate on the table, and he picks it up.

"Well guys I'm going to have to love you and leave you, my dad's picking me up in five minutes, which means in dad language he's already outside waiting for me." Bryan sighs, looking disappointed that he's going home already.

"I'll see you at college Maddie and I'll catch you later Danny." And he disappears out of the front door quickly, letting it slam behind him.

"You know that's the first time I've heard someone call you by your actual name, I had no idea it was Danny. Would you prefer it if I called you that?" Maddie asks, and I realise that she's right, I've never given her my first name.

"You know I didn't even think about it until you just mentioned it." I laugh, but quietly chastising myself for being such an idiot. "The Coach thing has only become a nickname recently since I started the volunteering, but I'd like you to call me Danny." I grin back at her, pleased that we're having this discussion, it somehow feels more intimate with Maddie now calling me Danny instead of Coach; which makes me sound about fifty years old instead of in my twenties.

"Well, it's very nice to make your acquaintance Danny." Maddie replies and stands up from the table and does a little curtsy towards me, going all Downton Abbey. Indeed, it is Maddie, indeed it is, I think to myself knowingly...

Chapter Ten

Maddie

Tuesday has come around so quickly, it's been such an unusually busy week for me, with college, volunteering at football practise and babysitting. I've barely had a minute to myself, I've really been looking forward to meeting Bryan for our night out to a bar, for drag night. It's been such a long time since I went out anywhere just for fun, that I can't remember. It was probably when I took Jack and Tommy to play crazy golf on the seafront, next to the other tourist amusements.

So I really don't exactly have many options when it comes to clothes to choose from, my current wardrobe is pretty sparce. In the end I decide to go with skinny black jeans a staple of mine, with a silver sparkly halter neck top which was one of my charity shop finds. I've tamed my curly hair and styled it and I'm wearing it down instead of the usual ponytail. Sam let me borrow her makeup, I really must get round to buying some of my own but I don't usually have spare cash to waste on things I'll hardly ever use. And I've set myself a two drink limit tonight because with my bus fare home that will be most of my baby sitting money gone from today, why do things have to be so expensive?

Bryan is waiting outside the bar when I arrive, just as we'd arranged previously. We both go inside together and I can tell he's already excited by the way he's fidgeting about. The bar is aptly named Dorothy's with its neon green sign and has a

Wizard of Oz theme, it's really quirky and I absolutely love it. The walls inside are painted different shades of green and there are framed pictures from the movie, with a giant one of Judy Garland taking centre stage. It's not a massive bar and only has a small stage at the end of the bar area but it's already really crowded and I'm not sure we're even going to get a seat at a table.

"What are you drinking Maddie first round is on me?" Bryan asks, checking his fake ID and grinning like a loon, I'm not sure if they'll even serve him. Although to be fair to Bryan he does look older than seventeen, and he looks good in his black jeans and tight fitting t-shirt, his blond hair is fashionably styled in that messy way. I've already noticed a few guys checking him out.

"I've got no idea, what tastes good? What are you going to have? I don't really drink if I'm honest." I smile back at him. I don't have much experience with alcohol, unless you count putting Nanna Jenny's empties in the recycling.

Bryan grabs a cocktail menu off a nearby table, "Let's have a look at the cocktail menu, ow look, they've got one called the Dorothy I wonder what's in that..." He starts to read the ingredients off from the menu, "Rum, orange juice, pineapple juice and apricot brandy, oh my God we need to try one of these!" Bryan shouts, getting excited. It's getting noisy in here already, and you can hardly hear each other over the jukebox playing various pop songs, they must have turned up the volume to get the atmosphere going before the drag acts come on stage.

I whisper shout to him, "Do you think they will even serve us alcohol? I know we're both nearly eighteen but I haven't got a fake ID, what if they ask me?" I looked towards Bryan worriedly, unsure how he's going to handle the situation, I could always drink cola instead.

"Don't worry I've got it covered, hey look, there's a table

down the front available, you go and grab it and I'll get the drinks." And before I have a chance to reply back to him, he's disappeared towards the bar, armed with the cocktail menu.

I manage to fight my way through the crowd to the tiny table that only has two seats near to the front of the stage, and sit myself down to wait for Bryan and the drinks.

"First time here my lovely?" A gorgeous drag queen asks me, and I'm almost lost for words, she looks absolutely stunning, perfectly made up beyond perfection. Wearing a sparkling green dress and killer heels, and her perfume smells like jasmine.

"Yes, I came with my friend, he's just getting the drinks in." I shyly smile back towards her, slightly lost for words at how phenomenal she looks.

"Well, my name is Dorothy and this is my bar so I hope you enjoy your evening." And she winks at me and gets up on stage and grabs the microphone, how did she make that move look so effortless in those heels?

"Ladies and gentlemen, good evening and welcome to Dorothy's and for tonight's entertainment, we have three of the best. Well, the best I could get at this short notice. "And the audience erupts into laughter, Dorothy continues to banter back and forth with the crowd like a seasoned professional, and the crowd is totally eating it up. I find myself completely mesmerised by her stage presence, and I wish that I had the confidence to do something like that myself.

"You have got to taste this drink Maddie..." Bryan appears and passes me a cocktail glass. The drink is a pinkie, orange colour with gold sparkles in which I assume is edible glitter, and a fancy straw made from bamboo. Nice to see they are environmentally friendly here. I take a small sip, my taste buds explode, it doesn't even taste like alcohol, I have a feeling these cocktails are going to be deadly.

Out of nowhere the lights go down, and loud music starts to play through impressive speakers. I immediately recognise the opening bars of Britney Spears, Crazy, Bryan is already grinning like an absolute loon again. I start foot tapping to the music and bouncing around in my chair. Within a minute we are both standing up on our feet dancing and singing along, with the rest of the crowd.

Dorothy is now strutting her stuff on stage, and lip syncing along to the song perfectly and adding some impressive dance moves for such a small stage, tonight is going to be so much fun, and I'm so glad I let Bryan talk me into it now.

Two hours later, I think I'm on my third or fourth cocktail. I'm not actually sure because I feel a little bit light headed and fuzzy but I'm having the best time. Bryan and I haven't stopped singing along and dancing all night. Bryan has really let himself go, not having a care in the world. I've seen him eyeing up a couple of guys so I'm sure we'll be coming back again another night. The drag acts have now finished, and the karaoke machine has been set up on the stage, and it's an open mic.

"Maddie come on we have to do a song I love karaoke and I've never had anyone to do it with me before tonight." Bryan excitedly shouts across the table, taking another sip from his straw.

"Oh my God yes! We have to do it, I've never done karaoke before." I think the alcohol might have slightly, if not taken all my inhibitions away, but at this exact moment in time I don't really care. We both walk up to the guy at the front, manning the karaoke machine. Then we both look through the songbook to see which song we can sing together, and decide to go with Madonna like a virgin because who doesn't love that song? We write our names down on the list, and the song we plan to sing, and wait for our names to be called out. As it turns out we are next up, and are called to come and get up onto the stage. The music starts, and we both start to sing along, following the words on the screen in front of us, although I know the song off by heart. After a few seconds I notice that Bryan has stopped singing and is just staring at me open mouthed, but I'm really getting into the music so I just continue to sing. The song finishes and the crowd erupts into applause, much to my surprise someone at the back shouts more, more. Bryan goes and whispers something to the guy in charge of the karaoke machine, and another song starts, Katy Perry, Wide Awake begins to play, Bryan knows I love this song. So I proceed to do my own karaoke encore. I don't realise at the time that Bryan has his phone out and he's filming it all...

The house lights come on signalling that its last orders at the bar, and Bryan looks at me and says "No more for you Maddie I'm cutting you off." I start to giggle, yep, I think I might be a little bit tipsy, just an incy wincey bit. Okay maybe a little bit more than that now that I'm standing up, I feel a little bit wobbly, the bus is certainly going to be fun on the way home, I giggle to myself.

We go outside the bar, ready to walk to the bus stop for the last bus home, and the fresh air just hits me, smack in the face. Wow, I do not feel good, in fact I think I might throw up. I start to wobble even more, and sway on my feet, why is the ground moving around so much? Bryan is looking at me with concern now, his smile has disappeared for the first time tonight. Yep, I can feel it coming, I'm going to be....

I bend over and start to vomit into some rather posh planters just outside the front of the bar this isn't good, and it certainly isn't pretty. Bryan now has his phone out and I've got no idea who it is he's calling, and at the moment I actually don't care. Yep, I'm going to vomit again...

Sometime, much, much, later, I hear voices in my ear, Maddie, Maddie. The voices are blurred together, and someone is shaking me. I squint my eyes open just a tiny bit and I can feel the world spinning, so I tightly shut them again." I don't feel so good..." I reply to the voices, and I lean over and start to dry heave. The voices start to talk again, and then I feel like I'm floating in the air. that can't be right, can it? I must be imagining things, or maybe I'm just dreaming.

"Let's just get in the damn car Bryan, I can't believe you let her get into this state in the first place. what were you thinking?" The voice sounds like Danny but that can't be right, why would he be here? I now feel like I'm being lowered down onto something soft, and I start to feel sleepy...

Danny

"I didn't realise she was such a lightweight we only had like four drinks." Says Bryan, going on the defensive over being so irresponsible, allowing Maddie to drink so much in such a short space of time when she's clearly not used to alcohol.

"Yes, four cocktails full of various shots of alcohol, and she's obviously not used to drinking unlike some people." I glare at Bryan, knowing full well he's been quite the party boy with the popular crowd at college, going to various parties.

"Hey, I can't help it if I like to party." Bryan replies, reading my mind, and looking guilty.

"Look, I'm sorry, I got mad with you. Your not doing anything I didn't do at your age. You did the right thing calling me. Do you know if Sam is home tonight or at work?" I ask him, knowing Maddie's foster parent would be horrified if she saw Maddie right now. I can't take her back to mine to sober up because my dad is at home, and he would ask awkward questions.

"Maddie mentioned she's working tonight; do you think we should call her?" Bryan frowns and looks at me concerned, probably thinking like me about the best course of action.

"I think I better stay with her tonight just to make sure she doesn't vomit in her sleep or anything. You can't do it, you're just as intoxicated you just hide it better." I reply, exasperated by the whole situation, but I also feel overwhelmingly protective over Maddie and her welfare .

"You're not going to say anything to my dad, are you? He can't find out I was here, my life will be over." Bryan is getting really panicked now, and appears to have broken out into a cold sweat.

"Oh, for pity's sake Bryan I know you're gay. It's hardly rocket science working it out. But I won't say anything to your mum and dad, that's a conversation you need to have with them. Don't worry, they love you." I smile back at Bryan and squeeze his shoulder in a show of support, even though I'm so mad with him right now.

Bryans now covering his hands with his face in angst. "I can't believe this is happening. Maddie's going to hate me. My parents are going to disown me. I'll have to live with you. And I will die a virgin." Bryan announces, clearly he's on his last nerve, and needs talking down.

"Stop being such a bloody drama queen, and you are never, repeat never, moving in with me!" I reply, I feel like shaking some sense into him right now.

Stopping the car, a few minutes later, I drop Bryan off a couple of doors down from his house. The covert operation so that his parents don't see my car dropping him off, that would take some explaining this time of night. But I expect his parents are in bed by now anyway, he's really going to have to talk to them at some point. And I hope things won't be as bad as he seems to think they will be, but who knows with Bryans dad.

I look over to the back seat of the car where Maddie is now gently snoring like Sleeping Beauty, and I drive over to her house. Parking the car out front, I hope and pray it will still be there in the morning, and doesn't get stolen. Opening the back of the car, and gently shaking Maddie to wake up, it looks like that isn't happening for anyone at the moment. Luckily her little handbag is being worn across her body and by some miracle she's managed to not lose it. I try and wake her one last time, but it's not happening, so reluctantly I open up her handbag and rummage around inside her bag, to find her front door keys. Bingo, found them, and I run up to the front door and open it first because it looks like I'm carrying her into the house.

Gently I lie her down on the sofa and take her shoes off, then cover her over with the throw blanket from the back of the sofa. I walk through to the kitchen to find a bucket, because you never know she might start vomiting again. This is not how I expected to be spending the rest of my night, but I strangely don't mind, and I'm really glad that Bryan decided to call me to help with his little problem. Tomorrow she's going to have the hangover from hell and then we're going to have a little chat about drinking safely and what potentially could have happened.

I don't expect Maddie had many little one to one talks given to her during her childhood, and it makes me wonder, who talked her through her first period? Or her first crush on a boy? No, she's been too busy playing mum herself. It's no wonder she let loose at the first opportunity, so I can hardly blame her for having some fun, and I feel slightly guilty for being so harsh to Bryan. Because he realised first that she needed to be a teenager, even if for one night only.

Leaving the lamp on in the corner I settle down into the arm chair which is surprisingly comfortable, grab the TV remote and put it on low, I think it's going to be a long night. At some point I think I must have dozed off but something disturbs me, Maddie is gently murmuring in her sleep but it's clear she's having a nightmare and is starting to become distressed.

I kneel down on the floor next to her and gently comb her hair off her face with my fingers.

"Maddie, Maddie, wake up sweetheart you are having a nightmare." She's not responding and I'm not sure what to do, and she starts to mumble something, I can only just make out what she's saying.

"Don't leave me, don't leave me, how will you find me again?" She continues to murmur. It's horrible to watch her in so much distress.

"Maddie I'm here, Danny's here, I'm not going to leave you." I say to Maddie gently, stroking her face with the back of my hand, her skin feels soft and delicate. I'm starting to run out of options. It's almost as if she's trying to fight the nightmare, and now she started to thrash around on the sofa I'm really worried. Suddenly, she's sitting bolt upright, and looks like she's about to vomit again. I quickly grab the bucket from the side of the sofa and hold back her mass of long red hair. I'm amazed at how much her little stomach can hold it's quite impressive really. Eventually she sits back, wipes her mouth with the back of her hand and takes a deep breath.

"Oh my God where am I? Shit, where's Bryan? Why is the room spinning?" She says as she leans over and grabs her head with her hands. I'm sure tomorrow she will have gaps in her memory about what happened tonight, another danger when you drink too much.

"Bryan called me last night from the bar, you were rather drunk and about to pass out. He wasn't in a much better state himself, but I dropped him off at home, and then brought you home in the car. I've just been dozing in the armchair. I was worried if you started vomiting again, that you might choke in your sleep. But you've just had a nightmare..." I answer Maddie, it must be a lot of information to take in, in her state. She looks up at me, shakes her head, then goes back to holding her head in her hands again.

"I have never been so embarrassed in my whole entire life. I don't normally behave like this and I'm so sorry." She looks up at me again, and her eyes appear slightly glazed over from the alcohol, or is she tearful? Shit, I hope not, I can't cope with her crying.

"You were having a nightmare before, do you want to talk about it? Because you seemed pretty distressed about it…" I ask her, and expect her to say it was nothing, but she surprises me.

Letting out a sigh she explains, "It's always the same dream I've been having it for years, it's about when I was a baby and how I was abandoned." And she shrugs her shoulders nonchalantly.

"You were abandoned? Where?" It can't be, surely not? No way can it be the same girl that I found as a baby I think to myself. But deep down inside I already know.

"All I know is what my foster parent Nanna Jenny told me, I was left in a box outside a church, but I don't know which church, or where. For all I know it's not even local. That's what I dream about." Maddie sadly smiles at me, and I now notice her blinking tears back. Why doesn't she let them fall?

It can't be the same girl, can it? Is Maddie the baby I found all those years ago? I can't say anything to her not until I know for sure even if I can feel the truth inside me, so I keep my mouth shut, hoping this secret won't come back to bite me.

"Do you think you're going to be okay now? " It's nearly six in the morning, and I know Sam will be home soon, it will take some explaining if I'm still here.

"Yes I'll be fine Danny and thank you, it wasn't my best moment I know that, I won't do that again." Maddie looks up and gives me the sweetest of smiles, making me feel ten feet tall.

"Take a couple of paracetamol and drink a pint of water, and my advice is take a sick day. I think you deserve one anyway, you can always work from home. Blowing off college for one day isn't going to hurt. But you didn't hear that from me." I grin at her giving her sound advice, I may have tried and tested a time or two. As I'm about to leave, Maddie stands up and hugs me, leaving a tender kiss on my cheek.

"Thank you, Danny." She whispers in my ear.

Chapter Eleven

Bryan

My head is absolutely pounding, and I currently have the hangover from hell, it's an absolute monster of one. Note to self, cocktails on a school night are a really bad idea, no way I'm making it into college today. Mum thinks I'm coming down with something, but I know dad is suspicious although he's not saying anything. He's totally sussed that I wasn't at study group last night, but he doesn't appear to want to call me out on it. Is he biding his time? Waiting for me to fuck up in some bigger way?

But I'll admit, last night was totally worth the hangover, it was an epic night. Except the end part, now I'm worried Maddie is going to hate me for letting her get blind drunk, in my defence, I had no idea she was such a light weight. But I was responsible for plying her with drinks last night, so I'm going to have to suck it up and grovel forgiveness if necessary. All I wanted to do was make sure she had a good time, and it got slightly out of hand, and that's totally on me.

Rolling over in bed and grabbing my phone from my bedside table, I decide to message Maddie. I need to check that she's okay and is still talking to me, before my paranoia goes off the scale, here goes nothing. Opening my WhatsApp messenger app, I start to type out a message to Maddie.

Hey girl, sorry about last night

And I press send.

Ping, a reply message arrives to my app almost immediately.

Why are you sorry Bryan?

My reply is immediate.

Because I got you drunk then had to call Danny for help

I press send again.

Ping, another message from her.

Not your fault, I had the best time. Going back to bed. Banging headache. Later.

This makes me smile, not because she's feeling hungover, but because she doesn't blame me. It looks like neither one of us is going to college today, and I smile again to myself because I know Maddie is a true friend, and I roll over and go straight back to sleep, snoring and dribbling into my pillow contently.

Maddie

Its nearly lunchtime, I've just taken a long hot shower and I feel slightly more human again. I totally confessed and told Sam about what happened last night. Although she was disappointed with me, she's glad I was safe and my friends looked after me making sure that I got home in one piece. But I'm officially grounded now for underage drinking in a bar and getting drunk. I've never been grounded in my life, and it makes me feel happy, that Sam cares about my wellbeing so much. However, I did leave out the part about passing out and Danny having to stay over and babysit me. Sam really doesn't need to know that information and I don't want to get him into trouble. I'm still allowed to volunteer at football practice and babysit, so it doesn't feel like much of a punishment, and I get the feeling that Sam is letting me off lightly.

There's a knock at the front door. Not expecting any visitors at this time, I wonder who it could be? Getting up from the sofa slowly because I'm still feeling delicate, I go and open the front door expecting it to be a delivery driver from Amazon or something. Instead a delivery driver I've never seen before hands me a takeout bag, and cardboard drinks tray. Before I even have a chance to say you must have made a mistake, the driver has gone. There's a receipt attached to the outside of the bag, with a handwritten message.

Thought you might need some refreshments after last night's little adventure, Danny.

Opening up the bag, I find inside a selection of croissants and various Danish pastries. They are from the expensive patisserie on the high street, the name is printed on the bag. Whenever I walk past the shop I always look through the window and dream of sampling the goods, but it's too expensive and extravagant for me to consider going inside. There are also two large black americanos, with a selection of milk and sugar, Danny has thought of everything. I'm totally speechless, not only has Danny sent me brunch, but enough for Sam too, he knew she was working last night at the hospital.

I shout up the stairs to Sam, as I know she's awake and getting up now, I can hear her moving around upstairs. Shouting up to her, I say "Sam, come down. I've got fresh coffee and Danish pastries here from the posh patisserie on the high street." Within seconds Sam comes wandering downstairs in her pyjamas, yawning out loud.

"Did you just say pastries and coffee or am I imagining things?" Sam yawns at me, stretching her arms at the same time.

"My friend Danny sent them to me, he thought I might need them after last night." I reply, showing Sam the note and looking guilty.

"Well, you better grab us some plates then. We might as well veg out on the sofa, I'm knackered and you look like death warmed up." Sam laughs at me, I knew she wouldn't stay mad for long.

The afternoon flies by watching old episodes of Big Bang Theory on TV, when I remember that I haven't thanked Danny for sending us both brunch. One problem. I don't have his phone number, perhaps Bryan would have it? Deciding to facetime him, because I want to witness if his hangover looks as bad as mine, I open WhatsApp and press the facetime icon. He answers a few seconds later.

"Hey girl, how you feeling?" Bryan smirks at me knowingly, he looks about as good as I feel. Which is definitely a little green still.

"Slightly better now I've had coffee and pastries, from the posh patisserie." I smirk back at him, feeling warm and fuzzy inside at the thought of Danny, taking the time to send me the surprise..

"You actually felt like going out to get pastries?" Bryan laughs out loud, then touches his head in pain, he must still have a headache.

"No, the Danish and coffee fairy sent me them." I smile back at him wickedly with mischief, knowing he's going to be jealous.

"And did this fairy happen to be the same one that came to the rescue last night?" He's looking rather smug now, like he knows something that I don't know.

And I can't help myself, blushing, I reply. "Might have been."

"Oh my god Maddie. Someone has it bad for you." Bryan replies, clapping his hands excitedly, and dropping his phone in the process.

"No, You can't be serious, he was just being nice. But I owe him about a gazillion favours now." I sigh out loud, Danny wouldn't ever be interested in getting romantically involved with me.

"If you say so girl. What's up anyway?" Bryan enquires and I can tell that he doesn't believe me. No flies on him then. Which makes asking the next question much more awkward.

"I was just wondering if you have Danny's phone number? I wanted to say thank you to him for sending me and Sam brunch, that's all, no biggie." I smile at Bryan, hoping and praying that he doesn't read too much into the situation,

"Sure Maddie. If you answer this one question…" Bryan smirks, knowing he's got me, because I really want Danny's phone number.

"Depends on the question Bryan." And I give him my sternest look back, not liking this game.

"Are you into him?" Bryan asks, and pauses to give me time to answer.

Letting out a sigh, I try to think. How on earth am I going to answer that question? I'm not even sure myself how I feel. Checking off a mental list in my head, I try to go through what I do know. Yes, I find him hot and I'm definitely attracted to him, and I really like him as a person. But do I like him, like him? Besides he's in his twenties, no way would he be into me, I'm only seventeen, okay, eighteen soon. It wouldn't be breaking any laws but I'm pretty sure it would be frowned upon. Look how I instinctively didn't want Sam to know he stayed over last night, even though it was completely innocent. So I answer with total honesty.

"I have no idea Bryan, no idea." And our conversation finishes, he nods and hangs up the call.

A few minutes later, Bryan sends me Danny's number…

Danny

Sweats dripping down my back, and I do the last few stretches to allow my body to warm down, finishing up my exercise routine. Opening the back door and grabbing a towel from the utility room, I walk through into the kitchen and open the fridge to grab a bottle cold of water. I like to run at least three times a week, and with the off road biking and football coaching I manage to stay fit without having to hit the gym.

My phone vibrates on the kitchen table, and I pick up my phone, taking a large swig of water at the same time. It's a WhatsApp message from an unknown number.

Hi Danny, got your number from Bryan. Just wanted to apologise for last night, I'm so embarrassed. But the takeout was certainly appreciated this morning, Maddie :)

Taking a deep breath, I lean against the kitchen counter. What am I doing? I Shouldn't be getting involved with Maddie like this, but I just can't seem to help myself. I put my phone down on the counter and stare at it. I don't know whether to reply to Maddie's message or not? I don't know whether to thank Bryan for giving Maddie my phone number, or strangle him for meddling. But it certainly just complicated things, because I know I'm not going to be able to help myself now. I pick my phone up again and open WhatsApp messenger so that I can reply.

Hi Maddie, No worries happy to help, You had me worried last night.

And I hit send. I decide to keep it short and sweet, I don't expect a reply straight away but that's what I get.

Didn't mean to worry you, but I'm glad you did. See you next practise:)

I'm pondering whether I should message her back or not when my dad walks into the kitchen.

"Danny you're home, everything OK? You look deep in thought son." My dad asks, with a quizzical look on his face.

"How do you know somethings wrong dad?" I answer him, letting out a loud sigh showing my frustration.

"Because you're my son Danny, and a father always knows when something's wrong, want to talk about it?" Dad asks me, not really prying, just asking out of concern for me.

"Dad, do you remember the little baby we found abandoned at the church? Well, I think I've found her again. I'm pretty sure it's a girl called Maddie. Do you think I should tell her about my theory, or wait until I know for sure? I don't think Maddie had a good time growing up and she's got a lot of responsibilities, it's complicated. And I know it's not really going to change anything for her, so do I say anything or not?" I look towards dad, hoping for some of his wisdom.

"That's a difficult one son, especially as she's not had a good time growing up. If it's not going to change anything, then I probably wouldn't tell her. Not at the moment, unless something changes." Dad answers with complete honesty, which is why I respect him so much.

"I think I'm going to speak to Father Christopher for some guidance as well, if the baby is indeed Maddie, she was found at St Peters Church. He might have more information that can help get some answers." And I stare out towards the window, thinking about all the possibilities.

"That sounds like a very sensible idea Danny, when was the last time you went to confession?" I take a deep breath, I wouldn't be going to confess my sins, just to get some answers. Although I have plenty of sins I could confess right now.

"Do I really have to answer that dad? Because I don't think you'll like the answer." And I swipe my hand down my face in frustration, I'm a terrible person.

"Then I think seeking Father Christopher out is the best thing to do in this situation Danny." My dad slaps me on the back, and leaves me standing in limbo.

Maddie

Why did I think messaging Danny was a good idea? I acted cool, and kept it casual, I just said thank you and left it at that. I do feel a little disappointed in his response, we didn't have a full blown conversation. But what was I really expecting?? At the end of the day, Danny is a colleague during after school activities, Jack and Tommy's Coach and I hardly know him. And it's totally wrong to have this kind of attraction to him, I understand that. But I can't help the way that I'm starting to feel about him. Why am I so drawn to Danny? The feeling is just getting stronger, and I have no control over it whatsoever. Am I just being a stupid schoolgirl? Yes, a silly little schoolgirl crush. That's exactly how Danny will view me, I must stop thinking about him. I'll have to distract myself but that's going to be very hard, especially since I'm going to be seeing him at football practice and he'll want to talk to me about Jack and Tommy. So it's not like I can even avoid him.

God how did I get myself into this hopeless situation? I pick up a cushion off the sofa and scream into it, but it's no use even this tactic doesn't work to calm me down. I gaze out of the living room window, and think about how much my life might have turned out differently, if I hadn't been abandoned in that box. Maybe it's time to try and find out where I came from? And finally get the closure I need, I don't expect a happily ever after scenario.

If I can convince Bryan to help me, it might speed up the

process. He goes to church, and it sounds like his family are pretty devoted so they must be on good terms with the Priest at his church. If I could get Bryan to introduce me to his Priest, then he might be able to help me find my family, or at least point me in the right direction?

I start to form a plan in my head, making mental notes and to do lists, it's something I've been exercising since I was a child I use it as a coping mechanism, constantly trying to solve the next problem in front me. That's what happens when you grow up in care, the child becomes the adult until the child completely disappears. This is another reason it's so important to get Jack and Tommy out of care, so they can at least have a better childhood, than my non-existent one. And no, this isn't a pity party, this is just a cold hard reality of my life, and I'm damned if I'm going to let that happen to the boys too.

Chapter Twelve

Bryan

I'm in the library at college in the social sciences section looking for a textbook, the library only has a few copies of the book I want to borrow, and it looks like all the copies are loaned out already. I've got an essay due at the end of the week and I need to bulk it out with some decent references. I'm trying to keep my grades solid because I don't want to disappoint my parents, or maybe it's a guilt thing because I know they are going to be disappointed in me eventually when they find out the truth. I find another book instead, and grab a couple of others just in case I need them, then return to my table, where I have my laptop set up.

"Bryan fancy seeing you here." Chelsea says as she plonks down her bag and a pile of books on my table, making the table jolt.

I sigh at her exasperated, I don't need her antics right now, "Chelsea I'm busy working I'm really not in the mood at the moment, I've got to get this essay finished and I'm on a deadline."

"Hey, I'm just here to work too. Thought you might want a bit of company that's all." She answers batting her eyes at me in her usual obnoxious fashion.

"Not really Chelsea, I'm being more selective with the kind of company I keep." And I turn back to my laptop. I really hate being abrupt, but I found it's the only thing that works with her, and I want to get rid of her quickly.

"Rude much, Bryan. I'm just being nice. I don't know what's got into you recently, or it might be the case of who's got into you?" Chelsea glares at me, clearly affronted by what I've just said to her.

"I don't know what you're trying to imply Chelsea, but you can stop right there. If you must know I'm sick to death of hanging around with shallow people, now if you'll excuse me, I have an essay to write, and I'm on a deadline." Abruptly I leave the table, in search of another textbook, hopefully Chelsea will get the message loud and clear.

Chelsea

Ever since he's been hanging around with that skank bitch Maddie, Bryan has been acting more weirdly. I'm not the only person that's noticed it, I'm sure. He was supposed to be my boyfriend by now, he was the one that instigated our friendship to start with. I know we only ever made out that one time, but I was sure it was the beginning of something, he shouldn't have led me on if he didn't want to be with me. All he needs is some gentle persuasion, boys never normally turn me down, and I'm not about to lose face now. I've invested too much time in him already. But he just keeps pulling further and further away from my grasp. He didn't even turn up to Ashley's party and he never misses those, there's only one person to blame. It's down to that Maddie girl, I just know it. She's somehow poisoned him against me. Where did she suddenly appear from?

Well, lookie what we have here. Picking Bryans phone up from the table, where he's left it sitting next to his laptop. I quickly scan the book aisles, and I can see Bryans deep in concentration with a book. He never locks his phone, because I've seen him with it enough times and know his habits.

I open his photos and videos to see if there is anything of

interest, and sure enough it doesn't disappoint me. I quickly forward one video in particular that looks interesting to my phone, but I can't play it with the sound on in the library. Then I replace his phone on the table in exactly the same spot, pick up my books and leave the library. I can't wait to witness the fallout from this video..

Maddie

Sitting on the floor in the corridor outside a classroom door is not an unusual occurrence for me. I often wait for the door to be unlocked, as I like to get to my classes early and get settled before the hustle and bustle other students bring into the mix. A few other people I recognise are loitering outside chattering and laughing at things on their phones. I look up from where I'm sitting on the floor reading a book, and a couple of boys make eye contact with me, I look down quickly and just ignore them. I'm used to ignoring catcalls in the corridor, and I'm pretty sure those are two of the worst culprits. College is supposed to have a zero tolerance policy on anything deemed offensive, but things rarely seemed to be enforced in my experience.

The teacher arrives and unlocks the classroom door, and we all start piling inside. We have assigned seats for the year and I sit next to a boy named Ben. I haven't said more than a few words to him all year as he's in the popular group, and doesn't really have a reason to interact with me. He sits down next to me and I get the usual nod and I nod back in acknowledgement. I notice Chelsea and Ashley enter the room, and I wonder how those two always manage to get seats assigned together? They sit two rows behind me which means I get to hear their mindless giggling all lesson, I'm so not in the mood for their crap today. I've got football practice later on and I'm really nervous about seeing Danny again, it will be the first time since the morning after I got drunk and I'm dreading it.

The teacher has written a so called lesson plan on the whiteboard in red marker pen, as if this is supposed to make us pay more attention. He barks a few instructions to us and then mutters something about photocopying some test, and disappears from the classroom. Giving half the class the perfect excuse to take their phones out and start messing around. I take out my worn copy of Dracula and start reading the chapters written on the board, even though I've actually read the book several times as its one of my favourites.

All of a sudden, students mobile phones start making pinging noises filling the classroom with the sound of notification messages, apart from mine, because I don't give my number out to just anyone and I definitely don't do social media. Maybe that makes me sad but I have more important things to think about than waste my time with that.

Noticing that most of the class have now gathered around a couple of desks at the back of the classroom, I wonder what amazing video can't wait until after class, but I'm not close enough to make out what it is. Someone shouts over to me "Katy Perry fan are you?" then someone else shouts "your tits look good in that top." Now I'm totally confused, what on earth are they talking about? I get out of my seat and walk over to the crowd and it immediately parts for me. Chelsea is smugly sitting at her desk holding up her phone so everyone can see it. It's a video of me singing karaoke from the other night, how is that even possible? Gasping loudly and going bright red, I die of embarrassment on the spot. Did Bryan video me singing, then forward it to all his friends? How could he? He had no right, I'm absolutely horrified that he could do this to me.

"Delete it Chelsea, all of you delete it you have no right!!" I'm pleading and shouting at everyone.

My teacher picks this moment to re-enter the classroom and shouts "Take your seats, I won't stand for this kind of disruption in my class." People scramble back to their seats, everyone apart from me. I'm visibly shaking now, and can hear whispering from every direction, my eyes blur with tears. I will not cry, I will not cry, the mantra repeating over and over in my head.

"That means you too Miss Reynolds. Now..." My teacher abruptly shouts.

I stagger back to my desk and pick up my backpack stuffing my copy of Dracula back inside and run past my teachers desk saying quietly "I don't feel well I'm going to the bathroom." And I don't even wait for him to answer me before I'm running out of the classroom, and down the corridor towards the girls toilets. Making it just in time I lean over the toilet bowl and vomit up my lunch, tears are now streaming down my face. How could Bryan embarrass me like this, I thought he was my friend? The toilet cubicle door opens and Ashley of all people peers inside to witness my meltdown, as I didn't have a chance to lock the door.

"Maddie, Maddie oh sweetie are you okay?" A look of genuine concern passes over her pretty face.

"Please leave me alone, I don't want to talk to anyone right now. Especially one of the mean girls click." I say as I wipe my face with the back of my hands, because there is no toilet tissue in the cubicle as per usual.

She gasps back at me clearly affronted. "I was only trying to help, the teacher sent me to check on you." She frowns.

I stand up and looking directly at Ashley, I say, "Go back to Chelsea and continue to take the piss out of me. I've got nothing to say to you." And I don't give her a chance to reply to me, I'm so angry right now, that she saw me at my most vulnerable, no doubt she'll report all the gory details back to the class. Grabbing my backpack, and storming past her out of the girls toilets, I decide to go to the front office and sign myself out for the rest of the day as being sick, and exit the building.

Taking a deep breath of fresh air, I walk towards the bike shed and unlock my bike with my hands shaking. I'm going to go straight home, I can't face seeing anyone else right now. All I want to do is hide under the duvet for the rest of eternity. Yes, that's exactly what I'm going to do.

Bryan

Typing the last paragraph of my essay with a sense of satisfaction, I then press save a copy and forward a copy to my teacher, finally turning off my laptop. Relief spreads over my body, I have just made the end of day deadline. I've been in the library most of the day, but it was totally worth it, and means I've narrowly avoided a row with my dad for not handing essays in on time. My stomach growls loudly, I even missed lunch today, and I've not had a chance to catch up with Maddie yet.

"Bryan, I've been looking for you all over college." Ashley approaches me and stands next to my table, as I continue to pack everything away.

"Why did you get let off your leash by Chelsea?" Its rather mean but not untrue.

"Look Bryan if you must know I was worried about Maddie, and you're the only person I've really ever seen her talking to her out of class." Ashley replies to me, crossing her arms over her chest in defence.

"Is she okay? I haven't seen her today, I've been stuck in here all day." I ask her now concerned, what could be the matter with Maddie?

"Something happened in class, and she got upset and left, I think she signed herself out as sick and went home. Just thought you should know, as she seems to be your friend now."

And Ashley turns around and starts to walk away.

"Sorry I didn't mean to be rude, its more to do with some of the company you keep." I call after her, and she turns back around to face me.

"Yes, that's the second time that's been commented on to me today," And she looks away from me again, either feeling embarrassed or guilty?

"What's wrong with Maddie, tell me what happened?" I almost demand, trying not to lose my temper with the girl.

"Someone shared a video of Maddie singing karaoke to the whole class, and comments were made. Nothing nasty, but she got really upset about it. She shouted at everyone to delete it. I don't think it helped that Chelsea was looking so smug. Then she ran out the classroom, by the time I caught up with her she was vomiting in the toilet and crying her eyes out." Ashley frowns at me, definitely looking guilty now.

"Show me, do you still have the video?" And she nods at me and takes out her phone, handing it over so that I can see. The video that is playing is clearly the one I took the other night when we were drunk. Shit. How has this happened? I didn't share it with anyone, the only reason I took it in the first place was to show Maddie just how good she is at singing. I go into my phone and see if I shared the video accidently with anyone although I find this highly unlikely. Shit, shit, shit. How did this happen? The video was clearly sent from my phone to Chelsea of all people. It doesn't take rocket science to work out what that bitch did, and she was in the library earlier today annoying me.

"Fucking Chelsea, when is that bitch going to accept it's never going to happen." I say out loud and Ashley shudders.

"I've got no idea what's going on here Bryan, but it had nothing to do with me." And Ashley holds both hands up and starts backing away.

I let out a sigh and say "Do yourself a favour Ashley, don't get further tainted hanging around with Chelsea. I learnt that the hard way, she doesn't make friends, she uses people. You're a nice girl when you don't hang around with her." Ashley clearly gulps at me with tears in her eyes and scuttles away with her tail between her legs. I need to find Maddie and fix this fast, before things have a chance to escalate out of control.

Chapter Thirteen

Danny

"Okay good practice everyone, Jack, and Tommy a word please. Rest of you hit the showers." I shout relieved that practice is over so I can speak to the boys.

"What's up Coach?" Jack and Tommy answer simultaneously in their usual fashion.

"I wondered if you heard from Maddie before practice, did she get caught up at college or something? It's not like her to decide to skip without saying anything." I try not to sound too concerned because I don't want to worry them both.

"No, we haven't heard from her. I can try and call her if you want?" And Jack walks over to his bag and starts to rummage around in it for his phone.

"Don't worry boys she probably just got caught up at college or something." I sigh, hoping that this isn't because of the other night when she got drunk.

Jack shakes his head tutting loudly, "She's got her phone switched off, I bet she's in the library and forgot the time."

"More likely that she didn't charge her phone up, you know what's she's like when she's working on a big assignment." Tommy sniggers, and both of the boys laugh together.

"Okay then, go hit the showers." I reply, knowing there isn't a great deal I can do about it now. My phone starts to vibrate in my pocket. I answer it swiftly without even looking at the caller ID, it could be Maddie.

"Hi, Danny, are you at practice?" It takes me a few seconds to recognise the voice as being Bryan, and a sense of dread passes me. If Bryans calling me, something is wrong.

"Yes, I'm still here." I answer, almost holding my breath at what he's going to hit me with next.

"Is Maddie still there, it's just I really need to speak to her and she's got her phone switched off." Bryan blurts out quickly, and I can easily detect the worry in his voice.

"She didn't turn up today and the boys haven't heard from her either. What's going on Bryan?" I ask as I look off into the distance across the football pitch, in case she still turns up even though practice is over.

"A video of her got shared around at college and she's really upset about it. I think she might think it was me. But honest to god Danny it wasn't me." He says franticly down the phone, and one thing I do know about Bryan is he doesn't lie, I've known him his whole life.

"I think you have some explaining to do Bryan..." I sigh, knowing that there is going to be some kind of teenage drama involved.

"I know, I know. I will as soon as I find her. Got to go." And Bryan hangs up on me, the little shit. I try to call him back and it goes straight to voicemail. Great so now he doesn't want to speak to me either. I can't do anything about it at this exact moment in time, I need to get this practice wrapped up. Equipment to put away and the boys changing room to check then lock up, so I'm stuck here for at least another half an hour.

So, I decide to send a quick message to Bryan instead.

Can you let me know as soon as you hear from Maddie and ask her to call me please. I don't know what's happened exactly, but I'm concerned.

CXXX

And I hit send on my messenger app, hoping he reads the message soon. A few minutes later my phone makes a notification ping and I receive a reply from him.

Will do Danny

The little shit, I'm going to kill him next time I see him, he just didn't want to speak to me and have an awkward conversation, using avoidance tactics, clever. No doubt he's at the bottom of this little drama somewhere along the line. But the question still goes unanswered, what exactly has happened and why has Maddie dropped off the radar?

As soon as I'm finished up here I'm going to find Maddie and make sure that she's okay, and isn't in any kind of trouble. Then I'm going to be having serious words with Bryan...

Maddie

Hearing a gentle knock on my bedroom door, I look up from my pillow, and wipe my nose on a saturated tissue.

"Maddie are you unwell? Can I come in?" It's Sam, she must have realised I was home from college already when she saw my trainers by the front door.

I wipe my eyes hastily with a fresh tissue from the box, and sit up. I never usually cry, it's one of the rules that I have for myself. No wallowing in self-pity is allowed for me, but things have been building up and the cork in the bottom of my stomach exploded out, turning me into an emotional mess.

"I'm fine." I just about manage to get out in between a sniffle and a hick -up, but Sam's having none of it, she's not going to listen to me, I can already feel it.

"You don't sound okay, I'm coming in." And she opens the bedroom door, as I predicted. I'm already in my Batman pyjamas and sitting on the bed cuddling my duvet surrounded by scrunched up tissues, gazing aimlessly out the window looking over the back garden. I don't want Sam to see me like this, no one gets to see me like this. Now Ashley, Sam and the receptionist in the office at college have witnessed me crying today. I don't want to face people ever again, I'm just going to curl up into a little ball to die, right here with my duvet.

"Oh honey, come here." Sam sits on the bed next to me. Then gently places her arms around me, I notice she does this slowly, it's like she doesn't want to scare me away. This thought makes me start sobbing harder, and I turn into her and put my head on her lap. Sam gently starts stroking my hair, and my sobs start to calm down a little, I don't recall ever being comforted like this before, and it feels nice.

"I don't know what happened today, but just talk when you're ready, no pressure." And she kisses my head, in a motherly gesture. It's such a sweet thing to do, but that's Sam all over, her caring nature. But she can't possibly understand how I'm feeling, and the deep down reasons behind them, not really. I feel so betrayed right now, by someone I was beginning to look at as a friend. I never usually sing in front of anyone apart from Jack and Tommy, but I was so drunk that night all my cares went out the window. Now people are going to taunt me, and take the piss out of my singing relentlessly at college.

Was this all some kind of an elaborate joke, instigated by Bryan? Befriend the foster care kid, get her drunk and take a video of her making a fool of herself? Did Bryan and Chelsea come up with the plan together? To share the video with the entire class at college, just for laughs. Oh my god, what if it gets put on social media, imagine the comments? I start sobbing again at just the thought of it, and my overactive imagination and paranoia has really taken hold in my mind.

Downstairs someone is knocking on the front door loudly, I can hear it even over my sobbing.

"Let me see who's trying to take my front door of the hinges Maddie, I'll be right back." Sam says standing up and leaving my bedroom.

"Okay." I manage to whisper back to her, already missing her cuddles, and I bury myself back underneath my duvet to hide my shame. I can still hear the whispers going around in my head, and I remember the crowd of students in the classroom, and start to imagine what they are saying. Box baby, box baby. Thrown away. Worthless. No one's ever going to love you. I close my eyes and think about Danny, he's so nice to me. But I bet he already has a girlfriend, and she's like one of those Disney princesses that birds sing around in the movies...

No. No. No. I totally forgot about football practice. I didn't even phone Danny to tell him I wasn't going to be at practice today. Didn't even bother to leave him a message out of simple courtesy. Now Danny's going to think I'm unreliable. I am a completely worthless waste of space.

How can things possibly get any worse for me today?

Bryan

Luckily for me I know where Maddie lives, and if she's not answering her phone then I'll go to find her. I've never been to this particular part of town before, and it frankly gives me the creeps. I like to think I'm not a judgmental kind of person, but how do people live here? Parts of the area look derelict or just downright shabby, and graffiti is everywhere and I'm not talking Banksy standard.

Parking the car outside of Maddie's house, I'm careful not to hit the curb, I only passed my test a few weeks ago. Mum lets me borrow her car because she mainly works from home now, I just have to run a few errands for her every week to keep her happy, and not leave the tank empty. Being able to use it gives me a sense of what freedom and independence would feel like.

I notice Maddie's bike locked up with a pathetic padlock I could break into in seconds. It's attached to a drainpipe at the side of the house, although I don't think anyone will be stealing it anytime soon. I need to make things right with her, and make her understand it's all been a big misunderstanding, and then I can deal with Chelsea once and for all. Losing Maddie as a friend would be awful, and I'm determined not to let that happen.

The front room blinds are open, but I'm unable to see inside the house because of the way the light reflects. Knocking on the front door loudly to get her attention, I start to wonder if I'm doing the right thing. A woman that looks like she's in her late thirties or maybe early forties answers the door, this must be Sam her foster parent.

"Where do you want me to sign?" She asks, and I look back at her with confusion, she must think I'm a delivery driver or something.

"Oh, hi, I'm Bryan. Maddie's friend from college. You must be Sam?" And I stand there rather awkwardly, shuffling on my feet. Trying not to look guilty.

"Oh, I'm so sorry. I thought you were the Amazon delivery. I'm expecting a parcel." She says looking slightly embarrassed.

"Is Maddie home yet? Do you know if she's okay? She turned her phone off and I was worried. Something happened at college today and I think she blames me. I really need to speak to her. Please?" I manage to blurt out as quickly as possible to Sam.

"Maddie's upstairs, currently sobbing her heart out. I'm not sure that's such a good idea, she's very upset and I've never seen her like this before." Sam gives me a full on glare, with her arms folded, she's pulling out the big guns and means business. Oh no. I hope she doesn't go full on Mumma bear, so I stand back slightly and put my hands up in a show of surrender. If I had a white flag handy, I'd wave it at her.

"Look, I haven't come here to cause any trouble. Maddie is my friend and I just want a chance to explain things to her. Please Sam, let me put this right." I sigh and run both of my hands down my face in frustration.

"You have two minutes, and if she wants you gone you go. I won't stand for any trouble. I'm only letting you in because she's talked about you to me, and I know she happens to think a lot of you." Sam opens the door wider and lets me inside pointing up the stairs. "First room at the top on the left. Two minutes, I'm serious Bryan." And she points at me. Wow, I really do not want to get on the wrong side of her, and I thought she was a nurse. Nurse Ratchet, more like.

Running up the stairs and gently tapping on her bedroom door, I notice Sam is still standing downstairs glaring daggers at me. Yep, definitely Nurse Ratchet.

"Maddie, Maddie, It's Bryan can I come in? Please?" I ask, and I can hear her crying inside her room, and my heart dips, I hate being the cause of all this. Well, some of it. Fucking Chelsea tampering with my phone...

"Go away. You've ruined everything. How could you, I thought we were friends." Maddie says and her voice sounds all scratchy and strained through crying.

"Maddie please. Let me at least explain things to you, I didn't share that video of you. It wasn't me."

The door opens slightly, and she stands there looking at me, her eyes red and her nose all runny. Maddie is what I call an ugly crier, but I'll keep that to myself. She dabs her bright red snotty nose with a tissue and quietly says, "You better come inside and explain then."

Walking into Maddie's bedroom I quickly glance back at Sam downstairs, but she's gone. Must of heard what Maddie said, I bet she has super hearing and nothing gets past her. Nurse Ratchet powers.

"Are you wearing Batman pyjamas Maddie?" I notice grinning at her trying to lighten the atmosphere in the room.

"This day just keeps on getting worse." Maddie replies as she looks down at the offending pyjamas and realises what she's wearing in front of me.

"I think they look cute on you, Batgirl." And I give her a another cheeky grin trying to get her to crack a smile.

"You didn't come here to discuss my questionable choice in fashion Bryan, so spit it out then go. I've had about as much as I can take for one day." And she pulls out a chair to sit on, leaving me standing there, Maddie certainly isn't going to make this easy for me.

"Okay, I deserved that. But I didn't post the video, please believe me. I stupidly left my phone unattended on the desk in the library. I'm pretty sure Chelsea went into my phone when I was looking for a book, she shared the video." I look down at the floor in utter regret, I need to take at least some of the blame for this.

"But why did you take the video in the first place Bryan? I was drunk, I was only singing because of that. It's so humiliating, now everyone is taking the piss out of me." Her eyes are tearing up again, I really don't want Maddie to start crying more. So I try to explain why.

"I took the video because you have such a good voice, I was going to show it to you when you were sober, but our paths didn't cross today because I was stuck in the library. Maddie I never intended to hurt you like this. But I'm going to put this right." I reply, hoping Maddie will believe me because I really do mean what I say.

"Why is Chelsea doing this? I don't even know her. I just don't get it." Maddie asks, with tears now running down her face again. I sigh out loud and sit down on her bed and she doesn't comment so I guess it's okay to do so.

"It was at a party, and I was drunk, one minute we were talking and the next minute we were making out, Chelsea instigated it. We never went past kissing or anything else. I stopped when it felt wrong. It just did nothing for me, it wasn't getting me excited or anything. I realised it wasn't just her, it was all girls. I'm just not into them like that. Chelsea was never the friend I thought she was, and now I can't get rid of her. She's obviously jealous of you, and the fact we're now friends. " And I smile sadly at her and continue "I've tried to let her down gently and that didn't work, and being downright rude to her doesn't seem to work either. But imagine if she found out I was attracted to men? The whole of Eastleigh-On-Sea would know." I sadly sigh, hoping that my explanation is enough for Maddie to understand.

"That's exactly how I feel now Bryan, about my singing." She replies curtly, and I totally deserve that.

"Touché Maddie. Touché." She's so right.

"Sorry, now I'm being the complete bitch. It's nothing like having someone potentially outing you. I'm sorry Bryan I didn't mean that." And she squeezes my hand, Maddie is now apologising to me, something that I don't deserve.

"Oh, come here." And I grab her into a bear hug which she reciprocates, snuggling into my chest.

"We really need to not get drunk like that again. But I promise you Maddie I really am going to fix this. Not sure how, but I will." And I pull back from the hug to smile at her, and she looks like she's starting to get some of her glow back.

"If it's going to cause problems for you Bryan just let it go,

Chelsea isn't worth it. Are you positive it was her?" Maddie asks, and I can't believe how understanding she's being.

"Chelsea was the only other person hanging around my table in the library, and she properly knows I don't have a passcode on my phone. I never saw the need in all honesty, but I'm going to rectify that right now." I take my phone out of my pocket and I proceed to put a passcode on my phone like I should have done when I first got it.

There's a gentle knock on the bedroom door.

"Is it safe to enter? I come armed with tea and chocolate hobnobs." Sam enters the room with a small tray with two mugs of tea, and half a packet of biscuits.

"Thank you, Sam, it's all good. Well not good, good, but at least I know it wasn't Bryans fault now." Maddie replies to Sam with a look of relief on her face.

"Good glad you kids have sorted it out. Have your tea and come downstairs when you're ready. I need a hand unpacking a delivery that just arrived at long last." Sam smiles and goes back downstairs.

"Sam really cares about you Maddie, you should of seen her before, she was ready to rip my head off for upsetting you." I say to her, shuddering my shoulders in fear.

"Who Sam? She wouldn't hurt a fly, she's a nurse you know..." And Maddie gives me a look of confusion.

"Yes, you did mention that..." And I just smile back at her knowingly, maybe Nurse Ratchet isn't so bad after all.

Maddie

Getting over my mini meltdown, it's amazing what a simple snack of tea and hobnobs can achieve. I actually feel really bad now, for blaming Bryan and thinking that he would do such a thing on purpose, I guess that I need to work harder on my trust issues . It wasn't his fault, even though I can tell he's not completely convinced, it was down to Chelsea and her selfish insecurities. I'm not one for causing further drama, so long as she leaves me and Bryan alone. I'll let it go, but this is the honest to god last time I do it, anymore and I'll be the one coming for her, personally. Guess I'll have to deal with people sniggering behind my back for a few days, until they move onto the next poor soul that they deem gossip worthy.

Thinking about my friend, I really wish that I could help Bryan feel more comfortable about his sexuality, but he's terrified about his family finding out, especially his dad. Surely being family, they wouldn't disown him like he thinks? But then look at what happened to me as a baby, and I can entirely see where Bryan is coming from.

"Are you going downstairs Maddie to help Sam, I'm too scared to leave it too long. She is one scary lady." Bryan says jokingly grabbing the tea tray, with empty mugs and a demolished biscuit packet, indicating we need to go downstairs.

Snapping out of my daydream I reply, "She really isn't scary you know." And I laugh as I start walking downstairs and into the living room. There is a massive cardboard box propped up against the sofa, the delivery driver must of helped her carry it inside the house. What on earth has she been buying now? Maybe it's something for the back garden?

"Great can you two unpack that box for me together please whilst I fold this washing. I want to get it in the airing cupboard before I go to work tonight." Sam says, pointing towards the box. Bryan gives me a look, and mouths "scary" to me, making me laugh.

"Sure Sam, what is it anyway? You have me all intrigued now. Is it a garden chair? Or maybe a mini-greenhouse, I know you have been wanting to get one." I say looking quizzically, trying to work out the contents by the size and shape of the box.

"Open it up and you'll find out, standing there playing guessing games won't tell you what's inside." She chuckles to herself and wanders into the kitchen to fold her washing.

"Guess we better do as the lady says, before we both get put into the naughty corner." Bryan laughs, nudging my shoulder with his.

"Guess we'd better then, seeing how you're scared of Sam ." I answer, giggling to myself. We battle through the plastic ties tightly wrapped around the large rectangular box, that's once I find the scissors. I swear to god those things have legs because they are never where you last left them. Next is getting through the tape and metal staples holding the box firmly shut. It's like they never want you to get inside it. Finally, we get the box open, and I still can't make out what it's supposed to be, inside all I can see is polystyrene packing material.

"Why don't we carefully tip the box on its side so we can remove the packing?" Bryan says.

"Good idea, but we need to be careful because it could be breakable." I answer. There might be glass or something equally breakable inside. We both nod in agreement with each other and get to work. The polystyrene is now tipped out onto the floor and all I can really make out are some metal handles poking out, and what looks like a wheel. Oh my god, she hasn't, has she?

"Sam if you've gone and done what I think you've done, I'm going to kill you!" I scream excitedly now ripping the polystyrene from the bike, yes, a brand spanking new mountain bike!!! I can't stop grinning from ear to ear. No one, and I mean no one, has ever brought me anything like this in my whole entire life ever. Everything I've ever owned, has either been a hand me down or from a charity shop. Don't get me wrong there is absolutely nothing wrong with that, but to have something new, something that's only mine. Well, that is special. I turn towards Sam, who's coming back into the room carrying a basket of washing, just in time to see the expression of pure joy on my now beaming face.

"I couldn't let you travel around the town on that death trap any longer. I also got you a proper cycle helmet, a decent lock and some lights." Sam smiles at me kindly, looking satisfied that her work here is done.

"I don't know what to say Sam, no one ever in my entire life has ever given me something this special. Thank you, thank you, thank you." And I sling myself at her, and pull Sam into a hug, kissing her on the cheek.

"Your very welcome Maddie, worth every penny to see that smile on your face. You most definitely deserve it with all the hard work you do." And she kisses the top of my head, and I suddenly feel blessed to have someone like Sam in my life.

"You're going to need some spanners Maddie, to put the handlebars onto the frame and attach the lights and I know just the person to ask. Danny has all that kind of thing, he takes his biking very seriously." Bryan grins at me knowingly.

"Shit, I just remembered. I totally forgot to let Danny know I wasn't going to be at practice today. I need to call him." I anxiously say to Bryan, feeling sick to my stomach that I'd forgotten again.

"No worries, I just messaged him that you're okay now, and he's coming over after practice to speak to you. I think he just wants to know for sure, and check up on you." Bryan replies nonchalantly, shrugging his shoulders, as if to say thanks, it's nothing.

"He can't come over right now, I'm in my bloody Batman pyjamas!" I shout thumping Bryan in the arm and running out of the living room to get dressed. I can hear them both sniggering at me together, as I run upstairs.

Danny

The notification sound on my phone goes with a familiar ping, I've got a new message.

Danny can you come over to Maddie's house asap. Bring bike tools, bike emergency.

Okay now I'm really confused, what's happened now? I can't keep up. So, I send a short message back to Bryan.

On my way over as soon as I finish up here, and you have some explaining to do.

The last few kids filter out of the changing room and I do a quick check to make sure nothing has been left behind. I'm always finding strange things left there, last week I found a plastic duck??? Finally I lock the door up, and make my way towards the car park, getting into my car. I decide to let my dad know I might be late for dinner tonight. Taking my phone out of my pocket I give him a call. His phone goes straight to voicemail which is strange, no one seems to actually want to talk to me today. So, I just leave him a message.

"Hi Dad, I might be late tonight, so go ahead and eat without me. There is a quiche in the fridge I got from the bakery yesterday, the salad is already made up and your low fat dressing is in the door of the fridge. You can microwave a jacket potato to go with it if you want. Don't worry about me,

I'll feed myself while I'm out. Call me if you need anything picking up. Bye." And I hang up the phone and get into my car. Wonder why dad didn't answer his phone? I'm sure it's nothing to worry about. Its only later on that night that I realise I should have worried...

The drive to Maddie's house from school is only a short one, and I always have my tools in the boot of the car in case of emergencies. I go off road biking most weekends unless the weather is particularly bad, and I don't like getting caught out. There are loads of places to cycle around Eastleigh-On-Sea or just beyond. My favourite route takes me across the hills near the cliffs, the view is spectacular. But you can't go up there if it gets windy, people innocently walking their dogs have been swept over the cliff in a gust of wind before now. It just isn't worth the risk. So, if the weather is bad, I normally just stick to taking the cycle route that goes around the town and down the seafront past the pier.

I arrive at Maddie's house and park behind Bryans car, blocking him in but parking is pretty dire in this street and I'm certainly not leaving my car further down the road. As I walk up the front path, the front door flies open and Bryan greets me.

"I saw you pull up, please tell me you have your bike tools? We have a bike emergency inside." Bryan laughs and disappears inside the house again, leaving me to just walk inside. I guess the invitation is implied as all social graces have appeared to have gone out the window today with Bryan and Maddie. God, I sound like my dad moaning...

"Danny thanks for coming, Bryan kind of volunteered you to help but it's totally okay if your busy or pissed at me for not turning up for practice today. This thing that happened at college kind of got in the way, and I might have had a slight over reaction to it and got upset. I promise I won't let you down again." Then Maddie whispers, "Sorry Danny."

"Hey I was just concerned you were okay when you didn't

show up, Jack and Tommy just thought you were in the library studying and forgot the time. So, no harm done. I'm just glad you're okay, but try not to worry me like that again." I smile at her reassuringly, feeling like a prick scalding her.

"As for you Bryan, I don't appreciate being cut off like that on the phone, then getting sent to voicemail. That really did have me worried." I glare at Bryan, crossing my arms over and tapping my foot, shit, now I'm really acting like my dad.

"Time was of the essence, and I was on a mission to find Maddie. But it all ended well, now we can do group hugs and sing kumbyya holding hands." Bryan announces, cracking up Maddie in the process. He's such a dramatic little shit, but you can't help liking him for it, I hope he never changes.

"Anyway, what's this bike emergency? Or is that just something you made up to distract me?" I look at Bryan raising my eyebrows.

"Oh my god, Sam is the best person ever, she got me a brand new bike. Brand new, with lights and everything. The only thing is you have to fix the handlebars to the frame and put the lights on. I could do it, but I don't have all the tools. Then Bryan volunteered you to help..." Maddie's gleaming at me in happiness, and Bryan does a little wave, cheeky shit.

"No problem happy to help." I reply laughing and shaking my head, these two are a right pair together, and I can see now why they are friends.

"Would you teach me how to fix it myself Danny? I think it's good to learn how to take care of things. That's if it's okay, or not, I can always YouTube it." Maddie babbles, and I notice she blushes at me slightly. This girl never stops surprising me. I guess she's so used to having to do things for herself, even though I'd offered to fix it for her, she wants to still help and learn at the same time. So of course I don't mind helping her out.

"And I'll order pizza, you need to save me from my mums corned beef hash tonight. I swear to god she's stuck in the nineteen seventies, it's the most disgusting meal on the planet. Save me." Says Bryan being as dramatic as ever, making a gagging sound for effect. We're all laughing loudly when a woman walks into the living room, this must be Sam, Maddie's foster parent. She's in a uniform, I didn't realise she was a nurse.

"Did someone mention pizza? Save me a couple of slices, I've been called into work early. There's been a pile up just off the seafront, several vehicles are involved. So it's just as well your having pizza because I haven't got time to cook dinner tonight Maddie." Sam says, with a worried look on her face. Then she opens her purse and tries to give Maddie some money for the pizza.

"It's my treat, put your money away. Let's get this pizza party going." Bryan pipes up excitedly, and Sam glares at him.

"Or minus the party, just pizza?" Bryan cheekily grins at her pulling out the charm offensive.

"Better." Sam replies, trying her best not to laugh.

"Oh, my goodness how rude of me, I'm Sam. I'm guessing your Danny the bike fixer." She says, holding out her hand for me to shake.

I laugh back at Sam in amusement, "Bike fixer, football coach extraordinaire. But it sounds like you have the really important job." I answer her back, indicating to uniform Sam's wearing.

"Yes, a job I need to get to asap. Nice meeting you Danny. Bryan, I'm watching you, these walls have eyes." Then she points to her eyes, then points to Bryan. Bryan salutes back to her standing to attention like a soldier.

"And don't forget to save me pizza, I will be thinking about that pizza for breakfast all shift." Sam grabs her backpack and car keys, and is out the door like a thunderbolt.

"Well, there's never a dull moment around here. I hope that accident isn't a bad one. Sam always takes it hard if she loses a patient. She doesn't let on, but I can always tell." Maddie sombrely says. Bryan as always lightens the moment.

"Okay I vote we get individual pizza because I know Maddie will want some veggie monstrosity and you just want the one with the hottest chillies on." Bryan directs at me, he's not wrong though.

"Bryan any pizza that has pineapple on is not a real pizza, it's just wrong on so many levels." I smirk at him knowing full well this will wind him up a treat, I know exactly which buttons to press, but it's Maddie who answers.

"For your information Danny boy I will also be having pineapple on my pizza." Maddie smiles at me, grinning cheekily.

I'm slightly speechless, only my mum ever called me Danny boy, and I haven't heard it in years. Her smile turns into a frown like she's picked up on something. I just shake my head at her to let it go, and she immediately drops it, she's so intuitive.

"Do you have any pizza menus Maddie?" Bryan asks and she shakes her head.

"Good, because I have Mario's Pizzeria here on speed dial." Bryan holds up his phone as he grins at us both.

"Well, you sort out the pizzas as you appear to know everyone's order. And Maddie and I will get onto fixing this bike together." I answer, picking up my tool box and opening the lid.

"Sounds like a plan Batman, and Batgirl of course." Bryan laughs and Maddie just glares at him for some reason, must be an inside joke, I feel like I'm missing something here...

Chapter Fourteen

Sam

Placing my bag in my locker, and putting my ID lanyard on around my neck, I carefully tuck the security card attached to the lanyard into my top pocket, so it doesn't flap around getting in the way. I pop a piece of minty gum into my mouth, just to freshen it up, and put my hair up into a twist and secure it with a butterfly clip, already knowing I'll have to put it up again at least three more times during my shift. Damn clip, never seems to hold my hair and it's too long to wear in a ponytail, but forget putting it in a bun, I can't cope with all the hair grips it involves. I change into my comfortable work shoes with the memory foam inserts, and I'm ready to go into battle. I open the doors to the orthopaedic trauma ward, my home for at least the next thirteen hours.

The ward Sister spots me, she's running around with a clipboard coordinating staff and patients into various bays, "Thanks for getting here early Sam, can you take charge in bay two please. We have at least six incoming patients from the emergency unit, some will need immediate prep for surgery. I'm not sure how many went to the ITU, and I know some are already in theatre. Ortho is in for a busy night that's for sure."

"Do you know yet what happened?" I ask the ward Sister, taking it all in, already making notes in my head.

"Apparently a van smashed into the side of a bus, then the bus smashed head on into a car which caused a multiple pile-up. There are three known fatalities with more expected." She discreetly whispers to me, not wanting people to overhear, you never know who's listening. I gulp. No wonder I got called in early it really was a bad accident, I expect some patients will be transferred to other hospitals if we don't have enough beds here. The ward doors open, and one of the emergency unit nurses and a porter are wheeling a patient onto the ward to be cared for.

"You take this patient Sam, I've got some extra Health Care Assistants into help but we are still short staffed. But holler loudly if you need me, I'm around." And she's off barking orders to one of the scared looking junior doctors, poor guy. He only started on orthopaedics two days ago, talk about a baptism of fire. I direct the staff into bay two and start taking handover from the other nurse.

"This is Thomas McKenzie, 56 years old and he was in part of the pile up. Observations are stable but he has sustained various injuries. We've got him in a head and neck collar because he's still waiting for a CT scan, but there backed up at the moment. He hit his head hard even though the air bags deployed on impact. Mr McKenzie was cut out of the car by fire crews, and he has a compound fracture of his right tib and fib, which will need surgery..."

And the nurse continues to give me all the gory details, poor guy. She finally finishes the handover, and I have my first patient of the night. Time to check his observations again, and get him comfortable, he's conscious so at least I can converse with him.

"Hi Mr McKenzie my names Sam and I'm going to be your nurse tonight, did you have a next of kin that you wanted me to phone and let them know you are here?" I ask him, taking out my small notepad I carry in my uniform pocket, to jot down any details.

"Yes nurse, please. Please call my son Danny for me..."

Maddie

"**O**kay Bryan, I've got to hand it to you. That was hands down the best pizza I've ever had. I don't think I will ever look at a frozen pizza the same way ever again, Mario's all the way." I laugh and agree with Bryan's choice of takeaway.

"Yes, Bryan I have to agree with Maddie, you can't beat a Mario's pizza." Danny just nods in agreement, wiping his hands on a paper napkin. Looking satisfied with the meal.

"Then my job here is done. Happy to have satisfied customers, all part of the service." Bryan grins, like he was the one that cooked the pizzas personally.

"And thank you for buying Bryan, I'll cook you dinner one night. Your invited too of course Danny." I shyly add on, hoping Danny doesn't think I'm being too forward with my random invite.

Danny chuckles and replies, "We are fast turning into a unofficial supper club, I feel all posh now."

Then Bryan adds "All we need now is a saucy book to discuss and we could add book club to that title, and really turn it into a housewife special."

"Oh, I see, your secretly into romance novels Bryan?" I prod, not knowing if he's serious or joking. It's difficult to know with Bryan sometimes.

"Hey, it's no secret, I love a romance novel as much as the next person. I'm just man enough to own it." And he winks at Danny, and we all burst out laughing.

"And on that note, I'm going to the bathroom if that's okay Maddie?" Danny asks me, blushing slightly at Bryans last comment.

"Sure, downstairs toilet is just through the kitchen." Danny wanders through the kitchen to find the downstairs loo.

"I still can't believe Sam got me a new bike. I know she said she was going to get me one, but I didn't think it was actually going to happen. No one's ever done anything like this for me Bryan. And then Danny coming over to help me fix it, and after I didn't turn up for practice today. It's like I've had my faith restored after everything that's happened." I smile at Bryan, the days turned out really well for me, and I have my friends to thank for it.

"Yep, it sure been a strange..." He doesn't get to finish his sentence because Danny's phone starts ringing on the coffee table where he left it.

"It's Danny's should I answer it?" I ask Bryan, looking at the phone ringing on the table.

Next minute Bryan yells through the kitchen door, towards the downstairs loo, "Danny your phone keeps ringing, do you want us to answer it?"

I hear a muffled "Yes I'll be out in a second, it's probably my dad."

So, I reach for Danny's phone sitting on the coffee table when it stops ringing, I'm just putting it back down and it starts ringing again. I can't help but notice the caller ID, and recognise it as the local hospital where Sam works.

"Hello this is Danny's phone he's just coming." Hoping Danny is on his way.

The caller answers back "Maddie? Is that you?"

"Sam, is that you? I'm so confused why are you calling Danny's phone?" I reply to her in utter confusion, why is Sam calling Danny's phone.

"Is Danny's surname Mackenzie?" The woman asks, it's clearly Sam. I fully recognise her voice now.

"Yes, it is, hang on he's just coming, I'll pass you over. Danny, its

Sam for you, I have no idea why.." And I pass the phone over to Danny wondering, I hope something bad hasn't happened.

Danny

"Hello its Danny McKenzie speaking, who's calling please?"

"Danny, it's Sam, we met briefly earlier, I'm calling from Eastleigh-On-Sea Hospital about a Thomas McKenzie. Firstly, he's stable and gave your name as his next of kin, but he was involved in a car accident earlier this evening. He's on ward one in the Eastleigh wing of the hospital." Sam explains calmly to me, but I'm feeling far from it right now.

"Oh god. My dad, is he going to be, okay?" I shakingly say, my mouth going dry, and my limbs feel numb. Maddie takes my hand, twining our fingers together and Bryan squeezes my shoulder in a show of support.

"Danny, there's not much I can tell you at the moment, but it's best you come down to the hospital, and please be careful if you're going to drive. We don't need you getting into a crash." Sam instructs me in her calm but firm manner. I can hear alarms going off in the background and before I even have a chance to reply Sam says, "Sorry I have to go, I'm needed." And the phone goes silent.

"What's going on Danny? Is your dad, okay?" Bryan worriedly asks me, fidgeting about, a trait he's had since a child.

"I need to get to the hospital, he's been in a car accident and I've got no idea what's going on. But I think it's bad." And I look at them both, not really knowing what to say or do next, I can feel the shock hitting my system.

"I'm coming with you." Maddie pipes up, still not letting go of my hand, and I appreciate the gesture.

"Me too. Maddie, you go in Danny's car and I'll meet you there. I need to go and get my dad, it's his best friend and he'll want to be there too." Bryan looks at us both, and nods, taking out his phone and firing off text messages.

"Okay, good plan Bryan. Come on Danny, are you going to be okay to drive?" Maddie asks looking into my eyes with so much concern it hurts.

Snapping out of my momentary trance, I fire off instructions to Bryan "Let's go. Bryan, ward one, Eastleigh wing, is where my dad is."

"On it." Bryan replies, for once completely serious dealing with the task at hand. Firing off another message on his phone, no doubt to his dad, David.

We all run outside to our cars, Bryan in his mums vehicle, Maddie and me take mine, and I drive in complete silence all the way to the hospital. My mind already thinking worse case scenario's. I can't lose my dad too. I just can't, not after losing my mum. Pulling up in the car park I put my head down on the steering wheel, closing my eyes and gripping the steering wheel tightly, my knuckles going white. I try to take some deep breaths, and I can feel Maddie soothing my back, rubbing it gently in little circles. She doesn't say anything. She doesn't need too. No false platitudes from her. But I'm relieved she's here with me, it's like I'm absorbing her energy and it's keeping me strong. It's really difficult to explain, so I put it to the back of my mind for now.

"Let's get inside Danny." She gently says, taking my hand again and leading me inside the busy hospital main entrance to find my dad.

"Okay, and thanks Maddie. For staying with me." I worriedly smile, what would I do without her?

Walking through the hospital is a complete blur, and without Maddie's guidance I'm not sure I would have made it in a timely fashion. But I suddenly find myself on the ward in a waiting room with a nurse walking towards me, and a sense of dread passes over. I try to work out in my head first what's she's going to say to me, and at that moment I pray to god that it's not bad news. I know I'm catastrophising about the situation, but I can't seem to help myself. But it's not me the nurse goes to, it's a family that's waiting for news too, and it doesn't look like they are receiving the good kind, and I gulp in dread.

"I'm going to find Sam for you Danny, wait here in case a doctor comes to speak to you." And Maddie, releases my hand and disappears towards the nurse's station immediately I feel the energy pull away from me as she lets go.

The waiting room doors open, and Bryan appears with his mum and dad in tow. They have been like a second family over the years and his dad David has been my dad's rock, especially after mum died.
Bryans mum, Joan, hugs me, which is then repeated by his dad. "Any news yet?" David asks, undoing the button on his suit jacket, and loosening his tie, he must have come straight from his office.

"No, I'm still waiting for a doctor to speak to me, I've only just arrived myself." I reply to him.
Maddie appears at the door and walks back over towards us with Sam. Finally, I might find out what's going on at last, I need to know my dad's okay.

"Danny is it okay to speak to you in front of everyone here, or would you prefer somewhere more private?" Sam asks me in her professional manner, but I wish she'd just get on with it.

"Yes, we are all family. Go ahead." I answer abruptly, eager for her to continue, but she takes everything in her stride.

"Your dad as you know was involved in a multiple pile up earlier this evening, he was unconscious at the scene and was cut from the wreckage. He was stabilised and brought to hospital with multiple injuries. I saw him briefly on the ward and he was conscious Danny and asked for you." She then goes onto continue "He has a head injury the extent is not yet known, but it's a good sign that he was talking to me. The compound fracture of his tibia and fibula needs to go to surgery, but he was just taken down to theatre with some internal bleeding in his abdomen. This is being treated as a matter of urgency, I'm sorry that's all I know at the moment." I gulp down, suddenly feeling nauseous, I'm speechless and don't know how to respond to that. And I just nod as way of reply.

"Don't worry son, he's as strong as an ox your father. He's not going anywhere." David says as he slaps me on the back in support.

I walk over to the nearest chair and slump down. I put my hands behind my head and look up to the ceiling. Why my dad? I'm finding it hard not to break down. I abruptly get up. "I'm going for a walk, I've got my phone on me." I say to no one in particular.
Maddie steps forward to come with me, but David grabs her arm and I hear him say, "Just give him a few minutes to get his head together."

Then I'm out the door and I'm walking, walking, keep on walking. It's all a blur, I hate hospitals, this is where my mum died. Is my dad going to die here too?? I know I'm catastrophising again, I can't help it.

Not knowing how I've even got here, I find myself outside, in a small courtyard area of the hospital grounds sitting on a bench, I'm in that much of a daze. It must be a break area staff use or just where people come outside for some fresh air, much like I am now. In fact, I'm pretty sure I've sat in this exact same spot before, and I try to search for the memory in my head…

"That's it Danny, wheel me out here, I want to feel the fresh air on my face."

"Are you sure you're going to be warm enough mum? You've only just finished chemo, should you even be outside?" I say to her.

"Just wheel me over to that bench, then you can sit next to me." She says.

"Okay but I'm not telling dad, and if he finds out you made me do it." I say cheekily.

"It will be our little secret Danny boy." My mum replies.

The memory of my mum makes me smile, god I miss her so much. I now remember I used to wheel her out to this courtyard all the time when she was in hospital. She hated being inside, she loved being in her garden tending to her flowers and vegetable patch.

This was the nearest she could get to being outside when she was really sick, no wonder I'm drawn to the space now. Its strangely comforting and I feel close to her here, another memory comes to mind. I think it was towards the end before she died.

"Danny, I want to talk to you about something and for you to try and remember this conversation in the future."

"Okay mum, I can do that." I reply to her, hanging on her every word.

"I'm losing this battle my little Danny boy, but one day you are

going to find a very special girl, of that I can be sure. And she is going to love you so much." She gently says.

"But I don't want you to go mum, I want you to stay." I say to her.

"And I wish I could, but I will always be here with you, here and here." She points firstly to my head, then my heart.

I can still remember. She died later on that day, this was her last time outside in the fresh air...

Enough, I think to myself. I need to be strong for my dad, moping about isn't going to help him get any better. Mum would want me to remain strong for him too.

I get up and take a deep breath, thanking my mum in my head for her strength because I know right at this very moment, she is here with me in my head and my heart, just like she said she always would be. I walk back to the waiting room where everyone is still gathered.

"We were just about to send out a search party for you." Bryans mum Joan says, and she looks relieved that I'm back here.

"I just needed some air, but I'm okay now." I reply to her. Maddie appears with a tray of coffee.

"Sam let me use her staff room to make coffee, so it's actually decent stuff. She always has a jar of it on hand in her locker for nightshift." And Maddie starts playing mum handing out drinks to everyone. The door opens again, and a doctor in scrubs appears, hopefully he can give us some news.

"I'm looking for Thomas McKenzie's family." He says expectantly, his eyes scanning the waiting room.

"Yes, I'm his son, and the rest are family." I quickly reply, so the doctor can get on with telling us the details, putting us all out of our misery.

"Your father's surgery went well, and we stopped the internal bleeding. For the moment he's stable, but he's going to require further surgeries in the coming days on his leg. His head injury will also need to be closely monitored so he will be moved to the ITU when he comes out of theatre recovery. He's a fighter, that's for sure." The doctor nods at me then says, "I need to get back to theatre for another case, but any further questions please ask one of the nurses." And he quickly disappears again. The hospital is manically busy because of the crash and I'm grateful he could speak to me.

"This is good news Danny, I'm going to find Sam for you. So, she can find out when you can see your dad." Maddie smiles at me, and I feel some relief, but I know dad isn't out of the woods yet. I still can't find my words, and David hugs me in relief.

"Told you Danny, strong as an ox, strong as an ox." David chants, looking relieved about his best friend. I now find myself laughing in relief, and I reply " You certainly did."

Chapter Fifteen

Maddie

I can't even begin to imagine what Danny is going through right now. He's obviously extremely close to his father and has a strong relationship with him, and considers Bryans family as his own. I didn't realise they were all so close, and I feel a pang of jealousy which is totally irrational given the circumstances. Bryan certainly kept that information on the down low, making me wonder if it's because he knows I'm developing feelings for Danny. Shit. I can't think like that, especially now with his dad lying in a hospital bed, talk about completely inappropriate, a time and a place, and all that jazz. I need to concentrate on being there for him as a friend, support him, and not add further complications to his life.

No, unwanted complications are the last thing he needs right now, complications from me. He just needs a friend to support him, so that's what I'm going to be, all I'm going to be. At the nurses station I ask for Sam, and another nurse goes to look for her.

"Maddie, there you are I was just coming to find you and Danny, they're about to transfer Mr McKenzie to the ITU, so Danny can go through to see him." Sam says, looking relived to have some positive news for me.

"I'll go and tell him." I answer, about to run off to relay the message to Danny, when Sam continues to speak.

"Only Danny will be able to visit with him tonight, and I doubt that Mr McKenzie will even be awake after his surgery, they'll have him under some pretty heavy sedation." Sam answers almost apologetically, I expect she's used to relatives arguing back with her when emotions are running high.

"Okay Sam. I pretty much thought that would be the case tonight. I've been living with a nurse long enough to know how hospitals work." I smirk at her, trying to lighten the moment, because I can tell just by looking at her, she's having a horrendous shift. Sam wears her heart on her sleeve I'm beginning to realise, and it must take a toll on her.

She gives me a hug and replies, "I've got to go kiddo, duty calls. Try to get Danny to go home after he sees his dad. He can't really do anything here at the moment and he needs rest too. As do you, Maddie." Sam adds playfully tapping me on the nose.

"Will do Sam. I'll see you in the morning, pizza for breakfast remember." I smile reminding her about the pizza request she made earlier.

"Believe me, thinking about that pizza is keeping me going right now." And Sam darts off again. Honestly, I don't know where that woman gets all her energy from, must be all the caffeine she drinks.

Finding Danny in the waiting room, I manage to persuade Bryan and his family to go home. But only after explaining at length, that only Danny would be the only person allowed to see his dad tonight. Plus the fact that would be unconscious until the morning, which seemed to satisfy Bryan's dad.

While we wait for Danny to see his dad, we both sit on some uncomfortable chairs in the ITU waiting room, allowing his dad time to get settled in by the nurses, and no doubt hooked up to various monitors.

Danny turns to me and says quietly, "Thank you for persuading Bryans family to go home, I love them to bits but..." And he looks at me.

So, I help him out by finishing the sentence off for him, "They mean well but can be a bit much, especially Bryan's dad, I get it Danny, no need to explain to me."

"Where did I find you?" And he looks right into my eyes, almost as if he's searching for something, just out of reach, and I gaze back into those big blue eyes of his.

Before I'm completely mesmerised by them a nurse appears in the waiting room, breaking the moment, and asks, "Are you Thomas McKenzie's son?"

"Yes, that's me." Danny replies, jumping out of his chair lightning fast.

"You can see your father now, we have him all settled into the ward. It's only one family member I'm afraid." And the nurse looks towards me, with apology written in her eyes.

"I'm a friend, don't worry I can wait here." I answer the nurse, and she politely nods.

Danny follows her through into the main part of the ITU, and I remain in the depressing little waiting room.
I notice a small television set on the wall in the corner, so I walk over and turn up the volume slightly so that I can hear it. The 24-hour rolling news station is showing scenes from the car pile-up tonight, and it looks really, really bad. It's strange seeing Eastleigh-On-Sea on a national television station, so that alone tells me how bad the crash was. They are now

reporting six people dead. Shit, this is my hometown, people I know could be dead. I can't afford to think like that, I refuse to think like that, and I turn the television off, angry it was on in the first place. Nobody needs to see that here in the ITU it's so insensitive. The news channel is sensationalising lives of the people involved in the tragic accident, and it sickens me.

"Thanks for turning that crap off, I was about to rip the TV off the wall." I turn around and see Ashley from college standing there, she's the last person I expected to see here tonight.

"What are you doing here?" I ask her, totally confused. The last time I spoke to Ashley I was running out of the bathroom at college. That seems like a million years ago now, in some distant past, when in fact it was only yesterday afternoon. Its only now I realise that she has tears running down her face, and she is visibly shaking, holding her phone in her hands.

"My mum was in the accident that's on TV. She's in the ITU, I don't know if she's going to make it." No wonder why she's an absolute emotional wreck, and my heart twinges in pain for her.

"I'm so sorry to hear that Ashley, do you have anyone with you?" I ask her gently, because it looks like she's all by herself.

"Dads on a flight back from Germany, he was away on business." She replies, tears dripping off her face, it's such a contrast to her normal appearance.

"You can wait with me then." I say and guide her towards the chairs, and dig a clean tissue out of my pocket for her.

"Thanks Maddie." She replies in a shaky voice wiping her face with the tissue, then asks. "How come you're here?"

"A friend of mine, his dad is also in the ITU, same accident, so

I've been waiting with him. They just let him into see his dad for the first time." I reply to Ashley awkwardly.

"Can I call a friend for you or other family, until your dad arrives?" I add, trying to help her apparent distress in some way. She looks away, and shakes her head dejectedly.

"I'm starting to re-evaluate my friends, I could have called Chelsea, but she would have loved the drama, and made something as awful as this about her." Ashley looks back at me tearfully.

"Forget about what I said to you yesterday, it was in the heat of the moment." I reply to her, feeling bad for causing her anxiety, especially now in this situation.

"I know, but it got me thinking, and I know you're right. I would actually rather be here by myself than have Chelsea faking her concern." And she takes my hand, giving it a gentle squeeze.

"Tell me how your mum is doing, that's what's important right now." I smile at her squeezing her hand back in comfort.

For the next several minutes I just let her speak to me. Ashley obviously needs someone at this moment in time to listen to her about what happened with her mum, and I don't mind being her crutch. I can't bear to see people in pain, physically or emotionally.

"...and then they brought her up to the ITU and I got to sit with her, then all these alarms started going off and I got told to wait out here." She finally comes up for air, and Ashley looks exhausted after telling me her tale.

"Do you happen to know your dads flight details? Maybe we can find out how long it will be before he gets here." I ask her, trying to distract her from her mum for a moment.

"He was on the flight before the accident happened, I had to leave him a voicemail on his phone. So, he won't get the message before he lands at Heathrow." Ashley answers me worriedly, clutching my hand for dear life now.

"No need for that honey I'm right here." An older man in a suit with a briefcase walks right up to Ashley and takes her in his arms.

"Oh Daddy, you're here." She sobs into his shoulder. Her dad mouths the words "Thank you" to me, and he guides her over to the nurses station. Poor Ashley, I really hope her mum is going to be okay, and all the other families involved in this tragedy. It's going to impact this community for a long time, and I feel like I should be doing something to help. But I've got no idea how I'm going to do that.

Starting to think about Danny again, I say a little prayer to god in my head that his dad is going to be okay, because I know his dad is religious. Taking a seat again, I pick up a magazine off a small coffee table and start to mindlessly flick through it. Anything just to pass the time while I wait. I don't even know what the time is anymore and I'm debating if I should see about finding some more coffee, when Danny enters the waiting room. I only need to take one look at him and the pain written across his face, and I find myself standing up and walking towards him. He doesn't say a thing, and I pull him into a hug, with no words spoken. I'm not the tallest person and my head only meets his chest, and I feel him rest his head on top of mine and his hands going around my waist.
We stand like this, I'm not sure for how long, when I break away from him slightly so that I can look up at his face into his eyes again.

"How is he doing?" That's all I ask him, and I patiently wait for his answer. Danny waits a few seconds, clearly thinking about what he's going to say to me.

"It's going to be a long road to recovery, all I know for sure is he's currently stable. The doctors are optimistic at least. I can't lose him Maddie, I just can't." And he walks away from me, leaving the comfort of my arms and I can see he's close to tears, but he's fighting it. I wish he would just let the pain out, holding it in doesn't help I should know.

"Why don't we go home Danny, you need your rest to help your dad. I'm pretty sure he would agree with me right now. Don't you?" And I look towards him, hoping that he will see reason and agree with me.

He turns around to me and replies, "What if something happens and I'm not here Maddie?"

"And what did the nurse tell you to do?" I ask him, knowing what the answer will be, thank you Sam. Listening to her hospital stories has helped me help Danny and Ashley tonight.

"She told me to go and rest. That they will call me if anything changes and that I can call the hospital anytime to check up on him." Danny replies and takes a deep breath, he just needed that gentle push in the right direction.

"As I thought Danny. Let's go home and get some rest, then you can be strong for your dad." And I take his hand and lead him out of the waiting room, out of the hospital and down to the car park.

Danny decides to make a small detour on the way home to get coffee and donuts, stopping at that posh patisserie on the high street. I think this must be a regular haunt for him.

I look at what's on offer behind the glass counter display and my stomach growls in hunger, I blush bright red in embarrassment, and Danny laughs at my stomach noise.

"Glad my empty stomach amuses you. I'm going to go with the banoffee donut and a decaf americano. And I'll think I'll get a blueberry donut for Sam to go with her breakfast pizza." Starting to open my bag to get my purse out to pay.

"Let me get this, you just stayed at the hospital all night with me. It's the least I can do." Danny offers, and I'm too tired to argue about who's paying, so I put my purse back inside my bag.

"Okay, but the next one is on me. And I wouldn't have been anywhere but with you last night." I answer him, trying my best not to yawn in his face.

Danny drops me off at home, and being the gentleman he is, he walks me right up my the front door, making it feel like we're returning from a date and not a night at the hospital.

"If you need anything, just call me. I'm here for you Danny, and your dad." I smile, meaning every word of it from the bottom of my heart.

"You're an Angel Maddie," He replies and kisses me on the top of my head, and I can feel my heart flutter, my legs shaky at the simple show of affection from him. Danny's left feeling completely breathless on my front doorstep. Boy oh boy, that will get the neighbours curtains twitching and the gossip mongers going around here...

Danny

Driving home on autopilot, I find myself sitting at the kitchen table staring at my phone. So many messages have been left, but I ignore them all except for one. Putting the call on speaker, I press call on David Johnsons name in my phone contacts. Dads best friend was like a second father to me when my mum died and dad was a grieving mess. He deserves to know an update about his best friend.

"Danny, how is he?" David says, skipping formalities and straight to the point, he's a typical highbrow businessman, the exact opposite to my dad, they are like Ying and Yang.

"He's stable, the surgery went well and they've stopped the internal bleeding. The doctor explained it better than I can, but he needs extensive surgery on his leg. So he's not completely out of the woods yet. Other than that, I don't know." I reply, trying to relay the information as quickly as possible, I don't feel like talking right now.

"Are you back at home yet?" David enquires, checking up on me like he did when I was a kid.

"Yes, I just got back. Although I don't even remember the drive, I'm so tired." I sigh out loud, and automatically start rubbing my eyes and trying not to yawn. Even that coffee I had didn't pick me up.

"Do you think they will let me see him later, I really need to see him with my own eyes Danny. He's like my brother." He says sounding abrupt, but I can hear the pain in his voice, and this is typical David.

"I arranged for you and the rest of the family to be placed on the approved visitors list, so you can see him in the ITU. But you can only go in one at a time for a few minutes, even if he's still unconscious. They are very strict about visitor numbers."

I explain, knowing he was going to ask me this, I checked with the nurse looking after my dad.

"Thank you, son, I will be heading over to the hospital soon then. Get a few hours shut eye and I will call you if there are any changes." David answers, and it's good to know that dad will have someone with him while I try to recharge my energy.

"I will, and thanks for being there for us both David." And I press the end call symbol on my phone.

Quickly deciding that it would be a sensible idea to send out a blanket text message, to all the well-wishers that have left messages for dad and me, or I'm never going to get any rest.

My dad is a really popular guy and is well known in the community but especially at church, and I'm really touched how many people care about him enough to get in touch.

Grabbing my phone, I climb the two flights of stairs up to my attic room bedroom. The same bedroom I've had my entire life. It's been redecorated several times over the years as I've grown up, but now resembles a bachelor pad, it even has a ensuite bathroom my dad had put in a few years ago to give me more privacy as a teenager.

The large open plan attic has what I refer to as my bedroom area at one end, and my office space at the other end. There I have my state of the art computers set up, so I don't have to travel far for work, although a have an actual office in town, I only use it if I have an important meeting.

Most things I do remotely from this room, I prefer it that way, less interactions with people, I'm not a recluse but I value my space. Especially when I'm working on something.

I've thought about getting my own place but I don't want to leave my dad on his own, he needs me, mums been gone a long time and he won't get any younger. Now he's had this terrible accident, so there is absolutely no way I'm leaving, life just hasn't been all that fair to dad. He's never dated since mum passed, and I'm sure he gets lonely. I'm pretty sure he's had one night stand's on overnight business trips. When he gets through this, I'm going to encourage him to date, he needs someone besides me.

Stripping down to my boxer shorts and sliding into bed, too exhausted to shower at the moment, I put my phone on my bedside table to charge on the cordless charger, I do love a good gadget. God, I'm so tired, but my brain just doesn't want to switch off right now, and I close my eyes in a vain attempt. My phone pings, yet another incoming message. I roll back over and grab my phone wanting to throw the thing against the wall. But then I notice who it's from, so I open the message.

Danny, checking you got home safely. Get some rest, and call if you need me.
It's from Maddie, my little Angel, without thinking I type out a reply.

Home safe and sound thanks.
And I hit send. My phone quickly pings again.

Sweet dreams, Danny.
I smile to myself, and I give Maddie a simple reply back.

You too, my little Angel.
Rolling over, my body completely crashes out like it's been given permission to finally sleep thanks to Maddie and her sweet words...

Chapter Sixteen

Bryan

Unbelievable, my mum's still making me go into college today even though we were at the hospital half the night, I feel like a cast member of the Walking Dead, full zombie costume and make-up, and now I understand why girls wear concealer under their eyes. But I'm not going to argue with mum, especially with Mr McKenzie in the ITU, I'd never sink that low. My dad and her are worried sick about Mr McKenzie, and how Danny's holding up.

My parents are so protective of them both, sometimes I'm sure my dad wishes Danny was his son instead of me, so no, arguing right now isn't a good idea. I've got no idea if Maddie is going to make it into college today, but I strongly doubt it, which means it's going to be a crappier day. And I don't want to call her in case she's asleep. But I'm glad she stayed with Danny at the hospital last night, those two are totally into each other, I'm willing to put money on it.

Mum won't even let me borrow the car today because apparently the roads are clearly not safe anymore, according to her, she really needs to stop watching the news. Then she went on this big rant about it and burst into tears, making me promise to be safe crossing the roads, like I'm five years old again. So I'm stuck getting the bus today, and I wasn't going to point out to her that one was also involved in the crash, I think that may have pushed her over the edge.

I decide to take a slight detour from the bus stop, and nip into the newsagents and grab an energy drink and a snickers bar because I missed breakfast again. No one in their right mind wants to eat bran flakes, I don't understand why mum stopped buying me co-co pops. The newspapers inside the shop all have pictures of the crash yesterday, and its more than I can stomach, especially when I recognise Mr McKenzie's car in one of the photos. How the hell did he survive that carnage? The scenes look horrific, and I leave the shop empty handed, suddenly losing my appetite.

Arriving at college I head straight to the canteen; I'm going to need caffeine to get through this day.
Unsurprisingly there is a sombre atmosphere in the corridors and it carries on through to the canteen. I decide on a coffee and bacon sarnie, that will keep me going for now, and I get in the queue to pay. Ben Chambers taps me on the shoulder in the queue.
"Breakfast of Kings I see." He nods towards my bacon sarnie, holding one up in his hand to show me.

"More like breakfast of the Walking Dead." I hastily reply, feeling dead on my feet.

"Late night?" And he wiggles his eyebrows, smirking. Not sure how he does that, but it looks cute, not that I'd ever tell him that. This is Ben Chambers we are talking about after all, he always has a girl hanging off his arm or a group around him. But I'm not going to lie, he looks totally hot in his rugby kit, those tight little white shorts...
I shake myself out of my Ben fantasy.

"I was at the hospital until late last night, my dad's best friend was in that horrible pile up." And I look down, feeling uncomfortable talking about it. Also the fact I'm totally into this guy, and he has no idea and never will.

"Hey, I'm sorry to hear that. Are they okay?" He asks with a look of genuine concern.

"He's in the ITU after going to surgery." I don't want to share personal details about Mr McKenzie, so I keep it basic.

"Ashley's mum is also in the ITU, Chelsea is blabber mouthing everywhere to anyone that will listen, but that's just Chelsea being Chelsea." He replies with a slight look of disgust on his face, turning up his nose, then shrugging it off.

"That's awful, does anyone know if she's okay?" I can't imagine my mum in the ITU, I'd be a complete mess. I may not see eye to eye with her all the time, but I love her and she's my mum after all.

"No idea, I don't know where she heard it from, but you could tell she hadn't got the details first hand. I'm surprised she's not at the hospital giving Ashley support. I thought they were meant to be best friends?" Ben replies to me, taking some change out of his pocket ready to pay for his food.

"Perhaps she finally saw the light with Chelsea." I reply without thinking, realising how tactless it sounds, but it's sadly true.

"What are you talking about?" He asks, slightly confused, wrinkling his eyebrows again but in confusion this time.

I sigh at him and say "Chelsea isn't a nice person, in fact most of that crowd aren't nice people. I finally saw the light, and maybe Ashley is now too." I answer, trying to gage what Ben's reply will be to that little gem of information.

"Strong words there bro, sure you feel that way?" He asks

looking totally surprised, because this is also the group of friends he hangs out with. The ones I used to also hang out with.

"Totally, wouldn't say it otherwise. Bro." I add on the end sarcastically. Not really wanting to have a full blown fight in the middle of the canteen with the guy I think about when I close my eyes at night.

"Those are my friends you are talking about, I thought they were yours too?" Ben glares at me, looking hurt, but I refuse to take back what I said to him.

"Look Ben, I don't want to fight about this, but I've had enough of that crowd. Especially after that stunt Chelsea pulled yesterday with Maddie." And I slap my money on the counter, and don't bother waiting for any change.

Ben calls after me as I leave the canteen, but I don't take any notice of what he says.
All I want to do is drink my coffee and eat my sarnie in peace, is that too much to ask?
I slam through the canteen doors, and bollocks, who do I immediately run into, but bloody Chelsea, the shit stirring little slapper.

"Bryan fancy seeing you here I.." She's about to start spurting out shit so I cut her off.

"Wasn't interested yesterday, definitely not interested today. And stay away from my phone. I know exactly what you did." I reply as I keep walking past her, not even bothering to stop, to give her my full attention.

"I don't know what you're talking about Bryan. What little lies has Maddie been feeding you?" Chelsea angrily replies, clearly not liking being called out for her stunt.

"Maddie hasn't said anything, so keep her name out of this. We have more important things to worry about than your pathetic antics. Understand this Chelsea, no one likes you, they just pretend to look popular. Now leave me and Maddie alone." And I storm off towards the library to finally get some peace, leaving Chelsea standing alone in the corridor for once speechless.

I throw my bacon sarnie into the nearest bin, I've really have lost my appetite now...

Maddie

Its nearly lunchtime by the time I wake up, and I want to at least make it into my last lesson at college today, then try and get back to the hospital. Although I don't want to overstep, Danny might not want me there today? Last night were extenuating circumstances, maybe I should just message Danny first? I can't stop going over in my head how awful that accident looked when I saw that news report last night on the waiting room TV. What must those poor families be going through right now. It doesn't bare thinking about...

Danny was just about holding it together, I'm glad I could be there for him, and I didn't want to leave his side this morning at my front door when he said goodbye.
I saw Sam briefly before I went to bed and she looked awful, she didn't say much to me. She didn't have to, and I wasn't going to push her. I can remember her once telling me that when things didn't get to her anymore it was a sign, she'd stopped caring. And she obviously cares. I just worry that she'll burn herself out one day, completely. That's what it appears to be

like working in the NHS as a nurse, who cares for them?

Rushing through a quick shower, I contemplate messaging Danny again, but instead decide that I'll just head over to the hospital instead, after my last lesson, I'll take my chances with him. Luckily, I don't have any babysitting commitments later.

Scribbling a quick note out to Sam so she knows my plan for the day, I leave it in the kitchen by the coffee machine. Sam's still sleeping, the poor woman's exhausted. Normally she gets up at lunchtime, but I'm not going to disturb her. Remembering the donut Danny brought her, I take it out of my bag and leave it next to the note. Totally forgot to give it to her this morning. And yawning out loud, I'm hardly surprised.

Grabbing an apple, cereal bar and a packet of ready salted crisps, I stuff them into my backpack and wheel my new bike outside. I carefully adjust my cycle helmet and I'm ready to make my way to college. I'm actually excited about riding this new bike for the first time, I didn't get a chance to last night after everything that had happened.
It's sunny, but that's deceiving because the colder weather is starting to kick in now, and there is definitely a chill in the air. I get onto my bike, riding down the short garden path and onto the road. I can't believe how smooth it feels, this is like flying, and I can't take the stupid grin off my face. People will think I'm a crazy person, let them think it, because riding this bike is amazing.

Eastleigh-On-Sea is great for cycle paths in most places except the route I need to take to get to college. So, I have to battle the traffic on the busy main road.
It's because I live on the dodgy side of town, or what's perceived to be dodgy, I guess it's a class thing. All the money on cycle paths gets spent elsewhere in the town and certainly not our

end of town. God, I sound like a bloody politician and I quietly laugh to myself. Yep, if people didn't think it before they will definitely think I'm a crazy girl on a bike.

Arriving at college, I take my phone out my backpack to check the time and see if I have any messages. Wow, that's the fastest I've ever ridden to college before, must be the new wheels and I grin to myself. Seeing no new messages, I take that as no news is good news. I bend over to lock up my bike when someone says, "Nice Wheels Reynolds."
And I turn around to see who it is. It's Ben who I sit next to in class, the one I ran out of yesterday.

"Oh thanks Ben it was a gift from my foster parent Sam, it rides like a dream." And I immediately regret oversharing, but my excited mouth ran away from me as per usual.

"I was talking to Bryan a few minutes ago. He seems to think he's too good to hang around with us now, and I think that has something to do with you." Ben doesn't seem very happy, but I can't understand why he has an axe to grind with me.

"It's up to Bryan who he chooses to be friends with surely?" I answer him, now standing at my full height which compared to Ben isn't that tall, so I put my hands on my hips in a sign of defiance.

"He suddenly has a problem with my friend group, and that only happened when you came on the scene." Ben replies sharply, looking down at me, but for some reason he doesn't scare or intimidate me.

"I'm going to make this short Ben, because I was at the hospital most of last night and my brain isn't firing on all cylinders right now. I can't speak for Bryan, but I do know that Chelsea has been saying nasty things about me. Yesterday, she got hold of Bryans phone and shared a private video of his. One that I happened to be in, and then she shared that private video with everyone in class to embarrass me." I reply angrily back to him, now waving my finger at him only a few inches from his face.

"So talk to Bryan." And as I start to walk away he grabs my arm.

"Get your hand off me now Ben, no one touches me without permission." I shout at him, realising I completely overreacted, the second I say it. Ben removes his hand looking guilty, then holds up both hands in the air, in surrender.

"Look, I'm sorry Maddie, it's just I'm trying to find out what's going on. Bryan stormed off before, and I just want to know why. I thought he was my friend, he just stopped hanging out with us. I totally get the Chelsea thing, she's a complete bitch on a good day, but we're not all like that you know." Bens now looking at me apologetically, because he realises I'm not the person to blame.

"And I'm sorry you were at the hospital last night. And I'm sorry I grabbed your arm." He quickly adds. Bens seems like a decent enough guy, but I don't really know him. Only from sitting next to him in class, and it's not like we really chatted or anything. And I won't share Bryans secrets, it's not my place, so if he's digging for information he won't get it from me,

"You still need to talk to Bryan, but I accept your apology." I reply, seeing no reason to blow this out of proportion.

"Let me buy you a coffee, in way of apology, you look like you could do with a pick me up." He grins at me cheekily, like we didn't almost come to verbal blows a few seconds ago.

"Okay. Do I really look that bad? Was the four hours of sleep not enough?" I laugh back at him, thinking I could do with some coffee, even if it's canteen coffee.

"Nah, I was just joking. You're a smokin hot girl any day of the week." Ben cheekily replies, wiggling his eyebrows at me.

OH, MY,GOD.
Is Ben flirting with me? This can't be happening right now, and I just agreed to coffee. Think Maddie, think.

"Sorry just remembered, I need to be somewhere, overdue library book, don't want a fine." And I literally run off, and hear Ben chuckling behind me.

Chapter Seventeen

Danny

I t's early afternoon, I've slept longer than I thought I would, and I guiltily pick up my phone checking for messages. Good. There are none from the hospital so dad must be okay, just some more well-wishers, and one from Bryans dad David, saying he still hasn't woken up yet because of the sedation.

None from Maddie, I'm slightly disappointed. But I shouldn't feel like that, especially as she went above and beyond supporting me at the hospital last night.

I need to get back to the hospital, but I really need to stop somewhere on the way, somewhere that is long overdue, even before the accident even happened…

Sitting down on the pew, a short time later, I look towards the front of Saint Peters Church. The stain glass windows looking beautiful with the sunlight shining through, I've always found those windows fascinating, even as a child. I feel the pew creak, besides me, Father Christopher sits down next to me, on what's basically a wooden bench with a cushion to sit or kneel on.

"I'm sorry to hear about your father Danny. Any news?" Father Christopher gently asks, he's known my dad along time, since before I was born when he was a young Priest starting out.

"Thank you Father Christopher. I'm going back to the hospital after this." I reply to him, not knowing really where to start the conversation.

"But you're not here about that are you?" He smiles, intuitively waiting for me to spill the beans.
I sigh and run my fingers through my dishevelled hair, and take a deep breath.

"No, Father. I need to talk to you about something else. Maybe now isn't the right time." And I start to stand up to leave, and come back another time.

"Danny, please stay because it's obviously something bothering you enough to be here." Father Christopher replies trying to encourage me to stay and talk about it.

"It was my dad that suggested it would be a good idea to speak to you. Before the accident." And I look off towards the stained glass windows again, my eyes blurring slightly with tears, but I quickly blink them away.

"Then it must be of importance Danny, because your father is a very wise man, and I've always respected him." Father Christopher answers, waiting for my reply, so taking yet another deep breath I dive into telling him.

"Do you remember the little baby that I found abandoned outside the church all those years ago, when I was a boy?" And I look towards him, knowing he'll remember it, it's not every day you find a baby.

"Of course, it's not something you forget easily, first time it's ever happened at this church to my knowledge.." He replies looking somewhat puzzled by my odd question, he obviously didn't expect me to ask him that.

"Well I think I know who the baby is. Well, she's not a baby now, she's nearly eighteen. In fact I've come to care very deeply for her, and I don't believe she's had a good life in the care system. What I need guidance on is, do I tell her I was the one to find her? Or just say nothing? What will it actually achieve? But I know Maddie has questions about where she came from, for that I'm sure." And I look towards Father Christopher hoping that he can guide me through this difficult conundrum.

"I wondered when this time would come, I just didn't think it would be you." Father Christopher answers looking surprised.

"What are you talking about Father Christopher?" I'm really confused now, I have no idea what you mean by that statement.

"I need to show you a letter Danny, one that was with the baby when you found her. It was inside the box, I only found it after social services had taken her away. I've kept the information to myself all these years. Come, it's in my office." Father Christopher replies standing up. And we walk together to his office round the back of the church.

Father Christopher takes a small key from a jar on his desk, and unlocks his desk drawer. Emptying the contents, he eventually finds what he's looking for, an envelope, yellowed with age; then hands it to me.

I carefully remove a letter from inside the envelope, the fragile paper is so thin it's almost transparent, and the handwriting is elegantly beautiful. I sit down on a small office chair to read what it says, and Father Christopher sits on the edge of his desk.

To the Father of this Church,
Please ensure that this child is placed in protection,
for she is no longer safe with us.

Just before her 18th year, a protector will come,
but they will also come for her.
Those who wish to cause her harm.
This must not be allowed to happen.
We must protect this Angel on earth.
For her future depends on it.
We will be watching.

"You found this with her and didn't tell us?" I look at Father Christopher confused, and also angry that he kept this information to himself.

"I believe the girl to be something of an enigma. And I decided that it was in God's hands. Ultimately if she was at risk as the letter says, she was safer hidden in the care system with no one having knowledge of this letter." Father Christopher replies, and my anger fades once I understand his logic behind keeping it a secret.

"So you definitely think it's the same girl then?" I answer, but I know deep in my heart already the baby was Maddie.

"You know she was abandoned at a church in a cardboard box for definite, and is nearly eighteen years old?" Father Christopher questions me.

"Yes, Maddie told me she was abandoned in a box at a church, I know she is eighteen soon, in the next couple of months. It's her isn't it?" I ask him, I need someone to confirm to me that my notion isn't completely crazy.

"I think it is Danny, no other baby has been abandoned here like that in the last eighteen years, and I don't believe in coincidences." Father Christopher states adamantly confirming my suspicions.

"Then I think that we need to keep this between us for her

protection, because as far as I'm aware no one else knows who this girl is. We could put her at risk if we go digging around for more information." I answer him, praying to god that I'm doing the right thing for the right reasons.

"My sentiments exactly Danny, let sleeping dogs lie." And Father Christopher nods to me, knowingly.

Chapter Eighteen

Maddie

Somehow, I manage to quickly escape from Ben, well, that might be a slight over exaggeration. It was probably darn right rude but I'm just not used to dealing with those types of situations. I hate dealing with conflict and try to avoid it like the plague, and I definitely can't cope with someone flirting with me. No, just no. Talk about completely out of my comfort zone.

This last lesson of the day is really dragging on, I swear this particular teacher loves the sound of his own voice and it's such a droning noise, it makes your ears want to block it out. And finally the bell rings signalling our escape, I need to catch up with Bryan before I head over to the hospital and fill him in on my conversation with Ben.

Quickly, I open my WhatsApp and message him.

Finished my last lesson where are you?
I hit send with my finger and within seconds, my phone pings.

In the library come find me.

Putting my phone back in my bag, I eagerly start walking towards the library to meet up with Bryan, when I hear that grating voice behind me.

"Got your claws into Ben now too? Wow, you got bored of

Bryan quickly, are you going to do the rest of the rugby team now too?" Chelsea sneers at me, almost spitting as she talks. Surely she must have at least one redeeming quality? Sadly she's yet to display such a interaction with me.

I refuse to sink down to her level, so I take the higher ground and decide to completely ignore her. Of course this tactic is useless, as she decides to follow me, spawning her poison down the corridor for everyone at college to hear.

When Chelsea is level with me I turn towards her and say, "You know Chelsea, if talking to a member of the opposite sex is getting your claws into someone, I guess you must be the ultimate expert on the matter." And I continue to walk towards my destination. People in the corridor are laughing at my come back, and Chelsea is going red with rage. It wasn't my intention to publicly humiliate her, but perhaps it's time for Chelsea to have a taste of her own medicine. She looks like her head is going to explode, I wonder if it will start spinning around like in that movie, I snigger to myself.

"I know what you're trying to do Maddie, and it won't work." Chelsea curtly replies, she's looking for a fight, so I make a point of stopping, then walk, and turn towards her. People in the corridor are watching and whispering, loving the free show.

"Let me make this crystal clear Chelsea, I'm not trying to do anything. I've got more important things to worry about. If you want to continue the spoilt little mean girl routine, carry on by all means. But stop trying to drag me, Bryan, Ben or anyone else into your childish drama. Because no one's interested." And I walk away from her, knowing that I held back, I could have said so much more. And I'm proud of myself for not being a doormat with her anymore.

Shouting after me Chelsea says, all red faced and angry, "You're going to regret trying to make a fool out of me, skank."

And I know it's petty but I shout back over my shoulder "It takes one, to know one Chelsea."

Slow clapping starts in the corridor and starts to get louder, and someone shouts "Round one goes to Maddie Reynolds."

Feeling even more proud of myself now for standing up to her, I perform a little curtsy to the small crowd that had been watching our spat. Chelsea has finally walked away, realising I'm not the easy push over she thought I was.
Reaching the library, I go inside and find Bryan at his usual table. He looks up, and stops typing on his laptop and smiles at me.

"I didn't expect to see you here today, you were at the hospital longer than me last night. Did you get any sleep?" Bryan asks with concern.

"Wow, I must look bad you're the second person to comment on it today. I think I got at least four hours, but I woke up and decided I could at least get a couple of lessons in today." I reply, trying to stifle yet another yawn.

"A whole four hours, sounds like caffeine is in order." And he pushes an open can of energy drink towards me.

I wrinkle my nose at it and reply "That stuffs disgusting, I think I'll pass. I was just coming to say I'm going back to the hospital. I want to check up on Danny, and I also saw Ashley last night. Her mums in the ITU too. She was by herself and wouldn't call anyone. I felt really bad for her, thank god her dad got there when he did." And I push the energy drink back towards him.

"Fucking Chelsea, some best friend she is. She should have been with Ashley. You know she's been telling everyone Ashley's mum is in the ITU, like it's the best gossip ever." Bryan replies looking at me with a look of disgust on his face.

"Ashley told me she didn't want Chelsea there because she would have made the situation about herself." I answer, my heart feeling a pang of pain for Ashley again, she doesn't deserve to be reduced to gossip.

"Well I think Ashley did the right thing, I'm so sick of Chelsea. Ashley is better off without her." Bryan replies, and I nod my head in agreement. I'm sick of Chelsea too.

"Changing the subject slightly, did something happen between you and Ben this morning, because I had the strangest conversation with him earlier?" I ask Bryan, tapping my fingers on the table not quite making eye contact with him at such an awkward conversation.

"I really don't feel like getting into it right now if that's okay, he's just upset I've stopped hanging out in their little group." Bryan sighs, I wonder what he's holding back from me?

"Figured it was something like that, he got funny with me at first. But don't worry it's all sorted. I already think you know who has been stirring up things today." I reply not wanting to bring up Chelsea's name again, but it's seemingly impossible today. You never know, I might be able to help, I think to myself not saying it out loud.

"Fucking Chelsea." Bryan huffs back, and he looks pissed.

"Yep, she tried to get into it with me just before I got to the library. She really doesn't seem to like me. I've never done anything to her, I don't know what her problem is." I say exasperated, because I'm damned if I know what I did to upset her.

"If that bitch starts anything else, I swear to god Maddie..." Bryan replies clearly getting annoyed, and I don't want him to get into any kind of trouble on my part.

"Don't worry, I handled it. Even got a little applause in the corridor." I smirk back, feeling ever so slightly pleased that people took my side of the argument.

"Tell me more..." He replies, and I proceed to fill him in on what transpired a few minutes before, in the corridor. And by the end of my torrid tail, Bryan is laughing so hard he's holding his sides in laughter pain.

We part ways, as I have my new bike to ride, and he's getting the bus. As I start to ride towards the local hospital, I'm using my lights for the first time as it's already getting dark. That's the problem with this time of year it starts to get dark so early. Perhaps that was the reason for the pile-up last night, people getting caught off guard, although I shouldn't really speculate on things, especially as I haven't got all the facts. I'm pretty sure it will be common knowledge soon, the police will already be investigating it.

A short time later I arrive at the hospital and lock my bike up in a metal shelter with bike racks, it's just off the main car park, and is poorly lit. Looks like vandals have been at it again. Sam is always complaining the car parks should have better security, and I hope it's going to be safe here.

I make my way into the hospital and up to the ITU, I know they won't let me inside to see Mr McKenzie because I'm not family, but I can let the nurses know I'm in the waiting room.

As it turns out, I don't even need to do that because I see Bryans dad in the waiting room.

"Hi Mr Johnson, how is Mr McKenzie doing today? And is Danny here? I just wanted to check how he was doing too." I ask, taking a seat opposite him in the waiting room area.

"Call me David, and I wanted to thank you for looking after Danny like that last night. Thomas woke up a few minutes ago, so Danny is with him. But I expect he will fall asleep again quickly with all the drugs he's got pumping through his system." Mr Johnson smiles at me, he has the same smile as Bryan.

"That's a good sign that he's talking, especially as he has a head injury. I don't suppose you have seen a girl about the same age as me with her dad around the ITU have you? Her mum was brought in last night, she was also involved in the accident." I ask him, hoping he's seen Ashley, and perhaps has some news to share.

"No sorry Maddie, I have been in and out the ITU taking turns with Danny all afternoon. We've become a unofficial tag team." He laughs, and I try to imagine him as a boy playing with Danny's dad.

"I'll leave a message at the nurses station for the girl, Ashley, we go to college together." And I take out my notebook and start to scribble down a short note. I walk up to the nurses station, and the nurse explains Ashley and her father have gone to the canteen for a break, but she would pass the note along for me.

Making small talk with Mr Johnson, I feel funny calling him David, because he's Bryans dad after all.
We don't discuss the accident, and keep things light. I talk about college and how funny Bryan can be, and I talk about

Jack and Tommy; and how I met Danny through their football and ended up volunteering too. He tells me about playing football as a boy with Mr McKenzie, and how they used to get into trouble at Sunday school for sneaking in comic books. I find myself laughing at all his stories, it sounds like they were both like Jack and Tommy at that age. And it makes me think of what Danny could have been like for some reason.

Excusing myself to use the bathroom, I return to the waiting room area and Danny is sitting there with the doctor talking. So I decide to politely hang back because I don't want to interrupt them. Finishing their conversation they shake hands and the doctor leaves the room.

"Everything okay with your dad? I couldn't help seeing you with the doctor just now." I ask, as I walk towards Danny, trying my best not to look worried.

"Maddie, David said you were here." And he stands up and hugs me. Wow, he smells great. Was not expecting that welcome, and I blush, taken aback by his sweet gesture.

"The doctor was just going over the surgery dad needs, and a specialist is coming from London to lead the procedure." Danny tells me excitedly, and I nod trying my best to take all of the complicated details in. I really need to start watching Grey's Anatomy or Casualty to pick up all the medical jargon, or I could ask Sam, she'll know.

"I hear your dad is awake now off and on, is he in much pain?" I ask Danny genuinely concerned, even though I've never met his dad, but he's a part of Danny, so of course I care. He must be a great guy, he raised Danny after all.

"They have him on some strong drugs, and he's slightly confused at times, but he knows where he is. Hopefully they can move him down to the main ward in a few days if he remains stable. But it's only early days." Danny looks away taking a deep breath, he looks exhausted too. At that exact moment my stomach lets out the loudest noise ever, much to my embarrassment. Twice in one day that's happened to me in front of Danny. Kill, me, now...

He looks at me with those startling blue eyes and says " When was the last time you ate Maddie?"

Looking guilty I reply, " I did have that donut this you brought me this morning, in all fairness I had every intention of eating at college, but I got caught up with things and totally forgot." That's my excuse and I'm sticking to it.

"Maddie, I'm so glad you came to the hospital again, but you need to take better care of yourself. Can't have you passing out or anything." He replies trying to look stern, but it's really not working for him, he just looks cute to me.

"I was worried about you." Shit, there goes my mouth again, always running away from me and spirting out whatever it wants.

Danny breaks into a the biggest smile, puts his arm over my shoulder and says, "Then let us worry about each other, I'm taking you for food. David is with Dad for the next half an hour. The nurse said dad needs rest before his surgery tomorrow. So I'm not going back tonight, they will call me if there's any change."

And we walk together out of the hospital, anyone looking at us would think we are a couple. And I find myself wondering if, I really wish that was the truth...

Chapter Nineteen

Danny

I should be thinking about my dad, and believe me, I am thinking about him, I haven't stopped. But when I saw Maddie in that waiting room, the relief I felt in my chest was palpable, she hadn't forgotten about me after all.

We get to the car park when Maddie declares that she rode to the hospital on her new bike, so we retrieve it from the hospital bike rack, then attach it to mine on the back of my car. I'm glad I had the foresight to add that accessory, as I have a sneaking suspicion that this won't be the last time I need to use it for her bike.

Without even thinking or even asking, I drive back to my house because I know I have healthy food in the fridge, and I want to give Maddie a decent meal for her troubles. She doesn't say anything, and spends most of the journey back, talking about a girl she goes to college with called Ashley; and how she ended up sitting with her in the ITU last night. Is there no end to this girls thoughtfulness?

This accident has had a massive impact on the whole community. I've so far managed to avoid watching the news or seeing a newspaper headline, but I know it will be a huge story for our small seaside town.

Pulling up, in my driveway, Maddie suddenly looks around like she's only just realised where we are, but she still doesn't comment, and we walk in silence into the house. Breaking the sudden tension I feel being home again, without my dad, I try to make small talk.

"So I've got a cheese and broccoli quiche in the fridge that needs eating, and I can throw in some jacket potatoes, and make a fresh salad." My dad was meant to have this meal last night. I look down at my hands and they are shaking, everything I try to do at the moment makes me think of him. How he could have died in that crash…

"I think your still suffering from shock Danny, go and sit down and let me sort out dinner." Maddie smiles and points towards the sofa.

"Thanks Maddie, that actually helps, I've got a ton of messages that I need to answer, dad has so many well-wishers." I answer her, glad to have an excuse to sit down but still be busy.

"Then go sit. Sofa, now. I've got this." And she disappears into the kitchen, it feels nice to be made a fuss over.

Sitting down on the sofa, I open up my phone and stare at the endless messages, so I write a another blanket answer which I intend to forward on. Not to be lazy, but so I don't have to keep repeating myself again and again. It makes me wince, I hope people don't think I don't appreciate their kindness.

My dad is stable and still in the ITU, so only family can visit at this time. Tomorrow he has another surgery, and it's important he has as much rest as possible. He has been awake for short periods and is aware he's in the hospital. Thank you for your kindness at this difficult time, Danny.

I press send, and place my phone on the table, and find myself staring outside through the gap in the blinds. Going over the last twenty-four hours in my head again. Could I have prevented my dad from going out, thus preventing the accident happening to him? Sighing to myself, I know he was only coming back from work, a journey he has taken a thousand times. If it was going to happen, it was going to happen. Dad would call it fate, and say everything happens for a reason.

Then I find myself thinking about the conversation that I had with Father Christopher earlier, and how Maddie is in danger. What is she in danger from? Who will be coming for her? And how I have I seemingly become her unofficial protector now? Protector from what though? Maddie's obviously been hidden for good reason. The endless questions, with no obvious answers keep going through my head, around and around. Until I hear the sweetest of voice's speaking to me, and I snap out of it.

"Danny, I said dinner won't be long. You seem like you zoned out. Hardly surprising really." Maddie sits down next to me, taking my hand, which is fast becoming a common occurrence between the two of us.

"I know I haven't met your father yet, but I'm sure he's a wonderful man if he's anything like you. Try not to worry, he's in the best place, the doctors and nurses will look after him. And it sounds like he's got some fancy specialist coming to work his magic tomorrow." She smiles at me, lighting up the whole room, then gets up and walks back into the kitchen.

"Do you want to eat there, and watch some TV? I'm sure there's a rerun of Big Bang Theory on channel four right now." She shouts from the kitchen, and I can hear plates and utensils clattering around.

"Sounds good to me." I reply without even thinking and grab the remote control to put the TV on channel four like she suggested. It's some home improvement show, but I leave it on anyway.

Maddie carries a small tray through with some drinks, condiments and knives and forks, she's even thought to fold some pieces of kitchen roll for napkins. She places it on the coffee table, then disappears back into the kitchen and returns with two dinner plates.

"This looks really good Maddie, thanks." I say, grabbing the salad dressing from the tray.

"No, thank you. You provided the ingredients, and wow, does everything you eat come from that posh patisserie?" She laughs with no malice meant.

"I must admit that dad and I are slightly addicted to that place, It's probably why I need to run so much, and the reason he still hits the gym." I laugh back. Then sigh. Will my dad ever get back to that level of fitness, what if he doesn't? No, I can't afford to start thinking about things negatively like that. It will help no one, especially my dad.
So we both start to eat, ignoring the elephant in the room.

It's comforting spending this time with Maddie, but I know I need to take her home. I've monopolized enough of her time already, and she's clearly exhausted, the constant yawning alone gives it away.

"Come on, now your fed, let's get you home." I smile at her, gathering the dishes and walking through to the kitchen, then loading the dishwasher.

"Not going to argue there, I feel like going into hibernation and waking up in the spring." She shouts back to me from the living room sofa. "I meant to ask you earlier, what are you going to do about football while your dad is in the hospital?

I'm sure the team will understand you cancelling for the foreseeable future." Maddie inquires as I walk back into the living room, picking up the remote control to turn the TV off.

"No, I can't possibly do that. I know my dad wouldn't want me to let the team down. If I'm needed at the hospital urgently, a couple of the other parents have offered to take over. I'll forward you their details, just in case." I answer her, glad she agreed to help me with football because I really need her help right now.

"Well, I will be there wherever you need me Danny, hospital or football pitch." Maddie replies as we walk outside and get into the car.

"Thanks, you're a good friend Maddie." I smile towards her, as I turn on the ignition to drive her home.

Chapter Twenty

Maddie

Danny, just dropped me off at home. And yep, I've totally been friend zoned. I don't know what I expected really, he's twenty-seven and I'm seventeen, it was never going to happen between us,

I just feel slightly deflated about the situation. No, I need to stop thinking like this. Danny's dad almost died, now is not the time to be having some kind of schoolgirl fantasy about a relationship with him. He needs a solid friend, so that's exactly what I'm going to be. I just need to totally ignore this invisible pull I feel towards him. Besides, he'd never be interested in me in a million years. The plain Jane, with no real future, okay strictly speaking that isn't entirely true. Jack and Tommy are my future, they are the most important thing to worry about right now.

"Sam, I'm home." I shout as I sling my backpack down, and I hear the bag of crisps I didn't eat earlier go pop with a large bang in my bag. Shit. Now I have to clean my bag out. Great, just great.

"What an earth was that noise?" Sam asks running into the living room looking around frantically for the cause of the loud bang.

"Don't even ask." I answer, as I start emptying the contents of my backpack out, so I can tip the offending crisps in the waste paper bin.

"How's Danny's dad doing? I was going to check after my shift last night, but the ITU was so chaotic, and I didn't want to bother the nurses, I think they had an emergency." Sam replies, picking some of the crisps I spilled off the carpet, waiting for my answer, so I go ahead and fill her in on what's happened today, and she quietly listens and nods.

"So anything new to tell me, I ask?" And Sam looks uncertain, I can tell something is wrong, this isn't a normal Sam reaction. Now I'm officially worried.

"So I don't want you to worry Maddie, but..." And before she even has a chance to finish that sentence I cut her off.

"That's never good, starting a sentence like that, because what it really means is that I need to worry." I reply, now feeling panicky inside, so I start to do my deep breathing.

"I had a visit from the landlord today. Okay, I won't sugar-coat it. He's sold the property and we have a week to move out." She looks at me with tears in her eyes, playing with her necklace.

"Shit Sam. He can't do that, there's laws and stuff, contracts??" I answer Sam, shaking with anger, we are about to be made homeless.

"Evidently he can, it was in the small print of the contract. Having the right to sell the property and break the tenancy agreement at short notice. That was why the rent was below market rate. It's done Maddie, nothing I can do about it now. I should have read the small print, I know better, but I was in such a rush the day I signed the contract." She can't even look at me, she's riddled with guilt.

"Sam this isn't your fault. How could you know this was going to happen?" I try to reassure her. Then I suddenly realise, if she can't find somewhere permanent to live quickly, I will get put with another foster parent, and I can feel the colour drain from me.

"First thing tomorrow morning, I'm going to go to the rental office and see what I can get in my price range. So Long as it has two bedrooms social services will be no problem." She says optimistically, reading my mind, a super power Sam seems to possess.

But I know the reality of this, rentals are really high in our little seaside town, even in the less desirable areas. Sam loves this little house, it's just so unfair, she won't find another one with a garden like this for the same price. She'll be making the sacrifice to keep me with her.

We sit and talk about it for the rest of the evening, coming up with no solid solution. This is just the icing on the cake to what has been a shitty week in Eastleigh-On-Sea.

Sam

Still in shock from yesterday's visit from the landlord, I can't believe how sneaky the landlord was. Hiding that away in the small print, about selling the property at short notice thus ending the tenancy contract making nil and void. It's totally my fault, I should have read the small print, if I hadn't been in a hurry that day. One things for sure, I certainly won't be making that mistake again.

Looking through the window of the properties and rental place in town, I put on my best smile and walk into the office, it's only been open a few minutes and I can see a couple of estate agents at their desks.

I decide that honesty is the best policy and explain my dire situation to the agent in charge of rentals. Which is a complete waste of time, as I can already predict what's she's going to say to me, just by reading the look on her face. But I do it anyway, because I live in hope.

"I'll be completely frank with you Miss Connors, you're not going to find another house for that price to rent. At very best it's going to be a two bedroom flat. And those go very quickly, do you think you could afford to pay slightly more? It might open up some more options?" The rental agent asks optimistically, tapping at her computer screen.

"It all depends how much, but I'm at my limit really already, and I don't qualify for any housing benefits because I apparently earn too much money." I say slightly sarcastically and I look down at my hands.

"Where do you work if you don't mind me asking?" The rental agent asks me, with a glint of hope in her eye.

"I'm a nurse at Eastleigh-On-Sea hospital." I answer, not really seeing how that could change anything.

"Well I think it's disgusting how much nurses get paid, my mum was a nurse before she retired, and I know how much she earnt, and how hard she worked for it. Let me go out back and see if any new rentals have come into the office. Give me a few minutes please, and help yourself to some coffee." And she points to a small waiting area with a coffee station set up for customers.

Danny, At The Same Time, In The Back Office...

"Oh, good morning Mr McKenzie, I didn't think you would be in today." Sheila, the rental agent greets me obviously surprised to see me here today.

"Just trying to keep busy, my dad has another surgery today, and I'm going back to the hospital in a little bit, so I thought I'd pick up some paperwork to take with me, the Wi-Fi reception isn't that great in the ITU." I reply looking up from my desk, one that I rarely ever use, and I can't even remember when the last time was.

"Well give him my very best wishes, and I will be baking some of those cheese scones he likes just as soon as he's feeling up to it." Shelia smiles at me, she's my longest employee at my company, and a jack of all trades. I'd be lost without her.

"If that isn't an incentive to get well soon, I don't know what is." I laugh back, knowing how much he loves those cheese scones.

"Do you happen to know if we've had any more two bedroom rentals come in since yesterday? I've got a sweet nurse out front and her landlord just sold the property she's been renting, and gave her a week to move out. But her budget is terrible, I wanted to try and find her something half decent, but it's going to be a real stretch." And I can see Shelia typing a million miles an hour at her computer out here in the back office.

"I'm pretty sure we can work something out with one of the landlords for a nurse wanting to rent, what's her name Shelia?" I ask shuffling through some paperwork.

"Her names Miss Connors, Sam Conners. She hasn't rented through us before. She certainly wouldn't have been stitched up like that by us, that's for sure." Shelia replies, with a look of disgust on her face that someone could be treated like that.

At first the name doesn't register, but then something clicks in my head. It can't be the same Sam surely? Not Maddie's foster parent? I get up from my chair and quickly poke my head around the office door to check if it's her, and a smartly dressed woman is standing there making coffee. As she turns around taking a sip from her cup, I can clearly see it is Maddie's Sam. Quickly I duck back into the office, so she doesn't see me.

"Shelia, that little two bedroom cottage I brought as an investment property, has the refit been completed on it yet?" I ask her with an idea in mind.

"Yes, Mr McKenzie it was finished last week. But the rental on that is three times her budget, so I wasn't even going to suggest it." Shelia says looking at me with confusion.

"I want you to offer it to her for the same rent as what she's previously been paying. If she wants to know why it's so cheap tell her it belonged to the present owners grandmother, and they wish to keep it in the family, and that they want someone living there that will take good care of the property. Tell her they now live abroad, and it will be a very long tenancy." I instruct Shelia, winking at her.

"Mr McKenzie, you big softie. Just like your father." And she kisses me on the cheek.

"Let's just keep this between us Shelia." I reply and go back to my paperwork smiling to myself, knowing I'm already keeping Maddie safe.

"But of course, Mr McKenzie." Shelia replies, "I'll get the contract drawn up now."

Maddie

Arriving home from college just after lunch, today is one of my half days, and I'm anxious to get indoors, to see of Sam has any more bad news for me. I push my new bike into the back garden, no way am I locking it to a drainpipe outside the front of the house, it's bound to get stolen there.

Not that I'm even going to be here much longer now Sam and I have been made homeless. I haven't stopped thinking about our dire situation all day. Two months until I'm eighteen, then I'm on my own anyway. Two months until I can apply to get Jack and Tommy.

I mentioned to Sam last night what my plan for them was in passing, we hadn't ever discussed it before. But it kind of came tumbling out of my mouth like some form of unstoppable verbal diarrhoea, sometimes I regret how much over share with people.

Sam didn't really comment much about my plan, she probably thinks it's just a pipe dream, maybe it is, but I can't give up on Jack and Tommy. I'm determined to find a way for the three of us to be together again.

Entering the kitchen from the back garden I immediately notice a large stack of brown cardboard boxes in all different shapes and sizes. What the hell have I walked into now??

"Maddie, great. Your home already. We've got so much to do before Saturday morning. I've found, us another house, I mean cottage, to move into and it was an absolute steal. I think the lady in the rental place, Shelia, very nice lady, but I digress. Anyway, I'm pretty sure she took pity on our situation, but after she learnt I'm a nurse, like her mum used to be, sorry, digressing again. Basically, Shelia put in a good word for me with our new landlord. The best part is that it's a long lease and the paperwork is water tight. The landlord can't just sell the property without giving proper formal notice, but it's a family property anyway, and they just want to keep it and not sell, plus they live abroad and won't be returning anytime soon. We can go and look together tonight when the keys are ready." Sam excitedly blurts out, grabbing my hands, and starts to jump us both around the kitchen in a dance of excitement.

"Oh my god Sam, I can't believe it. We're not going to be homeless, is this for real?" I answer, in utter shock, I think I've been through a whole roller coasters worth of emotions in the last twenty-four hours.

"Sweetheart, we were never going to be homeless, I can't believe you even thought that. You should have told me last night how worried you were. I just didn't expect to find somewhere so quickly. We must have a guardian angel looking out for us. Come and sit down, I want to talk to you about some things that you mentioned last night, because it got me thinking." And she leads me through to the living room, that is also stacked with an array of boxes which have already been packed. She must have been running on rocket fuel today, or twenty cups of coffee.

A sense of dread starts to run through my veins, I'm not ready to have this conversation yet, I know I'll have to move out in two months...

"I've been thinking all day about what you shared with me last night, about your plan to foster the twins. I want to help you Maddie, but I think my way might be easier and give you more options. The cottage we are moving into together on Saturday, how about you stay on as my lodger when you turn eighteen? I love living with you Maddie, and you feel like family to me now, and perhaps it's selfish of me, but I don't want you to leave. I can apply to foster Jack and Tommy, and we could all live together. The cottage only has two bedrooms, but it does have a small loft that has been recently renovated and would be suitable for a small bedroom. I'm not going to lie, it would be a squeeze and Jack and Tommy would need to share a bedroom. It also means you would need to be at home on the nights I'm working, but we could do this together. We could be a family. That's if you want me." And Sam looks at me tearfully, her eyes full of hope that I'll say yes.

Instead of answering Sam, I just sling my arms around her, and start to cry. But for once they are tears of happiness not sadness. We could be a family, we could be a family...

Taking a deep breath, I take a step back and look at Sam, and she's in tears as well.

"I don't know what to say. We could really do this together? Do you think that social services would let us?" I ask Sam, with a hint of doubt in my quivering voice and still full of tears.

"Honestly Maddie, we won't know until we try. But I'm already registered as a foster carer, and Jack and Tommy did live with you for years, so they already know you are like siblings and have that bond. You will be eighteen by then, so legally an adult, and we will have a loving, secure home waiting for them. Oh and I forgot to mention, the cottage is in a really nice area not far from the seafront. The boys would be able to walk to school, by themselves, we've got a really strong case already. Obviously Jack and Tommy need to express how they feel about living with me as a foster parent, but you already said there are documented issues with their current foster parent. I can call social services and get the ball rolling, what do you think?" Sam finally comes up for breath, smiling.

"I think it's a fantastic idea Sam, I don't know why I didn't think of it myself. I already know the boys will totally go for it. Sam you are a wonderful human being, I can't even begin to know how to thank you for doing this for us. I feel like this massive weight has just been lifted from my shoulders. I love the idea of looking after them both together. A real family at long last, that's all I've ever wanted." I sniffle and smile back at her, Sam pulls me into another hug.

Could things finally start to go my way for once?

Sam

We've picked up the keys to the cottage, and are just making the short journey to the seafront from the rental office in town. It's strange to think there was a major accident here just a couple of days ago, and I make sure to take extra care on the road driving. Maddie makes a comment about me driving like an old lady, and I have to laugh, because in this instance she's not wrong.

The cottage is situated in a small cul-de-sac and has off

road parking in a small driveway, the front garden is slightly overgrown, but nothing too horrific, and I do love gardening, and I can hardly wait to get stuck into it.

"Well this looks really nice, are you sure we have the right place? It looks way too expensive for us, no offense." Maddie says looking worried, like I've got the wrong place. I look down at the printout in my hand just to double check because I'm doubting myself now. It's definitely the correct cottage according to the printout, and Maddie's completely right. This is a really upmarket area, especially for the rent that I'll be paying.

"If they've made a mistake Maddie it's too late now, I've already signed the tenancy agreement. I just got the impression that they wanted a certain type of tenant and we fit the bill." I answer her honestly, being a nurse has given me an advantage for once.

Opening the front door into a small hallway, I notice a built in cupboard for coats and shoes. That will be a godsent with two boys, storage is always important.
The living room is open plan and a really good size, with the stairs leading up just to the side.
My furniture should fit in nicely here, and I can't wait to finally upcycle my old chesterfield sofa.
Maddie walks down to the kitchen just off the lounge and I follow.
It's about the same size as the kitchen I have at the moment, but then I notice another door. It's a tiny laundry room complete with a brand new washing machine and dryer. I can't believe my luck, I had no idea this was going to be included. My washing machine is on its last legs, and I've never had the luxury of a dryer before.

"I can't believe I'm excited about having a laundry room Maddie. This just made my life so much easier. I imagine those boys will generate a lot of laundry between them." I laugh looking excitedly towards Maddie, still not believing my luck.

"I think I've spent my life doing their laundry Sam, and especially now they both play football, and are constantly caked in mud." Maddie replies wrinkling her nose up, and I find myself thinking about how much she's already been caring for Jack and Tommy.

I open the back door onto a small decked patio. The garden is overgrown and needs attention, but it's going to be a fun project. You can even see the sea in the distance, the view is fantastic, and I can already imagine family BBQ's in the summer. I start to fantasise about building one of those brick ones, like I'd seen on a recent DIY show on TV.

"Let's look upstairs Sam." Maddie says excitedly, grabbing my hand and leading me upstairs.
I allow Maddie to lead me onto a small landing, both bedrooms are a fair size and I already know I'll have the one in the front of the house, because the other bedroom is slightly bigger so would be a better fit for Jack and Tommy. The bathroom is small and only has a shower, but the toilet is separate which is good. Maddie is looking really confused.

"Sam this is great, but how on earth do you get into the loft?" Maddie asks, turning around in circles.

Leading her back to the hallway, I pull down a small rope hanging from the ceiling.
"This reminds me of that scene in The Goonies, are we going to find one eyed Willies treasure map up there?" Maddie laughs, and I must admit it does feel like that. A built in ladder pulls

down easily when I gently pull the rope, and we both climb into the loft. You can only stand upright in the centre, but the actual space is bigger than I thought it would be. It even has a skylight, which is a bonus.

"So how would you feel about this being your room?" I ask Maddie, and I can already tell by the look on the face that she loves it.

With the biggest smile on her face Maddie replies "This is perfect Sam, just perfect."

"Then we better get home and continue packing, the rental lady Shelia kindly arranged for a removal van on Saturday at a discount price because her daughters husband can do the job, and I don't have a massive amount of furniture." I tell Maddie, thankful that I can give her a good home.

And tomorrow I need to set up a meeting with social services about the twins, because now I've seen the cottage I want to finally bring them all back together as a family.

Chapter Twenty-One

Danny

My laptop is open and I'm trying to get some work done, dad is still completely out of it after his surgery and the nurses keep popping in and out of the room checking his observations, so I'm finding it difficult to concentrate.

The Consultant Surgeon from London I paid a small fortune for privately said the surgery went well, and my dad should be able to get his leg back to full mobility but it's going to take intensive rehabilitation.

Hopefully tomorrow he will be well enough to be moved to a normal ward, and I've already arranged a private room for him. I just feel absolutely helpless and I want to do everything I can possible for dad. So he can get back on his feet as quickly as possible, and the sooner he can leave the hospital the better.

I'm just thinking to myself that I haven't heard from Maddie today yet when a message comes through on my phone, the girl must be psychic or something.

Sorry I haven't made it to the hospital today. How is your dad doing? Had a few issues at home and Sam needed my help, it's all good though.

I decide to call her, smiling to myself, rather than message her back. She's probably gone to see the cottage, but I can't let on that I know all about that. The phone rings and she answers.

"Hi Danny."

"Hi Maddie, thought it would be easier to call you, are you free to talk?" I ask her, my heart gently fluttering hearing her voice. Maddie never fails to have this effect on me.

"Yes it's fine if you don't mind me putting you on speaker. I'm in the middle of packing boxes. The short version is our landlord sold the house and gave us a week to move out. So we are moving on Saturday, can you believe it? Sorry, how's your dad, I should have asked that first." Maddie says breathlessly, and I can tell that she's getting herself all flustered.

"Dads surgery went well, but he's still knocked out and I haven't spoken to him yet, but I'm sitting here with him now in the ITU, he's observations are stable according to the nurses. So let me get this right, your landlord sold the house?" I ask Maddie, pretending to be surprised. She doesn't need to know that I own the cottage and I'm her new landlord, my name doesn't appear on the tenancy agreement. It just states Eastleigh-On-Sea properties and investments, the name of my company. The computer programming is my main work, and my company is a side gig that more or less runs itself with my staff at the helm a majority of the time.

So I allow Maddie to tell me all about the new cottage that she's moving into on Saturday, and how fantastic it is for her and Sam. I smile to myself when she tells me how excited Sam was about the new washing machine and dryer.

I arranged for them to be installed, that's why I didn't let Sam have the keys earlier, I needed to make sure the delivery had arrived. I've also organised the removal company, but they don't know that either. I like to keep things like this to myself, my mum would of called it something like spreading the kindness about. I don't need credit, it just makes me happy seeing other people happy. Especially when it comes to anything to do with Maddie. And after this epic shit show of a week everyone deserves some happiness.

"I can help you on Saturday if you want, so long as I'm not needed at the hospital. My dad should be on a normal ward by then, and he will probably have a gazillion visitors. And if I'm honest, I just want to do something normal that doesn't involve hospitals. Believe it or not, my dad would be the first person to understand that after everything with my mum." I whisper to her, on the phone, suddenly aware that my dad might be able to hear me.

"This is bringing up a lot of memories isn't it?" Maddie quietly replies, always so intuitive to my feelings.

"Yes it is, it's a lot to process. So moving heavy boxes around sounds like normality to me." I answer, smiling at the thought of spending more time with her.

"Then your help will be very much appreciated Danny, I'm going to try and rope Bryan in too. He can be the entertainment for the day, and he's scared of Sam which in itself is hilarious." She laughs, and I hear her tearing packing tape in the background.

"Not sure how much help Bryan will be, but your right about the entertainment factor. I'll be at football practice tomorrow, see you then?" I ask Maddie, selfishly missing not seeing her today.

"Yes I'll be there. Would you like to come to dinner afterwards? I'm stealing Jack and Tommy for a couple of hours after practice. Thought I'd rope them into packing some more things up, and then feed them." She asks me, and I'm suddenly feeling nervous. Am I allowing myself to get to close to her? But I find myself quickly answering her offer.

"That sounds great, I can have dinner with you and then come back to the hospital and see my dad." I reply a little enthusiastically, and blush. Good job Maddie can't see me right now.

"We have a solid plan then. See you tomorrow Danny. Call me, or message me if you need to vent. Bye."

"Bye." And we both hang up together.

"Save me some of that dinner tomorrow." My dad whispers to me, his voice hoarse from having the intubation tubes down his throat.

"Dad, thank god. How are you feeling? I've been losing my mind with worry." I move closer to the bed and hold his hand, slightly shaking with anxiety.

"I'm alive son. I'm alive. I swear to god I saw her though." Dad whispers again, and I give him a sip of water through a straw that the nurse left on the table for him.

"Saw who dad?" I'm pretty sure my dad's getting confused with all the drugs again, and my stomach churns with that same anxiety again. Do I want to know the answer?

"Your mum Danny. Your mum. She told me to go back towards the light, said it wasn't my time yet." Dad coughs slightly, then closes his eyes. He's out of it again.

"Oh dad." And I put my head down onto his bed and I silently cry for the first time in years.

Maddie

Climbing into bed totally exhausted, I think about the mountain climb of the last seventy-two hours of my life. The video of me singing being shared at college, the terrible accident, finding out we were being made homeless, the packing of boxes...

But only one thing really stands out from all this trauma, and that's my relationship with Danny becoming much closer than before. I can't seem to get him off my mind.

These aren't the thoughts of someone who just wants to be friends, am I kidding myself? I roll over again thumping my pillow in a bleak attempt to make it more comfortable.

Sleep, I needed sleep. As I lay there quietly contemplating I finally manage to drift off into a troublesome sleep.

"One more push, and the babe will be born. That's it. She's here."
Says a woman's voice.
"Please let me hold my Angel, just this once." And hands reach for the baby girl.
"Remember you will always be loved, my Angel." The young woman now kisses the babes head.
"We have to get her out of this Realm, before they find her, her father has spies here." A man's voice says.
"Remember Angel, remember me, when the dreams come to you. I love you."
The babe is taken away gently from the woman's arms, and the man with wings takes off into the sky, babe in arms to get her to safety.

The next part of the dream is a familiar one, the young boy and the baby in the box. The boy's face merging into that of a man, one that's still blurred. Why can't I see it? Damn, I want to see who it is.

Waking up with a start and looking at the time on my phone, I can see it's the middle of the night and now I'm wide awake now. Hang on, the dream. The first part of the dream, I've never had that part before. Practically leaping out of bed I run downstairs to find my backpack not even bothering to put on any lights, just relying on the moonlight coming through the blinds that were never shut last night. Finding it on the floor where I left it and digging in my backpack, I find my notebook and pen, then frantically I start to scribble down the first part of the dream, trying to remember as many details as possible. Finally I finish, and now feeling completely exhausted again I go back to bed and fall straight back to sleep.

My alarm wakes me at seven the next morning and I rub the sleep out of my eyes. Remembering last night, I reach straight for my notebook and read over what I wrote down in the moonlight. Good job that I can understand my hurried scribble. One vivid detail sticks out, a man with wings. A man with wings? Okay, that makes absolutely no sense what so ever...
Another word sticks out, Realm? This is fast turning into a fantasy world. Maybe I'm just over tired, and stressed out. This part of the dream can't be real can it? Could the woman really be my mother, and why did she call me her Angel? Too many questions and no answers.

But all I can find myself thinking about as I get ready for college is a man with wings, flying away with a baby girl in his arms...

Chapter Twenty-Two

Bryan

"**W**hat's up buttercup?" I say as I put my lunch tray down on the table and sit down next to Maddie, she appears distracted looking off into the distance. Something is obviously playing on her mind today, but she'll share if she wants to, I don't like to push, we all have our secrets after all.

"I see you braved the canteen food again, and what delights that sensitive palate of yours today?" Maddie laughs at me playfully, picking up on my terrible eating habits, I always have the best intentions to be healthier. But then something yummy will catch my eye, and all bets are off.

"Well, it was a toss-up between a scary looking egg mayo sandwich or this slightly less scary slice of Hawaiian pizza. Although it's certainly not Mario's standard." I smirk back at her, taking in the smell of the pizza and wishing it was indeed my favourite from Mario's. This would have to suffice for now.

"If your free later, and don't mind packing some boxes you can have dinner at mine tonight, Sam's already cooking for the boys. She won't mind an extra mouth to feed if it means more help" Maddie replies, her eyes shining with excitement like she has a story she's itching to tell me.

"I feel you have some new information to fill me in on here.."

And Maddie goes on to tell me all about what's happened to her in the last twenty-four hours with her living situation.

"...so that's why we're packing tonight. With Sam still having to work, and me at college all day it's going to be tight getting the packing done before Saturday morning. Even Danny is coming, but I think he just needs some time away from the hospital. He's putting on a brave face, but I'm worried about him." Maddie finishes, and pokes her fork around her chickpea salad, losing enthusiasm for her lunch. Now I get what's really on her mind. Danny. She's worried about Danny.

"Count me in, I can grab some more boxes if you want. Dads got some in the shed left over from a delivery he had. I was supposed to put them in the recycling but totally forgot, so this works for me too." And I take another bite of my pizza, as I give Maddie a cheeky grin.
"As for Danny, he'll be okay. I expect being at the hospital has just brought up stuff with his mum. That's what my dad said to mum last night. Have you spoken to him today?" I ask her, hoping that eases some of her worry about him.

"Not really, I got a brief message earlier to say his dad had a comfortable night and he'd see me at football practice." She smiles at me. Yep, definitely called it. She is so into him. So I smirk back at her, knowingly.

"What are you smirking about Bryan? You look like the cat that got the cream." She cheekily smirks back at me, pretending nothing is going on. But I can read Maddie like a book right now, she can't keep her feelings about him hidden from me.

"Nothing, just a general observation." I reply, playing it totally cool, not wanting to rock the boat. Okay, that's a lie. Maybe rock the boat a tincy, tiny bit...

"We're just friends, besides he's twenty-seven for god's sake. No way would he be interested in me. So just leave it alone Bryan, please." Maddie looks down, and she's visibly upset by my comment. Shit, it looks like I hit a nerve. I didn't mean to do that. I actually think they would make a great couple. But I don't say that out loud, not right now, and we continue to eat in silence.

"Sorry." I say after a few minutes, realising I'm going to have to be the person who breaks the silence, I don't like upsetting her.

"It's okay Bryan. Really, I'm just being over sensitive. So I'll see you at mine tonight, dinner and packing?" Maddie replies, not being the type of person to hold a grudge, and I admire how she forgives so easily. She's standing up to leave the lunch table…

"You can count on me. I'll be there." And she wanders off, waving over her shoulder to signal goodbye for now. I'm chewing the last mouthful of my pizza when someone sits down opposite me, I look up and see it's Ben. Oh shit, I'm really not in the mood for this right now. So I stand up.

"Please Bryan, I just want to talk to you, I want to apologise for the other day. I really do miss you hanging out with us all, it's not the same." Ben asks, almost like his eyes are pleading with me to say more, but I haven't got the energy for this right now.

"We both said some stuff Ben, but I can't cope with all the toxic, superficial shit anymore in that group of people. And I'm done with partying like that. I don't want to act that way anymore Ben. We're practically adults now, the world is real. Other shit is more important than who got off with who, or who's dad makes more money. I don't care about that stuff anymore. You know in the last three days my friend Maddie's been bullied, my dad's best friend nearly died, oh and not to top

Maddie being bullied she was almost made homeless." I finish my rant at Ben panting, getting everything off my chest all in one go. Well not everything, but I'm not about to confess those feelings to Ben in the middle of the canteen.

"Bryan I..." But I don't allow him to finish, I can't do this right now. That look he's giving me, like he cares. Or something more. Nope, I'm not getting caught down that rabbit hole. Because I really like this guy, but he's straight. I'm just wishing that he wasn't, I can't be his friend anymore, not with these feelings. I know I'm never going to get the kind of relationship that I want with him. So I just walk away, and leave him sitting at the table...

Danny

Unintentionally, I ended up sleeping in the chair at the hospital last night, and my backs as stiff as a board now. I didn't want to leave dad alone, but the nurse made me leave this morning, she hinted at me perhaps taking a shower. A polite way of saying I stink of sweat and hospital. I know the nurses will phone if there's a problem with dad, and David is heading over to see him later on this morning.

Finishing my run, and ironically all sweaty again, I feel less stiff and slightly more energised. Taking a quick shower before I leave for football practice, work has fallen by the way side today, but it doesn't really matter because I'm my own boss and my staff will keep things running for me. I'm also anxious to see Maddie again, I can't seem to get that girl out of my head, and the letter Father Christopher showed me.
There is a light drizzle, so it's going to be a cold, wet, football

practice with lots of mud. I'm just not feeling it today, but as soon as I spot Maddie pushing her new bike onto the field my day immediately brightens.

"Hi Maddie, your early today, see you brought all the good weather with you." I laugh, looking up towards the sky. The day is dismal, but seeing Maddie has brightened everything.

"My last lesson got cancelled for some reason, so I'm officially in the library studying and writing an essay right now." She laughs back, putting her new bike down on the grass like she doesn't want to let it out of her sight.

"The boys are just getting changed, I thought I'd do a couple of five aside games today, just make it a fun practice. Everyone in town is shaken up by the accident, and knows someone that was involved in one way or another. And if I'm honest I think that's as much as my brain can cope with at the moment." I say to her honestly. Today I'm finding it difficult to function, constantly worrying about my dad.

"No one even expects you to be here at the moment, but I think the normality is beneficial for everyone, I know it helps me." And she beams at me, that killer smile lighting up the dreary October day, and I feel her energy already working it's magic. Boys start emerging out of the changing rooms and I start doing a warm up with them, and Maddie for the first time joins in. I now notice she's dressed slightly differently today in a pink and black tracksuit. Normally she's just in jeans and a sweatshirt.

"I got fed up of standing in the cold watching, Sam lent me this to wear. Snazzy isn't it." And she laughs, doing star jumps with the rest of the boys. I notice Jack and Tommy are finding this particularly amusing. I do a quick head count of the team and notice we are a boy short today.

"Who are we missing today? Does anyone know I shout." And look at all the boys, I should be able to tell, but my poor sleep last night is taking it's toll on my brain.

"Zach has gone to the dentist, sorry forgot to tell you Coach." Jack replies, continuing the star jumps, his arms and legs flying in all directions.

"Right in that case Maddie, you can officially be Zach today." I laugh and point to the far goal, the position that Zach usually takes in practice .

Maddie does a quick salute, and jogs down to the goal to take up her position. And to be fair to her, she can certainly hold her own. It becomes clear to me that this isn't the first time she's played football with the boys, and her skills aren't half bad.
It certainly makes for an interesting practice and I'm disappointed when it finishes, Maddie is covered in mud and couldn't care less. She has rounded up the boys for water and protein bars, and they have slowly started disappearing into the changing rooms to get changed.

"You were great out there today, thanks for stepping in like that. The team has really taken to you." And I walk towards Maddie and stop, she's got mud on her face, and she looks fucking adorable. I gently wipe the mud off with my finger, and I can tell she's holding her breath, almost in anticipation. Right at that very moment, one of the parents calls my name, and we break apart from one another. That was close, I almost did something very stupid, I almost kissed her, and I think Maddie would have let me…

"I'll be right back." I say, and she simply nods at me and blushes. Running off, then starts to collect the empty water bottles.

Parents are asking about my dad, talking about how awful the accident was and how lucky he is. I know it's only out of concern, but it's the last thing that I really want to talk about right now.

Maddie must notice how uncomfortable I'm feeling, because she comes over to rescue me, and leads me off towards the changing room.

"Are you still coming for dinner tonight?" She asks, smiling brightly, cheering me up instantly.

"Of course, and I can give you Jack and Tommy a lift home as well, seeing as I'm coming over anyway. Do you want to go and load your bike up onto the rack while I lock up the changing rooms." I ask her, falling into the routine of getting her bike loaded up, and I hate her cycling when it's starting to get dark even with lights on her bike.

"Thanks that's great I'll phone Sam and let her know she doesn't need to pick Jack and Tommy up. I'm surprised that Mrs Thompson even agreed to let me have them round for dinner, but she's playing nice for some reason. I think that little chat that you had with her helped. Sam wants to spend some time getting to know the boys anyway." And she jogs off again towards her bike, still full of energy even after running around all practice.

Jack and Tommy appear from the changing room still full of ten year old boy energy, laughing and joking about with each other.

"Your both riding to Maddie's house with me, so try not to get mud all over my backseats." I laugh and throw Tommy my car keys, which he catches looking slightly startled, but grins as soon as he realises I'm trusting him with my car keys.

"Last one there is an idiot." Tommy laughs, with Jack running after him. I shake my head and smile to myself, and finish up putting equipment into cupboards and locking the empty changing room.

I get into the car and everyone is patiently waiting for me with their seatbelts on, and Maddie is flicking through my CD's and her eyes light up when she finds a particular one.

"Do you mind if I put this one on?" Maddie asks, already removing the CD from the case. With her hand lingering near the car stereo.

"Go for it, you don't have to ask every time, I like listening to the songs you pick ." I smile, happy that she feels comfortable enough to just flick through them, and I know whatever song she picks I'll be listening to on repeat later on tonight.

Maddie loads the CD and starts forwarding through the songs to find the one she wants to listen too.

The last song I ever expected comes on through the speakers, Need you now, by Lady A.

Jack pipes up from the back, "You used to listen to this all the time when we lived at Nanna Jenny's it used to drive her mad." Jack laughs at the obvious private joke between them.

"Yes ,sing along Maddie like you used too, it will make Nanna Jenny turn in her grave for sure. You know how much she hated country music" Tommy adds, laughing his head off.

"Picture perfect memories, scattered all around the floor, reaching for the phone cause, I can't fight it anymore, and I wonder if I ever cross your mind, for me it happens all the time.." She sings along, and it feels like those words are meant for me.

When it gets to the chorus, the boys start joining in horribly out of tune. But to me it all sounds perfect. It's one of those moments that you just want to keep in a bottle to last forever.

The second verse is coming up which the male vocalist sings, so I take a deep breath and go for it,
"Another shot of whiskey, can't stop looking at the door, wishing you'd come sweeping in the way you did before, and I wonder if I ever cross your mind, for me it happens all the time." And then we all sing the chorus together.

But my verse was just for Maddie, even if she never realises...

Chapter Twenty-Three

Maddie

Danny just sang the male part of one of my favourite songs. His voice is deep and sultry, country with a rock vibe, and sexy as hell. Talk about a massive turn on, oh my god, he never let on he could sing. And talking of singing, I just did it again in front of him without even thinking about it. Maybe my confidence is growing?

"Well that was a fun journey." He says parking up his car behind Sam's, smiling as he undoes his seatbelt and opening the door.

"You never thought to mention to me you could sing Danny?" I answer, still slightly in shock. He kept that little gem hidden. I've already memorised him singing that song, it almost felt like he was singing it to me. But that's ridiculous, just my over active imagination playing havoc again.

"I was a choirboy for a few years, so I can hold a tune just about." He smirks back, winking at me and gets out of the car.

"More than hold a tune Danny, that was amazing. You sounded better than the vocalist on the CD." I reply, and he pokes his head back into the car.

"Look who's talking Maddie, you're the one with amazing vocals." Danny replies, pointing at me making me blush in embarrassment.

"Hey what about us?" Jack adds, sensing my tension.

"Stick to football." I laugh back, and everyone joins in. Nice save Jack I think to myself smiling.
Entering the house together we pile into Sam's living room, and it looks like she's packed some more boxes up since earlier today.

"Sam we're back from football practice." I call out and she appears in the living room looking wrung out but happy.

"Hi guys, dinner is going to be about forty-five minutes. So if you fancy packing a few boxes for me? Danny, I was wondering if you would mind taking all the pictures on the walls down, then bubble wrapping them. There's a large box in the kitchen I've marked pictures. Boys, would you mind packing up my CD's and DVD's from that cupboard, there's already a box started." Sam replies, anxious to continue organising us all with jobs, and I giggle to myself.

I quickly butt in to her instructions, "Mind if I take a quick shower first Sam? I'll be five minutes tops." I laugh at her, pointing to her muddy tracksuit that she lent me that I'm currently standing in.

"Yes, sorry Maddie. I'm just going into work mode, I'm so used to organising things in a methodical way." And she blushes slightly, shit. I didn't mean to embarrass Sam.
There's a knock on the door, saved by the bell so to speak. So I decide to go and answer it.

"I come bearing boxes, what's for dinner?" Bryan chuckles, and starts carrying them inside.

"Bryan, you little darling, I need more of those." And Sam gives him a hug, "Dinner is macaroni cheese, mixed vegetables and garlic bread." She smiles, and wanders through to the kitchen.

Bryan follows her through and I can hear him saying, "Do you need any help out here…"

So I decide to leave everyone to it and go upstairs for my shower. I strip off in the bathroom and start the water to get to a decent temperature, and as the bathroom starts to steam up I get inside the shower stall. I grab my cherry bodywash that I share with Sam. We have a great routine really, and we borrow each other's things all the time. It's something I never had with Donna when we lived at Nanna Jenny's house. I wonder how she's getting on now? I haven't heard from her recently, she didn't reply last time I messaged her.
Stepping out of the shower, I wrap my body in a towel and start combing through my hair, I hate getting the knots out of my natural curls. My hair serum is in my bedroom, so I open the bathroom door to go and retrieve it from my room.

Danny is standing right in front of me, removing a painting Sam did from the wall, and I'm standing in just a short towel. I can feel my cheeks going bright red, and I quickly rush into my bedroom without saying anything. I'm mortified that he saw me in such a state of undress, how bloody embarrassing. Quickly getting dressed, I don't bother drying my hair and I grab my muddy tracksuit and socks, running downstairs and heading into the kitchen.

"Jack and Tommy, if you want me to wash your football kits before you go home I'm putting a load on now." I shout from the kitchen, trying to ignore any eye contact with Danny. But it's him that replies to me, I'll grab it out the car Maddie." And Danny disappears out of the front door, I expect he's embarrassed too.

Taking the washing powder out of the cupboard, and pouring some into the compartment at the top of the machine, I say, "I'm not going to miss this washing machine, it sounds like an aircraft taking off when it goes into its spin cycle."

"Well that sounds like it could be fun." Bryan pipes up, and wiggles his eyebrows jokingly.

Sam walks past and gently clips him round the ear, "We'll have less of that talk with Jack and Tommy around." She laughs, not really angry with his amusing innuendo.

"Two backpacks of muddy football kits, I'll go and scrape the mud off their boots in the garden." Danny says handing me the backpacks, with their dirty kits.

"No Danny, they should be scraping their own boots. Jack and Tommy kitchen now." I shout slightly annoyed, Jack and Tommy damn well know that's they're job to do, and I won't let them get out of chores like that.

Bryan is taking this all in, I just know he's going to ask me about it as soon as we are alone. But I don't really feel like sharing my embarrassment of Danny seeing me in only a towel. He probably thinks I did it on purpose to get his attention.
I'd never sink so low as to do something manipulating like that. But now I've snapped at him for offering to clean the boys boots.

"Come on boys let's do this outside, we don't want mud all over the kitchen." And Danny and leads the boys into the back garden, to get the mud off their boots.

"Okay spill, what's up buttercup?" Bryan asks, luckily Sam has gone upstairs muttering to herself, about boxes.

Grabbing Bryans arm, I lead him into the living room, to talk, "Bryan, I'm bloody mortified is what I am. I came out the bathroom in just a skimpy little towel, and Danny was on the landing taking a painting down. He saw me, probably thinks that I did it on purpose, in a bid to get him to notice me. I swear to god I didn't." And I throw both of my hands in the air and cover my face in frustration. Bryan just stands there and starts chuckling away at me. So I cross my arms over attempting to give him my best annoyed look, "It's not bloody funny Bryan." I shout out, clearly exasperated with his response to my dilemma.

"Your right Maddie, it's not bloody funny. It's fucking hilarious. I can just imagine the look on both of your faces." He continues laughing, holding onto his sides now.

"Why me? Why me?" I answer seeing that I'm going to get nowhere with Bryan, when he's in one of these moods.

"Maddie you do realise that he's totally got the hots for you?" Bryan says, being deadly serious now.

"Shoosh, keep your voice down Bryan. And you've got it totally wrong. We're just friends." I reply looking towards the kitchen door to make sure no one else heard.

"Okay, have it your way for now. But I'm never wrong about these things. I've called it several times at college, when people have got together as couples. Just call me the love doctor." And Bryan laughs again, in a know it all way.

I absolutely can't stay annoyed with Bryan, and by the time everyone reappears in the living room we are both laughing together…

Chapter Twenty-Four

Danny

O utside with Jack and Tommy in the back garden, I get to teach them both an easier way to clean their boots. Maddie got annoyed with me for some reason, and wouldn't make eye contact with me in the kitchen, and I don't think it has anything to do with Jack and Tommy. Perhaps she's embarrassed that I saw her coming out of the bathroom in just a towel. I'll be the first to admit that I'll be thinking about that image of her in just a towel when I take a shower later...

She has no idea just how attracted to her I am. But no, I absolutely cannot have those kinds of thoughts about her. It's just wrong on so many levels. It's not like the poor girl did it on purpose, she looked horrified. I'm just going to ignore it unless she brings it up, and save her the embarrassment. Pretend it never happened. Yes. That's the best thing to do. When we're finished outside, we walk into the living room. Bryan and Maddie are both in hysterics about something, so the moment must have passed thank goodness.

"Maddie, can you help me dish up dinner please, you'll have to all make do sitting round the coffee table on the floor I'm afraid. Bryan could you grab the bottle of cola out of the fridge and some glasses, don't worry Maddie I got the caffeine free, sugar free sort." Sam says, springing into action organising us all again, and I smile.

"Oh Maddie. Why did you go and tell Sam that, about the cola? Now we won't be all hyper when we go home to annoy Mrs Thompson." Tommy replies, looking disappointed with her, like she let out a massive secret or something.

"That's exactly why Tommy, I'm trying to stay in her good books." Maddie answers sternly, being completely serious. She really is doing her best to keep in the miserable old bags good books.

I enjoy watching their playful banter, it feels like being at Bryans house at Christmas time. Being with a family, instead of just me and dad. Thinking of dad, I grab my phone out of my back pocket and check for messages from the hospital.

Just one from David, saying dads doing well and they're moving him onto the main ward into the private room that I arranged tonight. Apparently they need the ITU bed and dad is stable enough to move. I smile and it's a huge relief things are going in the right direction, and I know he'll appreciate the private room, he likes his privacy like me.

Sam and Maddie both walk into the living room holding plates of steaming macaroni cheese. And my stomach growls in appreciation.

"They're moving dad onto the main ward later, he's doing much better. I'll go and see him after dinner if that's okay." I say as Sam hands me a plate, and my mouth is watering in anticipation.

"That's fantastic news Danny, I've set aside a small Tupperware container of macaroni you can take to him on the ward. It's nice and soft, and might tempt his appetite more than hospital food." Sam answers. Looking pleased with herself.

"Sam, he will really like that. It's one of his favourite dishes, mum used to make it all the time when I was little and going through a fussy stage. Dad got slightly addicted to it." I sadly smile when the sudden memory hits me by surprise, and I look towards Maddie for some reason. She smiles back in a show of support, there goes that intuition of hers kicking in again. I never really talk much about my mum. But for some reason I find it easier with Maddie around, the memories don't feel quite as painful.

"I'll pop in and say hello to him when I'm on shift tomorrow. See how he's getting on. I doubt he'll remember talking to me the night of the accident. Which is probably just as well." Sam replies, and heads back into the kitchen to fetch some more plates.

I turn to Maddie, "Sam's so kind, I can see why you get on with her so well." And I can see Jack and Tommy are taking this all in, quietly observing us.

"Sam's the best, I wish we got to live with her instead of you know who." Jack butts in grumpily, with his eyes downcast.

"Is it really that bad with Mrs Thompson?" I ask, and the boys look at each other, and Tommy shakes his head. Something is going on here. What don't Jack and Tommy want to share?

Maddie looks towards me with a worried look on her face, then asks the boys, "Has something else happened at home I need to know about?"

"It's nothing really, hardly worth mentioning, and it's not like the first time its happened." Jack replies nonchalantly, shrugging his shoulders.

"Jack don't say anything, you promised me." Tommy replies, putting his plate down on the coffee table like he's suddenly lost his appetite.

Maddie looks like she's about to explode at them in pure frustration, I can see it in her face, so I shake my head at her, and mouth "no don't".

"Tommy if it's something bad you need to tell an adult. We can help you, but if you don't speak up, we can't help if we don't know." I say, speaking with the same voice I use when I'm coaching. "Would you rather speak to someone in private? Would that be easier?" I ask him, trying not to pressurise him. Tommy nods at me, and I notice Jack puts a hand on his shoulder, in a show of brotherly support.

"Can I talk to you alone Coach?" Tommy asks me in a whisper, looking around the room.

"How about we go and sit in the car after dinner and have a little chat? Eat up now it's getting cold." And I nod towards his plate of food, I want him to eat first, taking the pressure off.

"I'm just getting a glass of water." And I walk out to the kitchen, using it as an excuse, hoping that Maddie follows me. As I turn around Maddie and Sam have both followed me in, my simple tactic worked and Sam closes the door.

"Sorry if I over stepped, but something is really bothering that boy, and has been for a while." I state in a low voice, looking at both of them worriedly.

"No, you did the right thing Danny, but you realise that you are going to have to share the conversation with us in case its serious enough that I have to phone social services." Sam replies, and Maddie looks close to tears.

"Hey, we'll sort this out. We're a team, and teams work together." I answer putting an arm around Maddie, it takes a village to raise a child and those boys have us all now.

"Let's just finish dinner, and we'll get through this, whatever it is, together." Absent mindlessly, I kiss Maddie on the head in front of Sam. Sam doesn't comment, and Maddie is too upset to really notice.

Bryan has worked his magic again and both of the boys are laughing at a story Bryan is telling them about a boy farting in class at college. The guy should be a stand-up comedian with the way he can make the most boring story sound funny, and he can certainly read the room. He's a great guy to have around, and he feels like the little brother I never had sometimes.
We finish dinner, with both boys going for second helpings, and Sam is beaming that her meal was clearly enjoyed by all.

Maddie and Bryan start gathering up plates, and Tommy turns to me and says "Is it okay if Jack comes too?"

"Of course it is Tommy. We're just going out to the car, be back soon guys." I shout out towards the kitchen. Jack and Tommy follow me out to the car and get into the backseats. I turn around in my seat so I can see them both, although it's getting dark now. Maybe that will make it easier for Tommy to say what he needs too.

But it's Jack that starts speaking first, "So Mrs Thompson, she's always given us the creeps. Like a bad feeling."

"She's always watching us, or just walks into a room without knocking." Tommy quickly adds, obviously more comfortable talking with his brother present.

"Sometimes I know she drinks alcohol, she tries to hide it, but Nanna Jenny used to do that, so we kinda know all the signs." Jack answers matter of fact, and it angers me that a child even knows about this stuff.

"Coach, I don't think I can do this. Jack can you tell him." And Tommy looks down at his hands, visibly shaking in fear now.

"One of the boys at school sent Tommy this video on his phone, basically porn. So Tommy was in the bathroom watching it, and he got, you know, down there." Jack replies and points to his crotch, blushing.

"You know it's perfectly natural for a boy your age to get excited at things, I don't suppose you've really had anyone to talk to you about it. An adult. That's what I mean." Jack and Tommy both shake their heads.

"Anyway Tommy was you know, enjoying the video, and doing stuff with his you know what, and Mrs Thompson just walked in the bathroom. She just stood there watching, told him to carry on." Jack answers, looking at Tommy, who now looks horrified.

"But I couldn't do it. She made me feel dirty, I just ran out the room and hid in the wardrobe. Jack had gone to the newsagents for crisps. He found a fiver on the way home from school that day, and wanted to get snacks for a movie marathon. I wish I'd gone with him now, but I wanted to watch the video alone. I was so scared, it just felt so wrong what Mrs Thompson wanted me to do. I didn't tell Jack for a few days, I was ashamed." Tommy replies, still looking down fidgeting with both of his hands.

"And did Mrs Thompson ever try to touch you, either of you?" I ask, I can't believe what they are telling me. I wasn't expecting this. This is child abuse.

"She opened the shower door the other day when I was in it, and I told her to fuck off. Then she tried to pretend she didn't know I was in there." Jack huffs in disgust.

"Boys this is really serious stuff you are both telling me, and I'm proud of you both for having the courage to speak to me. But there is absolutely no way you can ever go back to that house, with that woman. I'm going to speak to Sam about this because she is a foster parent and a nurse. Is it okay if I tell Maddie too?" I gently ask them both, trying my very best to stay as calm as possible, when all I really want to do is go and punch something repeatedly.

"Are we in trouble, don't let us get taken away from Maddie?" Jack shrieks out in distress. Tommy looks like he's about to go into a meltdown.

"No. No way are either one of you in trouble. Do you want to stay out here or come back inside with me?" I ask quietly, looking at them both patiently and waiting.

"You can tell Maddie." Tommy answers, his voice cracking and he immediately bursts into tears. It breaks my heart, I can feel the pain and despair radiating off of him.
"Stay here with him Jack, I'm going to get Maddie." And I walk back into the house, tearing up myself, and stop for a few seconds to straighten myself out.

"Maddie can you go outside and make sure Tommy is okay, he's crying his eyes out. Sam you need to get social services on the phone now and raise a safe guard on Jack and Tommy, for child sex abuse. I want a social worker, the police I don't fucking care here tonight. Those boys are never going back to that child abusing bitch ever again." And I start pacing round the living room.
The colour has drained out of everyone's faces. Maddie's already gone out of the front door without saying a word, and Sam has taken out her phone.

"Do you want to do this in the kitchen Danny?" She asks. And I nod.

"Bryan, can you phone your dad for me please, and ask him to stay on at the hospital with my dad. Tell him something serious has happened and I will try and visit with him later, I'm sure the nursing staff will let me after visiting hours as he has a private room." I say hastily, dishing my orders out. Bryan takes his phone out, and calls his dad.
"Then go and check on Maddie and the boys after that." I say and walk into the kitchen slamming the door behind me.

"Sorry Sam, I'm so fucking angry for them. Ten year old boys. Ten years old. She's been watching them for god knows how long. Bursting into the bathroom, opening the shower when they are in there. God only knows what else. They say she didn't touch them, but we can't be sure Jack and Tommy aren't holding back anything. But it's still abuse isn't it Sam?" I ask her red faced and angry, spitting my words out.

"Yes it is Danny, but try and calm yourself down for the sake of Maddie and the boys. They need you calm. I'm going to phone the on-call social services number that I have for Maddie, and see what they say. Your right though. Those boys are not going back there. If I'm allowed I'll keep them here tonight I will, but they might not let me. Whatever happens, they are not going back to that house. Why don't you go through and check on everyone, and I'll make some calls." Sam says, thank god she can stay calm in this terrible situation because I'm a wreck.Thank god Jack and Tommy opened up, now I need to make sure they stay safe.

Maddie

Running out to the car, I sling open the rear door and Tommy practically falls into my arms sobbing.

Jack gets out the other side, and slams his door. Looking like he's ready to murder someone.

Both the twins are so similar when it comes to facial expressions or mannerism's, and the fact they are almost identical in looks is where the similarities stop.

Tommy has always been the more sensitive of the two, always taking things to heart. Where Jack is definitely the protector of the two, and he was clearly going into full on protector mode right now.

Nodding to Jack, I manage to guide Tommy back into Sam's living room and sit him down on the sofa, sitting down next to him and putting my arm around his shoulder. I notice that Danny has taken Jack off to one side, and is quietly whispering to him.

Bryan, bless him, followed me outside and has been hovering the whole time. He's fidgeting at the side of the living room now, not sure what to do.

Tommy is slowly calming down, and his sobs are subsiding. I continue to hug him to me, gently rubbing patterns on his back like I used to when he was little.

"Tommy it's going to be okay. You don't need to talk right now. Just breathe. I'm here and I'm not leaving you again. Not this time." I know that I probably shouldn't have said that, and I'm in no position to make promises right now. But it just slipped out, and besides I mean it. No one is separating us again now, not after this.

Sam walks back into the living room a few minutes later with a serious look on her face.

"Bryan, thanks for coming with the boxes tonight it was much appreciated, but as you can see we have a few things to deal with right now. Could you run this over to the hospital for Danny's dad, just say Nurse Connors sent you with this." And she hands him the Tupperware container of macaroni.

"Of course, no problem. Call me later Maddie." And he quickly disappears out the door, obviously relieved to have been given the okay to go, and I feel slightly guilty that I'd basically ignored him. But Tommy is my number one priority at the moment.
Sam kneels down in front of Tommy, she could have sat next to him but she's purposely not crowding him.

"Tommy, you and Jack have been very brave tonight and have taken the hardest step. That was telling Danny about what happened with Mrs Thompson. This is very serious stuff your both dealing with, and I don't want either one of you to be scared. A police officer and your social worker are on their way here now. And I need you to tell them what happened, so we can stop this ever happening again. Do you think you can do that Tommy? You too Jack?" And she looks at both of them, Jack is now sitting next to Tommy looking just as scared.

They simply nod at her, and Sam gets up and walks into the kitchen and it's clear that she wants me to follow. And I notice Danny has followed too. Sam closes the kitchen door, and looks at us both.

"So as luck has it Jack and Tommy's social worker is the one on call tonight, which means she knows their history inside out and Maddie's connection to them both. She's had concerns for a while but hasn't had enough evidence to remove the boys. It sounds like Mrs Thompson had an answer for everything. But this is serious enough to get the police involved now, so they need to get a statement from the boys tonight. There is no question of the boys ever going back there. The social worker has agreed as a temporary measure the boys can stay with me. I'm going to have to speak to my manager and try to get either my shifts changed or take some annual leave early. But I absolutely can't be working nights without an adult in the house, and until your eighteen Maddie I'm afraid you don't count. Moving on Saturday is a pain, and I need to organise beds for them both. But we can get through this together. We will Maddie, I promise." Sam lets out a breath in relief, she's so confident, so strong, I wish I could be more like her.

"Let me organise getting stuff for the boys, honestly, all I want to do is help. Do you need me to stay once the police and social worker arrive?" Replies Danny, he's calmed down and is back to his normal rational self.

"They can really stay with us?" I manage to blurt out before bursting into tears myself, I'd been holding it in for Tommy's sake. Danny pulls me into a hug and I sob on his shoulder, my hands going around his waist, and I find myself hanging onto him for dear life.

"Oh Maddie. Yes, they are staying with us. I'm going to fight to keep them here. And Danny that is much appreciated, I'll pay you back. Beds and bedding, for Saturdays move. They can have my room for now. I'm going to check on the boys. You two stay here for a few minutes, and get your heads together. This interview isn't going to be easy, but you need to be strong for them." Sam answers, then quietly leaves the room. I pull back from Danny. God, I'm such an idiot. I haven't got time to break down like this. Sam's right we all need to be strong for the boys.

"Sorry Danny, I just needed to get that out of my system. I'm fine now. Are you okay? This is a lot, especially with everything going on with your dad." I ask him, looking up into his eyes. He gently tucks one of my curls from my face behind my ear.

"You have nothing to be sorry for, this has caught us all off guard. No one expected this to happen tonight. But I'm glad it did, that those boys won't have to ever go back to that woman. You were right about her Maddie all along. Social services should have taken more notice of you, and that's on them. Not you. This isn't your fault. So get that idea out of that pretty little head of yours. And please don't worry about me. Dads doing better. They wouldn't move him from the ITU otherwise." And he looks back at me, almost like he's holding something back.

But I can feel it too, the energy between Danny and me...

Bryan

Mum finally let me have the car tonight, as I agreed to drive to the hospital to pick up my dad after he visits Danny's dad. But I must admit that I'm glad Sam gave me an escape route out of there. Shit, that's some really dark stuff they are having to deal with right now, and I felt like a voyeur.

And it also made me realise that I need to speak to my own parents about things sooner rather than later. But not tonight. Remembering that Mr McKenzie was moved to the main ward tonight, I go off in search of him. Finding the nurses station I'm told that visiting is nearly over, so I mention that Nurse

Connors sent me and I hold up the Tupperware container. Smiling, the nurse points me in the right direction, and I knock on the door and I hear two male voices say, " come in".

My dad is sitting in a chair next to Mr McKenzie, who's sitting up in bed, it's the first time I've seen him awake since the accident.

"Mr McKenzie your looking better, your awake. I'm so glad you're okay. I had dinner at Maddie's tonight and Sam sent some macaroni for you. Danny was going to bring it but things have kinda kicked off tonight, so he's got caught up." It's difficult because I don't know how much I should tell them, it's not my story to tell. I'm pretty sure that I know more than I should at the moment anyway, being as I was in the same room, and I have ears.

"Is Danny okay?" Mr McKenzie asks looking confused, and probably worried about Danny now..

"Danny is fine. I can't really go into details but two of the boys that he coaches have told him some really bad things about their foster parent. So he's waiting for the police and a social worker at the moment. I can't really say more than that, it's not really my place too." And I look down at the ground awkwardly.

"Sounds like my boys doing the right thing. Don't worry Bryan, I won't shoot the messenger." Mr McKenzie answers, with a proud look on his face. He is so close to his son, I wish that I had that kind of relationship with my dad.
The nurse I spoke to at the nurses station gently knocks the door and comes inside the room.

"I thought you might want me to heat up that food for you Mr McKenzie, if it's something Sam has made then it's going to be tasty and you hardly touched your supper tonight." And the nurse takes the Tupperware container from me.

"It was good macaroni." I reply, wiggling my eyebrows up and down.

"Then you'd best get that heated up for me nurse, because I do love a good macaroni cheese." And Mr McKenzie smiles at the nurse.

"And where's mine? I missed dinner tonight." My dad laughs, jovially, holding his hands out for another container. He looks like Oliver Twist asking for more.

"Sorry dad, only patients get special treatment. You ready for me to drive you home?" I ask him cheekily.

"Yes son, but I'm driving, so hand over the keys." He replies, and we leave the room in good spirits together for once.

Chapter Twenty-Five

Danny

When Maddie broke down in my arms, I never wanted to let her go from my arms of protection. I can feel myself falling further and further for her. The need to protect her and those twin boys is immense, and no one is ever going to hurt them again, I won't allow it.

And first thing tomorrow morning I'm contacting my solicitor to make sure Sam has all the legal support she needs with getting custody of those boys, and they will never want for anything again.

Jack and Tommy are going to need therapy after this, probably Maddie too, shit me too. So much has happened over the last week, please god don't let anything else happen.

"I'm sorry about my minor breakdown Danny." Maddie says, instantly snapping me out of my thoughts, to look at her beautiful face.

"Stop apologising Maddie, please. Come on, let's go and wait for the police and the social worker to get here." I reply, leading her back into the living room.

Jack and Tommy are still sitting on the sofa together. I've never seen them look so scared before, if I ever get my hands on that evil bitch I'll be locked up for bodily harm.

Sam is hovering near the blinds, waiting for the social worker and police to arrive. We wait almost an hour before they get to the house, that agonising time spent in near silence with no one up to making small talk.

The police officer at least has a kind face, but the social worker just looks stressed, I'm not surprised considering how often Maddie raised concerns, they're properly in the shit now. Good, I have little sympathy for the social worker in charge of their case.

For the interview, the police officer explains that the social worker and temporary guardian will only be allowed to be present. But under the circumstances the boys can be interviewed together. So Maddie and I go upstairs to her bedroom and wait, because then they will want to talk to us to take our statements afterwards.

We're now upstairs waiting, sitting on Maddie's bed. I turn to her and say, "Why don't we pack some more boxes, keep busy while we wait?" And point to the stack of flat boxes propped up next to her bed.

"Sounds like a plan, why don't you do my bookcase, just write on the box Maddie bookcase." And she passes me a red sharpie pen from an old jam jar on her desk.

"So, these are the books you read then? Or are they just for show?" I ask her trying to get a conversation going to take her mind off things going on downstairs. Loving a good book myself, it's nice to see another thing that we have in common.

"I can assure you Danny that I have read every single book on that bookcase, and most of them more than once. I did some volunteer work last summer in a charity shop in town, most of those books they let me have for free because they had multiple copies of them, or I only paid a couple of pounds for the hardbacks. Some were in near perfect condition, it amazes me what people get rid of." She replies to me smirking. Oh I get it. Maddie likes a bargain.

"I've never really given that kind of thing much thought, so your big on recycling and reusing things?" I ask her, genuinely interested in what she has to say about the subject.

"It started off as need, when you don't have much you make do best you can. So spending a pound in a charity shop could be a book, a CD, or an item of clothing. Then I started to think, why pay more just because something is new? It's not like it's going to stay perfect. Plus you can find some really unique and retro clothing, I also like the idea of reusing something so it's not just going into landfill, saving the planet and all that." Maddie replies, and I find myself respecting her even more because those are solid, thought out reasons.

"A great philosophy, one I should perhaps adopt more." I say thoughtfully, thinking about how I never need to worry about money, skrimping and saving to buy the basics in life.

"Last year I managed to find two different Nike tracksuits, not a mark on them for the boys. I don't want them getting bullied for not having the same stuff as other kids. So I do as much as I can, and it became a bit of a hobby too looking around all the different charity shops." She looks away with tears in her eyes, and she blinks them away. Money I know is a emotive subject for Maddie.

"Stephen King fan I see, I read his books too. Admittedly on my kindle though, don't judge. I got fed up of always losing my page, or dozing off in the bath and ending up with a soggy book. Although I found out the hard way, Kindles are not waterproof." And I laugh, thinking about one of my first experience's with my new kindle.

"You didn't did you?" Maddie gasps in shock at the thought of me drowning my poor first kindle.

"I did, brand new kindle ruined in the bath the second time I used it, but at least when I got a replacement, it had saved my page." I chuckle, thinking of the palaver I had to go through.

"Maybe the universe is trying to tell you not to read in the bath anymore." Maddie replies, her eyes now twinkling with mischief.

"I think you could be onto something there." I answer, and we quietly continue to pack boxes, no doubt both thinking about the same thing.
Sometime later there is a gentle knock on the door.

"They are ready to talk to you next Danny. I'm going to settle the boys in my bedroom with a movie on my laptop. They are mentally drained, both of them, so I'd leave them be just for now." And Sam goes off to settle the boys.

"I'm up next then." And I leave Maddie in her bedroom so I can go and make my statement.

Sam

E ven with everything I've witnessed during my nursing career, and believe me when I say I've seen horrific things happen, that was hands down the hardest thing I've ever had to witness. Listening to Jack and Tommy talking about their short lives, and what's been happening over the last few months with that sexual predator Mrs Thompson, made me want to throw up. But this isn't about me. It's about them. Staying strong for Jack, Tommy and Maddie through all of this. I managed to get hold of my manager at the hospital, and I've been granted special leave until the end of next week, and she's going to change me to the day shift. I'm not sure exactly how I'm going to pay my bills yet but I'll cross that bridge when I come to it. I can always go to citizens advice and see if I can claim any grants or benefits, I will probably qualify for something taking on two more foster kids, I'm not going to worry about that now. It's a problem for another day.

"Looks like someone vomited pink in here." Jack comments as he takes scope of my bedroom, I'm letting them both sleep in here because I have a double bed. I can take the sofa for a few nights, so long as Jack and Tommy are comfortable.

"Don't be an arse Jack, Sam's being nice to us." Tommy replies, elbowing his brother. His eyes are still red and swollen from crying so much.

"You know, Maddie said exactly the same thing the first time she came in here. I am rather partial to pink." I joke, trying my best to lighten the atmosphere, and failing miserably. Although it is true, Maddie did say that the first time she saw my pink room.
I hand Jack and Tommy a t-shirt each of old bands I used to listen to, back in the day. They are the most masculine items of clothing I own, but better than nothing. Plus new toothbrushes, and fresh towels.

"Feel free to use any toiletries in the bathroom, and there is plenty of hot water. Sorry I've only got a t-shirt for you to wear tonight. If you give me your school uniforms, I'll wash and dry them ready for the morning. I'll be driving you to school tomorrow and speaking to your teacher. Don't worry, everything will remain confidential. Let me log you into my Netflix account if you promise to stick to PG rated movies or series, and I'll know if you don't, so I'm trusting you both. If you want anything I'll be in Maddie's room. Just leave your washing in a pile in the bathroom floor for now." I smile at Jack and Tommy as I log into Netflix for them.

"Why are you being so nice to us? I mean your nice to Maddie, but you get paid to do that. Is it a money thing? Because you can drop the act if that's it. We know the score, we lived with Nanna Jenny for years." Jack replies defensively. I can hardly blame him for acting like this, I'll have to work hard to gain their trust.

"Jack shut up! You'll ruin everything. Sam's okay, Maddie trusts her." Tommy shouts at Jack, getting tearful again, and Jack goes silent.

"You want the truth Jack? Here's the truth. I decided to become a foster parent because I can't have children myself, it took me a long time to come to terms with that. Then I read a leaflet a friend gave me about fostering children, and I decided it was something I wanted do to. So I've looked after many children over the years, sometimes for one night and the longest for almost five years. But one thing I can say truthfully, hand on heart, it's never, ever been about the money. Just give me a chance to earn your trust. Saturday we're moving into a lovely little cottage, think of it as a fresh start for all of us." I say, smiling at them both, my heart slowly being torn to pieces inside, because all I want to do is say and do the right thing.

"Okay." Is all I get from Jack. I can already see that I'm going to have my work cut out for me with Jack, he clearly doesn't trust me right now. I need to change that.

"Thank you Sam." Is the reply I get from Tommy, he is the more trusting of the two brothers.

But I'll take that as a win for now…

Maddie

Having just finished making my statement to the police, and telling the police officer and social worker anything the about the boys I can think is relevant, I feel mentally drained. Nothing got left out and by the time I finished the social worker looked pale and guilty as hell.

Good. I'm glad she's suddenly developed a conscience, maybe she'll take the next person that tells her about abuse happening more seriously. I can read between the lines, I know her hands were effectively tied up in bureaucracy, ridiculous red tape, but that didn't help Jack and Tommy. Things should never have gone this far.

Thank god Danny started asking questions at dinner, and the boys opened up to him. I'm never going to be able to thank him enough for this. He left a few minutes ago so he could quickly pop in and see his dad, he looked exhausted, but there was no point telling him to go home, and I hope he messages me later, or I could message him...

Jack and Tommy are settled down in Sam's bedroom, and bless her heart she's sleeping on the sofa tonight. Sam is such an amazing person, I'm realising now just how much she cares about me and the boys, and I'm kicking myself for not realising sooner. Thank god she came into our lives, we are truly blessed having her, Sam is going to be a fantastic foster parent to Jack and Tommy.

Looking around my bedroom, with boxes everywhere, I realise for the first time I'm actually going to miss this room. My first bedroom, one that was just for me and no one else. That Sam let me paint purple, and got curtains in the same colour, and the cute little throw cushions for the bed she made.

Sam did everything in her power to make me feel welcome and loved, and I'm only just realising now. I've been so caught up in my own head, she's been the first person that's really cared for me.

Then there's Danny. I don't even know where to start when it comes to him and my feelings.

My phone rings and I've got an incoming video call from Bryan, so I press answer, and his face comes onto the screen.

"What's up buttercup? Sorry it's so late but I was worried. I won't ask how things went but are you okay?" Bryan asks me, with a look of worry on his face. The poor guy got caught up in the middle of everything today through no fault of his own.

"Better than earlier thanks, sorry I haven't called. My brains gone to mush tonight, after speaking to the police and my social worker, I felt like saying, I told you so. But I managed to hold back." I reply. Still angry that I left the boys in such a dangerous situation, I don't think I'll ever stop feeling guilty.

"Don't worry, I won't repeat anything I heard. I didn't even tell my dad. Just kept things vague." Bryan answers, and I can see that he's feeling my pain for the boys. He's a good friend. The best.

"It didn't even cross my mind Bryan, I trust you. Your my best friend. I'm glad you have a good idea of what's going on, even if I can't really talk about it. But I need to protect Jack and Tommy's privacy as much as possible." I say feeling emotional, holding my tears back, trying to remain strong.

"I'll always have your back Maddie, and the boys. How's Danny is he still there?" Bryan asks, and I have to keep reminding myself how close those two are. They act more like brothers I've noticed the more time I've spent with them both together.

"He left a short time ago, he was okay, and he'd calmed down. Although I could still see how angry he was, he kinda wears his feelings on his face doesn't he? I'm glad Danny went to see his dad, I think he needed to after tonight." I answer Bryan, and twiddle a stray curl. The same curl Danny tucked behind my ear earlier.

"What was that look, I saw that look Maddie. You were thinking about him, you are so into him." Bryan grins at me knowingly, but I can't think about Danny right now, my brain really is a pile of mush.

"Please don't, not tonight, I just can't take anymore tonight." And I quickly swipe a stray tear away.

"Shit Maddie, ignore me I'm being an idiot. Forget I even mentioned it." Bryan replies now looking guilty, and I didn't want to do that. Fuck this whole day. I've officially had enough.

"It's okay Bryan, I just know in my heart it could never be a thing with Danny. He wouldn't be interested in some stupid girl at college. Nope. Just let it be." I reply sadly, a tear now dripping down my face, and I angrily swipe it away. Damn tears.

"I think your totally wrong about that Maddie, but consider these lips zipped on the subject unless you want to change the narrative." Bryan answers as he pretends to zip his lips, trust him to try and bring humour into the situation.

"Message received. Unless I change the narrative." And I give a sad smile to Bryan, and end the call.
There's a light knock on my bedroom door.

"Come in." I answer, grabbing a tissue and wiping my face.

"Maddie, can you come through to my bedroom and see Tommy please. He isn't doing so well at the moment, and I think you'll get through to him more than me. He's never been this upset before, he's crying again." Jack asks, standing there in Sam's old Nirvana t-shirt and his boxer shorts.

Following Jack into the bedroom, I climb onto the bed. Not saying anything, the simple act of being there for him. Holding Tommy in my arms, until he eventually wears himself out crying, then drifting off to sleep. Jack has fallen asleep the other side of Tommy, so I peel myself away from Tommy and creep out of the bedroom. Leaving them settled, in what I hope is a peaceful sleep.

My phone is flashing on my bedside table, as I pick it up I notice it's nearly two o'clock in the morning. It looks like Danny did message me earlier. Damn. I missed it.

Just checking in before bed. Call me if you need me, day or night, Danny

I smile at his simple message. And type out a reply, not expecting an answer this late.

Sorry I missed your message earlier, Tommy was having a hard time settling, but both boys are asleep now. Speak to you later. Maddie

And I hit send. My phone pings.

Thought something like that happened. Get some sleep. See you later.

I smile at his message, and can't resist sending a final one back.

Sweet dreams Danny x

Oh my god, I can't believe I put a kiss on the end of that message. My brain definitely isn't firing on all cylinders at this time of night. Ping. Shit. Another message.

Sleep tight, my little Angel x

Now I'm speechless, I wish it wasn't the middle of the night and I could call Bryan. No, I'm reading way too much into it. It's just a kiss, but he called me his little Angel again. I throw my phone to the bottom of the bed, pretend to ignore it, and roll onto my side.

Closing my eyes, I allow myself to process everything that's happened over the last few hours, eventually sleep wins...

Chapter Twenty-Six

Sam

It's been three days since we moved into the little cottage. Things are slowly settling into a routine. The social worker hasn't given me any updates yet on Mrs Thompson, but she did manage to get the boys few possessions back from the Thompson house. I thought it best that I keep Jack and Tommy in school to help maintain some normality for them both, and Maddie has been a huge help. But it's going to take some time before they both trust me. Jack still hasn't unpacked his bag, and I'm sure he thinks he's going to have to move again so it's not worth unpacking. Tommy is slightly more settled, and at least he's unpacked his bag, but he's not speaking very much. Jack does most of the talking for both of them.

Maddie seems to really like being in the loft space, we managed to get a small futon type bed and put it together in the loft, and she's got rails for her clothing. Danny is coming to put some shelves up for her books today, and I worry about those two being together all the time. But Maddie is practically an adult now and needs to make her own decisions, and mistakes. Maybe I should have a little heart to heart with her?

I'm now officially back on days at the hospital, and I'm picking up some extra shifts so I don't need to worry about my rent. Danny brought the boys new beds and bedding, and insisted it was a gift. Is he trying to get on my good side, or is he just that generous? Unfortunately I'm always suspicious, especially with men. I've been burned too many times myself. Saying that, my general feeling points towards Danny being a generous guy, so we shall see. But I'm watching him.

On my never ending list of things to do, I need to take Jack and Tommy shopping. The few clothes they have are either too small or worn out, Maddie did her best, I just never realised how bad things were. Social services have allocated an emergency grant to me, after their social worker picked up their meagre possessions, it won't go far but it will at least cover the basics.

"Jack, Tommy can you come downstairs a second please." I shout up the stairs, maybe I should have just gone up to see them? Too late now. Their bedroom door opens and they both silently come downstairs, like something else bad is about to happen.

"How are you both finding the new living arrangements?" I ask Jack and Tommy, as they both sit down on the sofa.

"Better than before, while it lasts." Jack answers, looking at the carpet, and swinging his legs trying to distract himself from me.

"I like it here." Tommy quietly replies, elbowing his brother. He's seems to be happy to be here at least.

What can I really say to that? So I take a breath and ask, " I need to take you both shopping after school, you don't have football practice tonight. I'll pick you up outside the gates." I say kindly, but firmly, this isn't a choice. They need to do this. Jack and Tommy look at each other confused.

"You both need new school shoes, trainers and trousers, jeans, hoodies, do you have winter coats that fit?" I ask looking them both, my head turning from one boy to another, waiting for an answer.

"You're getting us all that stuff? Sweet." And Jack nudges Tommy, smirking.

"Don't be so ungrateful Jack. She's being nice, she doesn't have to have us here, don't ruin it." Tommy replies, and I can see he's really not happy with Jack's reaction.

"We're only here because social services fucked up so bad, how long until we get fucked over again Tommy." Jack shouts back, and runs upstairs, slamming the bedroom door loudly.

"He doesn't mean it Sam, he's just angry." And Tommy leaves me standing there slightly speechless , running upstairs to find his brother.

This is going to take time and a lot of patience to get Jack to understand I'm not the enemy here. In the meantime I'm just going to have to deal with these outbursts. Maddie wanders through from the kitchen, she obviously overheard everything.

"Jacks just protecting his brother, he'll come around. But don't let him walk all over you. Don't let him speak to you like that Sam." Maddie says, blowing over her cup of coffee. She's turning into a remarkable young woman.

"I know your right Maddie, and I will. But I'm finding my feet here, this all happened faster than I expected. But I'm glad it did. And I'm glad that they are both out of that awful situation. I just want to wrap them in my arms and tell them it's going to be okay, but life isn't that simple. It's going to take me a long time to gain their trust especially Jack." I reply, and sit on the sofa, looking towards the stairs.

"Do you want me to come shopping too? Might take the pressure off you a little." Maddie asks, and it's kind of her to offer. But I need to do this, to prove to Jack and Tommy I'm serious about fostering them both.

"I thought Danny was coming to help you put the shelves up?" I enquire, trying my best not to pry.

"That's not until later on this evening, he's visiting his dad first, so I can meet you after college? Means you'll have to drop me off today so I can leave my bike here." Maddie replies, expecting me to want her to come as a crutch, but I refuse to do that today.

"No it's fine Maddie, this is something that I need to do with them, don't you have babysitting later?" I reply, not wanting to hurt her feelings either. She has enough to deal with.

"Babysitting got cancelled again, chicken pox is doing the rounds. I really need to find a better job, so if you hear of anyone wanting a babysitter let me know, mowing grass, anything." She answers clearly frustrated, it's tough getting a job at her age.

"You'll find something else. Just keep looking online, in the local paper, shop windows. You'll be eighteen in a matter of weeks. That will open up the job market." I smile. I've tried talking to Maddie about university but she won't listen, she doesn't want to leave the boys. Maybe she'll be able to find some kind of apprenticeship instead? I just need to continue encouraging her.
Jack walks back down the stairs, looking solum, so Maddie declares she needs to get ready for college, and disappears so we can talk together.

"Sorry Sam." That's all Jack says and he looks down at the floor.

"Apology excepted Jack. I only want to take you and Tommy shopping because it's something that woman should have done before the new school year. She neglected and abused her position as a foster parent in every way possible Jack. But buying you new clothes, this is a small thing that I can fix right now. Get you things that fits you, things you need. And I thought you and Tommy would like to help choose, rather than me just choosing it all, that's all." I answer Jack being completely honest with him.

"Maddie was right about you. We'll meet you at the gates after school." And he simply runs back upstairs. I think I finally made some progress with Jack, hopefully the walls are starting to come down.

Chapter Twenty-Seven

Bryan

Sitting down at the table in the canteen by myself, I slip in my earbuds and listen to some Taylor Swift, that will help cheer me up or possibly depress me further, depending on the song. Maddie's last lesson must have over run, she normally gets here before me.

I look down at my tuna and mayo sandwich and sigh, I don't even know why I chose it now, just for fuel, I don't even feel hungry.

My brains been in complete overdrive these last few days, and I need a distraction. I bring up my Instagram account and start swiping through, stopping on the account for Dorothy's. It's a job advertisement for waiting tables, and another for inhouse entertainment whatever that means. Without thinking, I send a message saying that myself and a friend would like to interview for the jobs advertised and within seconds I'm sent a reply to drop into the bar after five o'clock today.

This could be my perfect cover story to spend time at Dorothy's. If I have a job there busing tables, and earning some money, it would be fantastic. Even if it's just until I go to university, or not if I have my own way. It might help to get my parents off my back, and not raise suspicion spending time at the bar. I just need to get my partner in crime Maddie on board, but she'll be a piece of cake once I convince her.

"Hi Bryan, sorry I'm late, I had to run to the library quickly and grab a textbook for an essay." Maddie pants, like she was rushing to get here.

"No worries. Are you free straight after college? I wondered if you'd come and check this out with me?" And I show her the advertisement for Dorothy's bar.

"Looks interesting, but what's inhouse entertainment?" Maddie asks looking at me slightly suspiciously.

"Not a clue, but I want to apply to wait tables. It will give me the perfect opportunity to hang out there without the parents digging too deep." I reply to her, finally biting into my sandwich, disgusting. I really hate the food in this canteen.
Maddie takes out a salad container from her bag and a little pot of what looks like homemade dressing. Then she adds croutons and pine nuts. Watching Maddie prepare her lunch has become an artform, one that never fails to amuse me.

"I'm free after college, but I'll meet you there because I have my bike. And I need to be back for seven o'clock because Danny is helping me put some shelves up for my books. His dad has the power tools we needs, and doesn't mind us using them." And she digs her fork into her salad, fishing around for an olive.

"So Danny's coming over again." I smirk at her, with a glint in my eye, but I don't say anything, and don't supply my usual witty comeback.

"Yes, no comment. Next question." Maddie replies, so it's still an out of bound subject, duly noted.

"How are Jack and Tommy doing?" I ask instead, talking about something different.

"Subdued, is the best word I can think of. Sam's taking

them clothes shopping after school. They didn't have many belongings. Most of the stuff I got them when we were at Nanna Jenny's they had grown out of. I should have realised." She sighs, and pushes her salad aside, taking a gulp of water from her bottle.

"It's not your fault Maddie. Look, things are moving on, and they have you and Sam now. A cool new cottage to live in, you can make new memories with them." And I smile at her, eyeing her discarded salad, hoping she takes the hint.

"Your right Bryan, I need to stop dwelling on all the negatives and look at all the positives. It's just going to take me some time to get past the guilt. Bryan, eat the damn salad I've lost my appetite." Maddie answers, and she pushes her lunch towards me.

I don't care what it takes, I'm going to get Maddie and me a job today, and put a permanent smile back on her face. Because unbeknown to her, I know full well what inhouse entertainment entails, and it happens to be something that Maddie excels in.

What I now need to do is convince Maddie between now and going to Dorothy's after college, that she needs to sell herself in the interview to get this job, as far as I'm concerned those jobs are as good as ours.

So the for the rest of that lunchtime, that's exactly what I do, not realising that we are bring watched.

Ben, On A Nearby Table In The Canteen, At The Same Time...

Bryan hasn't acknowledged me in days, and I don't know how to get his attention. I've started to isolate myself from the so called popular crowd, but now I haven't got anyone to speak too. Of course I still get random girls trying to talk to me, but that's not what I want.

Why won't he notice me? How can I get back in Bryans good books, I'm ninety-nine percent sure he's in the closet like me itching to get out, and announce his sexuality to the world. I know dammed well he was listening to Taylor Swift a few minutes ago because even I could read his lips from here.

But I'm not brave enough to do this by myself, what are my Rugby team going to say? It would be nice to have at least one gay friend, I wonder if Bryan realises there are rumours going round about him? Should I tell him?

"And why are you sitting over here all by yourself?" Chelsea asks sitting down uninvited as usual, like a parasite clinging on for dear life.

"Free country, just wanted some alone time. As in fuck off Chelsea." I answer. I'm so sick of her fake concern, the girl is deluded.

"Suit yourself, but secrets have a habit of coming out if you know what I mean." She smirks, and saunters off to join the popular table.

"Shit." I say out loud to no one in particular, just as Bryan and Maddie walk past my table.

Bryan turns and makes eye contact with me briefly, and I hear him say to Maddie that he'd meet her later. Bryan walks back over to my table.

"You okay Ben?" Bryan asks, but not sitting down.

"Not really." I reply, being completely honest with him.

"I noticed you over here by yourself, not liking your usual company." Bryan replies saying it sarcastically, but then frowns when he sees that hurt my feelings .

"Something like that. But I give up, I obviously can't win with you." And I walk out the canteen abandoning my lunch, and head outside into the cold not expecting Bryan to follow me.

"Sorry Ben, I was being a dick. I'm just going through some stuff at the moment. Heavy stuff, and Maddie just gets me. It's nothing personal." Bryan answers, holding his hands out to his sides in an open gesture.

I turn around and sigh, "Me too, I'm going through some heavy stuff too. Don't worry about it." And I smile sadly and I start to walk off again, but at the last minute I decide to take a leap of faith and turn back towards Bryan.

"You need to know Bryan, there is a rumour going around a few people in the popular crowd that your gay. I thought you'd want the heads up, but I've been agonising over if I should say something or not. Just for the record, it doesn't bother me either way. So now you know." I say, and I notice that he's turned pale.

"Does this have anything to do with Chelsea?" Bryan asks me with pleading eyes.

"Honestly, Bryan, I have no idea if it was her that started the rumour, but this will give her something to talk about." And without thinking, I step forward, placing both of my hands either side of Bryans face. Carefully I bring my lips down to his, and gently kiss him. I step back and look into his eyes. "I'm scared too, but we could do this together." And he's standing there speechless, touching his lips.

"Think about it." And I leave Bryan standing in the cold.

Chapter Twenty-Eight

Bryan

"**M**addie, code red! We need to go, get in the car we'll come back for your bike later." I shout across the college car park. Maddie comes jogging over and gets into the front seat slinging her backpack in the footwell, and I immediately pull away in my mums car, skidding on the carpark gravel.

"What the hell is a code red Bryan? And slow down before you have an accident." Maddie exclaims as she fumbles with her seatbelt, trying to put it on. Somehow it's gotten all twisted.

"Sorry Maddie, I just had to get out of college asap. Ben kissed me." And I pull over mums car into a side road and stop the engine, before I crash the car.

"Wow." Maddie replies.

"Wow, that's all you've got? Maddie, I've secretly lusted after Ben for months. I didn't have the slightest inkling he might be into me, you know, that way, and he kissed me. Outside the canteen entrance at lunchtime. I've got no idea if anyone saw us, and if there wasn't already a rumour going around that I'm gay, courtesy of Chelsea's gossip, there certainly is now." I say slightly shaking, and gasping for breath, I think I'm having a heart attack.

"Totally getting the code red thing now, or maybe it should be code rainbow?" Maddie replies smirking at me, she picks now to be humorous?

"He kissed me Maddie." I'm clearly still in shock , my secret crush, the guy I've been lusting after kissed me. Ben. What did you just do to me Ben?

"So you said. Was it nice? Did your heart go all funny?" Maddie enquires, getting a dreamy look on her face. I bet she's thinking about Danny.

"Fuck, Maddie. What am I going to do?" I ask her, a boy kissed me. I've wanted this for so long, and now I've got no idea how to handle it.

"Absolutely not a clue, I can't even sort my own love life out." She replies to me, shrugging her shoulders.

"Good talk. No help whatsoever. Let's get to this interview." And I start the car and drive off towards Dorothy's, with Maddie still smirking like a Cheshire cat.

My life just became even more complicated, but Ben kissed me, he likes me too. That's all I can concentrate on right now...

Maddie

Ben kissed Bryan, I'm ecstatically happy for them both, it's been blindingly obvious for ages that Bryan has a thing for Ben. The fact that the feelings have been reciprocated by Ben, now that did take me by surprise, Ben has kept those feelings really well hidden up until now. I just pray he doesn't break Bryan's heart, but I have a horrible feeling in the pit of my stomach that the path to true love won't run smoothly with them, and they both need to be prepared to fight their corners. It makes me scared for Bryan now especially. What if his dad finds out? Will he react badly like Bryan thinks his dad will?

We pull up in the car park at Dorothy's and Bryan turns to me, "Follow my lead once we get inside." And he guides me towards the entrance of Dorothy's Bar, with his hand placed on my back.

Approaching a bartender inside, we are both pointed in the direction of the manager's office, the door is wide open and the drag queen I recognise as Dorothy is sitting at a desk tapping away on a computer keyboard. She is still in full make-up but not nearly as flamboyant as the other night. Her nails are bright green and her t-shirt matches, it has a large Dorothy's logo across the front in red glitter.

Bryan taps on the door to get her attention, "Hi, I messaged you on Instagram earlier about waiting tables and inhouse entertainment." Bryan confidently says, sticking his hand out to shake hers as he approaches her desk.

"Oh yes, I remember you two from the other night. The baby gay and best friend I'm guessing? You know I had to pay someone to hose out the puke from my planter out the front." She laughs, shaking Bryans hand and shaking her head, it appears she has a good sense of humour thank goodness.

"I'm so sorry, please don't get a bad impression about us. I really need a job, my foster brothers have just moved in with me and my foster parent and I want to contribute to bills and things. Sam's a nurse and her wages are crappy. And there I go over sharing again." I shut myself up before I say anything else damaging.

"What Maddie means to say is she's very keen to work in this fine establishment, as am I." Bryan quickly adds, giving me a calm it down look, he reads me so well.

"I have to say, you two are the first to reply to my social media advertisement and it achieved exactly what I wanted it to do. As you can see I'm not exactly old and past it, but I'm not getting any younger either. I need to attract a younger crowd into the bar, and know what's popular, keep my eye on the ball. So having a mix of some younger members of staff to train up is exactly what I want. How old are you both?" Dorothy asks us both bluntly, and I know we can't lie to her, she'd see straight through us, and I give Bryan a look to say keep it real...

"Total transparency. We are both eighteen in the next few weeks, but don't let that put you off. You can train us up, pay minimum wage and give us all the weekend shifts and bank holidays..." Bryan tells Dorothy, and she holds up her hand and cuts him off.

"So you were both drinking in my bar underage knowing full well you were breaking the law, which could have resulted in me losing my alcohol licence?" She asks us both, tapping her long green fingernails on the desk. We both look at each other, then answer.

"Yes" We both say together, no point in being dishonest now.

"And what makes you think that I would employ you both?" Dorothy asks, her eyes sparkling waiting for us to answer, it's almost like this is some kind of test.

"Because you just admitted that you need a younger crowd, and we can help you with that. Maddie's singing talent will bring in people from far and wide, and with my bubbly personality waiting tables you're going to make a killing."

Bryan answers confidently, and Dorothy looks impressed.

"You failed to mention anything about singing Bryan. I don't sing in public." I turn around to him annoyed that he's dropping me in it like this. Dorothy is clearly amused by our exchange and clicks her fingers to get our attention.

"I have no idea what it is about you two, but I got the same feeling the other night, before you puked in my planter young lady." And she looks at me directly when she says that.
" I like you both, I'll give you both a six week trial period. But, you will not, I repeat not, serve or drink any alcohol in this establishment until you turn eighteen. When you do, you'll do it responsibly, because it reflects on my bar." Dorothy puts her hands on her hips and turns to us both, grinning and chuckling away to herself.

"You mean we have the jobs?" I squeal in excitement and hug Bryan, taking him off guard, and nearly knocking him off his feet in the process.

"Yes you have can the jobs, just fill out these application forms so I can get you on the payroll, and I can get you some uniform t-shirts ordered to wear, and I'll write a job description for you both. I'll have to slightly alter them to incorporates your age for now until you turn eighteen. I'm taking a chance on both of you, so please don't let me down." Dorothy hands us both a clipboard and pen, with a pile of forms attached to each to fill in.

"Go out to the bar and fill those in for me, then I want a song from you Maddie, call it an audition. I want you on my stage singing again, the punters loved you on karaoke night. Go into the bar, and I'll be out in a few minutes." And Dorothy shoos us out of her office, and shuts the door.

"What just happened Bryan?" I ask him, still slightly overwhelmed by the surreal experience.

"What happened is we both got a job together!" And Bryan high fives me in his coolest way possible, which doesn't look cool, but I won't ruin the moment.

"I have to sing, you never said anything to me about singing, that was sneaky Bryan, very sneaky." I answer worriedly, hoping my nerves don't get the better of me. The last thing I want is a full blown panic attack.

"I'll admit that I had a good idea singing might be involved with it being called inhouse entertainment, but I wasn't one hundred percent sure. So I may have left that information out, my bad, but I didn't want you getting cold feet. But this is a real job with real money Maddie, and not just anywhere but here." And Bryan puts his arms out to his sides, and turns around slowly, giving me that dazzling smile of his.

"It's a good job your my best friend and I need this job Bryan. But can we keep the singing on the down low? I'm still not confident with it, and I won't have alcohol to aid me along this time." I reply sitting down on a bar stool and picking up the pen attached to the clipboard.

"Absolutely, whatever you want, I can do that for you. This is my dream place to work Maddie." Bryan does a little dance like the sugar-plum fairy, and I giggle at his absurdity. He's really good.

"Bryan did you used to do ballet or something? Because you are very light on your feet." I ask looking at him with interest, I'm going to steal some of his moves if I'm going to be up on stage.

"No, but I've watched Dirty Dancing with my mum about a

hundred times." Bryan laughs, doing some more moves from the movie. Now that explains a lot.

"Let's get these filled out before Dorothy comes out." I reply laughing, trying to concentrate on the stack of paperwork.

"So long as you promise to sing a Taylor Swift song, I can't stop listening to her at the moment." Bryan replies with a dreamy look on his face. I bet he's thinking about the kiss he had with Ben earlier, those two make such a cute couple together, no wonder he's gone all Taylor Swift.
It makes me think of Danny, and how romantic it would be if I could just go ahead and kiss him. But then I think about all the reasons that it could never happen, and I drift off into my thoughts while I robotically fill in the application forms at the bar.

"Courtesy of Dorothy, these are the mocktail version of a Dorothy." And the bartender pushes a drink towards us both, which we sip while we fill the forms in. Most of it is health and safety stuff, and I can see online tutorial training on the horizon with video's to watch, oh joy.

"Time for a song sweetie." Dorothy says as she sits down on a bar stall next to me. "We need to get rid of those nerves and now is a good time to show me what you've got. Tony, can you play Maddie a tune on the piano, pick out a song she knows please." She shouts down towards the small stage area to a guy that must be Tony. I didn't notice the piano the other night we were here, it must have been pushed to the back of the stage or covered over.
I walk towards Tony, and look back at Bryan who's now holding two thumbs up, and he mouths, "You've got this."

"Hi I'm Maddie." I introduce myself and shake hands with Tony nervously.

"Don't look so nervous Maddie, most of the stuff we play here at the moment is female Divas, but if a song is popular and gets requested a lot we usually add it to our set lists. Sometimes you can sneak something unexpected in, but you learn to read the crowd, and Dorothy and I will help you. Flick through this song book, these are all popular songs, pick one out for me to play." He asks smiling at me, he's an older guy must be in his forties and he's dressed impeccably in an nineteen twenties style suit.

"How about this one, I knew you were trouble by Taylor Swift. My friend Bryan is going through a phase at the moment and will love it." I answer handing back the piano music to Tony, grinning manically, but Tony just continues smiling.

"I might have to peer over your shoulder for some of the lyrics if that's okay." I add quickly, I'm not sure if I can remember all the words.

"No problem, Dorothy's always doing that. But don't tell her I've noticed." Tony winks at me.
He takes me through a few scales first, just to warm my voice up, which I've never really done before, but Tony puts me at ease and talks me through it, I feel like I'm learning with him already. I deliberately don't look at Bryan or Dorothy, and Tony starts playing the song on piano.
Starting to sing the first few lines of the song and I'm shaking like a leaf, but by the time I hit the chorus I'm starting to feel more confident, and by the end I know I've done a pretty decent job. Thanking Tony, I walk back towards Dorothy and Bryan blushing bright red, like it's the walk of shame. Bryan is grinning, but I can't get a read on Dorothy. She's tapping her nails on the bar again, when she suddenly jumps up, startling me and Bryan together.

"Punters are going to love you, we just need to polish you up and get rid of those nerves. Work out a set list, dress you up, and put you on stage. Can you learn songs quickly?" Dorothy asks me, tapping her long nails again, this time on a nearby table.

"I've always been pretty good at remembering lyrics, so I can't see a problem with that. But I'm not very confident on stage, as you can already tell." And I look down at the ground, blushing some more and mentally kicking myself.

"Maddie, I won't put just any singer on stage honey. Your voice needs some work, but overall it's fantastic. I actually regretted not getting your number the other night when I heard you sing, but I had a feeling you would be back. In my bar again." Dorothy smiles, and promises to work out a practice schedule for me around college, I might have to skip a couple of football practices but I'm sure Danny will understand.
Bryan and I shake hands with Dorothy again, and I leave the bar with a spring in my step, and Bryan doing one of his silly dances.

Getting back into Bryan's mums car we chat about our new jobs excitedly, and by the time he drops me off at college to collect my bike to ride home, it's already getting dark.
Looking at my phone I can see it's only just past six o'clock, so I have plenty of time to get home, plus the journey to the new house is much more pleasant. As I'm riding home on my bike it gives me a chance to clear my head. That's one of the things I really appreciate about the freedom of riding a bike, but my mind soon starts to wander towards Danny again, always towards Danny...

Chapter Twenty-Nine

Sam

That was an educating experience, shopping with Jack and Tommy for the first time. I think I've managed to get most of the things for them that they need, and now that I have an better idea of their sizing I can buy the rest online.

I never cottoned on before that each twin has their own colour scheme, and each one will only wear certain colours. They absolutely will not wear the same clothes unless it's a school uniform or football kit, which I can understand, they want to be seen as individuals. But my goodness did it make shopping for them harder than I expected. I've started writing down who likes what, so I don't get them muddled up. Luckily they wear their hair in different styles so at least I can tell who is who.

We walk into the living room with a pile of bags each, and I collapse on the sofa, my feet are killing me and I still need to cook the dinner. The boys have abandoned the shopping and disappeared upstairs again, so it looks like I'm sorting through this all alone.

I can hear a key in the front door, looks like Maddie is home, she's late tonight, I wonder what kept her?

"Looks like you brought the entire shop Sam, let me guess the boys have mysteriously disappeared and left you to sort it all out." She laughs and joins me collapsing on the sofa.

"Something like that. I'm absolutely shattered, what with moving house and coming off the night shift, my body doesn't know what time of day it is anymore. But it felt important for me to show the boys that they won't be neglected here. Did you know about the colour scheme thingy? You could have warned me." I laugh back at Maddie, giving her the evil eye.

"Oops, my bad, I totally forgot I'm so used to all their little quirks, I bet you've started writing them down to remember." Maddie replies, giggling away into her hand.

"You know me too well, I think it's a nurse thing. Writing stuff down to remember. I'm going to throw together a quick spaghetti bolognaise for dinner, do the boys mind eating that vegan mince you like?" I ask her praying she'll say yes, because then I can just make one big pot for everyone.

"One thing the boys are not, and that's fussy eaters. They usually devour whatever food is put in front of them, probably because they got used to not having consistent meals with Mrs Thompson." And she looks away with tears in her eyes.

"Come on, give me a quick hand, and we'll eat sooner." And I pull Maddie up from the sofa, and into the kitchen.

"Can you save some for Danny, he's coming over to do the shelves, but he's running about half hour late because he wanted to catch the doctor to ask about his dad." Maddie replies, she's obviously worried about Danny.

"Sure, it's nice he's making the time to come over with his dad in the hospital still." I reply taking some onions out of a bag to chop, and handing them to Maddie. We've made this dinner together several times and are totally in sync together with the preparation.

A thunder of feet run down the stairs and into the kitchen, Jack and Tommy have changed into some of the new clothes, so that explains why they ran straight upstairs when they came in from shopping.

"Fashion show." Maddie shouts laughing, and does a turn around motion with her finger.

"We wanted to say thank you for taking us shopping." Jack says, Tommy quietly nodding behind him in agreement.

"Your both very welcome and don't you look smart in those new tracksuits, would you mind taking the rest of the bags upstairs and I'll help you put them away after dinner." I reply, secretly bursting with pride with the progress I'm slowly making.

"That's okay, we can do it. Your cooking dinner. Maddie likes us to help too." Tommy replies, and they both go and grab the rest of the shopping, and thunder back upstairs again.

"I can see those two are going to keep me on my toes, but you seemed to have taught them well Maddie." I answer her, and she smiles back and replies "I love those two like little brothers."

Danny

Dads sleeping again and the doctor has given me an update on his progress. He doesn't need any more surgery, and he's going to start an intensive rehabilitation program, for his leg. I've got a private physio coming to work with him in the hospital, so I know he's going to get the extra care for my piece of mind. Nothing against the

NHS but they are so overstretched, and this takes the pressure off them slightly. And after everything that happened with my mum, I'm taking no chances with him. He's the only blood relative I've got left.

I'm looking forward to seeing Maddie, and I'm finding it harder and harder to stay away from her, so I'll use any excuse I can, to make sure that I can see her. Tonight it's putting up shelves in her loft space. Stopping on the way to her cottage, I pick up a couple of bottles of that horrible caffeine free, sugar free cola Maddie insists the boys drink, and a bottle of red wine and a house plant as a house warming gift.

Sam answers the front door and points upstairs towards the loft, Maddie's apparently already started without me. Too impatient, to wait for me to get started. She's certainly learnt to be self-sufficient.

"Small house warming gift for you Sam." I hand her the gift bag with the plant in, and a carrier bag with the wine and cola inside.

"You are too kind Danny, you already got the boys the beds, you need to stop spoiling us." And she kisses me on the cheek.

Whispering I reply, "After everything they've been through its nothing. I just want to help. They were so brave opening up like that. It's what my mum would have done if she was still here."

"Promise me one thing Danny, don't break Maddie's heart, because I'm not blind. I see how you both look at each other." Sam replies with no malice, but with genuine concern in her face.

"It's not like that Sam, we're friends." I answer her, slightly taken aback that she's called me out on our not so innocent relationship.

"Keep telling yourself that Danny." And she pats me on the shoulder as she walks into the living room, then shouts back "I've saved you some dinner for when you're finished."

"Thanks Sam." And I run upstairs taking two at a time, trying my best to process what just transpired between Sam and me.

A head pops out of the loft, "We're up here Danny." Maddie's grinning at me, "The boys wanted to help, so we're getting stuck in."

I make my way up the loft ladder and the room is certainly looking more organised than it was on Saturday, it's a squeeze but we all fit in the loft space.

"So I see you started without me then." I laugh, and sit on the floor by the futon, not wanting to ruffle up her perfectly made bed.

"Sam has made me watch that many home improvement shows, I feel like I could do this blindfolded. I just needed a decent drill to use." Maddie answers pointing to the drill case I thought up snuck up into the loft.

"Can I drill the holes, we've already marked them out?" Jack asks hopefully.

"I don't see why not under my supervision, watch me drill the first couple of holes, and I'll let you try." I reply, but looking at Maddie to make sure I'm not overstepping.
"Well if you don't need me, I'm going to go downstairs and start on my essay for college." Maddie laughs, and makes her way towards the loft ladder.

"Oh, I see, getting out of the work?" I laugh, but disappointed she's going downstairs, I wanted to spend time with her. But Jack and Tommy need more attention, especially after the last few days, so I won't be selfish.

"I know where I'm not needed, too many cooks and all that." And Maddie disappears down the loft ladder.

"Well, it looks like this is men's work then." Jack and Tommy both laugh at the same time as I teach them both how to put the shelves up, talking them through every step.

An hour later, we're all finished, and I'll admit that it was fun teaching both the boys how to handle a drill and use a screwdriver properly without rounding off the screw. This is the stuff me and dad did together growing up, so it's been a pleasure to step up and help, and I hope that I'll get asked again.

"Can you go and grab Maddie so she can see your handiwork." I say as I'm vacuuming up the last of the drill dust. Jack goes off in search of Maddie and I notice Tommy looking like he wants to say something to me.

"What do you think's going to happen to Mrs Thompson?" Tommy asks me, almost in a whisper.

"Honestly Tommy, I don't know. The police are investigating still, but I do know that she was taken in for questioning and they haven't released her yet. So the police must have enough evidence to still be holding her in custody." I reply, he's obviously deeply concerned about this. I need to talk to Sam and Maddie, and make sure they are both aware.

"That's what I thought." Tommy sighs and looks down at the floor, refusing to make eye contact.

"Tommy you're going to get through this, it's not going to happen overnight, but if you ever need to talk to me feel free." I reply smiling gently, he needs to know that I'm here for him, and I feel deeply protective of both of the boys now.

"I know, you're the best coach we've ever had." And he sniffles getting tearful again, "I'm going to my room if that's okay." And my heart breaks every time I have to watch that boy cry because of that woman's behaviour.

Maddie's head pops up through the loft hatch and Tommy charges into her, clinging around her waist barely giving her time to climb through the hatch. And the boy sobs, I don't say anything else as Maddie obviously heard us talking before, and I decide to go downstairs to speak to Sam in private. Explaining everything Tommy just said to me upstairs, as Sam reheats a bowl of spaghetti bolognaise in the microwave and hands it to me, indicating to me to sit down on the sofa.

"Sam I don't want you to take this the wrong way, but I know a really good solicitor that works pro bono on these sorts of cases. And he's really good, this woman won't get off with him involved."

What Sam and Maddie don't need to know is he's a top solicitor and I've already got the ball rolling on this, and I'm footing the entire bill.

"Really? That would be fantastic. It would devastate the boys if she gets away with this. I'll take all the help I can get Danny." Sam answers, and I'm glad we're on exactly the same page with this.

"I'll get him to contact you directly tomorrow." And I take another mouthful of spaghetti, only now realising just how hungry I am, it's the first time I've eaten today.

"Tommy's stopped crying, their watching Netflix on your laptop Sam, hope that's okay?" Maddie says and she sits on the corner of the sofa next to me, so our arms brush together.

"When is this nightmare going to end for them? I should have been there for them and I wasn't, I don't care what either of you say. This is on me. They got hurt because of me, I didn't protect them." Maddie suddenly leaps up and goes through to the kitchen, "Are we opening this wine or not?" she shouts, the anger is radiating off her.

"Calm down Maddie, and leave that bottle of wine alone, it was a housewarming gift, and I'm going to save it for a special occasion. You are not, I repeat not, to blame. Come here." And I watch Sam take Maddie into a bear hug, and I can already hear her heart-breaking sobs.

"I'm going to make a move before it gets too late, thanks for dinner. Call me if you need me." Sam's still hugging Maddie, and I feel like a voyeur, I need to get out of here, I can't handle Maddie being so distraught like this. It tears up my insides each time I know that she's hurting like this.

Starting my car, I don't find myself driving home, but find myself driving towards St Peters Church.
It's dark as I walk up the path towards the church and I can see a figure coming out of the door, as I approach closer I can see that it's Father Christopher.

"Danny, what brings you here so late? I was just about to lock up for the night. Let's go inside, and we can talk." Father Christopher holds the door to the church open for me as I walk through in silence. He flicks on the light switch, and a soft glow of lamps come on throughout the church, giving off a soft lighting and a welcoming feeling. Father Christopher sits down on a pew halfway down the inside of the church. I sit down on the pew in front of him and turn around to face him.

"Something on your mind Danny?" He asks me, patiently waiting for an answer.

"Too much, Father Christopher, too much." I reply, and turn my back on him, so I'm not facing him directly anymore. It's almost like being in the confessional, without the box, I feel like I can't face him right now.

"Well, I visited your dad today and I know he's doing much better. So I'm guessing this has something to do with Maddie." Father Christopher answers, awaiting my response. But nothing comes out of my mouth, I don't feel like talking, I just want to sit and clear my muddled head.

Father Christopher stands up and leaves a set of keys next to me, "Take all the time you need Danny. Lock up afterwards, and give me the keys back when you come to church next. I have a spare set at home." And I hear him get up and walk away, a few seconds later a door gently closes.

Father Christopher, he's a crafty one. He knows I don't go to church services much anymore, but I appreciate him letting me stay to find some peace. I don't know how long I sit there, staring at the shadows and flickering of the lamps that are designed to look like real candles.
Speaking out loud to an empty church I say, "I don't know how to protect her if I don't know what I'm protecting her from, I need to know what to do."

"Danny." I turn around but no one's there, it must be a figment of my overactive imagination. But I decide to answer the voice anyway, just for the hell of it.

"Who's there? Show yourself." I reply, slightly freaked out in the otherwise empty church, I really am losing the plot…

"Will you believe I'm real if I show myself?" The male voice answers, if this is a teenage prank, I'm really not in the mood right now.

"Whoever you are, stop playing around this isn't funny." I stand up, and turn around, trying to locate the unknown male voice.

"I'm going to reveal myself Danny, it's a great risk, but I feel it to be something you need, and I know you are worthy." The male voice answers again.

Sitting back down on the pew and waiting, a moment later I feel something feathered brush against my hand and sit down next to me. Slowly I turn my head and sitting right there, is a man with wings, a winged man? An angel? And for some reason it doesn't freak me out or even surprise me in the slightest.

"My names Uriel, a messenger from another realm, and a friend." Uriel says, and I notice he looks around the same age as me, he's dressed simply in black jeans and a t-shirt, but all I can stare at are the beautiful wings, the purest white you have ever seen.

"Have I finally lost my marbles? I'm looking at an angel." I reply, still staring at his wings.

"You haven't lost anything Danny, but I'm no angel. Not anymore." He answers, slightly tilting his head to the side looking at me.

"I don't even know how to react to this." I answer, okay, now I'm starting to really freak out inside.

"Be calm please Danny, for I have little time to speak with you." And he places his hand gently on mine. I nod back to him, suddenly losing my tongue, but hanging on his every word.

"The baby you found, the woman you now protect. Listen to her dreams and keep her safe." Uriel stands up, like he's about to leave.

"What does that even mean Uriel? Protect her from what? I don't understand." And as I try to grab onto his arm, my hand passes right through it, and he's starting to quickly fade in front of me.

"Her mother loves her, but her father will destroy her, remember Danny, protect her at all costs." Right before my eyes Uriel fades completely away making me wonder if I made up the whole thing inside my scrambled head. But as I look down, and into my hand there is a single white feather, I wasn't imagining things. This is real, and Maddie is in danger from her father...

Chapter Thirty

Bryan

Lying on my bed staring at my phone, I don't know why I expected a message from Ben after the kiss, I certainly haven't received one. Then why did he kiss me? Was it a pity kiss? I'm even doubting myself now having a internal argument with myself, and dreading going to college tomorrow. I really don't know if I have the guts having to face the music.

On the flipside of the coin, I do have a fabulous new job, and I get to spend time at Dorothy's now without raising my parents suspicions too much. They didn't comment much about me getting a job at first, until I mentioned Maddie had as well, and then it was congratulations all round. Go figure?

So much is happening at the moment, I don't want to bother anyone with my mediocre problems, especially Maddie while she's having to deal with so much at home herself. My issues are minuscule compared to what Jack and Tommy are having to go through, I feel sick every time I think about it.

As if by magic, or some force in the universe my phone starts ringing and the caller ID shows its Maddie, my bestie, so I immediately answer her, happy to see her calling me.

"What's up buttercup?" Which seems to have become my go to greeting with her now.

"Had a mini meltdown in front of Sam and Danny, I made a

complete fool of myself and needed to hear a friendly voice." Maddie sniffles down the phone, she must be really upset. This isn't like her.

"Sweetheart, big invisible air hugs coming your way right now. Tell your Auntie Bryan all about it." I reply, and let her offload what happened, and I'm glad of the temporary distraction from my own problems.

"...and then I stormed into the kitchen and said something like, are we opening this wine then. I don't even like wine Bryan, and the next minute I'm sobbing on Sam, blaming myself for things out of my control, and by the time I stopped, Danny had already left. He's going to think I've got a screw loose." She's still sniffling down the phone, and her tears are not abating. I either need to offer her words of comfort or change the subject completely.
So I go with trying to change the subject, this stuff she's dealing with is really heavy, and I honestly think she needs to think about something else for a little while.

"So in other news, Ben kissed me. How do I deal with that tomorrow at college?" I sigh and roll over onto my stomach, with Maddie on speakerphone I can see I still haven't received any messages from Ben on my phone yet.

"You could call him, or message him? If he kissed you I'm pretty sure that's an invitation to make contact. Or you could just walk up to him tomorrow and say hi, want to grab a coffee?" It's not the worst advice from her, and at least she's stopped crying now. Mission accomplished.

"I'm going to be a complete chicken, and wait until he messages me first or finds me at college. I'm going to be hiding out in that library tomorrow if you want me." Openly admitting my cowardly ways to Maddie.

"I can relate to that. Do whatever feels right for you Bryan. Did you tell your parents about the job? I totally forgot to mention it to Sam, with everything happening here." She answers, letting a small hiccup escape.

"Yes I told them, they didn't seem that enthusiastic about it until I mentioned that you have got a job there too. You don't think they suspect something do you?" I've taken her off speaker phone now, and I sit up on the side of my bed, drawing patterns in the rug with my big toe.

"Maybe? But I doubt it. It's probably because it's your first real job, plus it's in a bar. I expect I'll get much the same reaction from Sam at first. At least you didn't get caught being hungover and having to explain how you passed out. Shit now I'm worried about that. " And she chuckles down the phone, her hiccups turning into a snort of laughter.

"We make a right pair, that's for sure. They could make a reality TV series about us." I laugh back, trying to keep the conversation light.

"The Real Teens of Eastleigh-On-Sea." Maddie laughs back, snorting again, nearly in hysterics at the idea.

"Oh, I know a certain drama queen at college that would love that." I reply still laughing.

"Chelsea." We both shout out at exactly the same time.

"She would be centre stage, can you imagine it?" Maddie says, her snorts of laughter getting worse by the minute.

"Please, don't put those images in my head." I hysterically laugh back, clutching my stomach now.

"Thanks Bryan, for listening to me. You're a good friend.

The best kind." She answers, the pre meltdown Maddie has returned, thank god for small mercies.

"Right back at you girl. Thanks for listening too, I was thinking how I wanted to talk to you and then you called me. You must be psychic." I answer half-jokingly, half-serious.

"Funny you should say that Bryan, but I had an overwhelming urge to call you. Like we needed each other. Am I being too weird?" Maddie replies, and I can hear the anxiety back in her voice again.

"No, I don't think your being weird at all. I think we're in sync with each other, like girls and their periods, except without the period." I reply in a semi-serious voice, hardly believing I just used that analogy with her.

"Without the period? Really Bryan?" And she bursts out into hysterics again.

"And on that note, I'll see you tomorrow at college." I reply, chuckling away to myself.

"Not if I see you first, night, night, don't let the bed bugs bite." And Maddie hangs up.

Smiling to myself I decide to put my phone on silent, I'll deal with the outside world again tomorrow...

Chapter Thirty-One

Maddie

Hiding out in the library with Bryan in-between lessons and at lunchtime has been kinda funny, trying to keep a low profile with him, and hiding out from Ben of course. Bryan thinks I need to hide too in case Ben try's to talk to me about him. When did my life get so complicated?

And I still haven't spoken to Danny yet, he's not messaged me since my meltdown, probably taking a wide birth and avoiding me like the plague. I'm hardly surprised, I acted like a two year old, but I know I'll have to face the music eventually, and I'm not exactly looking forward to it.

Bryan and I are heading over to Dorothy's bar straight after college to start our induction training, I still haven't had a chance to speak to Sam about it yet. So I shoot her off a quick text message, telling her I'll be late home tonight, and to please save me some dinner. I'll fill her in about the new job later on, she'll just assume I'm late because I'm babysitting.

Bryan and I manage to avoid Ben all day, and we walk out to the bike shed together after the last bell of the day rings. Bryan has dug his old mountain bike out so he can ride with me. As it turns out his "old bike" is actually a top of the range mountain bike. Bryan goes on to explain that he goes out riding with Danny sometimes, but more in the warmer summer months.

As we're both going to Dorothy's at the same time he's decided to make an exception to the rule, and is riding along with me today, and I must admit that it's nice to have a companion for once.

Arriving at Dorothy's a little after four o'clock, we head inside the bar finding it almost empty. The bartender points us in the direction of a back room. This must be the staffroom, there's an ancient coffee maker, kettle and microwave inside, as well as a few lockers. We sit down on a surprisingly comfortable sofa and wait.
Dorothy walks into the room chatting with Ben, what's he doing here? And I notice Bryan has gone very pale and for once is completely speechless.

"Great your both here, after you left yesterday I had another applicant via social media, so I decided to hire a third person. Meet Ben, he's going to be on the bar because he's already eighteen. Bryan you'll be working closely with Ben today. While you're waiting the tables and taking the orders, Ben will be making the orders up for you. You'll then run them out to the waiting customers Bryan. You both need to memorise what's in each cocktail on the menu because customers always ask, and also learn the till system. I'll take you both through everything. Maddie I want you to come up with a set list with Tony and get some practice in, and then I'm going to go over hair and make-up, costumes, that sort of stuff. On Saturday night you'll all get to show me what your made of." Dorothy declares, obviously used to being the boss and dishing out instructions.

Bryan and Ben are both staring at each other, awkward much. So I decide to break the ice, " Hi Ben didn't see you at college today, we're all going to be working together then? That's a nice surprise isn't it Bryan?" And I grin at both of them, the universe certainly has a sense of humour today putting these two in the same room as each other.

"Fantastic, your all friends. Even better. Follow me boys, Maddie, Tony's down by the piano waiting for you." And she clicks her fingers and turns around expecting us all to follow.

Wandering down towards Tony, he looks up at me and smiles. Tony takes me through some warm up scales again like last time, and then we sit looking through more songs, eventually coming up with a short playlist. It will work for now until I can learn more songs.

Tony explains to me that Saturday nights are like a cabaret so it's always piano music and actual singing with no lip synching allowed. My act will be the warm-up with Dorothy being the main entertainment, and then we will pair up at the end and do a couple of duets, usually something from a popular musical.

It all sounds kind of exciting and I'm starting to feel more confident, and starting to look forward to Saturday now instead of dreading it. This is definitely the positive release I need to boost my mood.

"So I can hear your singing coming along nicely. Shall we venture backstage and have a play with hair and make-up?" Dorothy ask's creeping up behind me, she is so stealthy it scares me.

Backstage turns out to be a small room with a make-up table, and a screen to change behind, there's also a small rail with sequined dresses in various sizes.

"Do you have any heels?" Dorothy asks, and I shake my head, I really don't own that much in the way of clothes. I've never really had the need.

"Have a look in that box and see if there's anything in your size. Remember, you won't be wearing them long just on stage, we need you to look good, and heels make legs look longer. We can sort you out a clothing allowance for you later. Here try this black dress on, I think you'll pull it off." And Dorothy hands me a black sequined dress.

Rummaging around the box of various heels, I find a pair of silver high heeled sandals that fit perfectly and go behind the screen to change.

The dress looks far too small, but I somehow manage to wiggle into it and pull it down. It has spaghetti straps and I can't wear a bra with it, but there's at least some built in support. It's a long gown with a slit up each side showing off both legs, and the back dips low showing off my back. I feel very exposed and would never pick an outfit like this in a million years to wear. It's classy and glamourous, and I feel like an imposter wearing it.

"I'm not sure about this Dorothy, this dress seems way too small, it's very tight fitting. But the sandals are great." I answer, trying to say at least one positive thing, and slowly stepping out from behind the screen.

Dorothy whistles as I emerge from the screen, "That dress fits you like a glove, how do you feel?"

"Strange, I don't normally wear a dress, and I've never worn anything as revealing as this, I feel like I'm about to be whisked off to a movie premiere, you haven't got Chris Hemsworth waiting around the corner for me have you?" I reply looking down at myself, and I don't feel like me anymore, but I also feel different. Good different. It's difficult to explain, so I don't say anymore.

"Didn't you have a school dance or prom at the end of senior school? Disco in the canteen?" Dorothy enquires, crossing her arms over, waiting for an answer.

"I was with a different foster parent at the time, and there was no extra money for prom. What with needing to get an fancy dress and the price of the ticket. Besides, it's not like I had a date or anything, so I didn't go." And a pang of regret reaches my voice, because I wanted to go, even without a date. But money was too tight according to Nanna Jenny at the time, and I didn't want to be selfish taking food out of Jack and Tommy's mouth for the cost of a dress.

"Oh honey, that's got to be one of the saddest stories I've ever heard. Let me tell you, with that voice and outfit, you are going to be making some serious tips Saturday night." Dorothy beams at me.

"Tips, we get tips?" Confused by what she means.

"We always pass a hat round at the end of each act, and you get to keep those tips. Just like the waiting staff and bar staff get to keep theirs. I'm not like some establishments, I like to treat my staff fairly, and I don't take tips away from my staff." Dorothy clarifies for me. Holy shit, I could actually make some decent money here. I cannot screw this up, I will not screw this up.

"Hair up I think, with smoky eyes and dark lipstick, what do you think?" Dorothy asks me, like I have the first clue about make-up application.

"I don't have much experience with make-up I'm afraid, can I borrow some until I can buy my own please? But I'm pretty good with hair, I've watched a few YouTube videos to learn various styles." I reply enthusiastically, and I hope she doesn't judge me too much on my inexperience.

"You can do hair, and I'll do make-up then. The dream team."
She laughs, pushing me down into the chair in front of the
mirrored dressing table.

Bryan, At Virtually The Same Time...

Ben's here. Oh, my, fucking, hell. Fuck. Fuck. Fuck. After
successfully avoiding him at college for the entire
day, he's here in what was going to be my sanctuary,
now working alongside me. My new personal hell has just
transpired, I haven't spoken to him yet, and all he's done is grin
at me like the cats that's got the cream.

Dorothy has just gone through the till system with us both,
and we've got these little touch screen pads to take orders for
bar food. Apparently Saturday night is the busiest one of the
week, so I will need to bring my A game, which with Ben here
is making me nervous as hell, and I'm worried about making
stupid mistakes now.

Ben is learning to mix cocktails at the moment, and I'm only
able to watch which is frustrating as hell. So I'm trying to
memorise each ingredient, each cocktail, the names and the
prices. Luckily for me it doesn't take much to memorise things
under normal circumstances, so I'm just trying my best to
ignore Ben. But what I'm finding particularly hard is that he
looks as hot as hell mixing those cocktails and it's distracting
me. He's going to make some great tips and be given a few
phone numbers...

"I'm going to leave you boys to play while I go and play
hair and make-up with Maddie." And Dorothy sashays away,
true RuPaul style, turning back towards us she adds, "And no

taste testing the merchandise my baby gays." Then she winks sauntering off.

"So that's the new boss then." Ben says grinning like a loon.

"I can't believe you're here Ben, what the hell! This was going to be my sanctuary Ben. Now the gang will no doubt be popping in to see you. Rumours will be rampant, my parents will find out. Shit, shit, I'm going to have to quit before I even start." I can feel a full blown meltdown coming, and my eyes glisten with unshed tears of pure frustration.

"Bryan. Look at me. I don't share other people's secrets, especially yours, and I'm sorry if kissing you made you feel uncomfortable yesterday. I just wanted to taste those gorgeous lips, and got carried away. I'm in exactly the same position as you, I haven't come out of the closet, but I'm not exactly keeping it a secret anymore. If someone asks me straight out, I'll tell them I'm gay." Ben says forcefully, with no regret in his voice, this is a guy that knows what he wants, and isn't afraid of the consequences.

But that's exactly where we both differ, I know Maddie and Danny know about my secret, but they're my friends. I can't risk it getting back to my dad, because I know my dad, he will disown me. I don't care how much Danny tries to convince me otherwise, I've heard the little comments dads made about gay celebrities or how people dress. Mum never says anything, and the one time I tried to argue back, he shut me down so fast, so I left the dinner table.

"Bryan, Bryan, talk to me, you completely zoned out. I'm not going to even mention it at college about my job here. And I promise to not be reckless with my kisses, but I will kiss you again. I know you hid out in the library with Maddie at college today, and I allowed you your space. But I want to take you on a proper date, and not hide." And Ben squeezes my hand and then links fingers with mine.

Looking down at our linked hand, a sense of relief comes over me, no one in the bar is taking any notice of us. So I take a massive chance, I live in the moment and I stand up on tip-toe and gently brush my lips over Bens, kissing him lightly and then I stand back. My heart is pounding out of my chest, I kissed a guy in public and the world didn't end, the world didn't end...

"Well my baby gays, that little romance didn't take too long. Tony you lost the bet, I totally called it again! Hope your both learning those cocktails boys, because I will be testing you out." Dorothy smirks, walking up to us, and holding her hand out to Tony. He passes her a ten pound note, and he shakes his head walking off. I can't believe they made a bet on us.

"We're actually a couple already, is that going to be a problem? We can both be professional.
It's just been a difficult day for us." Ben replies confidently, still holding my hand, and I can feel my colour draining again.

"Boys, boys, boys. I've been through it all, and the fear of being found out is radiating off both of you. This is a safe space, an odd kiss here and there isn't going to bother my punters. But no X-rated stuff in any cupboards please." Dorothy laughs, without a care in the world, like she really has seen it all before.

"Now, I want you both to practice waiting the tables in here at the back, and she points to a section. I've warned them all your new, and I want to see how you get on." And she walks off towards Tony with Maddie in Tow now, and Maddie does a little wave to me.

"I guess we're doing this then, and I look at Ben." Looking right into his hazel coloured eyes, taking a gulp and then a deep breath.

Ben gives me the biggest smile back in reassurance, and kisses our linked hand. Have I just bagged myself the hottest guy in college? Yes, yes I have, and I mentally high five myself. The female population of Eastleigh-On-Sea is going to be crushed, this is not how I expected my day to go, and I grin back smugly savouring every moment.

Chapter Thirty-Two

Danny

Trying to get any kind of work done today is damn near impossible, my concentration is shot to pieces and I look towards the single white feather on my desk. Was it even real last night in the church? Did I imagine that angel like figure dressed in modern day clothing? Am I really that sleep deprived worrying about my dad constantly, and his rehabilitation? Then there's Maddie. Don't even start me on this whole I'm her protector thing. Then there's Jack and Tommy and the abuse allegations, which I have no doubt are true...

Which brings me right back to my present thinking, am I really seeing angels now?

Who can I even confined in about that? It's not like I can walk up to Maddie and tell her the message he gave me without sounding utterly insane. Father Christopher is my only option really, but I'm not sure if I can even share it with him. Would he believe me? And don't you have to report stuff like that back to the Pope? Miracles and stuff? Or have I just watched too many movies with catholic priests in, reporting back to the Pope? So it's just me, myself and I, for now at least.

Getting up from my desk, and walking away from my computer to go downstairs, without thought I grab my car keys off the kitchen table, and decide on the spur of the moment to go and see my dad at the hospital. Needing to speak to him, the urge is immense, and the urgency appears to also take my mind of everything else, slightly selfish I know, but it is what it is.

As I walk towards my dad's hospital room I can hear voices, and being nosey I stop just outside the door to listen. It's a woman's voice I recognise, but I can't quite put my finger on it.

"You did really well with the physio today, but she's concerned that your trying to do too much too soon. You don't want to undo all that good progress you've made do you?" The female voice says, she must be a nurse or a doctor.

"I know, I know. But I just want to get out of this hospital, and get some decent grub." I hear my dad moaning and laughing back.

"Then I'll just have to bring in some more macaroni cheese for you then, and build you up through food." She laughs back, and I can detect a cheekiness to her voice.

"And tell me Nurse Samantha, do all of your patients receive meals on wheels?" My god, is my dad flirting with the nurse, and is that nurse Sam??? Maddie's Sam????

Not being able to take the suspense anymore, I walk into the room unannounced and clear my throat loudly. Two heads turn towards me, with Sam's face going bright red in the process. As I suspected, caught in the act.

"I better get back to my rounds, call me if you need anything, and don't get out of bed by yourself. Danny, talk some sense into your father for me please or he's going on my naughty list." And Sam jots something on a clipboard at the end of his bed and leaves the room.

"Well, I didn't realise Sam was looking after you. Looks like you're getting special treatment." I smirk at my dad, who's looking tired but chipper today.

"Samantha looked after me the night I came in, and this is part of the ward she works on. She's Maddie's foster mum?" Dad asks, but I'm sure he already knows the answer to that, he's just deflecting the conversation.

"Samantha hey? Everyone else calls her Sam." And I grin at him smugly.

"I have no idea what you are implying son, it's a beautiful name and Sam sounds like a boy's name." He answers with a cheeky glint in his eye. It's strange, I've never seen my dad act like this before. Maybe that bang to the head did something to him, but dad flirting with nurses, especially Sam is just weird. I wonder what Maddie will say?

"Not implying anything dad, just an observation, but you better stay off of her naughty list." I reply as I sit down next to his bed pinching one of the chocolates out of an open box on the table.

"Do you mind? They were a gift from the church ladies, and I thought you were working today? I'm getting better you know. You don't have to be here all the time." Dad snatches the chocolates off the table and closes the lid so I can't pinch anymore.

"Well, excuse me for caring. I couldn't concentrate and I wanted to see you dad." I huff, much like a child does. Dads eyes soften and he offers me the chocolates back, and I shake my head.

"Danny, I'm okay, I'm not going anywhere. Not for a good few decades yet. But you need to try and get some normality back into your life. And I mean not just because of the accident. You need to start living again, your mother god bless her soul has gone, and has been for a long time. We're both guilty of being stuck in the past, but nearly losing my life has made me realise that life is so, so precious. Your young son, you need to go out. Make friends, get a girlfriend, get laid!" Dad answers, obviously exasperated by me.

"Seriously dad, I can't believe you just said that to me. I don't want a girlfriend, and who's to say I don't already get laid." Newsflash, I don't and haven't in a long time. Sometimes I might go to a bar and go back to a girls place, but I haven't done that since I met Maddie. Not that she's got anything to do with that...

"Okay, okay. I worry about you that's all. Promise me, if you find someone special, hang onto them." The pain in dad's voice is palpable.

"And what if I've already met her but it's too soon?" I answer, immediately thinking of Maddie and her age again.

"That's easy Danny, you wait until she's ready, and when she is, she'll come to you son." Does my dad even realise the advice he's just given me?

But I know in my heart the only girl for me will ever be my Angel Maddie...

Chapter Thirty-Three

Maddie

Today I've got some unexpected free time, my morning lessons at college got cancelled because the heating system broke down again. I'm up to date with all my college work so I decide to do some research on local churches, it's time to find out where I came from once and for all.

Not being brought up with any religion in my life, I wasn't aware that there are so many places of worship in my immediate area. But I instinctively decide to concentrate on Catholic and Church of England churches, because for some reason that's where I can visualise being abandoned.

Scribbling down the church addresses into my trusty notebook because we don't have a printer at home yet, and using google maps I can easily work out a route to visit each one. I've already decided in my head that it will be easier to visit each one on the list and speak to people face to face, rather than just phoning up each church asking questions. Taking my phone out of my rucksack I call Bryan, and the phone doesn't even get a chance to ring before he answers.

"What's up buttercup? Did you know college got cancelled today?" He answers in an even more cheerful mood than usual.

"That's why I'm calling. Any chance you can borrow your mums car today? I've got something I need to do, and I'll get more ground covered than I will on my bike, if I have four wheels instead of two." I say not giving too much away knowing that it will grab at Bryan's inquisitive mind.

"Sure thing, I can tell mum we're going to the library in town to study and don't want to lug our books on our bikes. Pick you up in twenty minutes." And he hangs up before I even have a chance to answer him back. But that's typical Bryan, a spur of the moment kind of guy, and I love him for it.

He eventually turns up forty minutes later, and I run out to the car before he even has time to get out and come to the front door for me. I put my rucksack in the footwell and fiddle around with the tangled up seatbelt.

"What took you so long? I rushed getting ready." I ask slightly annoyed, I'm anxious to get started on my list.

"Sorry about that. Mum had the car, she'd popped out food shopping early." Bryan replies apologetically. Now I feel bad for doubting him.

"No worries. Sorry, I'm just anxious about today's mission should you choose to except it." I laugh remembering he's the one doing me a favour and I should be grateful to have a friend that will drop everything for me.

"So where am I driving too? You have me intrigued." Bryan grins back doing that cheeky eyebrow wiggle of his.

I hand him my scribbled notebook and point to the list of churches. Looking totally confused he turns to me and says, "You do realise that I actively try to avoid churches where's possible, on account of being gay and probably now going to hell."

"I need to find out which church I was abandoned at, I want to find out where I came from. People are more likely to help me if I'm standing in front of them. Will you still come with me?"

My eyes fill with tears and I quickly blink them away. This is a very touchy subject for me.

"Hey Maddie. Of course I want to come, please don't get upset. Let's start at the top of the list." And Bryan pulls away from the kerb and drives towards the first church on the list.

By the time lunchtime comes we've already ticked off three churches from the list, and they are all definite no's. It appears that abandoning babies at churches is not something that happens in this area, which is a good thing. I mean, who wants to be abandoned?

"So the next church on the list is St Peters, that's my church. Father Christopher should be around and he's been at that church since I was a kid, so he should know all the history." Bryan chirps back at me enthusiastically. He can tell I've already started to get disheartened. I knew this wasn't going to be easy, but I hoped it would be.

Out of all the churches we have visited today this is hands down the prettiest of them all. We walk up the path to the entrance and I feel a strange feeling of familiarity, like I've been here before. The church is locked, so Bryan directs us around to a small building around the back of the church, where the office is located.

He knocks on the door, and I hear a male voice say "Come in, it's open."

"Bryan, I wasn't expecting to see you today. And I see you brought a friend with you." This must be Father Christopher. He has a friendly face and a deep baritone voice, and I notice he's dressed in normal clothes except for his dog collar.

"Yes, this is my friend Maddie. We've been visiting the local churches today trying to gather some information." Bryan gently pushes me forwards, and I shake Father Christophers hand.

"Very nice to meet you, do you have a few minutes to spare? I realise you're a busy man." I ask him nervously, and I'm getting a funny feeling in the pit of my stomach. Like something big is about to happen.

"Of course my dear. Please take a seat and tell me why you're here." And he indicates towards the chairs in front of his desk. Bryan and I sit down on the chairs, and Father Christopher sits on the edge of his desk.
Taking a deep breath I start my little speech again, one I've already said three times today. I practiced it last night, and I know it off by heart now.

"I grew up in the foster care system because I was abandoned as a baby. When I was younger I asked my then foster parent Nanna Jenny where I came from. At first she was reluctant to tell me anything. But she later told me that I was abandoned in a box at a church, but even she didn't know anything about the exact location. I went to social services to ask them, and they were no help either. So I have to ask you, was a baby girl abandoned here nearly eighteen years ago that your aware of? Or can you point me in the direction of someone that might remember?" Finally taking a breath, I wait for him to answer me.

"I expected this to happen one day. There was a baby girl abandoned around that time, I remember it clearly. The young son of one of my parishioners found the little girl in a cardboard box, it was a freezing cold day. They brought the girl into this very office, and I called for an ambulance where the girl was taken to the hospital. I visited her several times while they searched for her mother, but she was never found, nor came forward." He replies gently, taking off his glasses and placing them on the desk.

"I don't know what to say. That must be me? Surely? You say a parishioners son found me? I have vivid dreams about a boy finding me." And I start to hyperventilate. Not now, not now.

"Oh shit. She's having a panic attack. Maddie, Maddie, listen to me. Slow your boats. You're okay. It's okay. This is good news, you wanted to know, remember. That's it buttercup, slow that breathing down for me." Bryan manages to calm me down before I go full on panic. Father Christopher is now kneeling down next to me with a glass of water. With a shaky hand, I take the glass and allow myself a few sips.

"It sounds most very likely that baby was indeed you." Father Christopher answers softly.

"Then it's true. No one really knows anything. This was a waste of time, a waste of your time." I tearfully reply, and I run out of the office, around the church, and down the path. And I just keep running, and the shouting voices become more distant, and I keep on running away.

Eventually I stop running, and I find myself standing at the end of the pier having run a good couple of miles. The adrenaline in my body is starting to bottom out, and my energy level is at zero now. I realise that I don't have my rucksack or my phone, and I've abandoned Bryan and been extremely rude to Father Christopher.
Tears stream in rivers down my face as I realise I'm never going to find out where I came from, and a concerned barista from a nearby coffee hut comes out to see if I'm okay.

"Can I call someone for you honey? It's freezing on the end of this pier and you don't look like you should be alone right now." The barista asks me and I shake my head.

"No I'm fine really." And I wander slowly around, at the bottom of the pier, and stop at the railings to look out to sea.

I just need to clear my mind, get my head on straight. Yet the angry tears keep on coming…

Chapter Thirty-Four

Danny

It's good to get out in the fresh air and run, I much prefer the chilly weather for this type of exercise so I don't overheat as much. California Dreamin' by the Mamas and Papas pumps through my earbuds, the melancholy song, one of my mother's favourites. Taking a seafront route today so I can appreciate the crisp sea air, I decide to deviate from my usual routine and run down to the end of the pier. They have a great little coffee hut there and I could do with a couple of shots of expresso to perk me up, I didn't sleep well last night, my mind still a plethora of problems.

As I reach the coffee hut, I remove my earbuds, when I notice a girl with stunning long red hair standing at the end of the pier looking out to sea. I'd recognise that hair anywhere, it's Maddie, what on earth is she doing standing there in the cold?

"Maddie." I shout out several times as I go running towards her, she's either ignoring me or just can't hear. As I approach Maddie she doesn't move or acknowledge me at all, it's like she's switched off emotionally and really can't hear me. Reaching the railings, and standing beside her, I can clearly see her face now staring out to sea. The rivers of tears are flowing down her distraught face, my poor Angel is in a world of her own, and in obvious emotional pain.

"Sweetheart, what's wrong, your scaring me." And I gently

touch her hand, it's freezing cold like ice. Maddie still says nothing, she's in shock of some kind, and I don't have my car to take her home because I was out running. What on earth has happened now? Pulling out my phone from my pocket, I call Bryan hoping he'll answer today because I need his help. The phone rings several times, damn it Bryan pick up, I can't help thinking to myself. I'm about to hang up in frustration when he answers.

"Sorry, I was driving. I had to pull over to answer the phone, mum doesn't have hands free in the car." Bryan answers seeming flustered, and like he's out of breath from running.

"Bryan, I'm with Maddie. It's like she's gone into shock, I found her on the end of the pier completely by accident while I was out for a run. Can you come and pick us up please, I don't have my car. I'll meet you at the front of the pier asap." I shout, hoping he can hear me because the phone signal can be sketchy here, and I hope it doesn't drop out.

"Thank god, I was looking for her. Gimmie five minutes and I'll be there." Bryan hangs up, with no explanation as per usual, but at least he's on his way to pick us both up.

Untying my tracksuit top from around my waist, I gently help Maddie into it. It's massive on her and easily fits over the light jacket that she's wearing. What possessed her to be out here alone in the cold? Not wanting to pressurise her in such a vulnerable state, especially when she's clearly distressed, I don't start bombarding her with questions. Putting my arm around her instead, I guide her slowly along the length of the pier, and by the time we get to the front entrance, Bryan is already standing by his mums car waiting for us with the door open.

"Let's get her home Bryan, and out of the cold before it rains." Bryan nods and holds the door to the backseat open, and Maddie climbs inside without saying anything, I sit down beside her. Bryan starts the car to drive Maddie home. The sound of the engine is the only thing I can hear, otherwise the car is in complete silence. Maddie still has tears running down her face, and I notice she turns and stares out of the window. Catching Bryan's eyes in the rear view mirror, he looks as worried as I feel right now.

Arriving at Maddie's house, she silently gets out of the car, and almost robotically takes her front door key out of her pocket, then lets herself into the house. Leaving the front door wide open, we both follow her inside. Sam must be on shift at the hospital, and the boys will be at school this time of day.

Maddie turns around to both of us. "I've got a migraine coming, so I'm just going to go to bed. Make sure to close the front door when you both leave." She turns away leaving us both standing there, and disappears upstairs to her loft.

"What the hell is wrong with Maddie? You better explain to me what's going on right now, Bryan." I snap at him angrily and Bryan looks mortified.

" Maddie had this idea in her head about how to find out about her past. By asking at local churches about abandoned babies around eighteen years ago, she had made a list and everything. Anyhow, we ended up at Saint Peters and spoke with Father Christopher. He told Maddie about a baby girl that was abandoned nearly eighteen years ago. She realised it must have been her and freaked out, and then Maddie also realised that Father Christopher doesn't have any additional information to give to her. She had a panic attack, which I managed to calm her down from, but then she got really angry about it and ran off. She was like a bullet Danny, she ran so fast I stood no chance catching her up. Poor Father Christopher, he was beside himself with worry. So I was driving around looking for Maddie, when you luckily found her. She must have a guardian angel watching her somewhere." Bryan answers looking at me, directly in the eye.

Before my encounter with a real life Angel I would have called it blind coincidence, but nothing that happens seems to be a coincidence these days.

"You go home Bryan, I'm going to go upstairs to try and talk to her, I have some things that I need to say myself. Please." I wait for Bryan to argue with me, but it doesn't happen. He just silently nods and leaves, dropping Maddie's rucksack on the floor beside me.

"Oh, and Bryan. Give Father Christopher a call and fill him in. He'll only worry otherwise." I shout out as he walks down the garden path.

"Will do, and thank you for finding her Danny. I feel responsible for letting her run off." Bryan gets into his mums car with his shoulders down, his expression grim as he drives away.

Going into the kitchen, I fill a glass of water from the tap and find a box of paracetamol in the cupboard, I walk upstairs, then, carefully negotiating the loft ladder with a glass of water so I don't spill it, I enter Maddie's loft space. It's almost completely dark with the blackout blinds closed on the sky light, except for a simple string of fairy lights above her bed. Maddie's lying on her side quietly sniffling into her pillow, this isn't a migraine, it's despair. I'd recognise it anywhere, I've been there myself a thousand times before, when I first lost mum.

"Maddie, I brought you some paracetamol for your head. And I wanted to talk to you, I have a confession to make." I've got no idea if the timing is right but she needs to know the truth, at least some of it. Time to rip the plaster off, and hope for the best.

Sitting up, and wiping her eyes and nose on her sleeve, or rather my sleeve because she still has my tracksuit top on. Maddie must have put it back on because her own jacket is on the end of the bed, but if she finds comfort from wearing my things, I'm not going to mention that to her.

"Confession?" Maddie looks at me in utter confusion.

"I didn't confess anything to you before because I wasn't even sure it was you. But after seeking guidance, and speaking to Father Christopher, I decided to not say anything because it doesn't change anything for you now." I reply to her, hoping that she understands where I'm coming from.

"What are you talking about Danny? Your speaking in riddles." Maddie looks at me, still in confusion. Kneeling down in front of her, I take her hand, it's still freezing cold. Her tears have started to abate now, but she still keeps wiping her face now and again.

"When I was ten years old, my dad dropped me off at church one Sunday morning while he searched for a parking space, we were running late as usual. I can still remember how cold it was, well below zero." I pause for a moment and take a deep breath, Maddie is hanging on my every word, still looking at me in confusion.

"As I approached the doors of the church, I was pondering if I should wait for my dad, or to go inside, when I heard this cry. Down by my feet there was a cardboard box with a baby inside, I picked the baby straight up to get it to stop crying. My dad then arrived and took over, I fetched Father Christopher, an ambulance was called and the baby was taken straight to hospital. I gave a statement to the police, but I never saw the baby again." I take another breath and Maddie's just staring at me now, her tears have completely stopped.

"I can remember asking my dad about the baby on several occasions and later found out it was a little girl, I even asked him why couldn't we look after her. But my father was still heavily grieving at the time from the loss of my mum. I never saw the baby again. Not until now..." And Maddie drops my hand, like it's just burnt her.

"I told you about my dream Danny the night you stayed with me, that boy was you. You knew and said nothing Danny.

You said nothing. What other secrets you keeping from me?" Maddie stands up, and turns her back on me.

"I saw no point, it doesn't change anything Maddie. I didn't want to upset you unnecessarily." I reply, instantly knowing that I've said the wrong thing.

"Didn't want to upset me, didn't want to upset me! I had a right to know Danny, I shared my dream with you because I trusted you. You could of easily told me that night, you certainly had plenty of opportunity. So I'll repeat it again for you Danny, what other secrets are you keeping from me?" Maddie points her finger into my chest, as she says it angrily, I didn't think she'd react this badly.

"I can't tell you everything I know, not at the moment, and please don't ask me why." Is all I can answer her with, and her eyes start glistening with tears again.

"Rather you won't tell me Danny, it's bullshit is what it is." And Maddie crosses her arms in defiance.

"Maddie. Please.." But she interrupts me, her chest heaving, and her eyes have daggers in them now.

"Get the fuck out of my house, leave. I don't want you anywhere near me Danny. You know that I don't trust people easily, and I let you inside here." Maddie points to her head and then her heart, and her tears are at full flow again.

"Maddie, don't. Please, I care about you." I can feel myself choking up inside now too, I've hurt the one person that I was asked to protect.

"Go." She climbs back onto the bed, and curls up into a ball and starts to sob again, oblivious to the rest of the world around her.

Finding myself climbing down her loft ladder in silence, and then driving away with my tail between my legs. Feeling like my heart has just been ripped out of my chest and stamped on, and that I've somehow betrayed my friend. I find myself pulling over to the side of the road, and I scream "Why" and hit the steering wheel with my hands. Cars around me start beeping in annoyance at my inconsiderate and dangerous parking. But I'm not thinking straight, and the tears drip down my face and onto my shirt. I should have told Maddie, this is on me, and now I'm keeping all this other information from her. About how Maddie needs my protection from her father, and the encounter that I had with Uriel. How could I have read the situation so wrong? I need to speak to Father Christopher urgently again, and so I turn my car around and drive to St Peters Church, hoping I can find some answers once and for all.

Chapter Thirty-Five

Maddie

Crying must have worn me out, and I think I must of fallen asleep, I can feel something shaking me. Sitting up and rubbing my eyes I notice Tommy sitting on the bottom of my bed. Jack is noisily climbing up my loft ladder.

"You didn't show up to football practice Maddie, I was worried because you'd said you would be there this morning, is this becoming a thing now?" Tommy quietly says, he's still not back to his normal self, and I've let him down yet again.

"Sorry boys, I had a bad migraine, I took some tablets and fell asleep. Sorry, I should have at least texted one of you." I feel the little white lie roll off my tongue uncomfortably, and I hate deceiving Jack and Tommy.

"You don't look very sick Maddie, and why are your eyes all red and your nose is all snotty? Have you been crying? Who's upset you, I'll kick their arse ?" Jack replies and sits on the other side of the bed, there's no bullshitting Jack, he can see right through me.

"No one's upset me. I'm absolutely fine." I answer him back ruffling his hair, as a way of distraction.

"If you say so Maddie." Tommy replies looking at Jack, I can tell they are doing that psychic twin thing, and neither one believes my lame excuse.

"I was actually going to speak to you both about football. I've got this new job starting properly on Saturday at a bar in town, and I'm not going to have time to help with practices anymore. I will still try and come to watch your games, but it might be hard if I'm working. It's important to me that I can contribute to the bills and stuff to help out Sam." It's not the complete truth, but the thought of being near Danny at the moment I just can't handle, and my new job is my easy out, and a perfect excuse for the boys to drop football practice.

"That's great news Maddie." Tommy answers, and both boys bear hug me at the same time, and we all land in a heap on the bed laughing together.

"Don't worry about football Maddie, Sam said she's going to come to all our games." Tommy smiles at me, beaming with pride. Nanna Jenny would never have set foot onto a football field in the mud, she actively avoided any of the boys activities as much as possible, school nativity plays, parent evenings, so having Sam show an interest is a big thing for them.

"Your both sure it's okay?" I ask guiltily, feeling no better than one of Nanna Jenny's lame excuses, but Jack and Tommy both nod simultaneously in agreement.

"Good, that's good. Now go and shower that mud off yourselves before dinner, I'm going to start cooking in a few minutes. Sam will be home around six, and I don't expect her to cook dinner after working all day long." I smile at the boys, relieved that I've dodged a bullet, barely.

Walking into the living room I notice my rucksack on the floor, Bryan must have brought it inside for me after he dropped me off. I dig inside and find my phone and notice several missed messages.

The first one is from Bryan.

Maddie, call me. Worried about you.

The next one is from Danny.

You didn't show for football practice. We need to talk. I'm sorry.

Then there's one from Jack.

Coach is in a shitty mood because you didn't show up. Told him you're in the library to cover.

The final one is also from Danny.

Please call me, I need to explain.

I put my phone down on the counter and start to cook dinner, anything to take my mind off things. Chickpea curry and rice, nice and simple. The boys are going to moan but they always end up asking for seconds, and I've got some ready-made onion bhajis from the deli counter to butter them up.

Thinking about the messages from Danny, I almost scold myself with boiling water filling a pan from the kettle for the rice.

"Shit." I say out loud, just as Sam appears in the kitchen, she looks worn out. I can't remember the last time she had an actual day off doing absolutely nothing at all.

"Rough day kiddo?" Sam says, and kisses me on the cheek, and lifting the lid on one of the saucepans to see what's cooking inside.

"Your home early, I didn't hear you come in. I'm making a curry for dinner." I reply putting the pan with boiling water onto the hob, and emptying a packet of basmati rice into it.

"Smells good, Maddie. In fact anything is good if I'm not having to cook it. Are you okay? You seem a little off this evening." She asks me with a look of concern in her eyes, my puffy eyes always give me away.

"Had a migraine, but managed to fend it off with tablets and sleep." Guiltily keeping up the white lie, not even looking at Sam as I say it.

"Sure?" Sam asks, I swear nothing gets past this woman sometimes, and I hate lying to her.

"I'm sure Sam, it's nothing to worry about. Ow, I totally forgot to tell you yesterday, but I've got a job in a bar in town. I'm going to be singing cabaret songs on Saturday, and I get to keep all my tips. Bryan and Ben are waiting tables and doing bar work there too. The owner wants to attract a younger crowd, hence training up some younger staff. So I'll be able to give you some money towards the bills and stuff." I smile at her enthusiastically, glad to change the subject.

"Oh Maddie, that's wonderful! Your first proper job, go you. I'm so proud of you. How's it going to fit in with college and helping at football though? You don't want to overstretch yourself." Sam asks me, and I can see the cogs turning around in her head.

"College is fine because my shifts will work around it, and I've explained to the boys I'm going to stop the volunteering at football because of the new job and they are both fine with it. I'll still try and get to their games when I can." And the white lies continue to slide off my tongue about why I'm giving up football.

"Have you told Danny yet? He deserves to know." Sam replies, and I'm sure she's onto my lie. She can smell bullshit, from a mile away.

"Not yet, but I'm going to later on, after dinner. I wanted to speak to you and the boys first." I reply, stirring the curry so I have something to distract me, and totally avoiding any kind of eye contact with her.

"Okay. I'm going to take a quick shower before you dish up. And Maddie, if you need to talk to me about anything else, anything else at all, especially to do with Danny, I'm here for you." Bloody woman has super powers I swear.

Chapter Thirty-Six

Danny

Father Christopher wasn't at the church, so annoyingly, I didn't get a chance to talk to him. I'm back at home trying to get some work done on my computer, but I'm finding it difficult to concentrate after my altercation with Maddie. I've messaged her several times and she hasn't replied, and then she didn't turn up for football practice. She's totally Ghosting me. Jack even covered for her telling me she was in the library at college, when I damn well know college was closed today. But I could tell Jack and Tommy didn't know why Maddie hadn't shown up.

My phone pings, as if by magic because I'm thinking about her again, it's a message from Maddie. I quickly open it to read, and instantly regret it once I've read it…

I've got a new job, and it clashes with football. So consider this my notice. Maddie

I stare at my phone slightly shocked, this takes being upset to a whole new level. I knew she was angry but I didn't realise it was this bad. Never has Maddie been curt with me like this, and via text message. So I decide to call her on the spur of the moment. The phone rings once and a recorded message comes onto the line, "this number is unavailable" and then the line goes dead.   Maddie's blocked my number. I'm in total shock, and my heart is pounding in my chest. I feel devastated, this girl is destroying my heart and she doesn't even realise it.

How the hell can I protect her if she doesn't even want to talk to me, what if something happens to her? I don't know what to do now, and I feel slightly numb, like it's not real and I'm having some kind of out of body experience. I knew Maddie had trust issues, but I never imagined them running this deep.

So I decide to put on my running gear for the second time today and pound the concrete, try and sort my head out, and work out a plan for what I'm going to do about Maddie. By the time I stop, sweat is running down my back and my t-shirt is soaked, and I've subconsciously run to St Peters Church, seems I can't keep away from the place today.

Jogging up the path, I try the church door and it's unlocked, so at least I know Father Christopher is around. Going inside the smell of incense tickles my nose and I notice the church is empty apart from Father Christopher kneeling in front of the alter. Not wanting to disturb his prayer, I sit on a pew near the back of the church and patiently wait for him to finish. A few minutes later he stands, and as he turns around he notices me sitting in the pew.

"Danny, I didn't hear you come in. Something troubling you? Is this about my red headed visitor earlier today?" Father Christopher asks as he approaches me.

"How very perceptive of you Father, you should have been a detective." I smirk back at him cheekily.

"Well in this job you often find yourself doing detective work, and I was always a fan of agent Mulder, as you and your father know." He laughs back, no doubt reminiscing.

"I was more of a Scully fan, I had some very vivid dreams about her as a teenager. I blame my dad, making me watch that boxset with him." I smile, happy memories invading my head of me and dad spending hours watching the X-files together.

"Yes, your father got me hooked too. I ended up borrowing that boxset from him in the end. I always found their take on the Catholic church fascinating." He smirks, sitting down next to me, his bones creaking with arthritis. After a slightly uncomfortable silence, I start to talk about my reason for stopping by to talk to him.

"I know you spoke to Maddie today. I was the one that found her after she ran off earlier." I say nervously fiddling with my thumbs.

"Yes, Bryan called me to let me know she was safe and at home with you." Father Christopher answers, waiting for me to volunteer more information.

"I admitted to her that I was the one that found her as a baby. Maddie didn't take it well because I kept it from her. I didn't tell her about the letter that was found with her, and she didn't mention it so I assumed that you didn't tell her?" I ask Father Christopher, also in two minds if I should mention Uriel to him.

"No, I didn't say anything about the letter to Maddie. I'm sorry she reacted like that towards you, but I'm not surprised. She's obviously hurting right now, give her some space to digest what's happened. Finding out no one really knows where she came from must be painful to hear, she probably already knew on a subconscious level, but allowed herself to believe she would find out the truth, then suddenly not getting any real answers must be hard." Father Christopher replies, looking at me with sympathy.

"I wasn't prepared for her reaction. She's quit volunteering at football, she says it's because she has a new job, but she's also blocked my phone number. You didn't see her, she was distraught, and I left her there sobbing because she told me to go. I shouldn't have listened to her, I should have stayed. Perhaps I should have come completely clean and told her about the letter too. At least then she would know she was abandoned for a good reason. But if I do that am I putting her at further risk? I don't know what to do Father, please tell me what to do." I say, panting slightly, trying desperately to fend off my emotions.

"Danny, calm yourself. I can't tell you what to do. But do you want my advice?" He asks me.

"Yes, Father. That's why I came, for your guidance." I reply, calming down, my anxiety abating.

"Give her the space she needs, then revisit that conversation with her, explain your actions, and that you were only working in her best interest. But be prepared that she won't want to hear what you have to say. It's possible a happy resolution won't happen." Father Christopher sighs.

"And that's exactly what I'm afraid of." Gazing towards the stained glass windows, I blink away my tears.

Chapter Thirty-Seven

Bryan

Maddie's all but ghosted me for the last day or so, apart from the one message telling me she's fine, and will see me at work on Saturday night. I know she's been practicing her set list with Tony out of hours and in private, so perhaps she's just been too busy.

Actually, I know that's total bullshit, because Danny called me to ask if I'd heard from her, she blocked his number, which must be brutal for him considering how he feels for her. It's beyond obvious now, and I can't understand why he doesn't just tell her, it makes me feel like I should be banging both of their heads together so they start communicating with each other like adults. I kinda feel like I'm stuck in the middle of things, and it's not a comfortable place to be stuck between two friends fighting.

My day wasn't a total washout, I met up with Ben after college, and we walked hand in hand together around the pier. Not exactly romantic weather for a stroll because it was cold and dreary, but nobody was really around to see us together and make harsh judgements about our relationship. It was nice, it felt right, and I can feel myself falling hard for him. We're both together in this new relationship territory, which is scary and exhilarating at the same time. I'm mainly worried about my dad finding out, so I'm trying to shove it to the back of my mind for now.

Ben has much more confidence in himself, where I hardly

have any. He's more mentally prepared for any fallout our relationship may cause when it becomes common knowledge, but I know that I definitely don't, not yet. Although when we held hands earlier today I didn't care who saw us, all those negative thoughts went out of the window, Ben made me feel safe and wanted. My minds so confused right now, and I really wish I could talk to Maddie about all of this, I need my friend back.

I can hear my mum calling me from downstairs, "Bryan, Danny's here to see you."

Going downstairs Danny's standing in the hallway waiting for me, nervously standing with his hands in his pockets, this is not the confident Danny that I know, and I don't even need to guess what has him so riled up. But I decide to push his buttons anyway, because I'm annoyed he's the reason that my friend hasn't spoken to me.

"Danny, let me guess this is about Maddie. Before you say anything, I haven't spoken to her, all I've had is a message saying she'll see me at work tonight and she's fine. Which I'm guessing is girl code for I'm anything but fine." I answer him annoyed, and I want to know what he said that upset her so much.

"Shit. Okay, I just wanted to check. You know she quit football and blocked my phone number." Danny replies, and I do feel bad for him. Talk about having conflicting emotions, having friends fight really sucks.

"Yes, you told me that already on the phone earlier. I can give her a message at work tonight if you want me too, but it might be an idea to let her cool off first, you don't want to make her even madder than she is." I offer Danny my advice, hoping that he'll listen to me and doesn't attempt anything rash with her.

"Maybe your right, I'm sorry Bryan, putting you in the middle of this." Danny sighs, looking really stressed out, I'm not used to seeing him like this over a girl.

"It's difficult Danny, because I'm friends with both of you. But I refuse to take sides, I'm not doing that, so please don't ask me too." I answer him firmly, being completely serious for once.

"Nor would I ever ask or expect you to Bryan, at least give me some credit. So where's this new job you've both landed together? Or is that now a big secret too?" Danny asks sounding pissed off being left out of the loop.

"It's three of us actually, me, Maddie and Ben from college. My boyfriend." I whisper to him with pride and grinning like a loon.

"Boyfriend." He whispers back discreetly, and smirks back with his eyes twinkling.

"The job is at a certain bar we went to that time, I'll tell you about it, but not here. I'll catch up with you after church tomorrow?" I ask him, looking around just to check my mum isn't trying to listen in on our private conversation.

"I hadn't planned on going to the church service but I can meet you outside afterwards, and we'll grab coffee somewhere." Danny sighs again, I know he tries to avoid church, and now his dad is in the hospital it's easier for him not to go.

"Tomorrow then, see you outside after the service." I reply to him, and we both say our goodbyes.

"Danny not staying for dinner?" My mum asks as she appears in the hallway, obviously hearing the front door close and him leaving, she's so nosy.

"No, I'm meeting him for coffee after church tomorrow. He's got a lot on his mind at the moment." I answer, not giving anything away to my mum about our conversation, it's none of her business.

"That's nice of you Bryan." And she squeezes my shoulder and disappears into the living room, now I feel guilty for thinking shitty thoughts about mum.

"Don't worry about dinner for me mum, I'm getting ready for work and I'll grab something there later on tonight." I shout through the living room door not waiting for her to answer me, then I run upstairs taking two steps at a time.

Forty-five minutes later, I'm pulling up in my mums car into the car park at Dorothy's, she's let me borrow it again tonight. Honest to god, I drive it more than she does now. I offered Maddie a lift, but she said she was already there at the bar practicing for tonight's show.   Walking into the staff room I find Ben's already arrived and is going through a large box of t-shirts with Dorothy.

"Bryan, welcome. I've had a delivery of new t-shirts for you baby gays, so dig in, there are several in each size." She smiles at me cheekily, and I can't wait to get my hands on one of those t-shirts.

"Great, now I don't have to worry about spilling beer down my own shirt." I laugh back, excited to be working here. It's like a dream come true for me. Somewhere I can feel safe and totally be myself.

"I'll leave you both to get changed, and no funny business, I have eyes everywhere." Dorothy winks at us both and walks through to the main bar area.

"Well hello you." Ben says, as he closes the gap and kisses me passionately. I close my eyes as I feel his lips on mine and my heart pounds.

"And hurry up getting ready you two." Dorothy shouts from the bar, and we both jump apart at the same time.

"That was evil." I laugh. Dorothy is such a tease.

"Yes, we better do as the boss says." Ben replies, giving me a second kiss, even more passionate than the first. Slowly pulling apart, we don't say a word, there's no need too. It was all conveyed in that last kiss…

Chapter Thirty-Eight

Maddie

Staring at myself in the enormous mirror surrounded by bright lightbulbs, like something out of a Hollywood movie, I hardly recognise the girl staring back at me. Dorothy has given me a full makeover, and when I say full makeover, I mean full makeover. She insisted on doing my hair for tonight's show, and I'm surprised with her skills, she could easily be a professional hair and make-up artist. But it's good to have a mask to hide behind, a different persona. Perhaps that's what she was trying to achieve for me, to help take my nerves away.

I should be ecstatically excited for tonight's show, but all I feel like right now is crying again. My betrayed heart feels like it's broken into tiny splinters of glass. Even though I'm still very angry with Danny, I miss him like crazy, why does it hurt so much? I have no idea how we can get past this, he basically lied to my face, and he's still keeping things from me. Perhaps it's for the best, it's not like I ever had a chance with him. Maybe we're better off apart, and what happened yesterday was a blessing in disguise. I blink my tears away, not wanting to ruin my make-up and glad Dorothy used waterproof mascara on me, she was obviously prepared for my emotions more than me...

Slipping my silver high heeled sandals on my feet, I take a deep breath and close my eyes, mentally trying to prepare myself for tonight and praying I don't freeze up on stage. The last thing I want is a bad case of stage fright. A wolf whistle comes from behind me, and I turn around to see Bryan standing there in his brand new bright green Dorothy's bar t-shirt.

"What's up buttercup?" Bryan says, and I find myself almost slinging myself into his arms, and knocking him off his feet, I want to burst into tears with relief that he's here. But I must protect my make-up or Dorothy really will kill me.

"Bryan, my life's gone to shit again." I manage to just about say choking back my tears, managing to preserve my eye make-up.

"No it hasn't. You've just hit a crossroad that's all. We have a big night ahead, and I'm your official cheerleader. So all you're going to concentrate on tonight is singing and making some serious money. Problems will still be there tomorrow, allow yourself this one night Maddie." And Bryan kisses me gently on the top of my head and says, "You look stunning by the way. Like a Hollywood goddess."

"Flattery will get you everywhere." I laugh back. Bryan is just what I needed right now, a massive boost to my waning confidence.

"And good luck waiting those tables tonight, I hope you make a killing in tips too." And I kiss him back on the cheek, making him blush. Taking his arm, Bryan leads me through a now crowded bar and down onto the stage, where Tony is already playing some show tunes on the piano as background music. Dorothy is already waiting for me, and announces my name as I walk up the steps onto the stage.

"Tonight we have the official debut of Miss Madeline Reynolds, a young lady with a voice to die for, discovered here on this very stage on a karaoke night. And after some gentle persuasion she's agreed to sing for us all tonight, so please put your hands together and give her a warm Dorothy's welcome to Maddie." And Dorothy steps to the side of the stage, straightening her arm presenting me to a waiting crowd, and hands me over the microphone.

"Thank you, Dorothy for this opportunity, and Tony for helping me put together tonight's set list. Sit back, sip that cocktail and let me take you on a journey." The opening bars to Taylor Swifts, No body, no crime, starts to play. And I put on my best sultry persona, and start to sing. The nerves I had have magically disappeared, and I strut around the stage like I belong there. The crowd is eating it up, and Dorothy has a huge smile on her face. I continue through my set list and even get the crowd singing along with me at one point, and at the end of my set the crowd erupts into applause.   Dorothy comes on stage to take over from me, and I slip off the stage and perch myself on the end of the bar to chat with the punters, and grab a drink before our duets start, at the end of Dorothy's set.

I notice a guy slip out of the door on the other side of the bar, and I swear it looked like Danny. But no, I must be imagining things because he doesn't even know where I work, and he wouldn't show up here surely? Must be my overactive imagination, or me wishing he was here to see me perform for the first time.

Ben slides over to my end of the bar to serve me, "And what does the beautiful lady require to drink this fine evening?" He chuckles to me, grabbing one of the fancy glasses normally used for gin.

"Water please. My throats gone dry as a bone, and I've still got to sing again tonight." I reply, watching as Ben adds ice to the glass, a slice of lemon and some sparkling mineral water. He places a napkin underneath the glass, and pushes it towards me. Someone's been learning some bar skills...

"Your killing it out there Maddie. Told you you'd be okay girl." Bryan says as he slides in next to me, putting a empty tray on the bar and handing over another drinks order to Ben.

"I feel more nervous now I'm off stage, I can't believe I did that. If you told me a month ago I'd be singing in a gay bar I would have laughed in your face." I answer Bryan before he quickly runs off with his order, it's manically busy in here tonight.

"I swear I saw Danny just leave." I say, but I don't think Bryan hears me as he's already walked off with his tray now full of more drinks.

"He was here, lurking in the back. Snuck in just before you started singing. Couldn't take his eyes off you." Ben answers instead surprising me, and before I can answer him back he's off serving another customer.

I'm not sure how I feel about Danny being here watching me, I'm just glad I didn't realise he was here before I started singing. My nerves would have been totally shot to pieces. But he came. Even after my harsh words yesterday, and my cruel text message. He showed up for me. My heart starts to do summersaults again, but I still can't forgive him for keeping the truth from me.

Finishing my last song of the night with Dorothy, we both take a bow and we walk around the tables of the bar with a bowler hat cabaret style, collecting tips. It's nearly last orders at the bar and people are either drunk or tipsy, and tips are very generous considering it's my first night here.

Taking my make-up off with a baby wipe in the changing room, and unpinning my hair, I start to slowly feel like myself again, like I'm removing the mask I had on. Dorothy just sauntered into the room and slapped a pile of banknotes on the table in front of me.

"Your share of the tips, we had a good night. If you do that every time I'm going to be one happy bar owner. How does singing three or four nights a week sound? It will mean vastly extending your setlists, but most songs you'll be able to sing along to a backing track, so you don't have to be here all the time to practice." Dorothy grins at me enthusiastically.

"That sounds amazing, that money is all really mine?" I'm almost too afraid to ask, in fear that she'll take it back.

"Yes, all yours, tax free on top of your wages which get paid monthly." Dorothy answers, winking at me.

"This is going to help my family so much Dorothy. Thank you." And I give her a hug, having the money to help out Sam means so much to me.

I know the first thing I need to do with that money though. Pay Danny back for the boys football boots. Especially now since I'm no longer volunteering at football. I've effectively broken our payment arrangement, so this way I don't have to feel as guilty quitting the team like I did. Yes, that sounds like the best plan to me, that way I can cut all ties from Danny, for my own sanity…

Chapter Thirty-Nine

Bryan

My first night at Dorothy's has been busy and I've been run off my feet the whole time. Everything went smoothly, I don't think I made any massive mistakes, and my new boss appeared to be happy with how I wait tables. My tips reflected that, and I'm amazed at people's generosity. After dropping Maddie off at her house, Ben and I went for a short drive and parked up in the McDonald's car park. We ended up making out with each other, until a security guard came over and spoiled it. Tapping on our window for us to move on, spoil sport. So we called it a night, both feeling shattered from working. I dropped Ben off at his house, and then drove home feeling all warm and fuzzy inside, for once feeling happy with my life.

Surprisingly mum and dad are still up in the living room watching some old eighties' movie, and I spot an open bottle of wine on the table. I hope dad hasn't had too much alcohol tonight and that's a first bottle, not a second or worse. He tends to get louder and more obnoxious when he's had a few. Sitting down in the armchair they both look around, only just noticing I've got home.

"How's your first shift go sweetheart?" My mum asks eagerly, I can tell she was waiting up for me.

"Really, really well. Made some killer tips, so I'll fill the car up with petrol tomorrow mum." I smile at her proudly, feeling on top of the world for once.

"What an earth are you wearing Bryan?" My dad sits up and asks me sarcastically.

Shit, so much for keeping where I work a secret. I totally forgot to change back into my own t-shirt, and I'm still wearing my Dorothy's t-shirt. No hiding my new workplace from the parents now.

"This, oh, just my work shirt dad. I forgot to change out of it before I left." I reply innocently, trying to play things down but already predicting how things will go.

"Thought you said you got a job at a bar?" Dad asks, and I can already feel myself falling into a trap, this is what he does, to try and catch me out.

"Yes, that's right dad a bar in town. Well I think I'm going to go off to bed, long shift, I'm knackered."   Standing up to leave the room, I'm quickly thwarted by my dad.

"Sit down now Bryan. I haven't finished speaking yet." Dad snaps at me angrily, and I can see that my t-shirt is the perfect excuse he's been looking for to challenge me.

"What's wrong dad?" I ask, but I already know the answer, I'm far from stupid.

"That t-shirt your wearing, is that the place your working now?" Dad calmly asks, lulling me into a false sense of security, like he's trying to reel me in..

"Yes." I simply answer, no point in lying about it. That's not my style anyway.

"So you're working at that fag bar." He replies curtly, and my mum gasps at his use of language.

"It's a gay bar but its all-inclusive, and we don't say fag bar dad, it's offensive." I reply standing closer to my dad at the same time he does. It's a power play.

"No son of mine is working in a fag bar. Those people are abominations and it goes against all our beliefs." Dad says angrily, his face slowly going red, and I can smell the alcohol on his breath.

Mums pulling on his arm trying to calm him down, and she shaking her head at me. But for once I'm feeling brave, perhaps it's because of my new job, or perhaps because of Ben's positive influence. Perhaps a little bit of both.

"It's not up to you dad, I'm nearly eighteen and I choose to work there with my friends." I answer as calmly as I possibly can, shaking with anger inside.

"Like hell it is Bryan, you can quit tomorrow before you get tainted with that filth." Dad practically screams at me, spitting as he's saying it.

"And what's tainted supposed to be code for dad? What do you even want me to say? Do you want the truth, because I can give you the truth, right here, right now." I'm standing almost nose to nose with him now, my whole body radiating with a sudden adrenaline surge.

"Out with it Bryan, but once you say it, that's it. You can't put it back in that box." Dad screams in my face, and mum is now screaming at him to stop.

"I'm a dirty fag. I'm fucking gay dad, I've got a boyfriend and his names Ben." I shout back in his face, my sudden bravery starting to fade almost instantaneously.

The colour drains from my dad's face, but then he does something he's never done before in his life to me. He punches me smack in the face, and I land backwards, crash landing on top of the glass coffee table, smashing through the glass with my full force. Mum screams and comes rushing to my side. But then my dad pulls me up by my shirt tearing it in the process, grabs my arm, and aggressively pulls me through the front door, and he finally pushes me onto the gravel driveway outside. Blood runs down from my nose, and I can feel my hands and arms are covered in cuts from the coffee table, my knees are cut to shreds and covered in sharp gravel. Mums in tears shouting at my dad, but he's past listening, there is no reasoning with him, especially when he's this drunk.

"You are no longer welcome in this house, I don't have a son anymore, you disgust me." And my dad slams the front door, leaving me bleeding on the ground in the driveway, now a complete wreck.

Luckily for me, I still have my phone and my wallet in the pockets of my cargo trousers, and I manage to pull myself up painfully into a sitting position. I look at my phone and it's really late, who do I call, shit, who do I call?

I'm not sure how Ben would react to this tonight, I know he's gotten in fights on and off the rugby field and he's a big guy. I certainly don't want him getting into any trouble defending my honour.   I could call Maddie, but that would mean disturbing Sam and the boys too, which I won't do either. Danny's house isn't that far away, I'm sure I can make it there on foot. I don't bother making any calls, and I slowly drag myself up onto my feet, with blood still dripping from my nose. It starts to drizzle with rain, and I'm shivering by the time I make it to Danny's house half an hour later.   His porch light turns on automatically with the motion sensor, and I press his doorbell and wait, hoping he hasn't already fallen asleep. I can't see any other lights on in the house, shit, he must have already gone to bed. I'm about to turn away and leave when the front door opens, Danny's standing there in lounge pants rubbing his eyes.

"Bryan?" He gasps.

Danny, A Few Seconds Before...

Slumped at my computer, tired and frustrated I'm trying to write some code for a program I've got in development, not the Saturday night I imagined to have.   Earlier on tonight, I did manage to sneak into Dorothy's bar covertly to catch Maddie's first ever set, and she blew me away, even with us not speaking to each other there was no way I was going to miss that. Except now my concentration has gone to shit since then, and I can't stop thinking about her. I'm not sure why I tortured myself going to watch her in the first place. I also filmed some of it on my phone, and now I feel like a stalker, I've already rewatched it three times in the last hour. Maddie would be freaked out if she found out.   Really, I should get myself to bed, I promised to meet Bryan for coffee tomorrow morning, and looking at the time on my computer it's already well past midnight.

A notification comes through on my phone, someone's at the front door. Damn, must be important if it's this late, either that or the pizza delivery guy has got the wrong house again. Running downstairs in a half asleep jog, while rubbing my tired eyes and yawning, I attempt to try to wake myself up a bit.

Opening the front door, the last person I expected to find on my doorstep is standing there, Bryan. His t-shirt is torn and covered in blood, and his face is a bloody mess, and his nose looks broken. I can also see he has cuts and bruises on his arms and legs, some of the wounds are still bleeding, he must have been in a fight or been beaten up.

"Bryan." I gasp at him, speechless and shocked by his appearance, Bryan doesn't do violence. I already know he didn't cause this.

"Danny. Sorry it's late, I had nowhere else to go." He manages to blurt out, and I can tell he's clearly shaken and going into shock. I notice he's shivering, and there is a light drizzle of rain, his clothes are wet and he doesn't even have a coat on.

"Come in Bryan, do I need to take you to the hospital? Should I call the police?" I ask him, as I guide him into the living room to sit on the sofa, I need to get some answers about who did this to him.

"No. I'll be okay. Can I stay here tonight?" Bryan asks me in almost a whisper, and I can tell he's struggling to hold back his emotions.

"Sure, always. What happened to you Bryan? Are you positive I don't need to call the police? I should call your dad, he'll be worried." I reply to him, concern seeping from my voice.

"No, no. Not my dad, don't call him. Or the police. I just need to clean myself up and borrow a shirt until I can get some of my stuff." Bryan says looking at me with alarm and panic, like I'm suddenly going to do the wrong thing, and go against his wishes.

"Bryan, does your dad know about this? Help me out here because I'm confused." I already have a feeling I know his answer, and I don't like it one bit, I really thought his dad would stick by his own son.

"He found out Danny. Well he guessed, then I filled in the gaps for him. As you can see he took it as well as I expected he would. So I'm officially out of the closet. Congratulations, you officially have a gay friend." Bryan hangs his head down, his hands covering his face, and I'm not entirely sure if he's going to start laughing or crying.

"Shit Bryan. I'm so sorry. What an asshole, I honestly thought he would be supportive. What about your mum?" I reply, finding it difficult to keep my venom towards his dad out of my voice. David Johnson has been my dad's best friend since they were kids. How could he treat his own son like this?

"Mum tried to pull him off me at one point, but she always ends up siding with him. He's not a bad person Danny, he just has certain views on certain things." Bryan replies, and I can't believe he's defending him after doing this to him. My dad would never lay a hand on me in a million years. David's behaviour towards his son sickens me. I was the one that encouraged him to talk to his dad about his sexuality, I never saw this kind of reaction coming...

"That's it. I'm going round there right now, he's got no right to beat you up like this Bryan. It's assault, it's against the law. If my dad was here right now he'd be the one knocking some sense into him." I'm so angry for Bryan, he's like a brother to me, he's family as far as I'm concerned.

"Please don't Danny. I can't take anymore, not tonight." And I can see tears starting to drip down his face, I'll lay off tonight. But all bets are off tomorrow, David Johnson has got a few home truths coming his way.

"Come on then, I need to at least get you cleaned up and tucked up in bed for the night. We'll revisit this discussion in the morning." And I lead Bryan upstairs to the bathroom.

"Does that mean I get a bedtime story too?" Bryan smirks through his teary face, still cracking jokes, and trying to cover his pain with humour.

"Don't push it, I'll go and grab you some stuff to wear. Why don't you get into the shower, it will be the easiest way to get rid of all that blood, then I'll check those cuts for you and patch you up." I reply, still shaking with anger myself, needing a few minutes away from him to calm myself down.

Tomorrow I'm going to pay a visit to David Johnson, and I'm also going to tell my dad what kind of a man his best friend is.

Bryan

Rolling over in bed I feel sore all over my entire body, I think I got to bed eventually at about three o'clock this morning and sleep didn't exactly come easily. I look again at my phone, but I've got no missed messages. Not even from my mum, and that really hurts, I thought she'd at least see if I was okay? Why am I not surprised. Thinking about my parents I cringe. How my dad almost has two different personalities, and my mum covers for him like nothing's wrong and there isn't any kind of a problem.

I'm supposed to be working later on today, and all I have on me are my clothes from last night. I need to call Maddie, I was meant to be picking her up too for her shift, and now I'm car-less too.

Taking out my phone again, I shoot Maddie a quick message.

Dad found out about me. He threw me out. At Danny's house.

My phone pings.

Are you okay?

I quickly type a message back.

Not really. I'll see you at work. Sorry I can't pick you up.

Another ping.

I'll see you at work, Sam will give me a ride in. We'll talk later. Love you bestie buddy.

That makes me smile, and I message her back.

Love you too buttercup.

Danny knocks on my door, and walks in carrying a steaming cup of coffee and places it on the bedside table, then sits down on the bed beside me. I sit myself up and grab the coffee, and my broken lip stings from the hot fluid as I take a small sip.

"So about last night." Danny starts, and waits patiently for me to fill in the gaps.

"Mum and dad knew about my new job, I didn't lie, I just told them it was a bar in town. I made the mistake of forgetting to change out of my t-shirt before I got home, and it has the Dorothy's logo in large letters across the front, you can't miss it. Dad started making comments about no son of his working in a fag bar." And Danny openly cringes at the comment my dad made, it makes me physically sick every time I have to repeat the word.

"I had no idea your dad even thought like that, I feel like I don't know him at all." Danny replies sadly, shaking his head.

"Dad only does it behind closed doors, and he'd been drinking which makes him ten times worse. But I can't say I was surprised by his reaction, I may have pushed him a bit last night too, but he needed to hear the truth." I reply with honesty, and I don't regret telling him what I need.

"Pushed him?" Danny inquires, raising his eyebrow slightly.

"I told him I was a gay, although I put it into the crass language that he uses. That's when he snapped and punched me, and I fell into the coffee table. Then he dragged me out the front door and threw me on the driveway. It wasn't my best moment." I smirk at him, trying to cover my pain again with humour.

"I'm going to fucking kill him." Danny replies, shocking me, and suddenly he starts to pace up and down the bedroom, nearly wearing a hole in the carpet in the process.

"I don't want you to get into any trouble Danny, he'll turn it all around so it looks like your causing a problem. I just need help to grab some of my stuff, and a place to stay until I can sort something out." I answer Danny, feeling guilty for involving him in the first place.

"Do you think your parents will be at church right now?" He asks me, not really seeing why he needs to know.

"They never miss it, unless they are ill." I reply in confusion.

"We'll go over and grab your stuff then, my dad has a spare key for your house in case of emergency. And I'm classing this as one. Put some clothes on, we leave in five minutes." And Danny disappears out of the bedroom. I notice a fresh pile of clothes at the bottom of the bed, and I get dressed quickly, Danny's clothes are massive on me but I appreciate the gesture.

Within minutes we're both standing in my bedroom at my parents' house piling clothes into a large holdall Danny brought with him, and a large rucksack I normally use when I go camping. I've also packed up my laptop and college stuff, basically all the essentials I need to get by with for now. Just as we're loading Danny's car up with all my belongings, my dad's car pulls up on the driveway, we took longer packing than I anticipated. Or they left church straight after the service today.

"Get in the car Bryan. Now." Danny demands abruptly, and I scramble into his front passenger seat quickly, but I open the window a crack so I can hear what's going on.

"Danny." My dad says to him, and then he looks towards me and his face pales when he sees the state of my face.

"I don't want any trouble David, we just came to collect some clothes." Danny replies, offering no further information.

"He's staying with you?" Dad answers Danny, stating the fucking obvious.

"Yes. Frankly, I wanted to call the police for your behaviour last night. But for some reason Bryan's protecting you. I suggest you stay away from him unless you can come to your senses. My dad would be ashamed of you if he was here right now." Danny replies to him, not pulling any punches, and gets into the car. I can immediately tell that he was holding back, just by the way Danny's body is vibrating with anger.

My dad stands there, not saying a word, as my mum looks on speechless as usual, like the perfect Stepford wife. Danny drives us back to his house, and he doesn't say a word until we get there, I can tell he's deep in thought. Turning to me he says, "For the foreseeable future you are moving in with me and dad, you can have the guest bedroom you slept in last night, I'll get you a set of house keys cut tomorrow. You can't go back home, not with your dad being like that. So that's settled." And he stomps into the house before I have a chance to say another word.

Looks like I have a new roomie, and I have to chuckle to myself, because I distinctly remember Danny telling me he'd never live with me...

Chapter Forty

Danny

Walking into my dad's hospital room I break out into a smile when I see him sitting on the edge of the bed doing some leg exercises. I've dropped Bryan off at Dorothy's for his shift today and I'll pick him up later on, more for my piece of mind. I'm worried about him, and I have no idea if his dad will turn up looking for more trouble.

"Hi dad, looking good, great to see you doing some exercise and getting your lazy arse out of bed." I say jokingly, and I place a paper bag with fresh croissants on his table, along with some fancy coffee from our favourite patisserie.

"You remembered, thanks son. I can't tell you how sick I am of hospital food, it's driving me crazy. And this is the private room, what are the poor NHS patients getting?" He laughs, already tearing into one of the croissants, and letting out a groan of satisfaction.

"Dad something happened last night, and you're not going to like it, I think I'm still in shock myself if I'm being honest. I did not see this coming…" I say going serious, telling him his best friend is a bigot and a bully isn't going to be easy.

"I already know Danny. Jean called me just before you came, it was only a matter of time before something like this happened." Wow, Bryan's mum called my dad, I didn't see that one coming either.

"I'd like to say I'm surprised Danny, but David has been on the edge for a while now." My dad replies, perfectly calm and not at all in the least bit surprised.

"You knew Bryan was gay?" I ask him, trying to process all this new information in my head.

"Danny I've known that boy all his life, of course I knew. His mother knew too. His father was just too narrow minded to see it. I'm proud of what you did for Bryan. Taking him in like that Danny, and sticking up for him, against his father. God knows, someone needed to do it. It should have been me, but I'm at fault too, for burying my head in the sand." Dad takes another bite of his croissant, looking thoughtful as he chews.

"But your Catholic too, how come you don't think the same way? I don't get it dad, you need to help me out here so I can understand the logic." I ask him, feeling like a little boy again asking his dad to explain things in simple terms of understanding.

"Look, the Catholic Church is far from perfect, you only have to read about the various scandals over the years. So who am I to judge others for their lifestyle choices? And I love that boy like I love you Danny. I'm so angry with David right now with how he's behaved towards Bryan, and that hurts too because he's always been my friend. Life is complicated and messy, you should know that better than anyone Danny." My dad sighs, and I can see he's tiring and in pain, so I help him get back into bed properly, and adjust his pillows. Dad never ceases to amaze me, I'm truly blessed to have him, and to think I nearly lost him in that accident. My mind starts to wander off again, I feel like it's spinning out of control sometimes.

"How's Maddie? You haven't mentioned her in a couple of days." My dad enquires, he knows something is wrong, he can always tell and there's no point trying to hide it.

"We had a falling out dad, and she's not talking to me. It's all a bit of a mess now, and I don't know what to do..." I proceed to tell him what's transpired with Maddie, the only thing I omit is my encounter with Uriel. I'm starting to think that wasn't real now, a figment of my imagination, probably due to stress the more I think about it. So I'm glad I haven't shared that information with anyone, they'd think I'm off my rocker, losing the plot. When my dad starts to become sleepy, I make my way back to the hospital car park slowly mulling over the conversation I've just had in my head. It's only when my guard is down, that I can't help feeling like someone is watching me. Perhaps my lack of sleep is making me paranoid now, I'm going to need a psychiatric evaluation at this rate. Looking at my watch, I can see I've got plenty of time before Bryan finishes his shift, I think I'll drive home and have a nap, all I need is some sleep. But my worries seem to be multiplying by the minute, and I really wish I had Maddie to talk too...

Bryan

Holding my breath with sudden anxiety, and knocking on Dorothy's office door, I nervously wait for her to answer. My face is a mess, I've got two black eyes, and possibly a broken nose. I should have gone to the hospital like Danny wanted me too, but that would have meant the hospital would make a report about a domestic assault because I'm still technically a minor. Danny patched me up good and proper, the guy is like Bear Grylls with his fountain of knowledge. I have a large plaster across my nose, and both of my arms have a patchwork quilt of steri-strips and plasters on. I look a complete mess, but I avoided hospital and the police which is a relief.

"Come in." I hear Dorothy's voice answer, so I open the door a crack nervously, then walk in slowly.

"Shit sweetie, what on earth happened to my little baby gay?"

Dorothy instantly stands up and walks around the desk, gently taking my face and turning it side to side to check out all the damage.

"My dad doesn't agree with my new lifestyle, and threw me out last night. I'm afraid my new Dorothy's t-shirt got wrecked." And I look down at the ground, feeling completely ashamed, and on the verge of tears thinking about what my dad did to me.

"Hey, don't look down. I've been there myself, albeit a long time ago. Are you doing okay sweetie? Got somewhere to stay, can't have one of my babies out on the streets?" She asks in motherly concern, one that you wouldn't want to cross while protecting their young.

"Yes I've got somewhere, I'm not out on the streets quite yet. I'm staying with a close friend of mine. I'm not sacked for coming in looking a mess on my second day am I?" I ask worriedly, not sure what to say, I've got no excuses. It's not like me to be lost for words.

"God no. Why would I sack you, don't be so ridiculous Bryan. You can help me do an inventory of the stock today, so you won't have to face any customers. I can play waitress instead, I love winding up my regular customers." She replies, taking a new Dorothy's t-shirt in my size out of a box from a cupboard, then handing it to me.

"Thanks." I reply, and I go to the staff room to get changed.

Maddie and Ben are chatting next to the lockers, and it feels just like being at college for a moment, which puts me on even more of an edge, because I haven't had to face that challenge yet.

"Oh my god Bryan, I didn't realise it was this bad. You shouldn't have down played it like you did." Maddie slings her arms around me, nearly knocking me over, in what's become her signature move.

Ben just stands there saying nothing at first, taking in my face and then my arms. He looks at me with an pained expression and says, "What the fuck Bryan? I'm going to kill him." Ben takes me into his arms and kisses the top of my head. I can feel him tremoring with anger.

"I'm okay, it's not as bad as it looks." I reply looking up into his eyes, my big strong boyfriend wants to protect me, and I can't help feeling a burst of joy in my stomach. He's going all caveman on me, and I think I like it.

"You should have called me, I would have come straight away." Ben answers, his voice breaking slightly, and he holds me tighter against his chest. My big strong man.

"Same here, you should of called, Sam would have looked after you, we could have taken you to the hospital." Maddie agrees, which is exactly another reason why I didn't call her.

"Honestly, I was okay, it looks worse than it is. I didn't call you Ben because I didn't want to cause trouble for you at home, I know you haven't come out to your parents yet. And Maddie, I was just thinking of you, Sam and the boys. Danny's house wasn't far, and he patched me up and helped me get my stuff this morning from my parents' house. Danny basically told me I'm staying with him for the foreseeable future, he was adamant about it." I reply looking at both of them, my eyes glistening with held back tears and emotions. Danny my unofficial big brother, and saviour it seems.

"Your dad has to answer for this, he can't be allowed to get away with this shit Bryan." Ben answers, still keeping me in a close hug, like he doesn't want to let me go.

"Leave it alone Ben. You too Maddie. Please, for me, I can't take anymore today." And a few tears escape from the corner of my eye, and I swipe them away hoping no one noticed.

"If that's what you want Bryan. We won't do anything, will we Ben?" Maddie replies, glaring at Ben fiercely like a mamma bear.

"I won't do anything, promise, not unless you ask me too." Ben sighs, and he continues to keep me in that bear hug for I don't know how long...

Chapter Forty-One

Maddie

Bryan's dad has behaved in a despicable manner as a parent and another human being, and I'm glad he's got Danny looking out for him. For now I'm going to push all my problems to one side and be there to support Bryan through this rough period, because we haven't even delt with college yet. Chelsea and her little posse are going to be brutal, I already know Ben won't put up with any shit flung their way, but Bryan is more sensitive making him a easier target.

Meeting Tony at a table in the bar as arranged, he has a pot of tea and two dainty teacups waiting for us which makes me smile. He's such a gentleman, dressed immaculately again in another nineteen twenties' style suit, I'm guessing he has a fascination with that era. We need to come up with at least three more setlists for next week, so we have a good catalogue of songs that I can perform. I just need to add a few more songs, and memorise the lyrics, I guess years of singing in the shower is about to pay off for me.

There's a guy standing by the bar sipping a pint, and he keeps looking over at me. Not in a flirty way, more like a interested in what I'm doing kind of way, and it's weird. Looking in another direction, and trying to concentrate on what Tony's saying, I ask him, "Tony, who's that guy standing over there at the bar?" My curiosity once again getting the better of me.

"Don't know his name Maddie, but I've seen him around a few times admittedly not in a while. I think he used to date

Dorothy at one time, a long time ago, but I don't think it ended all sunshine and roses." Tony answers, continuing to flick through sheets of music, and marking some with a red sharpie pen.

"How's it going? Need any help?" Dorothy asks, sitting down at the table and sneaking a peek at my little notebook.

"Yes please, I'll take any help I can get, you know this crowd better than me. I want to try and make my own mark without alienating people. I'm thinking of throwing in a few songs that are currently in the charts, stuff people will recognise from the radio." I reply to her, hoping my ideas are following what she expects of me.

"That sounds like a fantastic idea Maddie, I'm thinking a set list of dance hits that you can perform as a warm up for our lip-synch battle next week would be a bonus too. Do you think you can handle that? It should be a packed out night, I'm going to advertise it all over social media, aiming at a younger audience." Dorothy answers tapping her nails on the table, and I notice her staring at the guy at the bar.

"You know him?" I ask Dorothy, ignoring her previous question, finding this far more interesting at the moment.

"He broke my heart. But it wasn't to be, I wanted more than he could give, so it ended." She replies solemnly, and I'm not used to Dorothy looking so vulnerable. She gets up and leaves the table walking back to her office, I assume, and I notice the guy follows her. I hope she's going to be okay. Maybe I should go and see?

"Don't worry about Dorothy, I can see that look on your face. She's a big girl and can handle herself, wait until you see her break up a bar fight. No one messes with Dorothy." Tony says, still flicking through his sheets of music.

"Oh for fucks sake. Not today." I announce louder than I mean too as Danny strolls into the bar, and orders a drink. He takes a table not far from where we're sitting working, probably on purpose. But the smug bastard doesn't say a word and takes out his phone and mindlessly starts scrolling.

"Do you mind if we finish this in the staff room Tony, there's a guy over there I don't want to have to speak to today." I ask Tony, feeling like a bit of a bitch, but I can't handle any confrontation with Danny today. Not at my place of work on my second shift.

"Sure Maddie." Tony replies and gathers up his sheets of music, and I grab my notebook, then we disappear to the break room to work.

I can feel Danny's eyes burning into the back of my head, and his energy fade as I leave the room. Already knowing it was a sign of weakness on my part, effectively running away from him like that. As I'm about to enter the staff room, I pass that guy that was standing at the bar earlier watching me. He must have finished speaking to Dorothy already, what I'd give to have been a fly on that wall...

Danny

Why did I think that coming into the bar early and waiting for Bryan to finish his shift was a good idea? But I know exactly why, I needed to see Maddie, she's like a drug I can't get enough of, and I feel like I'm going into withdrawal. When I spotted her sitting there working with her colleague , I completely chickened out and ignored her. Damn, I acted like a teenage boy and a complete dick. I carry on scrolling aimlessly through my phone, and Maddie and her colleague leave their table and go out back, clearly to avoid having to breathe the same air as me. Maddie hates me right now, and it's all my fault. Someone sits down beside me, in a chair at my table, I look up and much to my surprise Uriel is sitting there, minus his wings. I've actually lost the plot, I must be seeing things, and I start to rub my eyes.

"Hello Danny, needed to catch up with a friend, and I thought I'd check in with you and see how your ward is doing." Uriel enquires with a smile on his face, like this is the most normal conversation in the world.

"Have I gone completely mad? Didn't you have wings last time? And if you mean Maddie she's currently not talking to me." I answer him in a whisper, confused by his sudden appearance in a gay bar.

"You haven't gone mad, I still have wings you just can't see them at the moment, and you need to fix things with Maddie. Fast. Troubles coming, I can feel it. Has she experienced any dreams?" Uriel asks, tilting his head slightly to the side, looking at me like I'm the most interesting object in the room.

"Shit. I don't know about any recent dreams, and it's not like I can ask her if she's not talking to me." I snap back at Uriel, pissed off because I'm failing at being Maddie's protector, the important mission I've been tasked with.

"Then this will help." And Uriel passes an envelope to me, written on the front in beautiful handwriting, the envelope reads:

To my daughter

"Is this from her mother?" Uriel simply nods in response.

"By rights Danny, I shouldn't even be here talking to you, but her mother wanted the chance to explain her actions. I can't approach Maddie directly, but you can. I need to go now, I've already stayed to long and taken too many risks." Uriel stands up, and then leaves the bar abruptly.

Staring at the sealed envelope in my hands, I carefully place it in my jacket pocket. I need to speak to Maddie alone, and not here. Maybe I can get Bryan to invite her over to the house? I feel like the envelope Uriel gave me is burning a hole in my pocket, and I need to speak to Maddie as soon as possible. Bryan walks into the bar carrying a crate of artisan beers, and goes behind the counter to start filling up a fridge, so I pick up my empty glass and head over towards him .

"Bryan, sorry, I know you're working but can I have a quick word." Bryan stops filling the fridge, and stands up to greet me.

"Your early Danny, sure I've got a second." Bryan replies, clearly surprised to see me, as I'd previously arranged to meet him in the car park once his shift finished.

"I need you to get Maddie to come over to the house tonight, it's really, really important. This can't wait, tell her anything, but get her there." As I hand Bryan my car keys, he looks back at me in confusion.

"Drive her back to ours after your shift. And do not, I repeat do not, crash my car, scratch my car, or get any speeding tickets. I'll call a taxi home, and I'll meet you there." I instruct Bryan firmly, praying I'm doing the right thing.

"No problem, I'm on it." Bryan smirks at me cheekily.

"I'll repeat it again Bryan, do not crash my car." Bryan has the audacity to salute me, the cheeky little shit, I shake my head, take out my phone and call a taxi home. Hoping I'll see my car in one piece again and trusting that Bryan can persuade Maddie to come over to my house...

Chapter Forty-Two

Maddie

The setlists are just about completed, and I've got various backing tracks downloaded onto a USB stick so I can practice singing the songs at home. Stretching my arms out and yawning, last night's late night is finally catching up with me, and I've been having some weird dreams again. Nothing about me this time. But I can never quite remember them by the time I fully wake up, which is as frustrating as hell. Somehow I sense that it's important though, so maybe I'll have more success remembering tonight, perhaps if I light some scented candles and put on some of Sam's meditation music, it might help to relax me first.

Bryan walks through to the staff room, bless him, he really does look terrible today, I think it's brave how he's still managed to show up for work today. I'd be a wreck, hiding under my duvet.

"Oh good, I caught you. I really, really need to talk to you Maddie. It's vitally important, can you hang on until my shift finishes, I've only got half an hour to go." Bryan asks me wide eyed and pleading, there's no way I'm saying no. Not with what he's been through in the last couple of days.

"Sure, I'll wait for you here. I can do some more practice while I wait." I'm intrigued with what he wants to talk about that's so important, I expect it's to do with being kicked out, it's a lot to process.

So I take out my notebook, and start going through my setlist again. Half an hour seems to fly by, and as we walk out of Dorothy's bar into the cold evening air, I do the zip up on my hoodie and take my fingerless gloves out of my pocket to put on.

"Danny lent me his car, so we ride in style." Bryan laughs, wiggling his eyebrows.

"He lent you his car? Really? Wow." I'm really surprised because Danny loves his car, and as much as I love Bryan I'm surprised Danny would trust him with it.

"We'll go back to Danny's house to talk. It's not like I can go home." So Bryan and I climb inside Danny's car, and as Bryan starts the engine, it feels really odd with Bryan driving. Going back to Danny's house wouldn't be my first choice of venue, but under the circumstances, I need to push my feelings aside to support Bryan. Be the bigger person, and all that stuff that sounds good inside your head until you actually come to do it. I fiddle about with the settings on Danny's car stereo because I know it will wind him up to find it set onto a different radio station from his regular one. A popular tune comes on that just so happens to be on my setlist, so I don't waste the opportunity to practice, and sing along at the top of my voice. Bryan is finding this thoroughly entertaining, and joins in at the chorus. By the time we get to Danny's house we are both laughing and joking, and it almost feels like the last twenty-four hours didn't happen, it's starting to feel normal again. That's until I see Danny standing by the living room window, like he's been waiting for us both to arrive.

Danny opens the front door just as we are getting out of the car, this is now starting to feel like a trap, and I've been stupid enough to walk right into it. He steps forward, holding up his arms in surrender. It looks ridiculous, and I can't help but laugh at him.

"I come in peace Maddie, but this is really important. Give me a few minutes of your time. Please?" Danny pleads with me, still waving his arms around.

"I'm here aren't I? Even though you lured me into a trap, using my friend as bait to suck me in." I glare back at him, for using Bryan like that.

"Happy to be of service." Bryan salutes Danny, and saunters into the house going upstairs, leaving me alone with Danny. So maybe Bryan isn't so innocent after all.

Following Danny into the living room, I make a point of sitting in the armchair and not on the sofa so he can't sit next to me. Instead, Danny sits on the coffee table in front of me, reading straight into my tactic, so now we're face to face with no escape.

"Maddie, whatever you may think of me, please know this, I care deeply about you. Nothing's going to change that, not now, not ever." Danny speaks in almost a whisper, his voice full of emotion.

"Okay, I'm listening." I answer back in a similar whisper, staring into his eyes, knowing in my heart that whatever he's about to tell me is the truth.

"There was a letter left with you when you were abandoned as a baby. Only Father Christopher knew about it, but he recently shared it with me because I started to put two and two together. I realised you were the baby I found as a child, and went to him asking for information to try and confirm my suspicions. That's when Father Christopher presented me with the letter to read. The gist of the letter was that you were in danger, and had been abandoned for your own protection. Then I had an encounter with an individual that appeared to know all about you being abandoned. He basically told me that I needed to keep you protected." Danny gently tells me, keeping his voice low, like he doesn't want to scare me away and the whole time keeping eye contact with me.

Then he takes a deep breath and continues, " That same individual paid me another visit today, and he gave me a letter to deliver to you. It's from your mother, I've no idea what the contents of the letter say." Danny pulls an envelope out of his jacket pocket and places it on the coffee table next to him.

"I don't even know how to react to that Danny." And I stare at the letter on the table, wanting to know the contents, but terrified at the same time.

"Would you rather I give you some privacy to read the letter in private?" Danny answers, with no pressure in his voice.

"No, please stay. Could you read it out loud for me? I don't think I can read it myself at the moment." I blurt out, feeling my anxiety levels rising, and praying I don't have a panic attack. But isn't this exactly what I wanted? To know who I am, and where I come from? Find out the truth? So I nod towards the letter, indicating that I want him to read it.

"Okay Maddie, the front of the envelope reads, to my daughter." Danny carefully opens the envelope and unfolds the letter inside. He looks at me again, waiting a few seconds, and then starts to read the letter out to me.

Dearest daughter,

I never gave you a name and for that I am sorry. When I met your father I was on my first assignment, I was only supposed to influence him, but I fell in love with him instead. I became with child, and that was forbidden for my kind with a human. As a future dreamer, we see things before they happen, and this powerful tool can be abused by others. Your father is part of a very powerful family, which is why I could never tell him about you.   After your birth, I had you placed in his realm because it was easier to hide you in plain sight. I know you must be getting the dreams now slowly. Once you reach your eighteenth year they will fully manifest. You need to learn to read them, and act on them where necessary.

This is your gift, and also your curse. Don't go looking for me or your father, it will only place you in further danger.

The human boy that found you, trust him. He will help to protect you.

Know that I wanted to keep you, and I love you with all my heart.

Your loving Mother

Tears, that I had no idea had fallen, are now flowing openly down my face, and I start to hyperventilate. I feel like I'm starting to lose control, and my entire world has turned upside down, this is what I wanted, to find out the truth. But never in a million years did I anticipate an outcome like this, I'm in danger and need protection? Danny puts down the letter, and gently takes hold of both of my hands, he looks into my eyes, blurred by my tears. Almost immediately, my anxiety starts to subside, and my breathing slows down. I've started to calm down through such a simple gesture from Danny, and whether I want to admit it or continue trying to lie to myself, this is the effect he has on me.

"Danny, I can't get my head around this, I have so many questions right now. My mother talks like she isn't even from this planet, and that's just crazy. Do you think that she's mentally unstable or something? It just sounds so far-fetched." I ask Danny, gripping his hands tightly, not wanting to let go.

"After what I witnessed at Saint Peter's Church, I know it isn't far-fetched at all Maddie. Even though my brain keeps trying to tell me I imagined things, I know what I saw is true. You're going to have to trust me on that." Danny replies looking stressed, and I can tell, even now, he's still holding something back from me.

"What did you see at the church Danny? I need to know so I can begin to understand all of this, and trust you Danny." I'm pleading with him now, because I need to know more answers.

I want to be able to trust him again.

"The individual that gave me the letter, I believe to be an Angel. That's my only explanation Maddie. He goes by the name Uriel, the first time I saw him in the church he had wings. When I saw him today in public they weren't visible. I asked him about it, and he told me he was hiding them." Danny sighs, knowing how crazy this all sounds to me.

Wiping at my eyes with my sleeve, I pick up the letter from the table. I need to slowly read through the letter myself. Perhaps now I can begin to process the contents better. After reading it for the third time, I look up at Danny and say, "I need to speak to this Uriel about locating my mother."

Chapter Forty-Three

Dorothy

My nerves are on edge after my unexpected visitor earlier on today. I'd long blocked him out of my heart and my mind. My first and only real love... But you're not supposed to fall in love with Angels. It's a double no no, if you're a hot blooded male. On top of that, defining myself as a woman, but only using that pronoun while in drag, which is now most of the time, making it a complicated mess.

Uriel hadn't changed, hadn't aged a day, and here I am twenty years on, okay, I still look good, but not Uriel good. He's only here to keep an eye on Maddie, I knew there was something special about that girl. I just wish he'd come back for me, how I've thought and missed him over the years. I loved him with all of my heart, so, so, much. If I'm being honest with myself, I never really stopped.

Running a successful business is extremely hard work that never ends, which is why I'm doing paperwork at past eleven at night on a Sunday. Feeling a light shiver down my spine I know someone is watching me, and I feel Uriel close by before I see him.

"You go twenty years without so much as a goodbye, and then I see you twice in one day." I look up from my desk, and sure enough Uriel is standing there in all his glory, wings and all this time.

"I wanted to stay longer earlier, but the risk was too great, with

Maddie so close. She can't start asking me questions, it will only place her in further danger." Uriel walks further into the room.

"Say what you need to and go Uriel. I've already lost you once, and I can't go through that all over again. It nearly broke me the first time." I answer him, hugging my stomach, in an act of self-comfort, while tapping my foot on the ground nervously.

"I never wanted to leave you Dorothy. But I was forced to go back, and imprisoned as punishment. That's why I'm acting as a messenger now, call it an act of rebellion for what they made me lose. I didn't want to lose you Dorothy." Uriel says passionately and walks towards me.

"Stop Uriel. Stop right there. I can't do this right now. Twenty years is a long time, a lifetime. I can't drag all those feelings up and go through it all over again." I answer putting my hands up to stop him stepping further towards my personal space.

"Dorothy, I never wanted to hurt you. I will leave for now, for I fear other matters have become more pressing. I will return though, for you, my Dorothy. I've waited a long time." Uriel replies as he slowly begins to fade away from my reach.

Taking a deep breath, I find myself crumbling in a heap on the floor my legs given way. A sense of relief coursing through my whole body now. He didn't want to leave me, but I can't risk opening up my heart to him again. "Please don't come back, my love." I reply to myself, in a loud whisper. But not really meaning the words I say. In my heart, I'd take him back in a second if I believed he could stay this time...

Chapter Forty-Four

Bryan

Danny dropped me off at college, and I feel like he's babysitting me like he did when I was younger. He's given me instructions to follow if my dad turns up and tries to speak to me, but I'm doubtful that's going to happen. My face still looks a mess so I already know people are going to be looking at me and asking awkward questions. Questions that I don't have the answers too at the moment, and why should I have to answer? What happens in my personal life is not anybody's business but my own. Let them all gossip about me, so long as they leave Ben alone. The last thing I want is to bring trouble to his doorstep.

Ben instructed me to wait out front for him, he doesn't want me walking into college alone. I smile to myself at the thought of a big over protective boyfriend, ready to help fight my battles. Sitting on the wall outside the canteen, I start scrolling through Instagram to kill some time. Lots of mindless selfies from various "friends" posted over the weekend, and nothing of actual interest or significance to me. It's all false, filters and posed photos, depicting their fabulous lives, but none of it is real. Can't people see that?

I've had some time to think about my current situation, and I've come to some conclusions since the fight with my dad on Saturday night. He's actually done me a huge favour throwing me out, because now I don't have to live under his constant shadow. On tender hooks, constantly in fear of saying or doing the wrong thing in front of him. Never knowing which version of my dad I was going to get, if he'd been drinking heavily or not. Now I don't have to go to university, that was all coming from my parents, constantly trying to push my life in that direction. I'm free to pursue other options now and they can't do a damn thing to stop me. Danny always told me when I was younger, that with my cocky attitude and charisma that I'd go far in the business world. So I'm going to call him out on it, persuade him to take a gamble on me. I'm going to ask him straight out for an apprenticeship, and teach me everything he knows. That's my big plan, and I'm going with it. Whether it's a pipe dream or not, I have to at least discuss it with Danny, I know that my powers of persuasion will work on him.

"Oh my god. Looks like someone beat the shit out of you. Are you okay?" Chelsea asks, although her concern instinctively feels forced and completely fake. This is her deceitful way of digging for information, but luckily for me, I can see straight through it. I refuse to become fodder for the latest gossip in her vapid circle she calls "friends".

"Everything is rosy, nothing to see here, move along, Chelsea." I reply not wanting to deal with her shit right now, why can't the girl leave me alone. It's not like I've been encouraging her to speak to me.

"Rude. I was only asking. You probably deserved it anyway with that kind of attitude." Chelsea huffs and walks off, with that annoying sway to her hips. She thinks it makes her god's gift to the male species. Wrong, so wrong. There is nothing remotely attractive about desperation, which Chelsea has in spades. I can't help smirking to myself knowing that I've put her nose out of joint, and wonder what kind of rumours she's going to make up about my current appearance.

"Hey hot stuff." I turn and jump down from the wall when I see Ben approaching me, now he is a sight for sore eyes.

"Hardly, with this face, but I'll take it." I grin stupidly at him, happy that he's here with me. Ben grabs hold of my hand, and my heart starts pounding in anticipation. He gently kisses me, avoiding my broken nose, it's a massive gesture to have made outside college together. No doubt any number of fellow students have witnessed our little display.

"You sure you still want to do this? There's no pressure, I'm easy either way." Ben looks at me with concern, like I'm having sudden second thoughts, and will change my mind about us.

"I need to do this Ben, and can do it with you at my side. The cat's out of the bag now anyway with my parents, so I don't have any reason to hide it anymore. But only if you want too, I don't want to put any pressure on you Ben. Your parents don't even know yet. Shit, now I feel like I'm putting undue pressure on you." I look up into Ben's eyes, so confused suddenly. Doubting myself, and trying to detect any doubt in Ben.

"I'll let you into a little secret Bryan. My parents know, and are cool about it all. I didn't want to say anything before because I didn't want to come off as being insensitive to your situation with your dad. I won't lie though Bryan. I'm as nervous as you, coming out to everyone behind those doors in college, but I don't want to live a lie anymore. I want people to know how I feel about you, how I feel about us being together at last." Ben eyes uncharacteristically glisten, and he squeezes my hand in support.

Stronger together as a united team, we walk hand in hand into the canteen to have coffee before lessons start. Something we are doing together as a couple for the first time. Within seconds I can hear whispers throughout the canteen.

"Ignore it." Ben says, squeezing my hand in support again, and I can feel all the eyes just staring at us like we are some kind of exotic animals rarely seen out in the wild. Are gays really that rare in Eastleigh-On-Sea? Or are people genuinely curious?

We grab our coffees and sit down at a random table, and

attempt to make small talk, knowing everyone around is judging us at the moment. A couple of the guys on Bens rugby team blank him as they walk past the table, guys he's normally chummy with, and a wave of nausea unsettles my stomach.

"And so it starts." I sigh out loud to Ben, this is already causing problems for him.

"Don't worry that pretty little head of yours, I'll deal with them when I need too." Ben replies, squeezing my hand tightly again, he hasn't barely let it go since we entered college.

"You think I'm pretty, even all beat up?" I grin, fluttering my eyes back at him playfully.

"Of course I do." Ben leans over the table to kiss me, clearly making a statement to the gossiping onlookers, and I think I've died and gone to heaven. The hottest guy in college just kissed me in the canteen...

"I knew it. I fucking knew it." Chelsea shouts from the other side of the canteen, and I can't help but laugh at her annoying outburst, when we are making such an important statement. Trust Chelsea to try and ruin the moment.

"Well you have my full support guys." A quiet voice says, Ashley is standing next to our table. She looks pale and like she's lost weight she didn't need to lose.

"Thanks Ashley, we appreciate that. How's your mum doing?" I ask her, it's the first time that I've seen her in college since the accident. She sits down at the table, and places her coffee cup down.

"They took her off the ventilator a couple of days ago, and she's breathing by herself. But she still hasn't woken up yet. Dad doesn't want me to miss anymore college, and it's awful sitting there watching her breathe all the time, wondering if she'll ever wake up." Ashley looks away, and takes a sip of her coffee.

"Well we're here for you, and we mean that." Ben replies, and I smile at him because he referred to us as "we" making us sound like a real bonified couple.

"Thanks guys, that's kind. I was hoping to catch Maddie before class to thank her. The night of the accident she was there for me in the hospital when no one else was. And she left me the kindest note too at the nurses station. I haven't had a chance to catch her in person yet." Ashley answers, getting up as the bell rings signalling class.

"I'll let her know you were looking for her Ashley." I answer, as we all start walking together out of the canteen, finally going our separate ways to our different classes.

Reaching into my locker, and already running late, I become aware of someone standing behind me.

"Mr Johnson, I was hoping to catch you before class." I turn around to see Principal Parker.

"Principal Parker, is everything okay? I've handed all my assignments in on time as far as I'm aware, I was only late that one time." I ask him worriedly, it's never good to be on the principals radar, at least if I get in trouble now, I can ask Danny to deal with it. Instead of my dad and the relentless lectures I'd receive from him.

"Students always jump to worst case scenario's whenever I speak to them in the corridor. I wanted to check that you were okay? I couldn't help but observe what happened in the canteen, and notice your injured face. Care to tell me about it?" Principal Parker replies, and I'm not entirely sure how to answer him straight away. It takes me almost thirty seconds to come up with a semi reasonable answer.

"Someone took exception to my sexuality." I can't get my dad in trouble, mum would never forgive me, and I don't want him to get in trouble with the police.

"Look Bryan, as college principal I'm responsible for the care and for the welfare of all my students while at college on these grounds, and if another student was involved…" I cut Principal

Parker off quickly, I can't let him think that it was another student that did this to me.

"It wasn't another student, I got mugged on Saturday." I quickly lie out of my teeth, protecting my dad again.

"Did you report it to the police?" He asks me, and I'm sure he can smell the lie that I just deposited out of my mouth.

"Of course sir. I must get to class, I'm already late." Against my better judgement I start to walk off.

"Not so fast Mr Johnson. I won't put up with any kind of homophobia in my college, and I want you to report it to the college straight away if you get any further problems. That little display in the canteen was very brave of you and Mr Chambers. I can still remember the not so good days in the nineteen eighties, I'm not saying it's perfect now. But things have vastly improved, take my word for it from someone that knows. Come on, I'll walk you to class so you don't get marked down as late." And Principal Parker proceeds to escort me to class.

Chapter Forty-Five

Maddie

L unchtime can't arrive fast enough today, and I walk out of class chatting with Ben about revising for a mock exam we have coming up. Trying to work out some revision time together, where we can quiz each other. We are in the middle of making arrangements when Bryan catches up to us, and grabs Ben around the waist from behind and kisses him on the cheek, in a show of playful affection. A pang of wanting rushes through my head, of Danny doing to me what Bryan did to Ben. That's never going to happen…

"Thank fuck it's lunchtime, I'm starving. Canteen or chip shop?" Bryan asks looking between me and Ben.

"Canteen." Ben and I reply at the same time laughing, Bryan eats such a unhealthy diet, but he has one of those magic metabolisms, and never appears to put on any excess weight. Unlike me, I have to watch every morsel now. I put on a ton of weight when I moved in with Sam, although she said I was malnourished.

"I've got a salad with me. And you should try and eat some healthy food for a change." I reply, not trying to body shame him, but encourage healthier options.

"Yes, too many carbs for me. I need to keep this athletic body for rugby." Ben agrees, and flexes his muscles for purely Bryans benefit, which makes me giggle. Especially when a group of girls walk past swooning at him.

"Guess you guys win, but I'm still getting chips in the canteen, the blonde always gives me extra chips in my portion." Bryan replies all matter of fact, and we laugh out loud boisterously together.

Finding an empty table in the canteen, I start taking my lunch out of my backpack. Bryan and Ben are in the queue for food, and I smile when I see Ben put his arm around Bryan. They make such a cute couple, and my heart starts to ache for Danny again.

After I was tricked into talking to him yesterday we are at least on speaking terms again, and I unblocked him from my phone even though I have had any need to call or message him. The revelation about this Uriel character is hard to take in, and it's not that I disbelieve him or anything. I'm sure he believes that he saw an angel, but he's been under an immense amount of pressure with his dads accident, and I know he hasn't been sleeping.

But that still doesn't explain the letters appearance, and if it was delivered by this Uriel character I need to find him to get to the truth. Until then, I remain on the fence about things. My mind starts to wander, and I'm made to jump when Bryan drops his lunch tray on the table.

"Chips, really Bryan?" I say as I steal one, and dip it in my salad dressing before putting it in my mouth and chewing slowly.

"Hey, hands off my carbs salad queen." Bryan laughs, pinching a cherry tomato from my salad.

"Now, now, no fighting at the lunch table, or I'll be forced to punish you Bryan." Ben winks at him suggestively. I laugh and almost choke on a piece of carrot at the same time.

"No sexual innuendos at the lunch table or I might vomit up my salad guys." I laugh, still coughing slightly so I take a swig of water from my bottle.

"So I've been thinking. Maddie and I both have birthdays

coming up in the next few weeks and we both turn eighteen, we could do some kind of joint thing together?" Bryan grins at me enthusiastically, oh no. I don't do birthday celebrations.

"I wasn't planning on doing anything special Bryan, birthdays have never really been a big thing for me, especially when I don't have an exact birth date, just an estimated one the hospital gave me. I was going to let it pass by, like all the others." I say sadly, because it's the absolute truth. Growing up in foster care, birthdays got overlooked. Although I always tried to make the twins birthday special.

"Then we definitely need to plan something, we only turn eighteen once. I'm thinking we could ask Dorothy if we could do something at the bar? I can't think of a better place to celebrate." Bryan adds looking at me hopefully, hoping that I'll change my mind and get on board.

"That isn't a bad shout, Dorothy's would be fun. We could do it on one of the quieter nights and see if she'll let us do karaoke too. She might even agree to put on a buffet for us at cost price if we ask her nicely. I'm sure the chef wouldn't mind if we paid him in drinks for the night." Ben replies, quickly getting right on board with Bryans plan.

"Slow your boats guys, I'm not sure about this. Sounds like a lot of fuss over nothing to me." I reply seeing how this could escalate quickly, especially knowing how excitable Bryan is.

"All I'm asking is for you to think about it Maddie. I'm celebrating my birthday anyway, and I want to do it with my best friend too. So no pressure, but you're not getting out of this, so don't even try." Ben answers in an, " I'm not taking no for an answer," but in a light hearted way. It looks like we're planning a birthday party together. If you can't beat them, join them I guess...

Chapter Forty-Six

Sam

Things are finally starting to settle down into some kind of a manic routine. Having a bigger family to look after is a whole new experience for me, and completely different from looking after one child. What with my hospital shifts, the boys football and Maddie's new job, it seems to be working itself out into a complicated jumbled up pattern.

We've been living in the cottage for several weeks now, and I don't think that I've totally won the boys over yet. Tommy appears to have reverted back to his old self according to Maddie, but it's plain to see it's just a mask he puts on to make everyone around him feel comfortable. It's like he's in denial about what happened with his previous foster parent Mrs Thompson, and he refuses point blank to go to any counselling sessions I've organised for him. Even Maddie couldn't convince him to go, and I don't want to push him too hard. But I know at some point it's all going to come tumbling out of him, and I need to be there to catch him when he falls.

In the meantime all I can do is carry on as normal as possible with the boys, encouraging them to do their homework and chores, and trying to engage with them. I've been going to watch their football matches, ferrying them around various schools to play their games, and we've been ten pin bowling a few times. Jack wants me to take him swimming, so I'm going to have to suck it up and buy a new swimming costume, because the last one I owned was in the late nineteen nineties.

I never expected to have an instantaneous relationship with them, and having Maddie living with me already has been an immense help. Things are certainly heading in the right direction, thank goodness, I just need to continue to keep a particularly close eye on Tommy.

Maddie has been organising a birthday bash with Bryan at Dorothy's, the bar she works at with her friends, and she's constantly singing around the cottage practicing. It's something she never used to do before at the old house, apart from in the shower if she thought I wasn't around. Her confidence has grown in waves, but she still won't change her mind about going to university, she won't even apply to keep her options open. Maddie insists that she needs to be around for Jack and Tommy, and has this mindset about working to help to contribute moneywise. Now she's talking about picking up a second job once she leaves college to help support the boys. She's determined to help give them a better life. It's such a responsibility for a young woman her age, but once Maddie makes her mind up about something it's difficult to change her mind, and she loves those boys fiercely. The things that Maddie has experienced and witnessed while in the care system, has had such a profound impact on her, and her way of thinking. Her loyalty to Jack and Tommy is unprecedented.

That's why it's difficult to break down the invisible barriers Maddie has erected around her for protection, even though she is safe with me. I feel like I'm treading a close line with her sometimes, and I gently had to remind her the other day that ultimately I'm the boys legal guardian. Maddie didn't take offence, but I'm sure it must have felt strange for her after feeling responsible for the boys welfare for so long. I've noticed that she's backed off slightly from trying to be a mother figure to Jack and Tommy, and taken on a big sister role instead, which is much more healthy for a girl her age.

Maddie has stopped volunteering at Jack and Tommy's football practice, using her job as an primary excuse. She still attends the occasional game to support them both, but it feels like she's keeping her distance for another reason. I'm pretty certain there's more to the story than Maddie's actually giving away, and I've noticed that she doesn't spend any free time with Danny now. Perhaps they had a falling out that I'm unaware of? I know Maddie still goes over to his house sometimes, but that's always to see Bryan, who's now living with him.

That poor boy, being thrown out of his own home like that, his father should be ashamed. Bryan never went to the police and hasn't reported what happened, and ultimately that's his decision. Thank goodness Danny stepped in to look after him, and invite him into his home, as I understand Danny is a close family friend. It just breaks my heart when I think about it all, I could never turn my back on my own child like that.

Why is society so cruel to its young people?

Anyway I must stop procrastinating, my twenty minute break is over and I need to get back to work. I've got several patient discharges to sort out, medications to chase up from pharmacy, and my rounds to finish.

Thomas McKenzie is finally going home today, and although I'm happy that he's going home, I'm going to miss seeing him every shift. He's got a wicked sense of humour that matches my equally dark sense of humour most seasoned nurses seem to possess. And he constantly flirts with me, he's a very attractive man, a little older than me, but what's an age at this stage in my life? Obviously I haven't encouraged it with him being my patient, but I've found it very flattering all the same. He loves my macaroni cheese, and asks me every shift if I'll be bringing anymore and it's become a standing joke between us.

"Good morning, Thomas, big day for you, finally escaping from the circus. Are you looking forward to be going home? You must be itching to get out of here?" I laugh cheerfully, but also feeling a pang of sadness he's leaving.

"Can't wait Samantha, to get back into my own bed. No

more hospital food, Wi-Fi that works and sports channels to watch, and maybe the odd beer." Thomas grins back cheekily, winking. Yes. Definitely flirting with me.

"I can see written here in your notes that your continuing with a private physiotherapist at home that your son organised for you. That's certainly going to help get you back on your feet faster. Are you coping with the pain better?" I ask him, hoping for once Thomas will give me a honest answer, he hates taking any kind of pain relief, unless he gets desperately uncomfortable. Typical stubborn man, trying to put a brave face on for others benefit.

"Yes the pains manageable now, and I'm extremely fortunate. Danny insisted on the private physio, and we've got a gym nearby that I can use whenever I want, it's one of those twenty-four hour places. But I'm going to miss looking at your gorgeous face Samantha." Thomas chuckles cheekily, and I can feel the obvious magnetism that radiates from him. He's such a charmer, how on earth can he still be single?

"Thomas, behave." I smile back not really meaning it, and scribble some observations down on his chart, that I've just taken.

"Have dinner with me. I want to see you again Samantha. Out of this prison, just you and me together." Thomas asks me with sincerity, and I'm almost lost for words, he's asking me out on a date.

"I don't know what to say to that Thomas." I reply, giving him the best answer I can come up with on the spur of the moment.

"Say yes, it's not a trick question, you can't deny the almost walking wounded." Thomas replies, awaiting my answer on baited breath.

"Yes." I squeak out all high pitched like a teenage schoolgirl, which is totally unlike me, and I can feel my cheeks blushing bright red. Oh my goodness, I've just agreed to a date with a patient. Think. I need to think. Talk myself down.

"Fantastic, once I'm back on my feet, it's a date Samantha." There goes Thomas again with the cheeky wink, and I can see Danny picked up his charm from his father. Goodness. What is Maddie going to say when she finds out? It looks like I've finally entered the dating game again, oh my....

Chapter Forty-Seven

Danny

It's a big day today. My dad's finally coming home from the hospital, at one point, that first night of the accident, I wasn't sure that it would ever happen. But this is my dad we're talking about, he's strong and determined, and won't give up without a fight. He thought for his life in the ITU and operating theatre, dad will always have my respect for never giving up. I'm on my way to the hospital to pick him up. Going through my head is a mental list of the things I've put in place for him. Just so it makes his life more comfortable and easier, while he's on the mend and still receiving daily physio. It will be great to have him home again, and I'm happy I've got Bryan around to help my dad out too. It will help to keep Bryan out of trouble having dad's influence around.

Things have certainly changed for me in the last few weeks, since Bryan moved in. But I have to admit that it hasn't been as bad living with him as I thought it would be, apart from the fact he can't really cook. His idea of cooking is ordering from Mario's, cheese on toast, beans on toast, or oven chips. Hence, I'm in charge of cooking and he's in charge of loading and emptying the dishwasher. Which is working for us both, and we've fallen into a routine. Luckily we don't have to do any real cleaning, I have a lady that pops in twice a week to keep on top of that, which Bryan incidentally loves. He's vowed now to have his own cleaning lady one day, which I still find funny. I dare not tell him that I also employ a gardener, and a window cleaner, it might excite Bryan too much. Talk about strange life goals for a seventeen year old.

Bryan's tried to pay rent money to me from his part time job at Dorothy's, and I point blank refuse to accept it, stating that he's family. But I've noticed various groceries appear in the fridge and cupboard that I definitely didn't buy, so it's obviously his way of contributing. So I haven't said anything, I don't want him feeling completely powerless. He's got a kind heart, and wouldn't hurt a fly.

Bryan still hasn't spoken to his dad, but he did mention that he's been texting his mum, and they avoid the subject of his dad.

The only time I get to see Maddie now is if she turns up to watch one of Jack and Tommy's football games. Occasionally she comes by the house to hang out with Bryan, but they always go up to his room. I don't get much more than a hello and goodbye from her these days, and I miss her company. Ever since our falling out things haven't been the same, but at least she's not ignoring me now. I just wish she'd try to talk to me. I've tried giving her space, I've even texted her several times. Maddie gave me one word answers, which made it clear to me she wasn't interested in talking yet. I'm at a loss as what to do now, and I don't want to push her too far and risk losing her again. So I'm effectively stuck in purgatory with her.

On the upside, I managed to assist Sam with getting the ball rolling with the solicitor. Getting full guardianship of the boys isn't difficult for her given the circumstances, and their social worker is fully supporting the move. It's just a timely process, but the solicitor I'm paying for should speed up the process, and give Jack, Tommy, Maddie and Sam peace of mind.

With all this going on, I miss my sweet Maddie, my Angel...

"Hi dad, I've come to break you out of here." I announce , as I walk into dad's hospital room a few minutes later, he must be sick of looking at the same four walls, day in and day out.

"Danny, I'm all packed and ready to escape home, just waiting on my medication and to be released by the chief jailer." Dad laughs, he looks worn out from physio, but he appears to be in good spirits.

"You're not really getting out of prison dad, it's a hospital." I laugh back reminding him where he is.

There's a knock on the open door, and David Johnson is standing there. I know he's tried to visit a few times since he threw Bryan out that night, but dads refused to see him, having the nurses send him away, he must of snuck in. So much for security, I'll be sending a strongly worded email to someone higher up to complain. Shit. Now I sound like my dad, I'm not ready to turn into a grumpy old man quite yet.

"What the hell are you doing here David? No one wants to see you, you're not welcome here." I ask, absolutely fuming, my temper rising, and in a raised voice, the audacity of this man, showing up here at the hospital. Unwanted. Unannounced.

"Please, Thomas. I need to speak to you. Danny this is none of your business, stay out of it." David answers me, going slightly red in the face. The vein in his neck pulsing, looking like it might pop open with the tension vibrating from him.

"Like fuck it isn't my business David. Like the night I had to patch up your own son. After you broke his nose and he refused to go to the hospital, to protect you. The fact he's been living with me since it happened, and you haven't even tried to speak to him in a calm and civil manner. So it's my business David." I rant at him, doing my best not to lose it in front of my dad, in the hospital. This is not the right time or place to be having this type of conversation, and I look towards my dad with concern.

"Say your piece David, I'll listen to you. But I won't guarantee you're going to like my response, even though we've been friends all these years." My dad replies fiercely, sitting up in the chair straight with his arms now crossed over, and a fierce look on his face. I know the look well, it means that he won't take any kind of crap.

"Listen. This isn't easy for me being here. My own wife is hardly speaking to me, and the church congregation is treating us like we're leppers. Even Father Christopher won't look me in the eye." David says, looking like a broken man. A better person would feel sorry for him, but I'm not that better person.

"I'm sorry to hear that. But actions speak louder than words David. You broke your sons nose and threw him out like a piece of rubbish." My dad replies, staring at his best friend like he doesn't even know him.

"He's a faggot. Tell me, what else was I supposed to do? I've been a devout catholic all my life, it's wrong and it goes against everything I believe in." David answers angrily, pointing his finger at my dad in a way that I don't like. David better have the decency not to start a fist fight here, because I know who will come out on top. Spoiler alert. It won't be him.

"If you can't keep a civil tongue David get out now, I won't stand for offensive terms like that, it's not the nineteen seventies anymore." I answer before my dad gets a chance, getting right in David's face as I'm saying it. I'm not scared of him, I'm half his age and in fantastic shape, I also tower over him now.

"Both of you calm down, please. Before you both get thrown out." Dad instructs us, raising his voice slightly above his normal tone. How dad can remain so calm, I'll never know.

"Sorry. Gay. My son says he's gay and has a boyfriend. Who knows what filth their getting up to under your roof Thomas. It seems your own son has lost his mind too." David answers less aggressively this time, but choosing a full on sarcastic tone instead.

"David, I understand that what you are coming to terms with concerning Bryans sexuality is difficult for you, but he's still your son. What you did to him, it's not how we treat our own flesh and blood. You don't have to agree with his choices, but he's almost eighteen, nearly legally an adult. Do you want to lose him all together? Never see or speak to him? Because if you carry on acting like this that's what's going to happen. And for the record, leave Danny out of it, or there will be a problem David." My dad replies, offering his words of wisdom, and a veiled threat to his best friend.

"Why though? What did I do wrong as a father? How could he turn out like this, I don't understand." He looks at my dad with tears in his eyes, David genuinely doesn't get it at all.

"Listen to yourself David, it's all me, me, me. If you're asking me he's better off without you." I shout angrily in David's face, thinking about how broken Bryan was that night.

"Danny, that isn't helping son." Dad chastises me, but only half-heartedly because I can sense that he agrees.

"Sorry dad, but I won't apologise for my behaviour, you didn't see Bryan that night. Or how his been since." I quickly reply, taking a step back from David before I punch him myself.

"Is he okay?" David asks, the anger and sarcasm suddenly leaving is voice, but not convincing me.

"So now you suddenly care again, make your fucking mind up David." I shout loudly, finally losing my temper and throwing my arm back in the air in frustration, ready to take that first punch at David.

"What on earth is going on in here? Do I need to call security?" Sam asks, storming into the room with her hands on her hips, looking less than amused, and equally scary. She's not going to stand for any fighting going down in a hospital room.

"I think it's best you go David." Dad calmly instructs him, pointing to the door defiantly.

"Okay. I'm leaving. I didn't mean to cause any kind of trouble here. Sorry. I'm sorry." David leaves with his head down, the fight in him gone.

"Who was that?" Sam asks, looking between me and my dad.

"That was my best friend since we were kids, and Bryans dad." My dad answers Sam, shaking his head. This was the last thing my dad needed to deal with today.

"Oh." Is all she says, looks at us both again, and reading the room she discreetly disappears.

"Awkward." I reply, looking at my dad, not wanting to make eye contact with him.

"Promise me something Danny. Promise me no matter what, we'll always talk. I never want to end up in a situation with you when we're not even talking. Please son?" Dad sadly looks towards me, the weight of the world on his shoulders in that fleeting moment.

"I'd never stop talking to you dad. You've always been there for me. I'm sorry I reacted towards him that way, but you never saw the aftermath of what happened to Bryan. I know David's your best friend. He's been like an uncle to me all my life, and now I feel like I don't know him at all. Betrayed. Angry. But I have this overwhelming urge to protect Bryan. You would have done the same thing dad." I answer him feeling deflated, and like I've gone three rounds with Tyson Fury.

"Your right son. I would have stood up for Bryan that night, had I been there, even if it was at odds with my best friend. I don't agree one little bit with how David handled things. Why do you think I refused to see him the last three times he's come to visit? I didn't want to lose my temper with him myself." Dad answers, being completely open and honest with me about the situation.

"I can't speak for Bryan, but I don't think he'd want to go home now, even if his dad wanted him too. And his mums been so weak, she hasn't called him. Just texted him. How can they treat him like that? Their only son?" I ask my dad, knowing he won't have the answer, but still asking anyway.

"David's father, was not a good man. He used to beat him up, and he would poison his mind with negativity and hateful things. Even as a kid, I would call him out on his behaviour and we had many fights, back in the day. But we always managed to remain friends, and when his dad died most of that behaviour disappeared. Obviously, some of it got left behind." Dad sighs, and he looks like he's thinking about the past.

"Sounds like your trying to make excuses for him." I reply sadly, because there is no excuse for how David acted towards his son that night.

"Not at all Danny, not at all. I'm just giving you the facts that's all." Dad replies with no malice in his voice.

"Okay dad. I'm going to go and find Sam to apologise, and see about breaking you out of this joint." I reply to him grinning, changing the subject, itching to get home now.

"Sounds like a plan. My own bed awaits me and a home cooked meal." I hear my dad laugh as I go off into the corridor in search of Sam.

Chapter Forty-Eight

Maddie

So far my search for this Uriel character hasn't turned up anything, I haven't got a single lead, nothing, zilch. Danny doesn't know how to get in contact with him again, and in desperation I even went back to St Peters Church by myself to ask around the parishioners, and see if anyone knew or heard of him. I sat alone in the church for hours, watching people come and go, and appreciated the serenity. But it was pointless, nobody knew a thing, and I'm no closer to finding out any more information about my mother. All I have is this mysterious letter supposedly delivered by an Angel named Uriel.

Then there's the question of Danny. I desperately miss him and my heart feels like it's in pain being away from him. Since I stupidly quit volunteering for Jack and Tommy's football team in a moment of madness, I've hardly seen him. It's my fault, and I know I'm to blame. My overreaction to an situation that I didn't have all the facts for, and never really giving him any chance to explain himself. The damage to our friendship having been done, and the secrets now out in the open. Even when I venture over to his house to see Bryan, Danny either disappears out running or goes up to his room to work. Our crossing of paths usually consists of hello's and goodbye's, so I haven't seen him to have a decent conversation since he admitted to keeping secrets from me. After we first had our falling out, and after he'd given me the letter, he did try texting me. But my mind wasn't in the right place at the time to answer him back in more than one word answers, so I doubt he would be susceptible to one of my texts now after waiting so long.

Grabbing my phone off my bedside table anyway, I lay down on my bed. I've got nothing to lose at this point, and I decide to start with something simple, and I type out the four word message and hit send. Holding my breath, and silently praying to a god that I don't know even exists.

I miss you Danny

Closing my eyes and feeling emotional, a few tears slide down the side of my face. He's not going to answer, I've been too much of a bitch to him and left it far too long. Danny must hate me by now, and who would blame him? Acting like an immature teenager he no doubt sees me as, Danny doesn't want to be my friend anymore. All kinds of negative thoughts continue to flow through my mind, and the tears come more fiercely. The pain inside I feel is real, and I'm almost too distracted by my own pitiful sorrow when my phone pings.

I've missed you Maddie, can I call you?

Shit, he actually answered me, and the balls in my court, but what do I do? Almost like I'm on automatic pilot I type out a reply and press send.

Yes

Almost immediately, within seconds my phone starts to ring in my hand and damn, he's video calling me. I hastily wipe my eyes on a tissue, failing dismally at hiding my tears, and I answer the video call.

"Maddie, what's wrong sweetheart?" And my tears turn into gentle sobs, with absolute relief that Danny's still talking to me. I can't seem to get control of them, and they're not stopping now that I can actually see him on the tiny screen of my phone.

"I, I, missed you Danny." I struggle to get out my words to him, full of regret and emotions, there is so much I want to say to him, so much to try and explain. I don't even know where to start to begin.

"Oh Maddie. Please don't cry. Don't cry. It's okay, we're okay. We just hit a bump in the road that's all." Danny replies, but I still can't get my words out, my emotions have taken over. Everything I've been holding tightly inside is all tumbling out at once now, and there's no way I can stop now.

"That's it, I'm hanging up and coming over, okay?" Danny answers, and I nod back to him, choking on my tears, as he hangs up. Does this mean things are going to be okay between us now?

Fifteen minutes later I hear the loudest knock on the front door and Sam's voice say, "She's in her room, just go straight up Danny."

His head pokes up from the loft ladder and he looks alarmed at the state I must be in, surrounded by wet tissues and red puffy eyes from crying so hard. I'm surprised I didn't vomit I've been crying that hard, or go into a massive panic attack, but I think it's because I knew my knight in shining armour was on his way to rescue me...

"Come here Angel." Danny says gently and I feel his arms wrap around me in an consuming hug. The relief that I feel with him holding me in his arms is instantaneous.

"I've been lost without you Danny." I whisper to him. He gently kisses me on the head and strokes my hair tenderly with affection, my heart feeling like it's slowly knitting back together from just having this small contact with him.

"And I've been lost without you too, but I needed to give you some space Maddie so that you could work through things in your head, and understand why I kept certain things from you." Danny pulls back from me slightly and looks into my eyes, tucking the ever present stray curl behind my ear. "But I'll always wait for you Maddie, I'm not going anywhere. Where ever you choose to go, I will always be waiting for you."

"I'm sorry, I over reacted over everything. I can't lose you Danny. I should have listened to you, and given you a chance to explain to me. I'm so stupid, so stupid." And fresh tears start to cascade down my face, and wetting his shirt. But Danny doesn't appear to notice that, his eyes are only for me. I can feel it down to my bones...

"You'll never lose me Maddie, I can't explain it but our souls are intertwined with each other, nothing can break us apart now we've finally found each other." Danny holds me closer if that's even possible, rocking me in his arms gently, whispering reassurances in my ear, until the tears stop falling.

Having no idea how long he's held me like that in his arms for, it could have been five minutes or five hours, for all I know. But Danny's remained gently rocking me, while stroking my hair, and I feel like I could stay like this forever, and I'm almost afraid to let go in case it's just a dream . When I finally stop sniffling into his now soaked shirt, he pulls back and looks into my eyes. Tucking that stray curl again behind my ear, the way he always does. I must look an absolute mess right now, with my dishevelled hair and puffy red eyes, hardly an attractive look.

"You've got no idea how beautiful you are, inside and out Maddie." Danny says, and I can feel him looking at my lips, his eyes lingering. I wish he'd just kiss me, and I'm pleading inside my head for him to do it. But instead he turns away, and the moment is lost, I must of misread the situation. Probably for the best anyway, he can do so much better than me, a broken mess with too many issues to list, and problems.

"Sorry Danny, I didn't mean to react like that. Things are tough for everyone, and I've been keeping things bottled up inside, I guess everyone has a limit, and not seeing you was mine." I answer, instantly regretting my honesty, almost giving away my true feelings about him.

"It's okay Maddie. Friends again? For real this time? No ignoring each other?" Danny asks, with sincerity in his kind face, the one person I so desperately wanted to kiss.

"Yes, I'll always be your friend Danny." I reply, realising that I'm totally stuck in the friend zone with him, despite my feelings for him. But I'd rather have him in my life as a friend, than not at all, even if that's going to be painful for my now broken heart...

Danny

Maddie was in such an emotional state by the time I got to her house, I didn't realise that she was finding our distance so difficult. Perhaps I gave her too much space? Now I'm regretting keeping my distance for so long, I must of held her for nearly an hour before she finally stopped crying, and I hate seeing her cry. It rips into my heart every single time, stealing another piece away, and I was the cause of it.

This has got to stop, I can't continue to hurt her like this. I'd happily hand over all of my heart on a silver platter to Maddie. That way she gets to hold onto it forever, but now isn't the right time. I very nearly fucked it all up by kissing her. The way that Maddie looks at me, surely she must know what it does to me inside? So being the coward I am, I pulled away from her, and for a split second I could see the devastation in her eyes, which she then hid like an expert. But this is better for now, for both our sakes. I need to keep my wits about me to be her protector, even though I'm not sure what danger lies ahead. In order to do that I need to keep a clear head, and my discreet distance from her and ignore her obvious attraction to me.

We've settled on being friends and it will be better for her in the long run…

"I'd best get going Maddie, it's getting late, and Sam is probably wondering what we're doing up here." I smirk at her cheekily. "Only in my dreams" I hear her whisper so very softly. Maddie didn't want me to hear that, so I pretend that I don't.

Climbing down ladder from her loft I walk along the landing, then downstairs, which lead straight into the living room. I cough because I don't want to barge in unannounced, but it's difficult with an open plan layout. Three sets of eyes look up at me, Sam and the boys are sitting on the floor around a coffee table playing monopoly.

"I'm off now, nice seeing you again Sam, and I'll see you boys at football practice. Dads home so I don't want to leave him too long." I say to them all, as I head in the direction of the hallway.

"I'm glad you stopped by Danny, I haven't seen you around for ages. I've got some leftovers from dinner if you want to take them home for you and your dad, oh, not forgetting Bryan too." Sam smiles at me, getting up and going into the kitchen, so I follow her through.

"That's very kind of you Sam, my dad loves your home cooking. And I've got football practice tomorrow, so that will save me from cooking, and Bryans infamous burnt oven chips." I laugh back at her, feeling a sudden awkward tension between us. I have a feeling she wants to say something else, get it all off her chest, but she's slightly hesitant to do so.

"Have you sorted out whatever's been going on between you and Maddie, I couldn't help but hear her crying earlier on, and I was about to go up to her when you arrived." Sam asks handing me one of her familiar Tupperware containers.

"Yes, Maddie should be okay now. We had a falling out a few weeks ago, and then kind of made up but didn't. But I think we'll be okay now. We've both missed each other's company, and she's had a lot of difficult things to deal with recently. It obviously all got on top of her, but she's starting to find a better place now. She just needed a friend to understand, that's all." I answer, hoping I haven't trodden on Sam's toes comforting Maddie.

Sam sighs, and looks up towards the ceiling in frustration, going on to say, "I wish she would open up to me more, I try, but I keep going wrong somewhere. All I ask Danny is don't hurt her, she's been so sad recently. Maddie's good at putting on a brave face, but I can see through that. You seem to be one of the only people she'll open up and talk too, and I'll selfishly admit that I'm jealous. I try so hard to get through to Maddie, but she still doesn't completely trust me, even after all these months. Every person she's ever had in her life has let her down in some way. Be careful Danny, very careful."

I gulp slightly, Maddie must have been hurting so badly these past few weeks, and I feel totally responsible for her hurt. Another reason I can't get to close to her, and hurt her further.

"I'm looking out for her Sam, try not to worry. I can try and encourage her to talk to you if you want me to?" I ask feeling guilty, and I don't want to come between them both, Sam clearly cares unconditionally for her and I'm getting in the way. What a mess.

"No, you don't need to go that far Danny. I want her to come to me, she will when she's ready, I'm sure. Ignore my selfish insecurities, we all bare them one way or another, no one is perfect. You, Danny McKenzie are a good man, just like your father. You've done nothing wrong." Sam smiles back, squeezing my shoulder in support. I think we just came to some kind of understanding.

As I walk back through the living room Jack pipes up, "Coach, what's happening with football camp next year? Is it still going ahead." His voice is eager, and he's not the first boy to ask me about the subject.

"It's something I've been looking to organise for the easter holidays next year, but the usual facilities the school use are not available due to building work, but I think I've found somewhere better." I answer him, it seems nothing gets past Jack when it comes to school football.

"That's cool. Tommy and I have never been to football camp before, but I was talking to Maddie about it the other day and she said she would put some money towards it." Jack replies, and I notice he's looking straight at Sam, almost like he's trying to push boundaries. That woman has her work cut out for her with Jack and Tommy.

"Did she now; well it's something that we can discuss together as a family when it comes up. Give Coach a chance to organise it first, we haven't even had the Christmas holidays yet." Sam replies to him, making sure Jack knows who's ultimate decision it is.

"Where would it be?" Tommy asks with a glint of excitement in his eye, it's the first time I've seen real excitement in his eyes in weeks.

"There's a great facility on the Isle of Wight, that's where I'm aiming for, they have everything on one site, and there will be additional activities we can do there, to encourage team building, like abseiling." I answer, knowing that I'm going to make this camp go ahead now at all costs, even if it leaves me out of pocket. It's not like I can't afford it.

"Do you need a passport to go there? It's an island, and we don't have one." Tommy asks innocently. Bless this boy, I'm finding it very difficult not to laugh, and I don't want to make Tommy feel insecure.

So instead I gently chuckle back, "No, you definitely don't need a passport to get to the Isle of Wight, it's just a short ferry from the mainland." I notice even Sam is trying to keep a straight face, hiding behind her hand.

"Anyway, thanks for tomorrows dinner, I'd best get going." We say our goodbyes at the door, and I take the short drive back to my house. Hoping my dad has been behaving himself and keeping out of trouble, and then I remember Bryan is living with us, and I start to think about what he's been up to.

"I'm home dad, and I come bearing Tupperware containers from Sam for dinner tomorrow." I shout into the living room, carrying the various Tupperware containers of no doubt delicious food.

Dad slowly follows me out to the kitchen on his crutches, and sits uncomfortably on a stool at the breakfast bar, he's slowly finding his feet again around the house at least. I grab two artisan beers which have been locally brewed, out of the fridge, and dad grins at me. It's the first time I've let him have one since he got home. The pain medication he's taking is less potent than what they gave him in hospital, and having one beer shouldn't hurt.

"Just the one dad, don't want you falling over in a heap and breaking the other leg." And I flip the top off with a bottle opener, and hand him the bottle, condensation already dripping down the side.

"Thanks son, it's good to be home. Where did you get too?" Dad asks, taking a long swig of his beer and sighing in pleasure. He must have been looking forward to that, and it makes me smile, because dad is still here with me, alive and well.

"Popped over to Maddie's, hence the special delivery of Tupperware from your Nurse Samantha." I smirk unable to resist the comment, looking at dad to see what his reaction will be.

"That was nice of Samantha, that woman knows how to cook." He smirks back, taking another swig of beer to hide the grin in his face.

"Something going on between you two I should know about?

Do I need to give you the talk about being responsible and safe?" I answer laughing, treating my dad like a teenage boy, at the same time digging for information about his love life.

"Would you mind if there was?" Dad asks, suddenly turning serious. Shit. He must really like her, and here I am taking the piss.

"Dad, I don't expect you to be by yourself for the rest of your life. I know you've had girlfriends while I was growing up, with sleepovers. You just never had anyone that was serious as far as I could tell." I look at him saying it seriously, then add, "I know you loved mum, but she's been gone a long time, she wouldn't want you to spend your life alone."

"Thank you son. You don't know how much I needed to hear that from you." My dad smiles back, and we clink our beer bottles together. Sam's a great woman, and I can't think of a better person for my dad to get to know better. Everybody deserves some love...

Chapter Forty-Nine

Maddie

It's a few days before Christmas, and I've somehow managed to rope Danny into coming with me and the boys to pick out a Christmas tree from a local farm that grows them. This is all new territory for me and the boys, as Nanna Jenny's idea of a tree was an ancient plastic monstrosity, which was almost bare, and had seen better days about twenty Christmases' ago. No. Christmas was never a massive event for me growing up, just another day, much like any other. Sam was supposed to be with us today, but she managed to pick up an extra shift at the hospital, I suspect to help pay for what will be an extravagant Christmas for me, Jack and Tommy. So that's why Danny is with us instead, although I don't mind spending extra time with him. I'll use any excuse I can find to spend time with him...

"I'm going to pick up a tree for me and dad too, normally we don't bother but Bryan's been nagging me for days and I can't stand the wining anymore." Danny laughs, and I find it funny because I know exactly how sneaky Bryan can be when he wants something. I'm not surprised Danny has given in to Bryans unrelenting antics, he would try the patience of a Saint.

"Bryan said he'd break you eventually, he's been telling me about it all week, Ben and I bet on how long it would take him to persuade you. Looks like I won the bet, Ben owes me a coffee and a donut. I knew we should have bet money." I laugh back at Danny, who's now walking off shaking his head muttering expletives about Bryan.

"What size trees do we need to get?" Tommy asks me, and I already know what the little devils are up to. Sam warned me they might try and pull this stunt.

"Sam said no bigger than 4ft. But I say we go bigger at least 6ft, it's not like she'll take a tape measure out or anything." Jack smirks, full of mischief as usual, and I wouldn't put it past Sam to do exactly that.

"Sam will kill me If we go back home with a tree too big for the living room. I will have the final say, now go and find a good one please." I reply, slightly exasperated, crossing my fingers and already begging for mercy.

"Well, you shot him down Maddie, never knew you were bah humbug." Danny smirks, and I can already tell he's on a wind up with me.

"Ten year old boys, ten year old boys." I reply laughing back, starting to see the fun in choosing a Christmas tree, watching Jack and Tommy running around excitedly.

"I need a 6 or 7ft tree for my house, want to come over tonight and help me decorate it?" Danny asks me, his eyes glinting with expectation, this is the first time he's invited me over to his house since before our falling out. I've been over there loads, but always with Bryan inviting me to revise, or watch the latest craze on Netflix.

"If its later on tonight Danny, because I expect the boys will want me to help decorate our tree, when we get home. And we have to wait for Sam to finish work first." I reply, and Danny tries not to look disappointed, but he's failing miserably, and it looks really cute. Not that I'd ever tell him that.

"That's fine, I just need to keep Bryan away from the tree until then, or he'll decorate the whole thing himself in a coordinated colour scheme, you know how excited he gets." Danny answers laughing, and I can already imagine the chaos tonight. I'm sure that I'm in for an interesting evening of entertainment, Bryan style.

"What are you doing for Christmas day this year? I know you usually go to Bryans family for dinner with your dad. I'm going to take a wild guess here, that's not going to happen?" I ask, inquisitively with an plan forming in my mind that will make Christmas a happier occasion for our families, and a chance to make new memories and traditions. Because that's what Christmas is about.

"Maddie, what are you up too? My Spidey-sense is tingling." Danny laughs tickling my waist. Oh no. I'm really, really ticklish, and I know I'm about to embarrass myself if he doesn't stop. Which I doubt he will…

"Stop, I'm super ticklish, your evil, stop, and I'll tell you. Mercy Danny, Mercy." I laugh as I take a deep breath of air, once Danny stops tickling me. Evil guy he is.

"Sam was pumping me for information last night about how you, your dad and Bryan are spending Christmas day. Why don't I suggest to her we have a joint celebration? Look how much our families have become intwined this year. Me and the boys have never experienced a big family dinner round a table before. Do you think it's too much?" I ask Danny, half expecting him to shoot down the idea straight away because it is rather presumptuous of me.

"Actually Maddie, I think that would be perfect. We would have to host it at mine though because it would be a bit of a crush at your cottage. Do you think Sam and the boys would be up for that, especially as it's your first Christmas together in the cottage, I'm sure you could talk her into it?" He replies excitedly his eyes lighting up at the thought of spending Christmas with us, and I smile back at him.

"Would your dad mind?" I ask Danny, with my eyebrows raised in question, because I don't really know Danny's dad well enough yet, only meeting him in passing while over visiting with Bryan.

"Of course not, he'd get to spend time with Samantha." Danny laughs, enunciating Samantha, and wiggling his eyebrows knowingly.

"Oh yes, I totally forgot about those two having the hots for each other. I know they've been planning on going out to dinner together, but with Christmas it hasn't happened yet. And your dad does love her cooking, I'm betting her Christmas dinner is amazing." I smile back at Danny, my wicked plan forming in my mind, and I can see Danny is thinking on exactly the same wavelength as me.

"We found the best tree ever, come and look Maddie, it's over here, you have to see it." And Tommy excitedly pulls my hand towards a tree, to be honest, they all look the same to me, but I'm not going to spoil his excitement.

"Hey Coach, I found a beauty for you, it's absolutely massive!" Jack shouts to Danny, and he laughs shaking his head at me, trust Jack to do the exact opposite of what he was asked to do.

Half an hour later Danny is busy with the boys, teaching them how to strap two Christmas trees to the top of his car, which is hilarious to watch. Jack keeps letting go of the bungee straps, and I'm pretty sure he's doing it on purpose. I'm in the queue for hot chocolate at a small stand that's been set up outside the farm shop. I quietly laugh to myself, this is starting to feel suspiciously like a plot to a Hallmark Christmas movie. Sam is absolutely obsessed with them, and even has me and the boys sucked into the happily ever after of every movie that is basically the same. We have been watching them at dinnertime most nights for the past couple of weeks now. I've never felt more Christmassy in my whole life, bring on the mistletoe and mince pie.

Carrying the cardboard cup holder holding the four hot chocolates, I find myself carefully balancing it in my hands as

I walk towards an empty picnic table. It's chilly, but the winter sun is out and we're all wrapped up warm. Jack comes running over first with Tommy in pursue, they both have a sixth sense when it comes to sugar I swear.

"Hope you got extra marshmallows, extra cream on ours." Jack says, sitting down on the wooden bench of the picnic table and clapping his hands together in delight.

"I got extra on all of them." I smile, handing one to Danny as he sits down at the picnic table. He looks hot in his beanie hat, and I blush thinking about it. I've got to stop thinking about him like that. But with his gorgeous face, built body, and those blue eyes, he could charm an nun into doing naughty things. Oh. My. God. I have got to stop thinking about Danny like that, we're friends. Only friends.

"What?" He picks up on my blush, grinning at me, like he knows my thoughts are not of the appropriate kind right now.

"Nothing, just thinking about some stuff, nothing to concern you Danny." And I turn slightly away from him and take a swig of my hot chocolate getting whipped cream on my nose, and before I have a chance to wipe it off, he's there wiping it off with his finger.

It really has turned into a Hallmark movie today...

Chapter Fifty

Danny

After a manic yet enjoyable morning with Maddie and the twins, I need to at least attempt to get some work done today. But I've have this strange and overwhelming urge since early this morning to go to St Peters Church. The feelings been creeping up on from me since then, and it's got to the point that I can no longer ignore it. Its unnerving me, making me feel uncomfortable, and I know I won't get anything else done until I act on the urge. I find myself turning the car around and heading towards the church, instead of home to my computer.

Walking into the church no one appears to be around at the moment and I'm surprised that it's unlocked. Father Christopher must be around if the church is open, or one of the church wardens. Unfortunately, security even with a church has to be taken seriously, with some vandals causing some damage trying to break into a collection box a few months ago. I decide to sit in a pew half way down the church, and stare at the stained glass window as usual. It never fails to catch my attention, lost in the way the light projects through the medieval glass.

"Danny, you got my message." And I turn to see Uriel sitting next to me, wings and all this time, he is truly magnificent in this form.

"Are you only allowed to show your wings in church?" I blurt out, wanting to know because I'm fascinated, I don't think I'll ever get used to seeing his wings.

"No, only when I wish for them to be seen." Uriel replies, matter of fact, not in the least bit surprised by my question.

"Why did you summon me here Uriel? Is it about Maddie, and have you ever heard of using a phone? Believe me when I say it would be less unnerving." I ask him having a really bad feeling in the pit of my stomach.

" We do not use phones. Has Maddie mentioned any dreams to you recently? She needs to listen to what they are telling her. That's all I can tell you. Please ask no further questions, my time is limited here." Uriel replies looking behind him, and I notice that he fades his wings as another parishioner comes through the door.

"That's an impressive little trick." And I nod to where his wings have gone.

"Not really, it uses more of my energy hiding them. Talk to Maddie about the dreams she's having. Things are going to rapidly change. I must go." And Uriel starts to fade before I even have a chance to talk to him about what he means. But at least now I know I can warn her about these dreams, I just wonder how she's going to react to me seeing Uriel again. I know she's not one hundred percent convinced he's even real. Although Maddie hasn't openly admitted that to me yet, but I can certainly read between the lines.

Later on that evening I arrange to pick Maddie up from her house. I want a chance to talk to her alone before we spend the evening decorating my Christmas tree. Talking during the drive to my house, is the only opportunity I'm going to have of total privacy with her.

"You didn't need to pick me up Danny, I was going to walk round it's not that far, but thank you, ever the gentleman." Maddie smiles as she does up her seatbelt, and starts fiddling with my car stereo as usual, stopping on a radio station that only plays rock and alternative music.

"After I left you today something funny happened." I say sighing, not really knowing how to start this odd conversation about another meeting with Uriel. Uriel the Angel. The guy with wings...

"Are we talking funny, ha, ha, or, funny peculiar?" She asks scrunching her nose, and I can't help but notice how cute she looks, and how intuitive she is, sensing the direction this conversation is heading.

"Funny peculiar. I got this overwhelming urge to pay a visit to St Peters Church earlier today, so I turned my car around and followed my urge. It's not something I'd normally do, but let's face it Maddie, there's nothing normal about it." I answer her, with total honesty, not wanting to keep any more secrets from her .

"Don't tell me, our friendly neighbourhood angel? He's turning into Casper the friendly ghost." And she rolls her eyes, unamused at my declaration.

"I'm being serious Maddie. He was adamant that you listen to your dreams because things are going to rapidly change, whatever that means. Don't shoot the messenger, I won't keep secrets anymore. Look what it did to us last time." I answer, knowing how freaked out she can get about things. No one can blame her for that kind of reaction.

"My dreams are all fuzzy, and I can't remember them by the time I'm fully awake. But I keep seeing blood, always lots of blood." She whispers back, refusing to look at me. Shit. This danger is worse than I thought.

"Blood? Do you know whose it was? Any little detail?" I'm not entirely sure what else I can say to that answer, but I pray she can start remembering before it's too late. Whatever is around the corner can't be good.

"I can see them, but not clear enough Danny, almost a blur of jumbled up pictures and flashes that make no sense." She looks down nervously, and starts fiddling with her hands, and I'm aware that I don't want to cause her to have a panic attack.

"Hey, I didn't mean to upset you, I just thought it was better that you know what's going on. Not now, but another night, we should sit down and try and decipher the dreams together. After all, two heads are better than one." I nod and pull out onto the road for the short drive to my house. She doesn't answer me back, and I decide to let it go for now. I know how Maddie always needs time to process these things. But the thing she said about seeing blood is still niggling in the back of my head.

As I pull up the car to my house, and onto the driveway, Maddie turns to me and says, "So how excited is Bryan about decorating the tree on a scale of one to ten?"

Laughing, I reply, "Oh, you'll see, excited doesn't even begin to describe Bryan right now, he's like one of the energiser bunnies on acid."

Before I even open my front door I can hear the sound of Santa Baby, coming through the speakers of my stereo. Bryan must of found the Christmas CD's at the bottom of my collection, some of them I haven't played in years. I went through a stage of listening to them when I was younger, to try and get me and dad in the mood to celebrate Christmas without mum being there with us both.

The living room is a slew of cardboard boxes overflowing with various decorations, most I haven't seen in years. There's a plate of mince pies on the table and Christmas paper napkins, and I can smell mulled wine coming from the kitchen. Yep, Christmas has arrived in the McKenzie household whether I want it or not. But I remind myself that this is to help Bryan and the recent trauma he's gone through with his dad, and the fact that he's effectively lost his family. Plus it has the added bonus of raising my dad's spirits after his accident and lengthy stay in the hospital.

Bryan and Ben are digging frantically through a large cardboard box which is covered in dust, looking for the Christmas tree lights. We've always placed them on the tree first, before the real decorating can start. Dad is pottering about in the kitchen, and I can hear him awkwardly knocking into things with his crutches, he's yet to master manoeuvring around on them. And I smile to myself at the chaos already going on. We needed this. All of us did.

"What's up buttercup?" Bryan laughs, and he stands up from the floor to greet Maddie with a bear hug, which she giggles from as he tries to tickle her.

"Loving the Christmas jumper Bryan, very you." Maddie laughs pointing at it. The jumper has "Shantay you Sleigh", written on the front of it and a picture of RuPaul. It's classic Bryan humour, and I realise this is the first time he's been able to express himself in this way openly, it's so much more than a Christmas jumper.

"Ben brought it for me, early Christmas present." Bryan grins like a loonytune character towards Ben, and I can clearly see the affection in both of their eyes passing between them.

"I can see you decided to start the festivities without us. At least you found the boxes okay, saved me a job hunting for them all." I laugh shaking my head at Bryans impatience to start, not really bothered by it.

"Ow I love this song, I've been practicing it for my Christmas set at Dorothy's, mind if I play it again to sing along too?" Maddie asks, already with her finger fiddling with the remote control to the CD player, the girl has no patience with certain things.

"Go for it, it's already become a free for all. I lost control a while ago, go for it Maddie." I laugh, sitting on the sofa and picking up a mince pie off the plate, and stuffing half of it in my mouth.

I'll need to go for an extra run at this rate, I have a weakness for mince pies.

Maddie starts to sing along to Santa Baby, and I'm mesmerised with her instantaneously. She has no idea how sexy she is with the slightly husky voice she has added to the song, and when she starts doing a little dance and adding some actions too, I really can't look away. I have to pick up a cushion and place it over my crotch so I don't embarrass myself in front of everyone, I'm reacting like a horny teenager.

She sings, "Come and trim my Christmas tree, With some decorations brought at Tiffanys, I really do believe in you, let's see if you believe in me…" Maddie has no idea what she's doing to me right now. But Bryan whispers something into Bens ear. I know, that he knows, and has just told Ben, call it a guy thing. And Bryan winks at me, the cheeky devil he is. It's difficult not to blush, and I'm failing miserably.

At the end of the song Maddie turns to Bryan and says, "What do you think? Is adding the little dance too much? I got the idea from the Ariana Grande version of the song, she does the dance in her music video."

"Girl, you are making some tips Christmas eve with that song alone. Dorothy is going to love it, they will be eating out of the palm of your hand with that performance." Bryan replies, then asks me "What did you think Danny?" Talk about throwing me under the bus and putting me on the spot.

Maddie gazes at me expectantly, awaiting my reply, eyes twinkling knowingly. The girl is playing dirty. She knows full well what kind of reaction I had to her just now…

"Very entertaining Maddie, very entertaining." And I smirk back at Bryan, he's such a shit stirrer sometimes.

Dad calls through from the kitchen, "Can someone carry this tray through for me please?"

Ben leaps into action, "Coming Mr McKenzie." Ben appears a

few seconds later carrying a tray of mulled wine, a cinnamon stick, and a slice of orange in each glass of the red wine.

Dad always makes the best mulled wine, getting the exact mix of spices, using a recipe and the same red wine every time, he's perfected it over the years. I grab a glass off the tray and take a sip, delicious, the aroma alone making my senses go into overdrive.

"We better not have too much of this dad, or we'll never get anything done." I laugh, clinking my glass with Maddie's in a silent cheers.

As the evening progresses the tree is fully decorated, and mums precious collection of snow globes are placed on the shelf above the fireplace on display. We don't normally get those out anymore, but Maddie innocently came across the box and started unpacking it. And my dad whispered, "let her" so she remained blissfully unaware of the huge thing my dad allowed her to do. And I knew it would make my mum happy, even though she wasn't here with us anymore.

"It's getting late, and it's the last day of college tomorrow before the holidays, I should get going. Thank you for your hospitality Mr McKenzie." And Maddie picks up her coat getting ready to leave.

"I'll walk you back, I can't drive after a couple of glasses of mulled wine." I get up and grab my coat too, before she has a chance to argue.

"If you're sure you don't mind Danny." Maddie innocently smiles back, and I notice Bryan smirking at me again, I'm going to kill him when I get back home.

"No trouble at all, I need to walk off those mince pie calories." I laugh back at her, only half joking thinking about the unhealthy treat I allow myself at Christmas.

We walk along the pavement together, and I can see Maddie looking at all the houses that have decorated the outside of their homes with lights. More and more homes seem to do it each year, and it's pleasant walking along seeing them, but staring at Maddie's reaction to them is mesmerising.

"Do you decorate outside of your house Danny?" Maddie asks, looking at me wrinkling her nose up again in that cute way I'm growing to love each time she does it.

"I'll buy a wreath for the front door, and string some fairy lights up around the window, but that's as far as I'll go." I smile back at her, walking along taking everything in, perhaps I'll string up a few more this year, just for her.

"Our house looks like someone vomited tinsel everywhere, Sam let the boys go crazy with it, she brought a load from Poundland. Your house looks much more tasteful." Maddie laughs, the glow radiating from her excitement and bright personality shining through.

"With Bryan in charge, it was going to be ideal homes magazine worthy decorations all the way. My mum hated tacky decorations, she was a woman of class." I reply, thinking about my mums snow globe collection, and wanting to add to it for the first time in years.

"Tinsel gives me the creeps, I'm sure that's why Jack and Tommy encouraged Sam to buy so much. They totally did it on purpose." Maddie shakes her head, shivering dramatically at the thought of tinsel.

"I've had a great time with you today Maddie, I've missed spending time with you like this, our little moments with just you and me." I've probably overstepped the mark saying it, but I want her to know how I feel, even if it isn't exactly appropriate right now.

Maddie stops and grabs my hand intwining our fingers together, and we continue walking along the pavement, when she turns to me and says, " I've missed this too, I've missed you so much Danny."

As we get nearer to Maddie's house, I find myself wishing the walk was further so that I can spend more time alone with her. We stop outside her house, and I want to kiss her, but I know that I can't. I'm her protector, her friend. Nothing more.

"Goodnight Maddie." I say gently, and let go of her hand, and I can't help but notice the disappointment again briefly in her eyes, I'm still hurting her. Damn.

"Goodnight Danny." Maddie unlocks her front door and goes inside. Leaving me with my thoughts of her as I walk back home...

Chapter Fifty-One

Bryan

Getting to spend time like this with Ben is like a dream come true, but at the same time there's a huge whole in my heart, and even with what's happened I still miss my mum and dad. Hardly surprising really, I have spent my entire life up until now with them. Christmas is going to be different this year. Very different. I already know that I'm going to feel more laid back now that things are out in the open. What Danny did for me tonight I won't forget in a hurry. I know that he organised the Christmas tree, and allowed me invite Ben over to help decorate it. And Mr McKenzie is the polar opposite of my dad, he has no problem with me having Ben over to hang out, so we can spend time together. Why can't my own dad accept me like that? I wipe away a couple of stray tears, but of course Ben notices right away.

"Hey, Bryan. It's going to be okay you know." And he puts his arm around me, in a comforting hug and kisses my cheek.

"Don't, you'll start me off, crying like a girl Ben." I reply sadly, not wanting to turn into a blubbering idiot in front of my boyfriend.

"It's okay to miss them you know. Especially this time of year, it magnifies what your feeling inside. Have you thought about phoning your mum?" Ben asks with concern, and I can tell that Mr McKenzie is aware of our conversation in the room, taking it all in.

"Been texting her, but I'm not sure I can face talking to her yet. Everything is just so raw for me right now. She didn't stand up for me, and let dad throw me out. You don't know how much that hurts." I excuse myself quickly to the bathroom, so I can let the tears fall freely.

A few minutes later there's a knock on the bathroom door, and I open it expecting it to be Ben looking for me. But it's not, it's Mr McKenzie standing there wobbling on his crutches, so I open the door wider so he can come inside, the last thing that I want is for him to fall over. I put the toilet seat down, and he sits on top, so I lean against the sink. He hands me some toilet tissue to wipe my eyes and nose with.

"You know Bryan, I remember holding you as a baby for the first time, and your dad was so proud. There is no excuse for his behaviour that night, but I do know how his mind was programmed by his own father, and it's made a lasting indentation on his mind. I'm not saying he's going to completely come round to your way of thinking, but perhaps you can meet him halfway. And over time he'll see you for the wonderful man your becoming. Come here." He offers his words of wisdom, and takes me into a fatherly hug.

"Thank you. I really needed to hear that Mr McKenzie." I reply into his shoulder sniffling away, wishing that my dad could except me for who I am.

"Bryan, consider this your home. You are welcome here always. And I enjoy having another person around the house. Danny can get very bossy you know, so I need a wingman." He answers, and in that moment I really wish Mr McKenzie could be my dad.

Ben appears in the doorway to the bathroom, with a look of concern on his face.

"I was getting worried Bryan, only wanted to check on you." Ben smiles and puts out his hand to me, and pulls me into another hug with him.

"I knew girls gathered in the bathroom, but this is ridiculous." I laugh, pulling back and smiling at Ben, and then Mr McKenzie. This bathroom was not designed to hold three men.

"What's going on here then, mothers meeting in progress?" Danny enquires, loitering in the hallway, he must of just got back from walking Maddie home.

"Things just got a bit much for me, I was feeling sentimental over Christmas, probably overdosed on Hallmark movies and gingerbread men." I answer Danny, and shrug my shoulders nonchalantly.

"You doing okay Bryan?" Danny asks, and I nod because I don't want to start blubbering again, I'm losing the few man points I had, left, right, and centre here.

Bens phone pings and he announces, "mums outside to pick me up, you'll be okay Bryan? I don't like leaving you upset like this."

"For goodness sake you guys, I'm fine. Just a blip on the radar, that's all. Come on Ben, I'll walk you out." And I grab his hand and lead him to the front door, where I turn towards him and give him a pretty sweltering kiss if I do say so myself.

"See you at college." He whispers in my ear, and we say goodnight on the doorstep. I'm thankful to have such a supportive network of friends around me, I'd be lost without them right now.

Saying goodnight to Danny and Mr McKenzie, I go upstairs to my bedroom, in my new home. I've unpacked everything that I brought with me, and I wish now I'd now packed up everything, leaving nothing behind. But I wasn't exactly in a good place when I went and packed my belongings up that day. I automatically check my phone for any messages before I go to bed and there's another one from my mum, so I open it to read.

Things are not the same without you Bryan. I miss you

I try to decide what to message her back, so I go with my gut feeling.

I miss you and dad, I don't think things will ever be the same now.

Hitting send, it's several minutes before she replies to me, my phone pings.

Do you need anything?

Well, that's a loaded question, I can think of a hundred things that I want to say to her, but instead I type back:

Just pack up the rest of my stuff, I'll get Danny to collect it.

After I hit sent, I realise how cold that message comes off. But I won't apologise for it. I wait for a reply, and I can see she's typing something, but then she stops, then starts again. Either she's writing a book for me, or she keeps writing things and then deleting them. Eventually after ten minutes of this, my phone pings.

If that's what you want. It will be ready by tomorrow afternoon.

Nothing else. No I love you Bryan, that's all I get, so I turn my phone face down and roll over onto my side in bed and let the tears roll onto my pillow...

Chapter Fifty-Two

Maddie

It's the last day of college before Christmas, I've never understood the point of coming in because we don't have any proper lessons. We just do silly quizzes in class and eat junk food that we all bring in to share around, but it's a bit of fun I suppose and beats the normal routine. We finish on a half day at lunchtime and have just entered the final period of the morning.

Me, Ben and Ashley have made a quiz team, sadly Bryan isn't in this class so he's missing, from what has become our little group. An open bag of toffee popcorn is on the desk, and a bag of chocolate coins in gold foil wrappers. We're filling in a quiz on historical figures through the ages, and I'm falling asleep with boredom.

"I can't believe I got out of my bed for this today, and we still have another hour left, do you think we'll get let out early if we finish this quickly? I need to see Tony at Dorothy's about my set list for Christmas eve." I sigh, putting my head on the desk and catching a piece of popcorn in my mouth.

"You still fretting about that set list Maddie, it's fine. You don't need to make any more changes to it, and Tony will tell you exactly the same thing." Ben replies struggling to open his chocolate coin with his short fingernails.

"You know me, I fret about everything." I laugh, grabbing the chocolate coin from his hand and opening it for him, it was painful watching him struggle with it.

"What's the answer to question six? I say Henry the eighth ." Ashley looks up chewing her pen, I don't think she heard a word of our previous conversation, I'm not surprised with her mum still in a coma.

Over the top laughing erupts from the table on the back row, where Chelsea has surrounded herself with rugby players, the ones on Bens team that have been blanking him since he came out. Which has made team practices and games beyond difficult for him. But he refuses to be made to quit the team, and he has my deepest respect for sticking to his principles.

"I wish Chelsea wouldn't do that, it just comes off as false and desperate. Believe it or not she can be nice sometimes when she's not being a bitch, or trying to put on a show." Ashley sighs, looking sad, and I think she misses at least part of being friends with Chelsea. But since her mums accident, and the way Chelsea spread gossip afterwards, Ashley has been giving Chelsea a wide birth. Which apparently hasn't gone unnoticed, by Chelsea. Ashley has really gone through it with her mum showing no signs of waking up from her coma, and having a massive falling out with Chelsea was the icing on the cake. Although if you ask me, she's better off without her. So we've adopted her into our little friend group, and I get on really well with her. She's even asked me to put in a word at Dorothy's for a waitressing job.

"Okay class, ten minutes left on the quiz, and if your team finishes it, I'll let you go home early." Our teacher pipes up, obviously he wants to go home too.

"Best consult Dr Google then and get these answers locked down." Ben laughs, about to take his phone out to get the google search engine up.

"And no phones allowed, and that means you too Mr Chambers." The teacher replies, obviously overhearing Ben, and the class laughs. All except for Chelsea's table, they remain silent.

"What's their problem?" I ask turning to Ben, "Are they still giving you a hard time?"

"To be honest, I think it's Chelsea shit stirring more than anything else, you know what she's like. The guys from the team are just following suit because they want to get into her knickers." Ben laughs, and Ashley snorts because she laughs so hard holding onto her stomach.

"Come on guys, eyes on the quiz, I want to leave this hellhole." I laugh back, wanting to escape from college as soon as possible. So the three of us concentrate on the quiz for the next ten minutes and get to go home early, except I don't go home I make my way over to Dorothy's. Because I'm a sucker for punishment and can't resist tweaking my set list with Tony again. Call me crazy, but there's an extra song that I want to add for a special somebody who I hope will be watching me tomorrow night.

When I arrive at Dorothy's I notice that guy again, the one that's apparently Dorothy's ex. He's in the bar by himself nursing a beer, I wonder if Dorothy is aware he's here again? But as soon as he notices me he downs his drink and leaves the bar, strange. I wonder what that's all about, probably hates my singing, each to their own.

Tracking down Tony, he's agreed to add the song I want to the setlist for Christmas eve tomorrow night. Dorothy says it's one of her busiest nights of the year apart from New Years Eve, so I'm putting in maximum effort. It's a ticketed event to avoid overcrowding, and there's also an charity auction for the local hospice.

Unlocking my bike ready to ride home, my phone starts to ring startling me, so I answer it quickly without even looking to see who the caller on the other end is.

"Maddie, where are you?" Danny asks, I wasn't expecting a call from him today, and I immediately feel a wave of happiness flow through me from hearing his voice.

"Unlocking my bike in the car park at Dorothy's, why?" I ask, slightly flummoxed at his question.

"Give me five minutes, and I'll pick you up, we have a shopping list from Sam." Danny laughs, obviously on speaker phone in his car. I patiently wait for Danny in the car park, and sure enough within five minutes he pulls up in his car. Out he jumps, and we go through the usual routine of securing my bike to his bike rack. We've done it so often it feels like second nature now. Unfortunately I'm forced to sit in the back seat of the car, because Bryan is already sitting upfront.

"So what's this all about shopping for Sam?" I ask them both totally confused, because as far as I knew Sam and I had all of the Christmas shopping finished.

"It seems we weren't the only ones discussing the Christmas day festivities. Dad and Sam have decided to hold a joint celebration at our house, Sam's going to do most of the cooking, so I said we'd pick up the groceries. I'm picking up an organic turkey from the farm shop, and we can pick up the vegetables there too. Then I thought we could go to the supermarket at the shopping centre and get any other bits we need. Does that sound like a plan?" Danny asks turning around to me in the back seat grinning, no doubt because this is how we wanted Christmas to pan out.

"Yes that sounds great, I can't believe we get to be together on Christmas!" I beam at him and Bryan, and I can literally feel the excitement building up inside me.

"It seems my dad and Sam have been talking a lot on the phone and getting to know each other." And he wiggles his eye brows, this is new information to me. Sam never mentioned a thing. It appears a budding romance is possibly forming between the two of them.

"I don't know if I should be happy or horrified by the thought of those two dating." Bryan pipes up, and we both look at him bleeding daggers.

"Dating, I can't even think about that right now." I answer Bryan, slightly melancholy. And I notice Danny looking at me in the rear view mirror, with a flash of pain in his eyes...

The farm shop is busy, and while Danny queues up at the butchers counter, Bryan and I get the vegetables. We start filling paper bags with potatoes, parsnips, brussel sprouts and carrots. I grab a red cabbage and some cooking apples, and Bryan places a few onions in a bag. We'll get the garden peas from the frozen section at the supermarket. As we walk along looking at the shelves, I grab a nut roast mix, and a couple of boxes of stuffing. Danny meets us in the aisle with a turkey in a basket, and it fills the whole thing.

"See you got the biggest turkey in the whole shop, are you sure it will fit in the oven?" I laugh at Danny, hoping he hasn't made a massive mistake with it, or the meat eaters will be going hungry Christmas day .

"There's a lot of mouths to feed, and I need to make sure there's left overs for boxing day, you know, the day of cold meats and pickles." Danny laughs, picking up a bottle of organic sparkling wine, and carefully reading the label.

"I'll grab another basket for you Danny." I laugh back again, amazed at the amount of food and drink we need for essentially one day. He places two bottles of expensive red wine, and three bottles of equally expensive sparkling wine in the basket, then he grabs a dessert wine.

"What about Christmas pudding? It's not on the list." Bryan says looking confused, and I know the answer to that.

"Sam has made Christmas puddings and a Christmas cake, she's amazing, I don't know how she fits it all in the day." I reply proudly, because I love living with her. Sam is the best foster parent I've ever had.

"My mouth is already watering at the thought, I love Christmas pudding, it better be good because I am a connoisseur when it comes to pudding." Bryan declares, rubbing his stomach and licking his lips.

"Do you mind if I pop off to the Hobbycraft shop while you two get the rest of the stuff in the supermarket?" I inquire, looking at Danny and Bryan. It's the perfect chance to pick up a few items I'm going to need.

"That's fine." Danny replies, but Bryan, being his nosy inquisitive self asks, "What are you up to Maddie?"

"You'll have to wait and see won't you Mr nosy pants." I answer, not giving anything away, knowing that it will drive Bryan mad.

"How old are you? Five?" He answers back, and Danny just shakes his head and walks towards the queue at the counter.

Twenty minutes later we are all back in the car, shopping paid for by Danny of course. The bill was huge, and made my eyes almost pop out of my head, but Danny didn't even give it a second thought. Come to think about it, he never seems to worry about paying for things and how much they cost, am I completely missing something here? It certainly feels like I am, maybe I can quiz Bryan about it. It's not like Danny is a secret millionaire or anything, that's ridiculous. My over active imagination again…

In the shopping centre we go our separate ways and agree to meet outside Hobbycraft when I'm finished. I've decided that I'm going to make some Christmas crackers, and some name places for the Christmas table, as we seem to be going all out this year, and I finally have a reason and the money to go crazy with crafting. When I was at secondary school I loved it when we had our textile lessons, and I still have a little cushion I made and tie-dyed myself. Yes, I could spend hours upon hours getting lost in a craft shop. Shame I've got a time limit today with Bryan and Danny doing the last of the food shopping.

It's been great fun watching some YouTube videos learning new skills to practice, and I have a good idea of what I'm going to make. Now that I have a job at Dorothy's I can afford to buy the supplies with my tip money, and it's a great feeling to have. I spot a cracker making kit, which is perfect and I carefully place two kits in the basket I'm carrying around the shop. I need to make sure that I have enough for everyone on Christmas day. Adding some plain white card to the basket, and a set of double ended artist pens; one end has a fine tip and the other a larger one for shading. They are expensive, but for once I can afford to splurge on myself. Finding a section in the shop that has small items that you can put in the cracker as a gift, I can hardly contain my excitement. Choosing a cracker gift for each person, I add an extra couple into my basket for Jack and Tommy to keep them happy. Outside Hobbycraft, Bryan and Danny are sitting on a bench surrounded by shopping bags, it looks like they brought the entire supermarket, I knew I couldn't trust them alone.

"Let's get the car loaded up and go back home." I say smiling at them both, I've got crafting to get on with and I'm eager to make a start.

"Yes, let's. I'm totally over this shopping, it was murder in that supermarket. People are going crazy, it's like they're buying enough food for the next zombie apocalypse." Bryan laughs, grabbing his share of the shopping bags, as we walk towards the multi-storey car park.

"I couldn't agree more, you dodged a bullet Maddie, hiding out in Hobbycraft, that was a fantastic ploy to get out of all of the boring stuff." Danny replies totally overexaggerating my last minute trip to Hobbycraft.

"I can't wait to get home and have a long soak in the bath, so I can turn my body into a prune." Danny laughs, and I blush at the thought of him naked, surrounded by bubbles. Oh my god, I'm turning into a pervert now thinking about my friend naked. So I quickly change the subject…

"Well, I'm going to use the rest of the day doing some art and crafts, and I can practice my set list at the same time with the backing tracks Tony downloaded for me, so busy day for me. No rest for the wicked." I reply still blushing from Danny's previous comment, he must of noticed my reaction but he's said nothing. Helping to load the shopping into the boot of the car, I still can't get that vision of Danny out of my head…

"My big plan is watching Love Actually with Ben, and eating my own bodyweight in popcorn. We might watch Die Hard, I kind of promised I'd give the film a go, apparently it's a Christmas movie. Who knew?" Bryan beams at us both, and I nearly burst out laughing, at the fact Ben has convinced Bryan to watch Die Hard. Bryan obviously has absolutely no idea about the plot of the movie, I must remember to commend Ben on his ingenuity if Bryan actually follows through and watches the movie.

"You might as well make the most of it, because you are going to be really rushed off your feet at Dorothy's tomorrow night." I answer, feeling a pang of nerves fluttering in my stomach. It will be my largest set list to date that I've performed, and being a ticketed event people expect their money's worth in entertainment. Plus I really, really, really hope Danny comes to watch me.

This is going to be a spectacular Christmas to remember. Back with Jack and Tommy, having a foster parent that cares about us all, my new best friend Bryan, and of course Danny. Our relationship is officially only friends, but I still feel that's a grey area between us, yet to be decided.

Yes, it's going to be the best Christmas I've ever had, so long as I stop dreaming about blood and blurred bodies lying on the ground in the night…

Danny

It's Christmas Eve, and for the first time in I don't know how many years, I can honestly say that I'm really looking forward to it. The thought of having Maddie to celebrate with, warms my fractured heart, and it's like I can feel it slowly coming back to life again.

Sam has been busy in our kitchen most of the day, preparing the feast for tomorrow, while my dad has sat at the breakfast bar keeping her company and chatting. Those two seem to be getting along like a house on fire, and I can definitely see a spark between them.

I've been keeping Jack and Tommy entertained teaching them some basic coding on my computer setup in my room, so dad and Sam can have some time together alone. The boys are fast learners and are keen to learn more, soaking information up like sponges. Perhaps they could help me when I build my new computer, the one I intend to use for gaming? It's a project I've been thinking about for some time, but with dads accident everything got pushed to the wayside. Before I know it the afternoon has passed by, and I'm surprised how quickly time flew by, maybe I missed my calling with teaching? Coaching the kids at the school these past few months has been more fulfilling than I could have ever imagined. Gaining Tommy's trust, and him confessing to the abuse he'd been getting, has changed Tommy's and Jacks life for the better. Teaching would be a new challenge for me, but I'd need to get the qualifications first...

Maddie and Bryan have been at Dorothy's all day preparing for tonight's function, and neither one are giving much away. Maddie gave me a ticket for the event yesterday, and said it would be nice if I could come and see her set. I can tell Maddie really wants me to come and watch her perform, her confidence with singing has grown so much. She's no longer the shy girl who gets upset singing in front of other people.

Dad and Sam are taking Jack and Tommy to the cinema to see the latest Marvel movie tonight, so I really have no excuse not to go and watch Maddie. Dads only request to me is that we go to midnight mass together at Saint Peters Church, following our tradition for mum, and I'm not really in any position to say no. Midnight mass is a quiet affair, and Father Christopher normally keeps his reading short knowing people want to get home to bed, for a busy next day of festivities.

Taking the small square box out of the carrier bag, I carefully gift wrap it in Christmas paper and attach a gift tag with Maddie's name written on it. It's a small solid silver pair of angel wings on a necklace, which has been handcrafted especially for her. Although I'll never let that detail slip, I plan to give it to her tomorrow, I'm just going to put it underneath the Christmas tree and not make a big fuss about it. The Angel wings remind me of her, and have a bigger significance than she'll probably realise tomorrow when I give her the gift.   I continue to wrap the rest of the presents I brought, then when I'm finished, I take them all downstairs to place underneath the Christmas tree. I can spot that my dad has already placed some gifts underneath the tree himself, he must have done internet shopping, very sneaky.

Wonderful smells are coming from the kitchen, and there are gingerbread men sitting on a plate covered with clingfilm. I can see the turkey has been prepared, with written instructions for what time it needs to be put in the oven tomorrow morning. Looks like I'm getting up early tomorrow, and with midnight mass I won't be getting much sleep, but it's all in a good cause.

The house is silent, and I look at the collection of mums snow globes on the shelf above the fireplace. I'm glad Maddie found that box and unpacked it, the snow globes have spent too many years hidden away in storage. I find myself picking up a photograph of me and mum, I must only be about five years old in it, Maddie doesn't have a single memory of hers. I can understand why she wants answers about her mum, more so now than ever before...

By the time I arrive at Dorothy's the whole bar is packed out with people. A bouncer checks my ticket and stamps my hand with a green D, and I head inside and fight my way towards the bar. The whole bar has been transformed into a winter wonderland. Decorations hang tastefully from a large tree in the corner of the bar, and green fairy lights have been strung up with pieces of mistletoe from the ceiling. Candles in stylish arrangements, surrounded by holly are on each of the tables. The windows have been sprayed with fake snow in the corners, and a smell of mulled wine fills the entire bar. Cinnamon, orange and other spices, and it's a shame I won't be drinking any tonight. I can see why this has taken Maddie and Bryan all day to help with.

Christmas eve seems to be a very popular night to be out celebrating, and I can't believe how busy it is here. Now I can understand why Maddie was getting so worried and nervous about tonight, expectations are high, and people want a good night out. I can see Ben serving at an impressive speed at the bar and he looks like he's been doing it for years. Bryan is zooming around packed out tables, and I can see extra chairs have been brought in for tonight's show. Although there's no sign of Maddie yet, I expect she's still glamming herself up, not that she needs to, but I understand why. Ben catches my eye, and I make my way towards him, and order a soft drink because I'm driving. The stool next to me becomes vacant, so I slide onto it and sip my drink in anticipation, waiting for Maddie to come on stage.

The lights go down, and loud wolf whistles start to break out throughout the captive audience. Dorothy struts herself on stage, and does a short introduction, then announces the winning bids on the silent auction in aid of the hospice. A rapturous round of applause breaks out for each winning bid, and a photographer I recognise from the local newspaper is taking photographs.

Dorothy quietens the audience down again, and then announces Maddie to the stage, and I didn't see her creep around the audience to get there. My mouth goes completely dry when I see what she's wearing, a sexy Santa outfit, with sheer black tights and red high heels. Her hair is down showing off her beautiful curls, and pinned back with candy cane hairgrips. Her lips are painted in a dark red lipstick and her eye makeup is minimal. She takes the microphone from Dorothy and starts to sing Santa Baby, and I feel myself crossing my legs as I sit on the stool. I've never been attracted to anyone in my life more than her at this moment, and I can't do a thing about it. Luckily for me with the house lights down low, it saves me from embarrassing myself.

Her set continues when Maddie announces into the microphone, "I'd like to dedicate this song to a very special friend, you know who you are." And I swear god Maddie looks straight at me, knowing I've been there the whole time, and winks at me.

The opening bars to Mariah Carey's, All I want for Christmas is you, plays on the backing track. Maddie starts to sing, "I don't want a lot for Christmas, there is just one thing I need, I don't care about the presents underneath the Christmas tree, I just want you for my own, more than you could ever know, make my wish come true, all I want for Christmas is you…"

I gulp, I was not expecting that, and she's obviously spent a lot of time picking out this song for me with those very specific lyrics. But I can't take my eyes off her, and she can't take her eyes off me, and I feel something very real passing between us in that moment. It feels like it's just me and her and there is no audience in the room.

At the end of the song, Maddie blows a kiss towards me, and I feel a slap on my back, and I turn to see Bryan putting a tray on the bar. He bends to shout in my ear, "You are in so much trouble, that girl is totally into you."

Maddie is totally making a play for me, unapologetically so, it feels dangerous, and I kind of like it. I think I need to get out of here as soon as possible before I do something really stupid. Maddie has left me completely speechless, I really am in trouble as far as she's concerned, trying to remain honourable is becoming increasingly difficult and I don't know how I'm going to get out of this without hurting her feelings or mine. Either way, I'm totally and utterly screwed...

Chapter Fifty-Three

Maddie

The sweat is dripping down my back, from the bright overhead lights and the sheer volume of people here by the time I come off stage. Dorothy and I have just finished the evening's entertainment show with some duets as usual, but singing Christmas songs. The tip collection looks like it's overflowing tonight, and I'll be able to tuck that money away to go towards Jack and Tommy's football camp next year. Excitedly I look around the bar for Danny and I can't see him anywhere, because there are so many people moving around. So I decide to go and get changed out of this ridiculous outfit Dorothy insisted I wear tonight, convincing me it would be great for tips, and I can't fault her logic there.

Getting quickly changed back into my skinny black jeans, and a baggy Christmas jumper with a giant gingerbread man on the front, I don't even bother to remove my make-up, and make my way back into the crowded bar, the last place I saw Danny sitting.

"Hey Ben, have you seen Danny?" I shout, as he busily pulls pints and takes last orders at the bar before it closes down for the night.

"I think he's gone already Maddie, ask Bryan. He was talking to him about ten minutes ago." Ben replies as he continues to work at an impressive pace not keeping the customers waiting too long.

"Thanks, I'll ask Bryan." I shout back, and scan the room for Bryan, who's with a customer at the moment, so I patiently wait until he finishes.

"You were fabulous as always tonight, Maddie." Dorothy says as she clicks her fingers for a drink, and points towards the two of us. Ben places down two sparkling waters with lemon in, which have become our post set drinks, as we get so hot and dehydrated under the lights while on stage.

"Thanks Dorothy, I really love this job now. It's almost become more, I can't even begin to imagine not singing anymore." I reply, thankful for the water, while taking a large sip through a straw aware that I'm still wearing lipstick.

Bryan returns to the bar, and bangs his head against his empty tray. "My feet are so sore, all I want to do is collapse in a heap in bed." He announces in his typical dramatic Bryan fashion.

"Did you happen to see where Danny went? I wanted to speak to him." I ask Bryan, almost holding my breath with nerves after singing Danny that song. I know it was slightly on the nose but I'm pretty sure he understood the message.

"Danny sends his apologies for not sticking around, but he's taking his dad to midnight mass. They go every year, so do I usually." And I see a glint of pain pass in Bryans eyes.

Damn. Danny's already gone. I hope I didn't embarrass him tonight. All sorts of ugly thoughts start to go through my head, and I suddenly feel my chest getting tight. Not now, please not now. My head starts to go dizzy, and I feel faint. I obviously embarrassed my friend, I should never had sung him that song.

"Maddie, you need to breathe. Deep breaths, or you're going to pass out." And I can feel Bryan shaking me, I start to slow my breathing down, and feel the dizziness subsiding. I can't lose it here, I won't lose it here, not in my place of work. Taking deep breaths, I look up and find three sets of eyes looking at me in concern, Bryan, Ben and Dorothy.

"Sorry guys, I didn't' mean to scare you like that. I get panic attacks sometimes, especially when I overthink things." I reply looking up at them all guiltily, and I feel like such a silly little fool.

"Come on missy, I'm getting one of the bouncers to drive you home. I expect the heat and the crowd overwhelmed you, happens to the best of us." Dorothy says, putting her arm around me and guiding me towards one of the bouncers.

"I'll see you guys tomorrow, don't worry, I'm fine." I shout over my shoulder to Bryan and Ben. How on earth am I going to be able to face Danny tomorrow?

Danny

The sound of the church choir and congregation singing Silent Night sends my mind wandering off, I stand up from the pew holding my hymn sheet not even attempting to sing along with everyone. My dad notices, and nudges my arm, them raises his eye brow at me in question. So reluctantly I start to join in, but only going through the motions for show and to keep dad happy. Looking up, I scan the congregation and can see Bryans parents near the front of the church. I'll be avoiding them like the plague on the way out of here once the service finishes.

Slipping back into my daydream, I think about Maddie singing tonight and how perfect she was. I feel like a coward running out on her like that before saying goodbye, but I really did need to get my dad to mass. And I had no idea how to act appropriately towards her after that performance, I'm going to need at least ten cold showers when I get home as it is, thinking about her in that sexy Santa outfit.

As the service comes to an end, I make a point of darting up first, and using the excuse to dad that I'm going to bring the car around to the front of the church, so that he doesn't have so far to walk on his crutches. He is still yet to get the hang of them, and his leg will be fully healed before he does at this rate.

Walking at a brisk pace in the frigid wind, a dark figure catches up to me. It's Uriel, no wings this time, too many people around I expect. This is exactly what I don't need right now, another one of his little visits.

"We have to stop meeting like this Uriel, I haven't had a chance to speak properly to Maddie about her dreams yet, so please don't hassle me about it." Aiming my frustrations towards him, I haven't got time for his riddles right now.

"From her mother, call it a gift." Uriel hands me a small glass bottle, with an ornate stopper in the top, it looks like it's made from some type of crystal that I've never seen before.

"What's in it?" I ask suspiciously, putting it in my jacket pocket before anyone spots it, and starts asking questions.

"Add one drop into any liquid then drink. The dream that she seeks answers for will become more clear. It will assist her until she gains more control over her gift. Do not worry, it isn't dangerous. All Angels use it in the beginning." Uriel replies, matter of fact as usual. Blissfully unaware of the bombshell that he's just dropped on me about Maddie.

"Pardon? Did you say Angels? Maddie isn't an Angel." I reply alarmed by this sudden revelation, no wonder she needs protection. But what possible help can I be? Surely she would be better protected by one of her own kind?

Uriel sighs. "I've said to much already."

"You can't leave it like this, it concerns Maddie. How can I possibly protect her if I don't know the entire truth?" I snap back at him, trying to rein my temper in, I've had about as much as I can take from Uriel. With his riddles and revelations.

"Very well. Her mother is like me, once an Angel, but defied the rules instructed to her. I suppose you may term our kind as fallen angels. Forever banished in another realm, forbidden from returning to earth. Maddie's father however is human which complicates things more, his family is very powerful. He is not a good man, and must be kept away from Maddie at all cost. I must go, my powers fading. Use this information wisely." In typical Uriel style, he fades away leaving nothing there. To say I'm in shock is an understatement. But it does explain a few things about Maddie, like her beauty inside and out that almost glows off her, and the voice of a literal Angel, my fallen Angel through no fault of her own.

Reaching my car parked in the next street, I drive around to the front of the church to pick up my dad, when I notice him standing propped up against the wall of the churchyard talking to Bryans parents. Great even more drama, is there no end to it tonight?   When dad notices me, he makes a fast exit from David and Jean. David giving my dad an awkward hug, followed by Jean doing the same thing, and she passes him a gift bag of presents.

"Sorry I got held up Danny, but I couldn't ignore them. Especially on Christmas eve, the season of goodwill." My dad says, as he slowly folds himself and his crutches into the car, with little finesse.

"What did they want? Haven't they done enough damage to Bryan mentally, and physically?" I ask dad bitterly, not feeling a scrap of sympathy towards them. They get to spend Christmas alone, that's on them and nobody else.

"No need to be like that Danny. I'm just trying to keep things civil. It's difficult for everyone." Dad replies, wiggling in the seat to get his leg comfortable. I realise he's caught between a rock and a hard place, but that changes nothing for Bryan.

"Tell Bryan that." I angrily retort, then instantly feel guilty getting mad at my dad, it's not fair on him, he never caused this situation.

"I know son, I know. I think it's hitting them that Bryan and you and me won't be there for Christmas this year." My dad answers sadly, because through all of this he must be missing his best friend, it's all such a bloody mess.

"If Bryans dad wasn't such a bigot then it would be happy families as usual." I answer exasperated, I refuse to defend Davids actions.

"Danny, what's wrong son? Talk to me, it isn't just this that's upsetting you, I can tell." Dad looks concerned now, turning towards me in his seat, his seatbelt restraining him pulling tightly.

"Everything, nothing. I don't know. Just things I can't talk about right now." I reply, running my hand through my hair in frustration. Where do I even begin to explain things?

"Does it have anything to do with a certain young lady? Is that's what's got you tied up in knots? I've seen the way you two look at each other." Dad smiles, knowingly, and I nod back sadly.

"She's seventeen dad. Seventeen." I answer knowing it's a weak answer because she turns eighteen this week, and would it be such a big thing if we did get together?

"And your mother god rest her soul was ten years younger than me, may I remind you. She was nineteen when we first started dating." Damn it, he's right. Dad always has an answer, smarty pants.

"I'll deal with it dad, let's just get through tomorrow first." I sass back at him, feeling slightly lighter than I did a few seconds ago, my dad. Ever the wiseman.

"It's technically already tomorrow, it's past midnight Danny. Merry Christmas." Dad laughs back, he's such a smartass.

"Merry Christmas dad." And I continue the drive home...

Arriving home, I say goodnight to dad, making a fast escape upstairs to my room. Checking the time on my phone it's really late or very early, depending how you look at it. I notice a message I've not yet read, opening it I can see it's from Maddie sent about an hour ago while I was at mass, my phones been on silent.

Sorry I missed you before you left, thanks for coming. Merry Christmas Danny

I smile to myself, and I can't wait until I see her later on, and I type out a reply.

Merry Christmas, my sweet Angel

Morning can't arrive soon enough as far as I'm concerned.

Chapter Fifty-Four

Maddie

Feeling my futon bed bounce on both sides, I can feel myself coming out of a strange dream, something important that I need to remember, bodies, blood, I reach for them but as soon as I open my eyes the vision is gone. My memory drifts away again out of reach, I can't seem to reach it, and the harder I try the less I remember.

Jack and Tommy are sitting on either side of my futon with large stupid grins on their faces, full of mischief and joy. A very different picture from last Christmas at Nanna Jenny's house, when we woke up freezing cold because she refused to put the central heating on, and we had no hot water because the boiler was broken. Gifts were my latest charity shop finds and dinner consisted of turkey dinosaurs, I kid you not, and chips. Nanna Jenny didn't believe in making a fuss. So not exactly the Christmas dreams are made from.

"It's Christmas Maddie, come downstairs and see if Santa's been." Tommy laughs, tugging at my arm in excitement, he's going to pull me off the bed at this rate.

"Firstly, what god forsaken hour do you call this? And secondly, you haven't believed in Santa since you were six years old and Nanna Jenny told you that he didn't exist, just so she could get out of buying you presents." I laugh at the tragic truth, and realise what a rotten childhood Jack and Tommy have had.

"Sam's already up, and said we can eat anything we want for

breakfast, so I'm having chocolate." Jack replies cheekily, with a smirk on his face, because I would never have let him get away with that.

"How do you even know you'll get any chocolate?" I answer joking back, knowing damn well he's got chocolate and lots of it.

"Because we saw Sam wrapping up selection boxes the other night before she yelled at us to get out of the room." Jack laughs back, cocky as ever. She better had brought me one too then, I mumble to myself half asleep.

The boys annoyingly don't let up bouncing on my futon until I throw back the covers and slowly climb out of bed, and put my slippers on. I follow them both down the loft ladder and make a sharp exit to use the bathroom first, and I can hear them both loitering outside the bathroom door giggling together, how do they expect me to pee with an audience outside the door? So I shout at them both to go downstairs and wait for me, and seconds later I hear a thunder of feet running down the stairs. Looking in the bathroom mirror as I wash my hands, I notice something different about myself and I smile. I'm actually looking forward to today's festivities. It will be my first proper Christmas with presents, a real tree, a massive feast, and most importantly a real family.

Excitedly, I practically bounce down the stairs, and start to sing Underneath the tree by Kelly Clarkson, Jack and Tommy drag me down to the Christmas presents underneath the tree, and   we   all   sing   along   together. Sam is sitting on the sofa looking smug, blowing over a hot cup of coffee. She has a huge smile on her face like she knows what's coming next.

"Stockings to open first guys." And Sam hands each of us a medium sized stocking each, that she had hidden down the side of the sofa, very crafty of her.

Each stocking contains a small selection box of chocolate,

chocolate coins, gourmet hot chocolate sachets, candy canes and marshmallows. At the bottom of each stocking is a mug with our name on, they have been hand painted, Sam's crafting skills are by far superior to mine.

"Promise me you won't make yourself sick before dinner, or put yourself into a diabetic coma." She laughs and adds, "Can't help my nursing humour."

For the next half an hour we all exchange presents, Jack and Tommy receiving by far the most, and I almost feel like crying watching the enjoyment in their little faces. By the end of it all, the entire living room carpet is a sea of torn wrapping paper and gift bags. Sam brought the boys a laptop each to make it easier for when they do their homework, and so she can have her Netflix back to watch in her room at night. She got me a kindle that I'd been debating on buying myself, and downloaded some books that she thought I might enjoy reading. We got Sam her favourite perfume, and a voucher for a spa day, having that tip money certainly came in handy.

"Right troops, chop, chop. We need to get ourselves showered and out the door by ten, I thought we'd walk to Thomas's so I don't have to drive later on. The dinner isn't going to cook itself, and I need to check Danny put the turkey in the oven for me." Sam orders us like an army sergeant ordering the troops into battle, we do rock, paper, scissors to decide who gets to use the shower first. I don't know how I manage it, but I lose against Jack and Tommy every single time without fail. Those two are little scam artists and I'm sure that they do that psychic twin thing, so I lose. Of course getting last shower means I'll get the least amount of time to get ready, so I lay out my clothes ready on my chair, and grab a bag of presents from underneath my bedside table.

I'm nervous to give Danny his gift and I really hope that he likes it, and I smile again at the thought of spending the rest of the day with him. Adding a little mascara and lip-gloss to my face, I've managed to get ready in record time even by my standards, and I chuckle at how impressed I am with myself. I'm wearing a sparkly purple dress, which I intend to reuse on stage at Dorothy's, but for today's purpose it makes the perfect Christmas dress. I've matched it with some cute purple candy cane print tights, and the candy cane hairgrips that I wore last night at work. Not having a cardigan that will match the dress, isn't a big deal so I don't bother wearing one, my winter coat will suffice on the short walk to Danny's house.

Finally we're all leaving the house and walking towards Danny's, Sam locks the front door and turns to Jack and Tommy. "Remember to behave yourselves today boys, I know your both very excited, but we have been kindly invited into Mr McKenzie's home."

"Of course Sam, we love going to Coaches house, he's the best." Tommy replies, and I chuckle again because I know Sam was talking about Danny's dad. But she just smiles at me knowingly and doesn't correct him, and that's another reason Sam's so great.

Jack and Tommy start to run ahead, "Don't go to far ahead." Sam and I both shout out at exactly the same time, we burst out laughing, because it's not the first time that its happened.

"So you and Danny's dad are dating now?" I enquire, it's not something Sam and I have spoken about, but if it makes her happy then I'm happy for her.

"I was worried about how you might react, and I was also worried about our age gap." Sam answers softly, as we walk along the pavement a cold December chill in the air.

"I can say exactly the same thing about me and Danny, although we're just friends." I reply, aware we have the same worries as each other now which is kind of funny.

"Maddie you are eighteen in a matter of days, and pretty soon no one will even think about your age gap. It's an awkward age, that's all it is. Don't worry about me, Danny is a good guy, he's given me no reason to doubt him. I'll admit that I did have them at first, but he's since proved me wrong." Sam smiles, she has basically given me a blessing to pursue a relationship with Danny. This is perfect, not that I need her permission, but it's nice to know she'll support me in my decision.

"About you and Danny's dad, I don't know him well but I think you should go for it Sam. You deserve to be happy. You do so much for everyone else around you, do something for you for a change." And we hug in the middle of the pavement, like it's the most normal thing in the world to do on Christmas day morning.

"Come on hurry up slow coaches, you two are taking ages." Jack shouts from halfway down the street. "We're coming." Sam and I both reply at the same time, which cause us both to burst into hysterical laughter this time. Great minds, and all that...

Bryan

"**M**erry Christmas bro." I shout as loudly as possible, and bounce onto Danny's bed, already knowing it's going to piss him off, Danny is always grumpy first thing in the morning.

"Fuck off it's way too early, Bryan. I went to bed late, and got up at stupid o'clock to put the turkey in the oven so we can have dinner, and I've earned some more sleep." Danny replies throwing a pillow over his head, and desperately trying to ignore me, but he should know me better than that by now. I take no prisoners...

"Danny, it's almost ten thirty, Maddie is due anytime lazybones, shall I tell her to come straight up here when she arrives?" I shout back at him, only half joking, because I would totally do that to my good friend. That's what bro's are for right?

"Shit. I slept through my alarm, why didn't you wake me Bryan?" Danny answers as annoyed as he gets up and walks towards his ensuite bathroom, naked, slamming the door behind him.

"Meet you downstairs Mr Scrooge, nice butt by the way, must be all that off road cycling keeping it all fit, and easy on the eye." I shout at the door just as he slings it open again.

"Sorry, Merry Christmas Bryan. Lack of sleep, I won't be long. And stop looking at my butt, it's weird Bryan." And he shuts the bathroom door again more quietly this time.

Today feels strange. Waking up on Christmas day, with no stocking on the bottom of my bed, it hurts inside my chest. I miss my parents, and I feel sad when I should be full of joy. But I'm determined to put on a brave face, I won't bring anyone down today, even if it is going to be hard. At least Ben is coming over later, after he's had dinner with his family, so there is a silver lining, I just wish that it didn't come at such a cost. And winding up Danny is so easy, he walks right into it every, single, time…

Taking my phone out of my pocket and looking at it for the twentieth time this hour, I still see no message has magically appeared saying all is forgiven and to please come home. Do I put my phone on silent and ignore it? Or do I keep obsessively checking it for messages? I decide to do nothing and put it back into my pocket, and go downstairs to wait for Maddie to arrive.

"Merry Christmas Mr McKenzie." I say as I enter the living room, admiring my handywork on the Christmas tree decorations, Danny's mum had really good taste, it's a shame I never got to meet her.

"For the hundredth time, call me Thomas. I think we've outgrown Mr McKenzie, and Merry Christmas to you Bryan. Is

Danny coming, I want to open some presents, and I'm getting impatient, he knows I hate surprises." Thomas laughs, giving me a hug, wobbling on his crutches. He still hasn't got the hang of them, even the physio can't understand why he can't coordinate.

"Danny's gone in the shower, so he won't be too long." Answering, already feeling guilty at the meagre gifts that I've gotten for everyone, I'm trying to save most of my money from my tips and wages at Dorothy's in case things don't work out here and I need to move. Danny's dad doesn't strike me as the kind of guy that would throw me out, but you never can tell. So I've gone with getting humorous gifts for everyone this year, I'm pretty sure Jack and Tommy will appreciate theirs, Sam not so much. But who doesn't find the occasional stink bomb funny? And the radio controlled mouse is hilarious, and I have it on good authority that Sam hates mice. Prepare for chaos.

"In that case can you go and grab some more chairs out of the garage or Jack and Tommy won't have anywhere to sit for dinner. We don't keep the full set in the dining room because we rarely need to use them." Thomas asks me politely, and I give him a cheeky salute in acknowledgement.

"Sure thing Mr, I mean Thomas. I'll do it now." And I slip my shoes on and go outside to the garage by the side of the house. I press the button on a remote control and one of the doors automatically opens. The McKenzie's don't use the double garage for cars, it's more of a storage area. Typical. The chairs that I need are right at the back behind some boxes, so I slowly start shifting stuff around. Locating the two chairs I need, I move them onto the driveway and start rearranging the boxes back. Trust Danny to get out of this, I bet its revenge for me waking him up, or not waking him up soon enough. Can't win either way on that one.

"Boo!" Maddie and the boys jump out at me as I back out of the garage, scaring the living daylights out of me.

"You scared the sh…" I start to say, but then notice Sam standing there and change it to "I mean you scared the stuffing out of my turkey." And I laugh hugging Maddie, and she silently mouths back, "the stuffing out of my turkey???" A look of total confusion on her face.

"What's that noise?" Tommy asks looking around, and he shushes everyone.

"Nice try Tommy." I reply laughing, the little sucker won't have me falling for his scam, I know what ten year old boys are like, I was a ten year old boy once upon a time.

"No seriously. That scratching noise, its coming from over there." Tommy answers annoyed, and walks towards the wheelie bin at the bottom of the driveway.

"Be careful, it might be a rat." Sam pipes up, hugging herself because she hates anything rodent.

"I'm sure it's nothing." Being the big brave man, I walk over to the bin and open the lid, with Tommy now peering from behind me. Inside a plastic carrier bag, something is moving around, and a pathetic little meow comes from inside the bag. Gently lifting the bag out of the bin, I notice that the top has only been tied loosely, like it was done in a hurry. Opening the bag carefully up, two tiny sets of green eyes look out of the bag back at me.

"Someone's dumped a kitten in our bin." I can't quite believe my eyes, who would do such a heinous thing?

"No, surely not." Maddie exclaims, and everyone crowds around as I lift the tiny creature out of the bag and cuddle it into my jumper.

"Poor little thing is shivering. Who the hell dumps a kitten on Christmas morning? Let's get inside to see if it's okay, and into the warm." I find myself bubbling with anger that someone dumped it like a piece of rubbish. Taking the kitten inside the house, I now realise how very small and probably hungry the kitten is. I've got no idea how to care for it, and I hand it off to Maddie while I do a quick google search on hand rearing a kitten.

"According to this, kittens can't drink normal milk and need a milk replacer or lactose free milk, you can use a syringe and let it slowly suckle. There's pages and pages of advice." I look up at Maddie, worriedly, still having no idea what to do with the little fur ball.

"Don't panic Bryan, I had cats growing up, and I've fed newborn babies, this is just a furry one with four legs." Sam answers taking the kitten from Maddie, her nursing skills taking over, and gently checking the animal's body for injury on her lap. I suppose she's the most qualified person to deal with this.

"Can we keep it?" Tommy asks, with his eyes sparkling, I know Maddie's told me before the brothers desperately want a pet. But it's never been the right time for them.

"Bryan, you're the one who found the kitten, so it should be up to you to decide if Tommy would be a suitable candidate to adopt the kitten now." Sam replies grinning and giving me a knowing look, I like her style.

"Well I've always wanted a kitten, but it's Christmas, and way too much responsibility for me. You go ahead Tommy and adopt it, so long as you think you can handle it. Jack could help as well I suppose, and if it's okay with Sam." I grin back at her, Jack and Tommy are on tender hooks now, waiting for Sam to give her decision.

"So long as you care for it together boys, it looks like we have another addition to our family." Sam announces, and I think I just witnessed some Christmas magic in front of me.

"This is the best Christmas ever!" Tommy pipes up, hugging his brother Jack. Looking at them both makes me realise my issues are minuscule compared to what they've been through.

At least I got to have a childhood and my parents loved me. I need to man up, accept my situation, and make the most of it.

Thomas points Sam in the direction of the medicine cabinet in the bathroom for a medicine syringe they have in a first aid kit, one that I'm unfortunately familiar with. While I go and retrieve the lactose free milk out of the fridge that Danny insists is better than normal milk. It's pure luck that we even have something like that in the house, until we can see a vet. Personally, I think it's because Danny is a health freak at times.

We all watch intrigued as Sam gently wraps the kitten in a towel, and teaches Jack and Tommy how to feed the kitten with a syringe. This is not how I imagined Christmas morning to be, but it's kind of perfect right now...

Chapter Fifty-Five

Danny

With the excitement of finding the kitten settling down, normal Christmas morning has resumed. We've decided to wait until after dinner to open presents, and with the kitten to keep the boys occupied, and with Sam and dad pottering about in the kitchen, no one seems to mind.

Needing to speak to Maddie before dinner, I find myself making a lame excuse about showing her something on my computer upstairs, and she follows me to my room without question.

"Sorry I left last night before saying goodbye, but I had to pick up dad to take him to midnight mass. I thought you were amazing Maddie, you blew it out the water with that performance." I grovel apologizing for running out on her like I did last night. Being a total coward, I don't admit to using midnight mass as an excuse, because I can't possibly share my real feelings with her.

"That's okay Danny, I did wonder if everything was okay though? You look like you want to say something else to me?" Maddie looks into my eyes like she's searching for the truth, always so intuitive.

"I'm working through some stuff in my head Maddie, it's really not you. So please don't worry." I answer, giving her one of the lamest excuses possible, inwardly cringing to myself.

"That sounds suspiciously like the, it's not you, but me speech

Danny." Maddie replies looking hurt, but quickly masking her reaction like she always does.

"Give me some time Maddie, that's all I can ask for now. Friends?" I ask her, inside wanting so much more, but now is not the right time for us to start that kind of relationship, and I hate myself for blatantly shooting her down like this. But something bad is coming, I can feel it.

"Okay Danny. If that's what you want. I can wait, I'll always wait for you." And she kisses my cheek, with her eyes glistening with tears, leaving me standing in my room, contemplating my decision for the millionth time. But right now protecting her is far more important, and I think about the blood she said she saw in her dream...

Christmas dinner turns into organised chaos, with everyone seated around the dining room table and one of dads Michael Buble CD's playing in the background. Dad sits proudly at the head of the table to carve the turkey, which is nice, because for years we've been at David and Jean's house. It's good to be celebrating at home again after all these years. Sam's busy filling wine glasses with sparkling wine or in Jack and Tommy's case cola. Maddie is passing her handmade crackers around the table, insisting that everyone pulls them at the same time, she's putting on a brave face but I know I've really hurt her again.

Then I find myself thinking about mum, I wonder if she's watching us all from heaven? Seeing my dad with a smile on his face after his accident, and his growing attraction towards Sam. I know mum would approve, she would want dad to be happy again and not alone.   Bryan is slightly subdued, and I notice that he keeps looking at his phone. I'm hoping he will perk up when we do presents and Ben arrives. Everyone is hiding pain of some kind...

"Ow, I forgot to bring the nut roast through from the kitchen." Maddie announces, getting up from the table.

"I'll get it for you Maddie, you're a guest." And I dash off before she gets a chance, and retrieve it from the kitchen for her.

"You can make walls with that stuff, I heard the recipe is in a construction manual and not a recipe book." Jack laughs, wrinkling his nose up, and pinching a piece of turkey off the platter. I notice the table trying not to laugh at Jack's proclamation, me included.

"Nothing's wrong with my nut roast, it's tasty and delicious if you bothered to try it." Maddie sasses back to him, not really upset by his previous comment.

"Do you mind if I try some?" I ask her, feeling brave. I hate nut roast with a vengeance, but I'll do anything to make Maddie happy, and her eyes light up. Well almost anything...

"Of course, there's plenty, for some reason no one else ever eats it." She smiles, and shrugs her shoulders. Then scoops a ginormous piece onto my plate, and I try not to shudder.

"Suck-up." Bryan whispers to me smirking, and I give him the evil eye, not wanting Bryan to give away my deceit.

"Who's for brussel sprouts and chestnuts?" Sam asks, holding up a large dish full to the brim.

"No." Jack and Tommy both reply at the same time, and Jack makes a gagging sound.

"I second that." Bryan replies, looking equally disgusted by the little green balls.

"Seriously boys, sprouts are lovely. You've never had my sprouts, I put butter on them." Sam replies, putting her hand on her hip, and my dad nearly spits his drink out.

"Get your mind out of the gutter dad." I laugh, and Sam blushes, suddenly realising the sexual innuendo she just implied.

"Let's read out the cracker jokes, they better be good Maddie." Tommy pipes up, picking up the joke from inside a pulled cracker. Jack snatches it out of his hand.

"Okay, why is Santa so damn jolly?" Jack asks, looking at us all sitting around the table bursting to tell us all the punchline.

"I don't know." Everyone repeats at once.

"Because he knows where all the naughty girls live." And the table once again descends into a scene of utter chaos.

"Where did you get those jokes from?" I whisper to Maddie, she's placed herself in the seat next to me with the cute little penguin placenames she also made.

"I thought a few slightly rude jokes, using my inner ten year old boys humour, would be well received." Maddie replies discreetly.

"Good call." I answer, gently squeezing her hand underneath the table, and she clings onto it for a few seconds.

After a hilarious Christmas dinner thanks to Maddie's cracker jokes, which Jack then decides to continue on by googling even ruder jokes, we settle down on the sofa and the floor to open up the Christmas presents. I pass two identical gifts from underneath the tree to Jack and Tommy. Inside each gift is a new football training kit and an envelope, and I watch carefully, as they open the envelopes with confusion on their faces.

"Coach this is amazing, I can't believe it! We get to go!" Jack and Tommy shout excitedly and hug each other, while the rest of the small gathering look on with confusion.

"What is it? Inside the envelope?" Sam asks, turning towards me, and I can see Maddie peering over Tommy's shoulder to see what's written inside.

"It's a written confirmation that next year's football camp on the Isle of Wight is fully paid, and that a schedule will follow in the new year." Maddie looks at me tearfully, and then gazes happily at Jack and Tommy.

"That's a very generous gift Danny." Sam replies, looking equally shocked, I think I've left her speechless for once.

"Jack and Tommy have worked incredibly hard, and brought the team together this season. They more than deserve to go to camp. So it's the least I can do. Really." I smile back at everyone, feeling all eyes on me. Now all I need to do is finish organising it, but they don't need to know that finer detail.

"We won't let you down Coach. We've wanted to go for so long. Thank you." Jack looks close to tears himself, I knew they wanted to go, but I didn't realise it was this bigger deal.

"No. We won't let you down. We'll work even harder. Thanks Coach, you're the best." Tommy adds, sniffling, the more sensitive of the two brothers. Everyone starts chattering about the football camp, so I take the opportunity and hand a small box from underneath the Christmas tree to Maddie, while people's attention is drawn away.

"This is just a little something, it reminds me of you." Handing over the box to Maddie, she looks at me in wonder, then carefully removes the paper and opens the box inside.

Maddie gasps, "Oh my god Danny, it's beautiful. I love it! Help me put it on please." Maddie lifts the delicate silver angel wings necklace out of the box and hands it to me, then gently pulls her long hair to one side. I undo the clasp, and place the necklace around her neck, my fingers brushing her skin and sending shock waves through me. Maybe this wasn't such a good idea after all?

"And this one is for you Danny, I hope you enjoy it. It's one of my favourites." Maddie hands me an gift and I start to tear off the wrapping paper carefully.

"I found this in that little second-hand bookshop in town. It's a hardback copy from the 1970's, it's not rare or anything, but I really liked the artwork on the cover. I know you like Stephen King too." Maddie blushes, and looks away. I've already torn the paper off the book, holding it in my hand. She's written inside in beautiful handwriting:

To my dearest friend and so much more, I hope you enjoy this book as much as I did, all my love, Maddie xxx

"It's perfect Maddie, your perfect." And I kiss her gently on the cheek, and I feel her breath quicken as I do so, I wish it could be a different kind of kiss. Noticing now that people have stopped talking, and the spotlight is on both of us. Dad is smiling giving me a knowing look. Trying to ignore the obvious attention on us, I hand a present to Sam.

"This one's for you Sam, but it's from me and dad. We pooled in together, hope you don't mind." Passing her an envelope with a rather large voucher for a local garden centre. We didn't pool together, I totally made that up. Dad's going to kill me, but he needs to up his game to impress the lady.

"Oh, and this one too." I say handing her another gift, a gardening journal so she can keep track of the seasons, and whatever gardeners do.

"I don't even know what to say." Sam gets up from the sofa and hugs me, and then hugs my dad. My dad is staring at me and I can't help but notice the twinkle he has in his eye. Definitely scored dad points with him. Maddie puts her head on my shoulder and closes her eyes, she doesn't say anything, she doesn't need too.

The doorbell rings, and Bryan automatically jumps up, the first time I've seen him genuinely happy today, because I can see through his clown act. Hearing from the hallway voices that must mean Ben has arrived, Bryan should perk up now.

"Merry Christmas everyone. This is for you Mr McKenzie, thanks for having me over on Christmas day." He hands my dad a bottle of his favourite whiskey.

"Your very welcome Ben, the more the merrier, and I will

certainly be merry now." My dad laughs holding up the whiskey bottle to the rest of the room.

"One small glass on those pain killers Thomas, you had wine at dinner. Or you'll be off your face." Sam points, putting on a over exaggerated nurses voice.

"Well, that told me nurse Samantha." Dad laughs, and wiggles his eyebrow. Oh my god, dad is blatantly flirting with her, I can't deal with dad flirting, it's all kinds of wrong...

"I'm going to load the dishwasher up." I say to no one in particular, escaping the room rapidly.

"We'll do more presents when you come back." I hear dad shout from the living room after me.

Maddie follows me to the dining room, and we silently start clearing down the table together in perfect harmony with each other. Maddie starts humming a tune, and before long she's singing Heigh-Ho, Heigh-Ho, from Snow White and the Seven Dwarfs.

After several minutes of this I whisper to Maddie, "I've got another gift for you passed on to me by Uriel, follow me out to the garage with one of the spare dining room chairs. I need to speak to you privately." Indicating to Maddie to follow me by picking up one of the dining room chairs. She complies with no question and follows me outside with another chair, everyone else is too busy to notice as they fuss over the kitten again.

Inside the garage, I close the door with us inside and I sit down on one of the chairs I've just carried so Maddie does the same. Might as well make ourselves comfortable. Before Maddie has a chance to ask me any questions, I take the small bottle out of my pocket.

"According to Uriel, this is a gift from your mother to help you decipher your dreams. Apparently all Angels use it in the beginning." And I let that sentence hang there for her to fully take in, after a full minute I decide to continue.

"Uriel keeps insisting that you need to listen carefully to your dreams, if you put a drop of whatever this potion is he gave me, into any fluid and then drink it, it's supposed to help you decipher the dream." I know I've just dropped a bombshell on her, and I don't know how she's going to react to this.

Maddie takes the bottle from me, and holds the clear glass bottle in the air to inspect it. She opens the stopper and sniffs the contents, then replaces it.

"It doesn't smell of anything suspicious, could be water or arsenic in there." Maddie replies with suspicion in her eyes, and I honestly don't blame her for thinking like that.

"I don't think Uriel wants to poison you. He's trying to help, I know he takes risks coming here to give me messages for you." I answer, desperately trying to reassure her, but failing miserably as usual.

"If that's the case Danny, I don't understand why he doesn't approach me himself. It would save all this cloak and dagger stuff." And she waves her arm around the garage in discontent.

"Apparently it isn't safe for you and him to meet. Please don't shoot the messenger, I'm only trying to help Maddie." Hoping she now doesn't take out her frustrations on me, I don't want to fight with her.

"Sorry Danny, it's just a lot to take in. My brains a mess too. We make a right pair today." She sighs and hugs me, and I take the opportunity to feel her body close to mine.

"Its okay Maddie I get it, I really do. But sooner rather than later, you need to try this potion to see if it works. I know your struggling to see a dream at the moment that you think is important, and Uriel said…" But Maddie abruptly cuts me off from finishing my sentence.

"Uriel said this, Uriel said that, and now a unidentified liquid you actually want me to try. And it implies something else Danny, being given this liquid to use, a liquid Angels use in the beginning. Are you crazy Danny, just listen to yourself right now! I'm not a bloody Angel, they don't exist." Maddie is starting to get mad with me now, I didn't expect her response to be like this. She doesn't believe me, this complicates things even more.

"Maddie I'm sorry. I should not have brought it up today, especially as we are meant to be celebrating Christmas. Can we agree to disagree for now? Put this conversation in a box until you have time to digest it properly?" I ask on baited breath, not wanting to ruin the day any further for her.

"Okay Danny. I can do that. Sorry I called you crazy, that was a low blow even for me." Maddie replies taking a deep breath, and straightening the bottom of her dress as a distraction.

"Don't worry about my ego, I've been called far worse for far less." I answer gabbing her hand to lead her back into the living room with all the others.

As complicated as things are now, I refuse to leave her side in this, and I will protect her from whatever threat comes her way. I'm going to give her some space again to digest this information about the liquid Uriel gave me to pass onto her. Maddie needs to have a few days to process, I'm fast learning this is something that she has to do, there's no point pushing her too soon. Then I can persuade her to try the potion, and if it works we can attempt to decipher her dreams. The recurring one she's having about the blood and bodies is very worrying. But it's pointless to speculate it could be interpreted to mean practically anything at this stage, with so little information available. Which is exactly why Maddie needs to try the potion, and around and around in circles I go.

What if my sweetest Angel Maddie actually turns out to be a real bonified Angel? Or what if Maddie's , and I have gone crazy? With all this happening now I'm more determined than ever to keep her safe from whatever threat is coming...

Chapter Fifty-Five

Bryan

Snuggled up on the sofa with Ben, I feel the most relaxed I've been all day. A random Christmas movie is on the TV, another Hallmark one I think, but no one is really watching it. Sam is showing Tommy how to feed the kitten again which they've decided to call Holly, I just hope that it doesn't turn out to be a boy, or it may have gender identity issues. It seems to be pretty content now, and has taken to sleeping in Tommy's hoodie pocket at the front. Much like a joey lives in its mothers pouch on a kangaroo. Everyone else is playing monopoly around the coffee table, it looks like a picture perfect moment, and I discreetly snap a few candid photos on my phone with no one noticing. I'll share them with Maddie later, they would look good in an old fashioned photo album. Feeling my mind wandering, I think about all the gifts I've received today from people that care about me, and how fortunate I am.

Ben gave me tickets to see the stage show Wicked in London, we are going to go together in the new year, and plan to have a day trip to London on the train. I can hardly wait, I've always love musicals but it was another dirty little secret I had to keep from dad. Danny and Thomas gave me a top of the range laptop. Danny says if I'm serious about learning from him, I need the basic tools to progress. He hasn't said an outright yes or no about taking me on as an apprentice to learn what he does yet. Danny said it's a big decision for him to make, and he doesn't want me to rush into anything because of my parents. So I guess until Danny gives me a definitive answer I'm still in limbo. At least I have a few months left at college first, and of course I have my fabulous job at Dorothy's. Maddie has made me a playlist for every mood, according to her, and I'm pretty sure this is her way of trying to get me to listen to rock and alternative music. One playlist is purely Taylor Swift, which she's called the Swifty Listey, which Maddie said is great for dancing too. Another list is alternative love songs, full of bands I've never heard of but Maddie assures me I'll love. Maddie has even paid for a Spotify account for the whole year so I can listen to whatever I want, that girl is making some great tips.

By my feet is a giftbag from my mum and dad, that Thomas discreetly gave me after dinner in private. Thomas spoke to them both after midnight mass, although he didn't elaborate on what was said, and I didn't have the guts to ask him.

"Open it Bryan, try not to overthink it, you're not going to be able to relax until you have." Ben quietly says. So I pick up the bag and stand up, indicating I'm going upstairs to my room. Firstly I take Bens hand and lead him upstairs with me. If I'm going to open this gift, I'll need his moral support. I place the gift bag on my bed, and look at it staring. I take my phone out of my pocket and see I don't have any messages. It hasn't rung all day, I don't know what I expected to happen really. But it makes me feel so desperately sad, and I could easily cry right now, in fact it won't take much to push me over the edge today.

"I don't know if I can do this Ben, why did they even send me a gift? Why throw me out like I'm worthless then do this? I don't get it, I don't get them." I look at Ben, with both my hands shaking, today has already been so overwhelming.

"I've got you Bryan." Ben replies and takes my hand and kisses it gently, he is literally all that is keeping my head above water, because I'm sinking. Without him I'm sinking. Ben is my rock.

Sitting on the bed I take the present out of the gift bag and tear off the paper. It's a photograph from last summer, it's when we went down the pier one Sunday after church for a stroll. My mum asked the girl in the coffee hut to take a photo of us three on her phone. In the photo we look like a real family. A tear slides down my face and I take a gulp. Even though they have hurt me, I still love them both unconditionally, even though they will continue to hurt me.

Also inside the bag, is what I assume to be a Christmas card, so I wipe away my tears and open the envelope up. It's not a card, it's a short note from my mum. With my hands shaking I read the note, letting Ben peer over my shoulder, so he can read it at the same time as me.

Dearest Bryan,

The way your father reacted was wrong, he realises this now. But he can't except your new lifestyle, and I find myself struggling with it too. Never in my wildest dreams did I imagine spending Christmas apart from my son. The house is empty without you here. But coming home isn't an option now, you made your own choice son, and now we all have to live with it.

Give us time, we love you. Please don't forget that. If you want to call me after you read this I promise you I'll answer.

Merry Christmas, love from mum

The note is sending conflicting messages to me from my mum, it appears that she has firmly taken my dad's side as I expected, but still wants to remain in contact with me. I wish she could be a stronger woman and stand up to him, but that would mean going against her own husband. Something that is very taboo with my mum, as she also comes from a strict catholic background. I always wonder why they never had more children, perhaps my father's temper is the reason why.

He's never hit my mum, I don't believe he would ever sink that low, mind you, he hit me, so all bets are off the table.

I look at Ben our eyes meeting, and he nods his head at me in support. Taking out my phone I press my mums number and wait for her to answer, and it only rings three times before she picks it up.

"Bryan." I can hear her voice breaking over the phone.

"Merry Christmas mum." I manage to blurt out, holding back a sob.

"You read my note.." She practically whispers, is she trying to disguise the emotion in her voice?

"I did. Thank you. I miss you both too." I say, I'm sure she can tell I'm crying now, and we both remain silent for a few seconds.

"I need to go, but I love you. Your father loves you, but he can't cope with everything right now." She whispers back, and I can now tell she's definitely crying too.

"Love you too." I reply, and she hangs up the phone.

Ben turns me into his arms, my emotions now running free. My heart is breaking up inside of me, and I just want this day to be over with now. Trying to think about my future, a future without my parents in my life, because I don't think that I can cope with this toxic half in, half out attitude from them at this current moment in time. Not unless something drastically changes, attitudes drastically change.

"Bryan, listen to me. Give them time, please don't give up, I can feel how sad you are and its slaying me. I love you, and I can't bear to see you like this." My mood almost automatically perks up.

"You love me?" I ask him gazing into his eyes.

"Yes Bryan, I have done for months, from afar of course. Don't say it back yet. Say it when you really feel it. I can wait." Ben replies, kissing the tears away from my face, and all I can do in that moment is reply, "Okay Ben."

Chapter Fifty-Six

Maddie

I t's that weird time of year, the days following Christmas and in-between New Year when nobody really does much except eat leftovers and watch reruns of Friends on TV and worry about how much weight they might have gained over Christmas. When the sales start on boxing day and the shops start selling off things at a fraction of the price you paid for them before Christmas. When you start pondering in your head about New Years resolutions. And if your unorganised, trying to rush through any unfinished essays for college, lucky for me, the last one doesn't apply.

But this year is different for me. I'm living with Sam, Jack and Tommy in a lovely little cottage, not forgetting our new addition Holly the kitten. Who incidentally is into absolutely everything, and loves attacking feet for some reason. I've got a fabulous best friend, Bryan who is funny and supportive, and never fails to bring a smile to my face. Also in what I consider to be my circle is Ben, who's now Bryans boyfriend, and Ashley, a stray we recently picked up into our little group. Then of course is Dorothy my mentor and boss, but also my friend, and of course Tony, a talented musician that I spend many hours with making set lists and practicing songs. But one person I could not possibly live without now is Danny. How do I define my relationship with him? Friends, of course, more than friends, yes, but he's not my boyfriend. Nope, I'm currently friend zoned by him, but he's giving me other signals leaving me completely confused...

Today is mine and Bryans birthday party which we organised together, strike that, Bryan did most of the organising, I merely agreed with him. Who knew Bryan would take party planning so seriously? We're holding it at Dorothy's, she's kindly letting us have the whole bar for a private party. Dorothy doesn't normally open much before New Year anyway, most people are saving the serious partying up for New Years Eve, according to her, so we really are very lucky to have such a generous boss. As far as invites go, we have invited a few select people from college that we're friendly with in our classes, and in the spirit of things Bryan has invited Ben's rugby team. Most of them don't actually care that Bens gay, just that spiteful little group Chelsea has managed to brainwash, but they won't show up. Ashley is here too, and she's brought her dad with her. They both needed a break from the hospital, and I can see Sam chatting to them both, no doubt talking about Ashley's mum. She still hasn't come out of her coma, and they have been talking about moving her into a long-term care facility.

Looking around the bar, it's decorated with rainbow streamers and pink and blue balloons with eighteenth birthday printed on them, and our names on a banner handmade by Sam and the boys. The buffet table is overflowing with finger food prepared by the chef at Dorothy's, all the usual suspects, sausage rolls, mini quiche, mini pizza, you get the idea, anything in mini, and he kindly prepared a vegan version of most things just for me. The massive cake sits pride of place, made by Sam, she was beside herself with excitement when Bryan and I asked her to bake the special cake for us, and she didn't disappoint. One side of the cake is a rainbow design with an realistic energy drink can and snickers bar sitting on top, and the other side is decorated with musical notes and little books made from fondant icing, to reflect each of our personalities. Which is absolutely perfect as far as I'm concerned.

Jack and Tommy are currently running around the tiny dancefloor, hitting each other over the head with balloons, and I can see Dorothy waving her finger at them both in gest, she love's a good party as much as the next person.

Tony is on the stage setting up the karaoke machine for us all and he's kindly offered to keep it manned for tonight's low key entertainment, the whole atmosphere is very relaxed and laid back. Bryan and Ben are already flipping through the karaoke folder listing all the songs available to sing with a backing track. I have a sneaking suspicion about what song they are going to sing together, and I chuckle to myself, hardly able to wait.

"Laughing to yourself Maddie, looks like you need another drink girl, it is a party after all." Danny laughs and hands me a glass of champagne. Danny insisted we had some as it's our eighteenth and we can now legally drink alcohol, and even though I don't know the exact date of my birthday, I feel like it could be today, and it's strange to think I'll be considered a legal adult now. I don't feel any different, but people will see and treat me differently now, well most people, not my friends obviously.

"Cheers Danny. I was just laughing because I think I've guessed which song Bryan and Ben are going to sing, and if I'm correct, it's going to be epic." I chuckle again and nod towards the stage, where Bryan and Ben are both preparing themselves to sing. Music starts, and it looks like I was correct, the opening bars to Don't go breaking my heart, by Elton John and Kiki Dee, come over the speakers. Danny and I both look at each other and burst out laughing, because we know this is going to be bad, really, really bad, and I don't mean bad as in good. No. I mean bad, bad. Lost without a cause bad, you get the idea

Ben's deep masculine voice comes over the speaker first "Don't go breaking my heart" followed by Bryans best impression of Kiki Dee singing in a high pitched, "I couldn't if I tried."

"Shall we go and rescue them from themselves?" Danny laughs, shaking his head. Ben does not have a singing voice bless him, and he's completely out of tune.

"No. I say let them have their moment together." Smiling at them both having fun on the stage, they were clearly made for each other and meant to be, and I'm so happy for them both.

"So what are you going to sing tonight?" Danny asks me, taking a sip of his champagne, a cheeky smirk appearing on his gorgeous face.

"I thought I'd take the night off and give other people a chance to sing for a change." I reply, smirking back at Danny, sipping more Champagne, the bubbles going up my nose.

"Well, you have to sing at least one song with me." Danny smirks back, knowingly. No way can I refuse a request to sing with Danny.

"Depends, what did you have in mind?" I laugh back, and taking another sip from my glass, the bubbles going up my nose again. I must slow down, or I'll be drunk before I know it, and that didn't end so well last time.

"Wait and see Maddie. I can guarantee it will be a song you know, trust me, you know you can." Danny replies, giving me a cheeky wink. He grabs my hand and we make our way together, towards the stage, so we can go on next.

When the song finishes, I hear Danny's dad shout out, "Thank god that's over, my ears are bleeding." And everyone laughs, including Bryan and Ben. They both know it's meant in jest, and how bad they sounded.

"Guess we're up next then Maddie." Danny whispers the song we're about to sing to Tony so he can set it up on the karaoke machine ready. I start to feel slightly nervous, what on earth has Danny chosen for us both to sing? I can't even begin to guess...

As the opening bars to the song starts, I turn to Danny and say,

"Please tell me you didn't.."

Danny just laughs back at me and starts singing "Stacy's mom has got it going on, Stacy's mom has got it going on..."

It's not exactly the most appropriate song to sing together as a duet, and it's an interesting choice for Danny, but together we make it work. We sound really great singing together, and it's good to see Danny letting loose for once. The bar is laughing at the song choice too, joining in singing on the chorus. Jack and Tommy have just about lost it laughing so much, and Bryan and Ben are doing a really bad waltz on the makeshift dance floor in front of us. By the end of the song I feel myself losing it too.

"That's the last time I ever let you pick the song Danny McKenzie." I say as he leads me off the stage for the next couple to take over, it seems a trend has now started, bad karaoke duets.

"Oh is it indeed, we'll have to see about that Maddie Reynolds." Danny cheekily turns towards me with a sparkle in his eye, it looks like he's going to say something else when Jack comes running over towards us, hyped up from the party and full of excitement.

"Are we doing the cake yet? I'm starving, Maddie." Jack asks trying to be all serious. He's already demolished half the buffet from what I've seen, I'm surprised he hasn't been sick yet. How can his stomach possibly have any room left for cake???

"After this song." Sam replies and ruffles the hair on his head, appearing at his side. The pair seem to be getting along better, and Sam appears much more relaxed with him now. Being a foster parent suddenly to twin boys, has been a shock to her system, but Sam adjusted well to the situation. The boys really enjoyed spending Christmas at the McKenzie house. It's great for them to have all these positive male role models around them, something that they have never had before. The couple on stage finish their song, and Dorothy takes over grabbing the microphone.

"For those of you who haven't entered this fine establishment before, welcome to Dorothy's. I met Bryan and Maddie when they answered a job advertisement on social media, and I have to say I'm glad they did…" Dorothy is interrupted.

"And Ben." Bryan shouts out towards her.

"Yes and Ben, but it's not his birthday if you let me finish Bryan, always so impatient that one." Dorothy answers, and everyone laughs, she's such a funny hostess.

"As I was saying, having fresh young people in this establishment has brought a great vibe and one I hope continues long into the future. So raise your glasses and wish Bryan and Maddie a happy eighteenth birthday. Up on stage, I want you both up here with me while we sing happy birthday to you." Dorothy demands in her usual way, and Bryan and I are both pushed by a gathering crowd up onto stage.

The crowd begins to sing happy birthday, as Sam carefully carries the cake onto the stage with the candles lit, she must have arms of steel carrying that heavy cake. We blow out the candles together, and I already know what my wish is for, Danny, I just want to be with Danny…

Chapter Fifty-Seven

Bryan

We've been on the dancefloor most of the night, or doing really bad karaoke, Ben has gone to the bar to get some water. I can feel the sweat dripping down the back of my neck, my arm pits feel disgusting and sweaty. Standing in the unisex toilets at the sink I splash water on my face trying to cool down I'm also ever so slightly tipsy, but I'm not full on drunk, I want to remember my eighteenth party after all. Ashley is applying lipstick in the mirror chattering away to me, how she can balance in those heels is spectacular, they must be at least six inches, adding height to her small frame. A wave of nausea comes over me.

Fresh air, yes, I need fresh air, not really thinking about it I stumble out of the bathroom. and instead of going back into the bar I head out of the side door. This is where the rubbish and recycling bins are kept in the alleyway. I slump against the wall to take a breather for a few seconds. Not appreciating the distinct aroma of rotting food waste, and how it's now making me feel very nauseous, I walk further out onto the street, and sit on a low wall just a little way from the bars main entrance. This is better, the smell has gone, and I can feel myself cooling down already, the sicky feeling abating. I close my eyes for a short moment, taking some deep breathing to wane off the feeling of sickness returning.

"Look who it isn't, the boy who turned Ben to the other side." I hear a voice say, and I open my eyes to see four of the guys from Bens rugby team, ones that weren't invited to the party. Bollocks, I seriously don't need their crap right now. It's not like I can take them on, they're all massive guys, hence being rugby players.

"Forget our invitation in the post gay boy? Or are we not good enough for your little party?" Another voice replies, in a condescending fashion, and it becomes plainly obvious that they are out looking for trouble. They all look a little worse for wear, it's obvious that they have been out on the town already tonight and I can smell the alcohol on their breaths. But me being me, I can't let a comment like that just go, maybe I'm feeling braver because of the alcohol, who knows?

"Is that honestly the best you've got? Gay boy? Hardly an insult, what are you five? Or have all those knocks to the head during rugby damaged your ability to use adult vocabulary." I reply really not thinking about any possible consequences to my actions, and I let my mouth run as usual, I don't stop there, my comebacks keep on flowing...

"You weren't invited because you've been arseholes towards Ben since he came out. I don't know what you're so afraid of, he's definitely not into your type, he prefers a pretty boy like me." I answer blowing on my fingernails, and batting my eyelids at him, I can't help antagonising this tosser.

"Watch your mouth you fucking pussy, your kind make me sick, and now we have to deal with a pansy on the team." He replies back briskly, taking a step towards me, into my personal space.

"Nope, no pussy for me. Definitely not into that." I answer defiantly squaring up to him and refusing to back down to a bully again, I think I know what's coming though.

Oh shit, is all I can think as the first punch strikes my stomach winding me, and I collapse down onto my knees, heaving in pain. Before I have a chance to gain my bearing, a fierce and frenzied attack rains down on me. Someone grabs the collar of my shirt and starts punching me in the face repeatedly, tasting blood I spit it out, hopefully in one of the bastards faces. Then the kicking starts, in my back, my abdomen, repeatedly, over and over. This isn't one on one, this is four on one, it was never going to be a fair fight. Feeling a kick to the side of my head, that's when I finally black out...

Ben, At Exactly The Same Time...

Two bottles of still water please, the bartender hands me two bottles, I think it's time to sober my boyfriend up a little, he was starting to look a bit green when he went to the toilet to freshen up. He disappeared with Ashley, so he should be fine, I think the champagne and excitement of the occasion has gone straight to his head. It's gotten really hot in here tonight, it must be from all of the dancing. Bryan is relentless on the dancefloor, I'm glad he wanted some water, it gives me a five minute reprieve from further dancing.

Walking back over to where I left Bryan standing, and in typical Bryan fashion he isn't there anymore. I notice Ashley back in the bar but with no sign of him, and I hope she's not left him alone puking his guts up, damn I should have gone with him. Scanning the room I can't see him anywhere, so I decide to check the toilets and see if he's in there. He better not be puking, I told him to take it easy on the champagne. Checking the stalls in the toilets doesn't take long, he's nowhere to be seen, so I walk back into the corridor to think where he could have gone to.

That's when I notice that the side door where we keep the bins is slightly ajar. Pushing the door open I walk outside feeling a sense of dread. No one is in the alleyway and I'm about to turn around and go back inside when I hear raised voices coming from the street. Walking towards the noise, I can see four guys kicking and punching someone on the ground.

"Hey, what the fuck you do think you're doing?" I shout as I walk towards then, and realise that I know these guys. They're from my rugby team, guys I used to be friends with, and hung out with, until a few weeks ago, when they turned on me because of my sexuality.

"Looks like we got two fairies for the price of one tonight lads." The obvious ringleader shouts back, stopping briefly and standing up straight, shaking out his hand, looking for a fight. I can take this idiot any day of the week and he knows it, until he reaches into his pocket and brings out a knife. Three of the guys jump me at the same time, and I don't stand a chance, not even managing to get in a single punch back. Fighting them as much as I possibly can, and trying to desperately shake them off me. Two of them are holding back my arms, and another has his arm round my neck in a choke hold. The fourth guy walks towards me grinning like he's off his face on drugs, the knife glinting in the streetlight.

"You don't want to do this guys, stop now before someone gets hurt." That's when I notice who's lying on the ground and my world shatters, it's Bryan and he's not moving...

Epilogue

Maddie

This has been the best birthday party I've ever had, okay, the only birthday party I've ever had, but it's still the best one. I've been singing and dancing all night, and I've eaten way too much cake to be considered healthy. Looking around the bar I can't see Bryan or Ben, did they sneak off somewhere the sneaky devils I laugh to myself. I bet they're making out in the stock cupboard, they better hope Dorothy doesn't catch them.

"If I catch you laughing to yourself one more time tonight I'm shipping you off Maddie." Danny laughs, nudging my shoulder and handing me a bottle of water, and I realise that it probably came off as being a tad bit psycho. As if to prove my point, Sweet but Psycho by Ava Max comes on full blast through the speakers, karaoke is over and it's time for a good old fashioned disco.

"Thanks, it's got really hot in here. Does Dorothy have the heating up full blast tonight or something?" I reply taking a large swig of water and handing Danny the bottle back.

"Let's go out the front and get some fresh air for five minutes, I need a breather." Danny replies and grabs my hand leading me through the crowd on the small dancefloor, we don't get any strange looks, people are getting used to seeing us together all the time.

Like the gentleman he is, Danny holds the door open for me,

and I skip through and say, "Why thank you kind sir."

"Don't tell me, Sam's been making you watch Downton Abbey again?" Danny grins, and shakes his head.

"You know me so well, kind sir." I answer laughing back at him, at the ridiculous use of old English.

"I'm glad we've got a chance to be alone tonight Maddie. There's something I've been wanting to say to you all night now about us…" But Danny never gets the chance to finish that sentence, because we hear raised voices just down the street, and four familiar figures running away…

Danny

Something is kicking off down the street and not just a fight, something really bad, I've got a horrible feeling. I need to go and investigate in case anyone needs help. Four lads don't run away like that unless they have something to hide, I think I recognise a couple of them, but I'm not sure where from. They scarpered off pretty fast when they saw us outside the bar. Maddie, I need to protect Maddie.

"Maddie go inside and call the police, something bad is kicking off down the street. I'm going to take a look." I kiss Maddie on the forehead quickly, and run towards the corner of the street near the alleyway at the side of the bar.

Two figures are on the ground and neither one of them are moving, and that's when I realise. It's Bryan and Ben, they've both been attacked and it looks like they've had the shit kicked out of them.

Shouting for help frantically, and trying to get further attention from the bar, I look around my surroundings assessing for any further danger. Switching onto some sort of built in, automatic pilot, I kneel down next to Bryan and check for a pulse, and see if he's still breathing. Finding a weak one, and not wanting to move him, I move onto Ben. I reach for his wrist to find a pulse and that's when I feel that his t-shirt is wet, shit it looks like someone has stabbed him. Pulling his t-shirt up, I can just about make out with the light from the streetlamp that he's been stabbed near his kidney. Without thinking I apply pressure to the wound.

"Ben. Stay with me mate. Come on. Wake up." I say to him trembling with fear, and his eyes open slightly.

"Bryan." That's all he manages to say.

"He's breathing Ben, hey, stay with me Ben. Helps coming." I answer in a stricken voice. Where the hell is Maddie, I hope to god she's getting help.

Maddie

Running back into the bar, I shout at the top of my voice "Someone call nine, nine, nine, something is kicking off outside, I think someone might be hurt."

"I'm calling them now." Dorothy shouts back, like this isn't a unusual occurrence.

Turning around and running back outside, and down the street to Danny, I hope to god he's not in danger.

"Oh fuck, what the hell?" I shout when I reach Danny, his hands are covered in blood, the blood, oh my god, the blood and the bodies. It was them, Bryan and Ben, that's what my dream was about. But it's too late I'm too late..

"Maddie can you snap out of it and help, check Bryan again, make sure that he's breathing. I can't take my hands off this wound." Danny answers frantically, and I realise I could have prevented this from happening, listen to your dreams, but I didn't did I? I should have tried the potion like Danny wanted me too.

"Bryan, Bryan." I shout shaking him, and I can't find a pulse. He isn't breathing, if they die, it's all on me.

To be continued in book two...

About The Author

Clare Kirk-George

Living on the South-East Coast of England with her husband, two children and a couple of crazy Siamese cats, Clare decided to start writing fiction later in life. Inspired by her love of teen romance books, television, movies, fantasy and science fiction. On a depressingly bleak day in January she took the plunge and purchased her first ever laptop computer. Determined to start getting her ideas transferred from a ratty old notebook, into something readable. Six months later Clare had completed her first book, The hidden Angel's daughter. Deciding to self-publish so others could become immersed with, and join her on a journey that originated from a lucid dream she had...

Being a huge music fan, following various genres, pop, rock and alternative music, not forgetting her love of musicals. Clare likes to listen to music while she writes often integrating it into the story.

Printed in Great Britain
by Amazon

41810753R00284